# Secret to an Earl's Heart

## (MERRY MEN OF ETON BOOK 2)

### TEAH KEMP WEIGHT

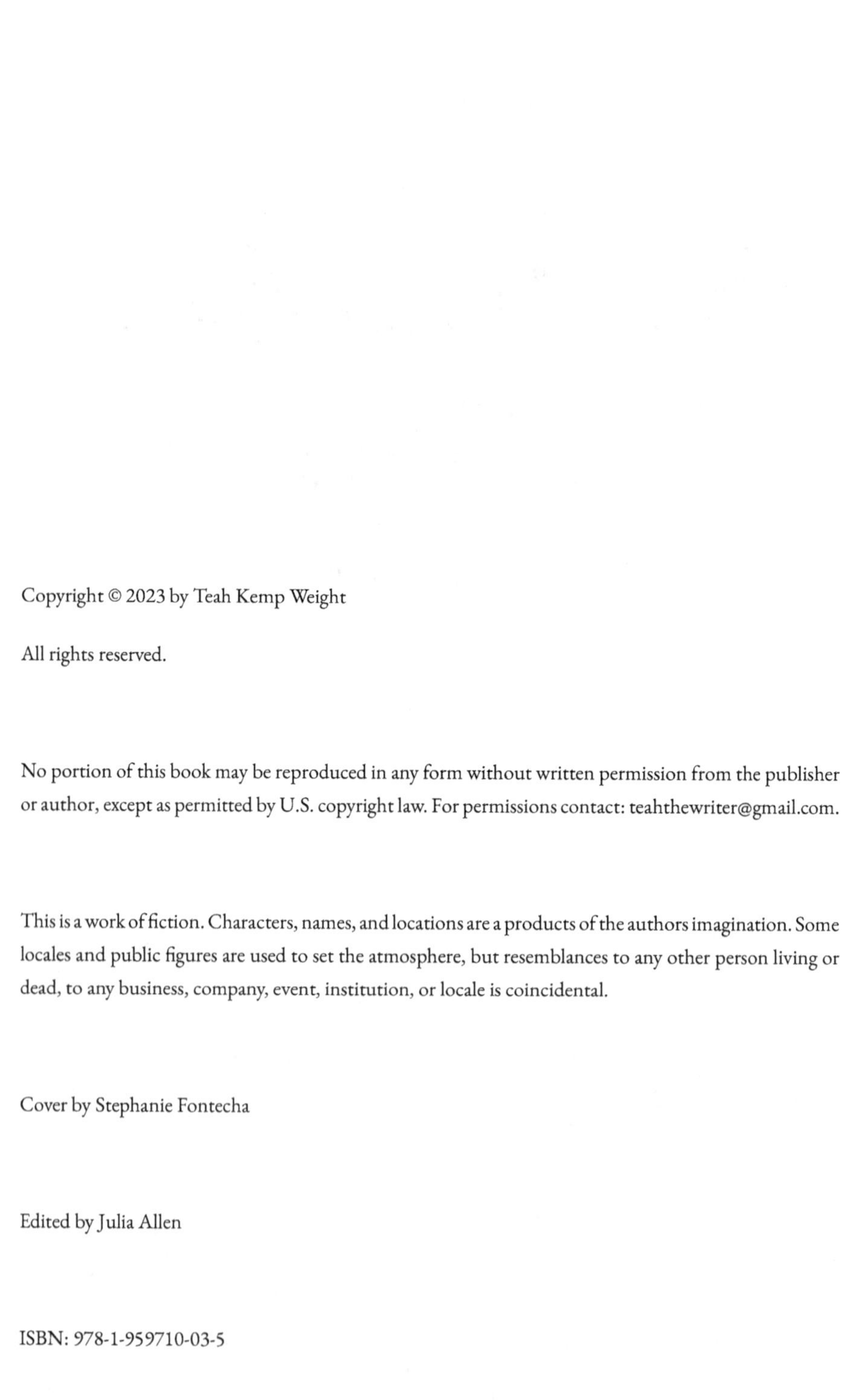



ISBN: 978-1-959710-03-5

# Contents

# Cast List

1. Lord Penbrose (Nicholas Fairchild)- New Earl of Penbrose and member of the Merry Men of Eton.

2. Mrs. Phillips- Housekeeper at Penbrose House.

3. Lady Julia Fairchild- Nicholas's mother.

4. Lord Hamdon (Anthony Kempton)- Nicholas's childhood friend and a member of the Merry Men of Eton.

5. Lady Hamdon (Emma Kempton)- Anthony's very pregnant wife.

6. Sir Richard and Lady Bawden- Guests who get brief mentions.

7. Miss Eliza Bawden- Daughter of Sir Richard and Lady Bawden.

8. Wilson- Butler at Penbrose House.

9. Mr. Bradley Lenning- Nicholas's friend and one of the Merry Men of Eton.

10. Mr. Arthur Greenwald- Childhood friend of Lady Evelyn and Lady

Julia.

11. Miss Sybil Greenwald- Daughter of Mr. Greenwald. Turned down an offer of marriage from Nicholas two years prior to the house party.

12. Maria Porter- Sybil's lady's maid.

13. Mr. Williams- Member of the House of Commons and friend of Mr. Thomas Fairchild and Lord Brock.

14. Mrs. Williams- Mr. Williams's wife.

15. Miss Williams- Oldest daughter of Mr. and Mrs. Williams. Also a close friend of Miss Cattering.

16. Miss Lydia Williams- The youngest daughter of the Williams. Also friends with Miss Cattering.

17. Lord Brock- Friend of Mr. Thomas Fairchild.

18. Miss Cattering- Lord Brock's daughter.

19. Miss Diana Cattering- Niece of Lord Brock

20. Mr. Martin- Neighbor of Nicholas Fairchild.

21. Lady Evelyn Burtrum- Older sister to Lady Julia and the dowager Marchioness of Caraway.

22. Lord Caraway (Edward Burtrum)- Lady Evelyn's son the Marquess of Caraway.

23. Lady Caroline Cartright- Married first daughter of Lady Evelyn.

24. Lady Olivia Burtrum- Second daughter of Lady Evelyn.

25. Lord Ansley- Viscount that has been invited to the house party to help

further Nicholas's cause in Parliament.

26. Miss Mary Fairchild- The sister just younger than Nicholas.

27. Aida O'Brian- Upstairs maid in Penbrose House.

28. Mr. Thomas Fairchild- Uncle to Nicholas Fairchild through his fathers side.

29. Mr. Tom Fairchild- First son of Mr. Thomas Fairchild.

30. Mr. John Fairchild- Second son of Mr. Thomas Fairchild.

31. Anna and Eva- Mentioned only. Nicholas's younger sisters that are away visiting their mother's brother at the time of the party.

32. Lieutenant Fredrick Marshall- Mentioned only. Final member of the Merry Men of Eton.

33. Mr. Brown- Clerk at the Mercantile in Kettering.

34. Mr. George Morris- Magistrate at Kettering.

To my daughter,
May you never lose your fire.

# *Chapter One*

## NORTHAMPTONSHIRE, ENGLAND, JUNE 1815

Where in heaven's name was his mother? It had been her idea, after all, to hold this large house party. Nicholas Fairchild wandered from room to room. The first guests would arrive at any moment, yet she still eluded him. He let out a low growl.

His extensive responsibilities had been overwhelming enough as the new Earl of Penbrose without this extravagant social event. Would he be forced to play hostess as well?

Chiding himself for his scowl, he stopped a passing maid for the third time.

"Do you know where I might find Lady Julia?"

"Yes, milord, she be in the formal dining room with Mrs. Phillips."

"Thank you." Perplexed, Nicholas directed his steps toward the dining room. He had checked that room when he'd first entered the main level of the house three-quarters of an hour ago. This impromptu game of hide and seek was beginning to wear on him.

It really would have been much easier to ask the butler to locate her and remind her she was needed to greet guests, but Nicholas had been so sure he could run her to ground when he had set out on this hare-brained quest.

He trudged back up the stairs from the kitchens. Hopefully this would be his last destination. If not, he planned to leave a message with a footman like any *sensible* gentleman would. Then he'd await her arrival in the front parlor.

Two doors down the main level corridor, the dining room door stood ajar. Voices filtered out, igniting a spark of hope and relief, but it was short-lived. In the dining room, he found only the housekeeper and a couple of maids.

All occupants ceased their activity with his entrance and dropped into quick curtsies. The maids' eyes immediately fell to the floor. Only his housekeeper, Mrs. Phillips, maintained eye contact.

"Mrs. Phillips, have you perhaps seen Lady Julia... recently?" he added as an afterthought.

"Yes, my lord. She was on her way to the front parlor. It is almost time for your guests to arrive. I believe she expected *you* to be there by now." Her words, while said respectfully, also held a small level of rebuke as if he was the one who was not where he should be.

"Thank you," he said shortly. Spinning on his heels, he marched out.

In the front parlor he found his mother comfortably seated on a cream-colored sofa. A soft smile graced her lips as she glanced up from her embroidery.

"There you are," she said evenly. "I was beginning to worry I would be required to greet our guests alone."

"Me?" Nicholas spluttered. "I've been searching nearly an hour for you!"

"For me?" She leaned back to take him in.

His conscience pricked. All the planning of the event had been carried out by his mother. Of course she would see to her duties. Why had he doubted her? Unease settled in his gut at the answer. He had never hosted an event of this magnitude, and he needed her to guide him.

Carefully, he tried for a less accusatory tone. "Yes, you. Do you have mystical powers that allow you to jump from one room to the next without me ever seeing you, because you are never where anyone saw you last."

A smile pulled at his mother's mouth as she arched her eyebrow. "Oh? And where would I have gained such power? I'm too old to have a fairy godmother, and I've not met any nymphs or dryads lately."

Nicholas tried not to smile, but it was a losing battle. His mother sat ever so properly, stitching calmly as if she had not just spouted nonsense. The tension that had built over the last hour slowly seeped out with the moment of levity.

He loved that his mother appreciated a little nonsensical conversation as much as he did. She may be staid and proper in public, but in the privacy of their own home, she often enjoyed a bit of whimsical fancy.

"You mean, you have not seen a single nymph? One that could have led you to a magical stream that grants endless gifts," he asked.

"Now that you mention it, I may have crossed one such stream in the garden."

"I knew it!" Nicholas declared. "Your sip from it must have also given you the gift of timeless beauty, for you are looking especially well today." He gave her his most charming grin.

Her bright blue eyes sparkled as she swept a chocolate brown curl out of her line of sight. While her hair had gained several strands of grey in the past three years, it only highlighted her natural beauty. Her trim figure belied the fact she had birthed six babies. Nicholas and his three younger sisters, the children who had survived infancy, were the only evidence of her travail.

She chuckled. "And you, my son, are a shameless charmer, but I will gladly take your flattery. Now, perhaps we should both adjourn to the entry as our first guests are coming up the drive."

"They are?" he asked surprised. "How have you divined that?"

"Years of listening for little boys and girls getting themselves into trouble has made my hearing quite keen."

Nicholas was dumbfounded. He could fair well believe it. He'd never been able to get away with anything when his mother was about. Most larks had happened when only his nursemaid was present.

He listened intently for carriage wheels on the gravel drive, but no sound reached his ears except those of a busy house being prepared for a large gathering.

His mother laughed. "Actually, I saw the carriage turn in at the lane. I *am* facing the window, after all. You will hear them coming soon enough. They are halfway up the drive."

"You could have continued on with that ruse, and I would have been none the wiser."

"I know, and I would have too, had your look of astonishment not pushed the laughter right out of me."

Nicholas was glad to see his mother so happy. She was not always so. The loss of his father three years ago still weighed heavily on her. For the moment, it seemed the prospect of a house party was lifting her spirits. Now if it could only lift his. But the responsibility of hosting so many people for three whole weeks was taxing. Not to mention that many of them still silently opposed his sudden ascension to his grandfather's title. But the late Lord Penbrose's will had been firm.

Offering his arm to his mother, they made their way to the front entry to greet their first guests. As luck would have it, his good friend Anthony, Lord Hamdon by title, and his wife were the first arrivals.

He clapped his old school chum on the back. "It is nice to see you, old man. It seems an age."

"Who are you calling an old man? And it has only been a twelve month. If you had come at Christmas, it would have been less."

"Yes, but then I would have been forced to witness your disgusting happiness as an old married man." Nicholas grinned. Turning to Lady Hamdon, he said, "And how are you faring, my lady? If the old curmudgeon is not treating you well, just tell me and I'll pound some sense into him."

She laughed lightly. "He is tolerable as long as he is free to move about, Mr. Fairchild—excuse me. Lord Penbrose, now."

"Yes, *Lord* Penbrose," Anthony said, a gleam in his eyes.

Nicholas supposed he deserved that, after all the times they had heckled Anthony about his title.

Lady Hamdon took a tottering step forward to greet his mother, and both men reached to steady her. They were rewarded with an icy glare.

Anthony had alluded to their growing family in his letters, but seeing it with his own eyes made it all the more real. And from the size of the petite woman's middle, she was quite progressed in her pregnancy. No wonder Anthony had only agreed to attend the party for two weeks.

As soon as Lord and Lady Hamdon had been escorted to their rooms by the housekeeper, the next group of guests, Sir Richard Bawden and his family, were announced. Such went the whole of the morning until all but three sets of guests had arrived.

Due to the chaos of the morning, a small repast was sent on trays to the guests' rooms as each arrived. Thanks to this bit of genius from his mother, Nicholas found himself free for a much-needed reprieve shortly after noon.

He enjoyed people well enough, but the constant hours of meeting and greeting made him long for a moment of silence. Sitting down at his study desk, he noticed a recent copy of the London paper had been delivered. Bless Wilson for his thoughtfulness. It had been placed directly on his desk where the faithful butler knew he would likely turn for some peace and quiet.

Picking up the *Gazette*, he engrossed himself in news of Napoleon's current march. How had that scoundrel escaped Elba? Current events sucked him into another world until a knock came at the door nearly an hour later.

"Enter," he called unceremoniously.

"My lord," Wilson said from the door. "Your mother sent me to inform you more guests are coming up the lane."

*At least she has the sense to send the butler instead of traipsing around like a fool.*

"Thank you, Wilson. I shall be there directly."

He straightened the newspaper and laid it on his desk. Tugging his jacket on, Nicholas appraised his appearance in the looking glass. His clothes were not too rumpled. He ran a hand through his wavy brown hair and tried to straighten a few stray locks. When he was decent enough, he made his way to the front of the house.

In the vestibule, he noticed his mother's strained expression. Perhaps the day's activities were taxing her as well. She turned to him with a tight smile, and for some reason, his shoulders tensed.

On closer inspection, she appeared more nervous than strained. A nearly imperceptible movement at her side indicated she was rubbing the fabric of her skirt together with her fingers, an action only employed when she was worried about something. Perhaps these next guests were particularly important for their acceptance into Society. Then again, Lord Brock and the Williamses had already arrived. Weren't they the main people she hoped to convince?

The knock came at the front door, and his mother stiffened. Definitely nervous. Wilson took his place by the door waiting for his cue. Taking a deep breath, his mother gave a slight nod, and the butler opened it.

The auburn-haired gentleman on the other side of the door grinned at Wilson's tall frame. He simpered in twirling a quizzing glass. "Have you missed my lustrous presence, dear Wilson? I am sure you have not opened this door for a more finely clad gentleman all day."

The corner of Wilson's mouth tipped up slightly, breaking his stoic butler demeanor as Mr. Bradley Lenning stepped past him. Nicholas glanced briefly at his mother and saw confusion on her face. But just as quickly, her posture relaxed and excitement entered her eyes.

"Bradley!" she exclaimed, stepping forward to embrace one of Nicholas's oldest, closest school chums. "We have missed you, dear boy."

"Boy, Aunt Jules? I am a man of five and twenty. That is hardly a boy."

"And yet you still call me Aunt Jules as if you were ten. Boy you have been, and one of my boys you shall always be, whether you are five and twenty or five and fifty."

Bradley wrapped his arms around the smaller woman with great affection, completely inconsistent with the dandy persona he'd tried to affect. While he dressed in brighter colors than most, he was no fop.

The man could not, however, resist bucking societal mores. Nicholas assumed putting on airs was his way of making light of the stodgier gentlemen in society. Whatever the reason, it brought Bradley no shortage of pleasure and was often his entrance of choice.

Bradley dropped his feigned pretenses, his grey eyes becoming serious. "How have you been, Aunt Jules? You appeared quite drawn out when I entered."

"Your line, my boy, is, 'Why, Aunt Jules, you look exceedingly beautiful today!'"

He chuckled. "Pardon me, I have quite forgotten my training, but that truly was going to be my second line of address. I must have gotten the order mixed up."

"Yes, but you are too perceptive and honest to deliver them properly."

He searched Lady Julia's face. "Has the day been that straining?"

With a sigh, she stepped away from the arm he had kept draped over her shoulders. "Only the expected pressures of hosting such a large house party."

Confused, Nicholas stared at his mother. The party had been her idea. He'd thought it was her greatest desire. He never would have agreed to such a venture, societal pressure or no, had she not been so persistent. Why did it now seem like a burden?

Then her face brightened. "But being able to have so many wonderful people to converse with over the next few weeks should prove most diverting."

"Speaking of wonderful people," Bradley said, "you must introduce me to that enchanting creature who arrived nearly the same moment I did. I am sure they will be at the door any moment, but I was too excited to see you to wait."

*Enchanting creature?* Many ladies had passed through his door today, far more in number than gentlemen, in fact, but he would not consider any of them enchanting.

The sheer number bothered him. Could his mother be on a quest to find him a wife? Was that why she was so nervous? Maybe she had pinned her hopes upon this next lady catching his eye.

If so, she would be sorely disappointed. He was not particularly interested in forming an attachment any time soon. He had more important matters to see to at present.

Another knock sounded on the door, and Wilson opened it to reveal an older gentleman with grey hair and a walking stick. Next to him was a tall, slender, dark-haired beauty who would take any man's breath away. One who had stolen Nicholas's breath as well... when he had first met her.

*How could this be possible?* Standing in the door was the last woman he would have ever expected. Miss Sybil Greenwald—the woman who had captured his heart, then sworn she would never speak to him again.

# Chapter Two

There Sybil stood, silhouetted by the sun. Nicholas's gaze stayed riveted on her as she stepped through the doorway. Had it really been two years since he'd seen her last?

Time had enacted very little change upon her. Her high cheekbones and angular jaw were perhaps more pronounced, but it only enhanced her beauty. His heart leapt in his chest of its own accord as he watched her emerald green eyes sweep the large entry with its vaulted ceiling and marble floors.

He had a moment to absorb the reality of her presence in his home before those enchanting eyes landed on him.

The momentary shock on her face would have amused him under different circumstances, but standing here in his own home, he was not at all amused. Why was she so surprised? Surely she had heard he was the new earl. Pain lanced through him with the memory of her rejection.

Her raised brows dropped, and her expression turned dark, those bewitching eyes flashing with the fire he loved––had loved, he reminded himself. He was sure his harsh words from their last conversation were probably playing in her head at this very moment. But when his mother started to speak, Sybil recovered herself quite nicely with a forced smile.

"Penbrose, allow me to introduce Mr. Greenwald. He is a dear friend from my childhood. And this is his daughter—"

"Miss Sybil Greenwald," Nicholas interrupted, causing his mother to stumble over her words.

Why his mother thought she needed to introduce the Greenwalds, he didn't understand. She knew very well he was acquainted with them. She knew the whole complicated story, in fact, as he had related every detail to her two years ago upon his return from London.

To invite Sybil, of all people— it was completely ludicrous. He clenched his hands. Why had he not insisted on seeing the guest list?

"Yes. Well," his mother said sweetly, but he could see the wariness in her eyes.

Nicholas realized neither he nor Sybil had performed the social niceties required of them. She just stood there. His dream in real life. But she could not be his with how things had ended.

Taking a deep breath, he did his best to stuff down the confusing emotions roiling within. "Welcome to Penbrose House, Mr. Greenwald, Miss Greenwald."

"Thank you, my lord," Mr. Greenwald said. "We are grateful to be here. Your mother's invitation was most welcome."

Nicholas watched as the older gentleman smiled toward his mother. How were they acquainted? His mother had never indicated before that she was on close terms with Sybil's father.

Sybil remained stock still in front of him, and he wondered if she would give him the cut direct in his own home. He would not put it past her. She seemed to be deliberating, then with great effort, she finally dropped into a short curtsy, saying nothing.

Nicholas glanced at his mother, and she cleared her throat nervously. "And may I introduce a dear friend of ours, Mr. Bradley Lenning."

Mr. Greenwald gave a brief bow to Bradley and Nicholas took the opportunity to examine him. During their brief acquaintance, the shorter, portly man had never appeared as amiable as he did just now. He had not been rude, just indifferent, or maybe even a little distant. What might have changed in these past two years?

"And where is Mrs. Greenwald?" Nicholas tried to infuse politeness into his words, even though his feelings toward the woman were anything but kind.

The Greenwalds both appeared distressed at his query. His mother frantically cleared her throat again. What had he done? Why did they all act as though he had said something uncouth? Then the color of Sybil's dress registered in his mind and humiliation burned his cheeks at his blunder. Lavender was a color of mourning.

Mr. Greenwald broke the silence at the same moment Nicholas's mother started to speak. They both stopped.

"It is your tale to tell, Arthur," she said.

Surprised at his mother's use of Mr. Greenwald's Christian name, he glanced quickly between them, then settled his gaze on Mr. Greenwald.

"My wife... passed away, just over a year ago." He winced as if the admission caused him pain.

How had he not known this? Why had news not reached him? How callous he must seem. He looked at Bradley, but his friend just shrugged. Bowing his head for a moment, Nicholas tried to summon the right words.

"My condolences and my apologies. I had not heard of her passing. I never would have...I did not mean to..."

Mr. Greenwald saved Nicholas from the mess he was making of the situation. "It is quite all right. Please do not trouble yourself. No offense was taken."

Mrs. Phillips entered at that moment, rescuing him from further embarrassment. Bless his housekeeper for perfect timing. He was going to need another hour alone in his study and probably a stiff drink to recover from his recent guests' arrival.

"Ah! Mrs. Phillips." Turning to the Greenwalds, he said, "Mr. Greenwald, Miss Greenwald, this is our housekeeper. She will show you to your rooms. If you have need of anything during your stay, please let my staff know." Nicholas made a brief bow and turned to leave.

"And what am I, last evening's scraps?" The twinkle in Bradley's eye was all too knowing. He was not truly offended, just stirring the already simmering pot for good measure. Nicholas glanced at Mrs. Phillips who hesitated as she looked between the Greenwald's and Bradley.

"Oh, no," Nicholas said to Bradley, "not last night's scraps. More like three-day old porridge."

Bradley's bark of laughter eased his tension.

"You know this house as well as you know your own, Lenning. You will be in your usual accommodations. I believe the footmen have already deposited your belongings there. Your man probably even has your things put away and your togs set out for supper."

"On my word, you must have high expectations of Peters. He is quite amazing, I assure you, but he is no miracle worker by any means."

His mother cleared her throat, *again*. At this rate the whole of the party would probably assume she had a head cold. He glanced at her, and she tipped her head toward the housekeeper who had an uncertain expression upon her face.

"Oh, forgive me. Mrs. Phillips, please show the Greenwalds to their rooms. I will show my reprobate of a friend to his quarters since he seems to have forgotten his way around."

Mrs. Phillips nodded, her lips quirking the slightest bit before she battled them into submission. "Right this way, if you please," she said as she led the pair up the staircase to the right of the entry hall.

Nicholas was quiet as the Greenwalds left the entry. Tension returned to his neck and back. The beginnings of a headache throbbed as he watched the retreating figures enter the upstairs corridor. "You will need to explain this, Mother, but at present I am in need of space to calm myself."

She nodded, her guilty expression speaking volumes. Nicholas did not think she had invited the Greenwald's to be unkind. His mother was, at her core, unfailingly thoughtful. At the moment, though, he wished she had kept her well-meaning intervention to herself. In fact, he was quite at a loss to understand how she found this invitation kind *or* thoughtful.

"I will be in my study if anyone should ask for me."

"Does this mean I do not get my personal escort to my room from the Earl of Penbrose? I am wholly disappointed!" Bradley said with mock censure.

"On the contrary," Nicholas said, "the Earl of Penbrose thought you would follow him like a puppy to his study, and once there join him in imbibing some much-needed fortification. Then make your merry way to your quarters."

"I am a puppy, then?" Bradley asked, trying to cover a smile.

"Most decidedly. Why else would you be at my heels everywhere I go?"

Bradley scoffed. "Hardly. Do you share your liquor with dogs, then, Nicholas? My, you are in want of company! I wish you had told me sooner. I would have come a fortnight ago had I known you were in such dire straits."

"Well, I guess it is good you are here now," Nicholas quipped, "since our gamekeeper has been quite on the outs with me since I brought back the last pointer completely soused."

The burst of laughter from both his mother and friend dissipated the tension that had hung over them. Nicholas could not help joining in.

Turning to his mother, he said in a softer tone, "Might I meet with you in my study in about an hour's time? That will give us some time to talk before we are required for tea."

"That will be fine," she said. After bidding farewell to Bradley, she made her way up the stairs.

Nicholas smirked at Bradley. "This way, Bradley. Come!" He patted his leg for emphasis.

"All right," Bradley said, hanging his head and slouching forward like a scolded puppy, "but only because I get a treat."

# Chapter Three

Sybil stared out the window of her guestroom, questions whirling about in her head. It was a well-appointed room to be sure, but she would not be able to appreciate it until her emotions settled. For the moment, the light green papered walls, white-washed furniture and dark green damask curtains held no appeal. The only thing that held her attention was the view from the window seat.

From her perch, she could see the stables and fields behind Penbrose House. In the distance, a small rise drew her notice. Beyond that, she imagined freedom. Freedom from this house. Freedom from its occupants. Freedom from the surprising presence of the handsome gentleman to whom she'd sworn she would never speak to again. Freedom from the deep and all-encompassing embarrassment she felt every time she thought back on a certain heated conversation in London.

Sybil hated being embarrassed. Embarrassment made her angry. She knew all too well her embarrassment stemmed from being terribly hurt, but she hated hurt just as much. And, of course, it made her angry. So did sadness, pain, and jealousy. In fact, anger seemed to be her ever present first response. It would flash up from her soul before she could stop it, but like candle wax it would melt away revealing the real emotion beneath.

For years she had tried to stop the impulse, but to no avail. Eventually, she had learned how to mask her initial reaction so others hardly noticed. Only those close to her knew of the flash and fire that burned within.

Now an hour after her shock, the anger had completely evaporated, and so she sat embarrassed, hurting, and entirely alone.

The last person she had expected to see in the entry hall of Penbrose House was Nicholas Fairchild. One look at his impressively tall form standing as the new Earl of Penbrose and the words from their last conversation began ringing in her ears.

*How could you say such a thing Nicholas? No! My answer is no. And I promise you, I will never speak to you again.*

That she was in his home was embarrassing enough, but that she would also be required to go back on her own word was even more humiliating. Sybil hated breaking a promise, even if it had been a ridiculous one spewed in anger. If it had not been his home, and if her father had not just regaled her with childhood tales of people she now knew to be Nicholas's mother and aunt, she would have given him the cut direct to save herself the embarrassment.

Fate, though, was a fickle friend and had placed her in just the position that would not allow her to do anything but break her angry promise.

It did not mean she could not try. Angry or not, it had been a promise and she would hate to make a liar of herself. Perhaps she could just avoid him for the rest of her stay.

Sybil scoffed at her own logic. Three weeks? Could she really hide away for three weeks? Perhaps it would not be too bad. She had hidden from most of society for the last year. Of course, that had been in her own home, and she had been in mourning.

But this was not her home, and there were rules of propriety to which she would be required to adhere. The first of which was not to give slight to her host and hostess.

She did not need any more rumors following her about. It was bad enough that all of London had erupted with suppositions when Nicholas had abruptly left two years ago, and she had been the target. It was truly unfair that women carried all the blame in Society's eyes and men none.

Sybil tried to rid herself of the memories of that awful journey home. Her father's worried face. Her mother growing increasingly ill with each mile. And the heartache. Oh, the heartache. A swift departure like that was something she did not want to repeat.

Nicholas's mention of her mother today had caused fresh pain to rip through her like a lightning bolt. Strange how with one sentence, her grief was as powerful as it had been in the first few weeks after Mama's death.

She knew he had not meant to be cruel. He had not known of her mother's passing. They lived so far away from one another. Besides, she had not spent her time waiting upon word of him— even if his beautiful face had filled her nightly dreams. Gracious, she had not even remembered he was somehow connected to the Earl of Penbrose. So why would Nicholas have been pining after word of her or her family?

And how was it that after two years, she still only thought of him as Nicholas? Using his given name in her mind was an intimacy she really could not afford. She needed think of him as Mr. Fairchild. Actually, Lord Penbrose would now be the correct title.

Did he ever think of her as Sybil? A tiny seed of hope sprouted before she could uproot it. They had never actually given each other permission to use Christian names, but in the heat of their last conversation, they had both resorted to the informality.

The *why* was beyond Sybil. In a time when emotions were so high, they should have become more formal, not less. Perhaps her heart had been trying to reach through to her head, but it had not worked.

Unfortunately, anger had been the victor of that day so long ago and had continued to prevail for the first few months after leaving London. But over time, the good memories had returned. She could not count the times Nicholas's compassionate hazel eyes had invaded her thoughts or the soothing cadence of his bass voice had repeated words of encouragement in her head.

Their parting had hurt, but the memories of the few months they had traveled in the same circles, laughed with the same friends, and danced at the same balls were the only things that had carried her through the dreadful year as Mama's health had faded away.

But after Mama's death, even those memories could not penetrate the darkness that had engulfed her. The frivolous concerns of Society had pained her. Visits and letters from friends had couched flippant sympathies among news of current gossip. To them it was like nothing had ever happened, even though Sybil's world had turned upside down. Eventually she had retreated within herself and refused the company of others. Perhaps that was why she had not heard of Nic— Lord Penbrose's ascension to the title.

She had become used to being alone, both in body and mind. Alone had eventually brought her comfort. So why was it not comforting today? She had desperately wanted to be alone an hour ago; why not now?

A maid came and delivered Sybil's small repast, pulling her from her unproductive introspection.

"Thank you," she said as her tray was set on a small table.

"If you need anything else, miss, please let me know." The maid bobbed a curtsy and left.

When she had consumed most of the meal, Sybil took her cup of tea back to the window seat to watch the stables. The grooms and stable boys were coming and going at regular intervals. With so many visitors, there must be quite the abundance of horses in the stables. The men and boys down below definitely had more than enough work to keep them busy.

Snippets of the conversation with Papa in the carriage came to mind. He had spoken of the fine accommodations her mare, Tempest, would find in the Penbrose stables. He had even promised her a glimpse of the earl's famous Friesian stallion.

She wondered how many stalls the large building contained. Were Tempest's accommodations as good as Papa had promised? She hoped her high-spirited mount was not causing too much trouble. Tempest often became restless when surrounded by new horses.

An urge to see the earl's collection of fine horses overcame her. At least there was one thing to look forward to during this ill-fated visit. Now was not the right time, though. With all the commotion below, she would just be in the way. Perhaps tomorrow after things settled, she would get a peek. The prospect of visiting the stables lifted her spirits. If only men were as agreeable as horses.

And now her thoughts had come full circle. Bother. Just when her mental wanderings were getting more pleasant, Nicholas—Lord Penbrose, she mentally corrected herself—had intruded again. Regret for her own brash actions mixed with the pain of his parting words pierced her tender heart.

He was obviously not pleased to see her here. One glance at his face had told her he was just as surprised at her presence as she was at his, but why? Had he not approved of the guest list? It was his house party, after all.

And that dark look he had cast her when his mother began introductions— he had not even allowed the poor woman to complete what she was saying. Sybil felt sorry for her.

A familiar fire lit Sybil's chest as she recalled his condemning expression. It was not her fault she was in his home. And he could have at least been civil to his mother if not to her.

Forcefully, she pushed thoughts of him from her mind before memories of their past could consume her.

Perhaps Papa would consider a removal after learning the earl's actual identity. Sybil had not had time to speak to him before he had been led away to his room, but she was sure he would understand her distress. If he had known that Lady Julia Hensmoore from his childhood was actually Lady Julia Fairchild, she was sure he would not have pushed for this ill-fated trip.

At least she hoped he would not have. Things had been uncomfortable between them this last month, ever since the anniversary of her mother's death.

Her father, who had mourned so deeply, had gained a sudden enthusiasm for socializing again. She could not account for the swift shift in mood. One day they were all in black and the next he was begging her to move into half-mourning and attend a house party.

Another knock sounded on the door. "You may enter."

Her lady's maid, Porter, entered the room carrying a freshly pressed gown.

"I see you have been quite industrious, Porter. The gown does not look at all like it has spent the last two days stuffed in a trunk."

"Yes, miss. It was fortunate that they already had a press warm for me." Concern crossed Porter's features as she turned from laying the gown on the bed.

Sybil had tried to hide her distress, but her maid knew her too well. She pasted what she hoped to be a believable smile on her face. "You really can work wonders, Porter."

The maid took her cue and did not ask any questions. Waving away the compliment, she began helping Sybil undress.

Porter held out a gray gown for her to step into. Moving from full to half-mourning had been hard, even though Sybil had spent longer than necessary in black. Mama's loss was still so acute.

As she appraised the color, she had to admit it was nice to see something other than black. While the gray was still a reminder of her loss, it gave just the barest hint that light was coming back into her life.

In time, she would add more shades back into her wardrobe, perhaps even bolder ones. At nearly one and twenty, the white dresses of a debutante were far behind her. It may not get her the attention Papa wished, but it was not as if she intended to marry now anyway.

With Mama gone, she was the only one left to care for Papa. She knew he hoped she would marry someday, but for what? The estate was not entailed like most of Society assumed. All Tave Hall property would revert to her upon Papa's death, so why the sudden desire to thrust themselves into the social whirl again? There was no need to haphazardly throw her at someone to keep her from destitution.

"How much time do I have before I am required downstairs?" Sybil asked while the maid fastened the tiny buttons on the gown.

"They have planned to have tea at four, and a late supper this evening."

Sybil reached over and pulled her timepiece off the dressing table. It would seem she had forgotten to wind it during all those tedious hours in the carriage. Oh well, it was not the first time she had forgotten, and it surely would not be the last.

Looking in the mirror as she sat at the dressing table, she watched Porter as she crossed to the bed. A slight smirk gave away the maid's amusement.

"No use holding it back, Porter," Sybil said in mock exasperation.

The maid stopped, an amused smile blossoming on her face. "Would you like me to tell you the time, miss?"

Grabbing a handkerchief off the table, Sybil crumpled it into a ball and threw it toward her maid. Porter laughed as the piece of cloth landed halfway between them

"You know very well I need you to tell me the time, Porter. I promise someday I shall remember to wind it, but apparently today is not that day."

They had been through this exact scenario so many times she could not count. To say she was quite terrible about winding her timepiece was an understatement. Porter had offered to do it for her, but Sybil took pride in maintaining at least a small level of independence, and her timepiece had become a symbol of that.

Apparently, it had also become a symbol of her ineptitude in that independence, as about every third day she ultimately forgot to wind it.

Porter seemed to enjoy their little game as much as she did. In fact, Sybil was quite sure her maid knew exactly when the timepiece had run out because she was prepared for their comical exchanges.

In truth, these exchanges had become something quite dear to Sybil since Mama's death. Porter had become somewhat of a friend, perhaps even her only friend now. What did that say about her if she had to pay someone to be her friend? All the same, she was grateful for Porter's friendship and loyalty.

There was a time it had not been so. As much as Sybil loved her maid now, she was ashamed to remember her treatment of Porter that first year she had been employed at Tave Hall.

Mama's warning still haunted her to this day. "Servants are people too, Sybil. They have feelings and lives outside of service. If you treat them with respect, they will be loyal to you and keep your secrets. If you don't, the whole neighborhood will know of your misdeeds by the end of the week."

What a revelation that had been. True to her mother's words, Porter had returned Sybil's respect, kept her secrets, and had been the most loyal maid a woman could ask for.

Watching Porter arrange her dark hair in the looking glass, Sybil wondered if her maid felt same.

Porter broke the silence that had reigned over the room. "Are you all right, miss? You are not usually so quiet."

"I am fine, Porter. Only revisiting old memories."

"Good or bad, miss?"

"A little of both."

"Hmm..." the maid said, using her teeth to open one of the pins wider.

"Did you know that Mr. Nicholas Fairchild is the new Earl of Penbrose?"

Porter retrieved the curling tongs from the fire and began silently twisting strands of hair about the hot iron. Sybil wondered if she had missed the question.

Finally, the maid took a deep breath. "Yes, miss."

Sybil's eyes shot to her maid's face in the mirror. "Did someone in the kitchens tell you?"

"No, miss. I've known for about a month." Her focus did not waver from the curl she had just formed.

Shocked, Sybil pulled away from her ministrations and turned to face her. "Why did you not warn me? I could have avoided this whole situation."

Porter looked down at the floor. "I was just following orders, miss."

"Whose orders? You are *my* maid! You are supposed to follow my orders." The woman flinched at her outburst, and Sybil mentally upbraided herself for using such a harsh tone. She tried to soften her words. "Pardon me, Porter, but I truly do not understand."

Porter continued to stare at her feet, her brows pinched, her lips compressed. Eventually, her head lifted and she locked eyes with Sybil.

"Mr. Greenwald asked me not to."

"My father knew?" Sybil yelled in surprise, then clapped her hand over her mouth hoping none of the other guests had heard her.

Porter stood still, her face a mixture of compassion and resolve. Calmly, she placed her hands on Sybil's shoulders and turned her back around so she could resume styling her hair.

"Why would he do this?" Sybil lamented. "He knows the whole of things. Why would he choose to put me in such a situation?"

"I don't know, miss, and honestly, it's not my place to say. He being the master of the house, I had to follow orders."

Her father's unusual behavior in the carriage now made sense. When she had asked him about the new earl, he had gone off on some tale about Lady Julia and her sister, Lady Evelyn being his childhood friends. It had not seemed completely out of line since he had explained that Lady Julia was the new earl's mother. But no matter how many questions she had asked, he had not been able to supply her with the surname for the family. She had supposed that time and his age were the culprit, but now she was sure he had deceived her on purpose. If she had only studied Debrett's Peerage more... or had a better memory for names and titles.

"I shall get to the bottom of this," she huffed out. "How could he have been so duplicitous? If he thinks I will stay after such a deception, he is sorely mistaken."

"And give slight to an earl, miss?"

"Yes, Porter. *This* earl I would slight. If we are lucky, we will be back in the carriage at first light tomorrow morning."

"But miss—" Porter stopped when she saw Sybil's determination. "Yes, miss. Would you like me to leave the rest of the trunks packed?"

"Yes, Porter. I shall make Mr. Greenwald see reason." Her father did not deserve the endearment of papa at this moment. She was far too upset with his lies. Sybil wrapped her anger around her like a cloak of armor, trying not to examine too closely the pain that lay beneath.

Porter's worried face loomed in the mirror. "If I may, miss, might you wait to speak with him until after tea? It is nearly four, and the guests will be gathering in the drawing room."

Sybil thought about her maid's words. "Yes, it would not do to make a public exposition of myself. There will be talk enough when we leave early. Best to act the part this afternoon. Perhaps there will be some time to speak with him before dinner."

"Yes, miss." Porter put the finishing touches onto Sybil's hair. "Would you like the pearls or the silver locket this evening?"

"The pearls please."

Finally finished with her ensemble, she surveyed herself in the mirror. Honestly, the grey did very little for her complexion. The circles under her eyes seemed darker, and the fleck of red that usually appeared in her dark brown tresses looked completely absent. At least her anger had done some sort of good. Her cream-colored cheeks now glowed with a rosy, pink hue.

Porter walked to the bed and retrieved a shawl.

"I do not need the shawl today, Porter. It is quite warm."

"Yes, miss."

At the door Porter turned. "Will you be alright, miss?"

Sybil's wall of strength crumbled and her shoulders drooped. Dear Porter knew the pain she was up against. More than once, the maid had patted her back as she'd cried into her pillow those first few months after her first and only season. She was unsure how much her maid had understood of her blubbering, but apparently it had been enough. Taking a deep breath, Sybil raised her shoulders and with them, the defenses she would need to carry her through tea. "I shall be fine, Porter, but thank you for asking all the same."

Opening the door, Porter whispered, "Good luck."

Sybil only nodded her head, but she stood a little taller, ready to face her demons.

# Chapter Four

Nicholas sat quietly at his desk; Bradley having left to his rooms a half hour past. Thoughts swirled in his head much like the brandy in his glass. He had not drunk himself silly with Bradley as he had suggested. They'd both known his earlier claim for the ridiculousness it had been. He could not hold his liquor at all, and since he did not want to be a tosspot for the rest of the day, he still held the single glass of brandy he had poured for himself well over an hour ago.

Just as he was about to take a sip, a light knock sounded on the door. He put the glass down. His mother must be especially nervous if she was knocking on his study door before entering.

Nicholas walked to the door and opened it. His mother stood on the other side, straight and tall. The hand fidgeting at her side gave her away. It would not do to have her defenses up before they even began talking. He would need to approach this discussion carefully.

"Ah, Mother, prompt as usual, I see," he said, forcing some cheer into his voice.

Her brows furrowed, suspicion in her eyes. He had caught her off guard. Good. Now she knew how he felt.

She entered the bright, cheery room, taking up her favorite chair by the fire. The two wingback chairs upholstered in leather had been one of the few things

Nicholas had brought over from Fairfield Manor five months ago when he had taken up residence here. A small table sat between them with a vase full of flowers cut this morning from the garden.

Taking the chair opposite his mother, he cleared his throat. His mother shifted in her seat and he watched her for several seconds as she stared into the empty fireplace.

"I know you must—" she said at the same time he said, "Mother, I—"

Nicholas chuckled and gestured to his mother. "Ladies first."

"It is times like these that I wish gentlemen did not defer to ladies. However, since I have created this situation, it is probably best that I explain. A little over a month ago, I spoke with your cousin Edward."

Nicholas nodded at the mention of his cousin, the Marquess of Caraway.

"He told me he had been corresponding with a Mr. Greenwald after a chance meeting in London a few years ago and was curious what I thought of the gentleman. Honestly, I had not seen the man since before my marriage to your father, and had heard very little of him since, except, of course, what you relayed to me after your return two years ago."

A familiar rock settled in Nicholas's chest at the mention of that season. It had been the best and worst time of his life.

"But Arthur and I were children together," she continued, reaching up and gently caressing a daisy from the arrangement on the center table. "He is six years my senior, but I have many a fond memory of him, much like an older brother. He and your aunt Evelyn were the best of friends and consequently were always getting into this scrape or that. Since our fathers were friends, we spent many glorious summer months at one another's estates. I'm not sure my mother thought they were glorious, though. She used to complain that Evelyn would send her to an early grave with her wild ways."

"Aunt Evelyn?" he asked incredulously. "Are we conversing of the same Aunt Evelyn? Marchioness of Caraway?"

A bubble of laughter escaped his mother's lips. "The very same. We were not always as proper as we are now, Nicholas. We were children once, you know."

"I understand that, but I cannot reconcile the idea that Aunt Evelyn was anything but a sweet, docile, perfect little girl. As long as I have known her, she has been nothing but the perfect paragon of lady-like propriety: calm, collected, soft-spoken, well-organized. Honestly, Mother, are you sure we are speaking of the same woman?"

"Quite, Nicholas," she said with a smirk. "Evelyn mellowed a bit as she prepared to leave the school room, but she was still quite enthusiastic and gregarious."

"Really?"

"Oh, yes." She smiled, but it faded a moment later.

"What changed that?"

She sighed. "During Evelyn's first season, she received an offer of marriage."

"Is that not a good thing? That is what the season is designed for, after all. So unmarried gentleman and ladies might meet and make an advantageous match?"

"It is, but Evelyn was determined not to marry her first season, or second or third, for that matter. You see, she had grown quite attached to a young man who would not be in a position to offer for her until at least her fourth season."

"This fellow that offered, did she turn him down?"

"No."

"Why ever not? It would not be the first offer of marriage to be rejected. It is done all the time during the season."

"Nicholas, it was a different age. A great deal of marriages were still arranged at that time. And while arranged marriages had been going out of style, there were still ways a woman could be coerced into accepting a man. Such was the case for Evelyn."

"The man... coerced her?" he sputtered out.

"No. Our father did. He was so enamored with the idea of his daughter becoming a marchioness, he demanded she accept. When she balked, he threatened to ruin the man she loved by revealing some indiscretion from his youth."

"So it was Caraway she was forced to marry?" Nicholas already knew the answer. It seemed strange. His aunt and uncle's marriage had not been as affectionate as his parents', but they had never seemed at odds.

"Yes." She slowly shook her head. "Caraway, however, did not know of the coercion. I think if he had, he would have called the whole thing off. After asking permission of our father, he was obliged to rush home to his estate in Sussex as his daughter from his first marriage had become suddenly ill. Not wanting to wait until he could return to town, he paid his addresses to Evelyn in a letter. Evelyn's response was thus carried through letter as well. The only reason it contained an acceptance was because our father stood over her as she penned it, dictating to her every word she would write."

Nicholas snorted with disgust. "I am now quite grateful I never met the man. How could someone be so unfeeling to his own daughter?" He rose and paced in front of the fireplace. "It still seems odd that Caraway was none the wiser. Didn't he take her measure when he saw her next?"

"They did not meet again until the day they took their vows. Caraway believed Evelyn happy to receive his offer, so he assumed her quiet solemnity only stemmed from a case of nerves."

Picking up the family Bible that lay on the table between them she traced the letters on the leather cover thoughtfully. "He enjoyed the vivacious young woman he had come to know in London. Losing his first wife had been hard. He hoped Evelyn would breathe life back into his home, and especially into Elsabeth, poor girl. But on the day of their marriage, the woman he knew no longer existed. Caraway tried to make her happy. He was very kind and far more understanding and compassionate with Evelyn than most men would have been. However, she never did fully regain her zest for life."

"What a tragedy." Nicholas sat back down. "But they did not seem wholly unhappy."

"No, I believe your aunt and uncle eventually became fond of one another. She has truly mourned him, and it has been difficult since his passing."

"So, where do Mr. Greenwald and his daughter come into this picture?"

"Edward told me that when he was a boy, his mother would tell them bedtime stories of her childhood exploits with Arthur. It was the only time he claims she was truly animated. Lately, Evelyn has become especially melancholy, and Edward is concerned for her. He believes that perhaps seeing her childhood friend again might bring back some joy and pull her from her doldrums."

Pieces of the puzzle started to fall into place. "This was all for Aunt Evelyn's sake, then?"

"Partially," she said slowly.

"Partially?"

"I have to admit, I knew who Miss Greenwald's father was when you returned from London two years ago."

The tension returned behind his eyes and he rubbed at them in frustration.

"But you were hurting," she continued, "and I did not want to cause you more pain by bringing up the acquaintance."

"I see." Silence stretched between them.

She took a deep breath. "In inviting Mr. Greenwald, I knew I would be forcing you to face Miss Greenwald, and for that I am sorry. But it is my hope, however vain, that perhaps by seeing her again you might be able to overcome the feelings that have kept you trapped these past two years."

A pulse of irritation pushed Nicholas to his feet again. After walking the length of the room, he pivoted, angry words ready to fly from his lips. Then he noticed his mother's tense shoulders and rigid posture. Inhaling deeply, he prayed for patience.

"And why would you believe that I have not moved on? That I am trapped, as you call it?"

"You have not looked twice at another woman since that first season in London, Nicholas. You threw yourself into your father's estate upon your return, taking his cause and making it your own. With your grandfather's passing and the presentation of this title, you have become even more obsessed with your work. I barely see you anymore. You are gone more than you are home." She crossed her arms over her chest. "You are constantly meeting with this lord and that preparing for the next parliamentary session, and you rarely go out with us. If it were not for Mary's upcoming season, or to further that bill you and Caraway are so set on, I do not believe you would accompany us anywhere. You are not getting any younger, Nicholas, and you need an heir. Especially, God forbid, if you should meet an early death as your father did."

"Father was not particularly young."

"Young enough to leave you to run an estate before you were ready. You cannot tell me that you would not have liked to have him for just a few more years. You could have obtained more experience in estate management, learned more about his fight for humanity."

He could not argue with her that on that score. He *had* wished for more time. It was his father's early demise that had sent him to London two years ago for the very reason she had declared. He had only meant to get a taste of Society that year, but then he'd met Sybil. She had been a ray of sunshine in his darkness.

After a year of mourning, he had not expected to be as happy as she had made him. They had laughed, talked, jested, even debated. Every moment with her had lightened his spirits to an almost euphoric level. He had been so sure she felt the same, sure that she had returned his regard. But apparently she had not, and the world had crashed back down around him.

"Mother." He chose his words carefully. "You could have warned me of your plans."

"Could I? I am quite sure if I had apprised you of my plans, you would have fled like a fox before the hunters."

Her imagery made him smile. He had to agree—he probably would have. "Perhaps."

It was astonishing that she could still read him so well. Nicholas took a deep breath and let it out slowly, doing his best to let his worries go with it. "I guess the only thing to do now is brave the lioness in her den."

"If I recall, we are in your den, Nicholas."

"Very true." He smiled. "All the more reason she will want to take a piece out of me."

"You say that as if you think Miss Greenwald might bite your head off."

"I would not be at all surprised if she did. She does have quite a temper."

A gleam entered his mother's eyes. "Somehow, I do not think you view that as a bad thing. You always did enjoy a bit of spirit."

Nicholas squirmed. Surely it must be time for tea. Pulling out his pocket watch, he checked the time, comparing it with the clock upon the mantel.

"Well, Mother, might I escort you to tea?"

Smiling, she rose and took his arm. "I would like nothing else. I do not know about you, but I am famished. I was a bit too nervous with our guests' arrivals to eat much today."

"Well, then," Nicholas said with a lift of his eyebrows, "let us hie ourselves to the drawing room before you expire of hunger."

"Lead the way, Penbrose." After only a few steps, she halted, pulling him to a stop. "You know, I do not think I shall ever get used to calling you Penbrose. It was your grandfather's title for so long, it feels exceedingly odd to call anyone else by the same name. Especially since we all expected Hepton or Thomas to inherit."

Nicholas patted her hand. The shock of inheriting after his grandfather's death still had not worn off for either of them. But with Lord Hepton's death preceding his grandfather and the piece of crucial information revealed in the will, the line of inheritance had clearly been his father's. "I completely understand. Nearly six months with the handle, and I still forget to respond half the time I am addressed. It can be quite embarrassing. I have great hopes that with time, I will fit into the name. I have quite the shoes to fill."

"Yes, you do. However, I believe you bring something to the title that your grandfather often lacked."

"And what might that be?"

"Compassion," she said wistfully. "Your grandfather, for all his greatness, held little respect for anyone who did not have a title or fortune to their name. You, my boy, will change this title for the better, I am sure of it."

"Thank you, Mother. Your faith in me does my doubtful soul good."

"You are quite welcome, Nicholas—Lord Penbrose," she amended. "Now let us go face your lioness."

# Chapter Five

Even though Sybil had left her room with her head held high, her confidence had faded on the long trek to the drawing room.

When she finally entered the room, Mr. Lenning stepped up and made a flourishing bow over her hand that both entertained and unnerved her. She was not quite sure what to make of this man. His dress and mannerisms put her in mind of a dandy, but the designation did not quite fit.

"How are you this fine afternoon, Miss Greenwald?"

"I am well, sir. And you? Did Lord Penbrose give you your escort as he promised?"

"He did not." An exaggerated expression of dismay crossed his face. "I am saddened to say the earldom is destined for doom for his dereliction of duty."

Sybil ducked her head to hide her smile. "Is showing one's guests to their rooms the duty of an earl, then? I had always thought it the duty of the housekeeper."

"Oh, no, my dear." He raised his rust-colored eyebrows. "Have you not heard? It was the newest law passed in Parliament that any earl possessed of such a long-standing friendship should be required to act as escort to said friend's accommodations."

"Really?" She played into his dramatics by adding a faux look of shock. "And what is the penalty if he does not?"

"Two thousand pounds, but I am sure the finest colt from Mirage would do just as well."

"That is quite a sum! I am assuming that Mirage is the Friesian stallion I have been hearing so much about."

"He is indeed."

"And how much does a colt from the famed sire usually cost?"

"Two thousand pounds, of course." he said triumphantly.

This *did* surprise Sybil. She had never heard of an animal going for such a sum. "Why, that is what many people live upon in an entire year!"

"And many much less," he said with a look of consternation.

Seeming to collect himself, Mr. Lenning continued lightheartedly. "This is why Lord Penbrose will surely bring down the earldom. He cannot afford to pay me such a sum each time he forgets his duty, you see."

"Ah, I do see." Sybil enjoyed the moment of light-hearted flirtation. "Well, for the sake of the estate and title, let us hope he remembers his duties before he drives the family coffers into the ground."

Her smile faded when her father stepped to her side. "I have some people I would like to introduce you to, my dear." Then he turned to Mr. Lenning. "Please excuse us."

Mr. Lenning gave a polite nod and turned to speak to another guest.

Crossing the room, they came to a stop in front of an older gentleman and what appeared to be his wife and two daughters.

"Mr. Williams, Mrs. Williams, might I introduce my daughter, Miss Greenwald?" Her father asked.

Mr. Williams gave a slight nod and her father continued. "Sybil, this is Mr. and Mrs. Williams of Whitney. Mr. Williams is a member of the House of Commons."

Bows and curtsies and general niceties were exchanged all around and Mr. Williams introduced them to his daughters, Miss Williams and Miss Lydia Williams. The two girls looked so close in age that Sybil would have been unsure who was older had Mr. Williams not denoted them by title. Both had heads full of golden-brown curls, slightly crooked teeth, and chocolate brown eyes, but while Miss Williams's complexion was completely clear, Miss Lydia had a smattering of freckles speckling her nose and cheeks.

"It is a pleasure to meet you both," Mr. Greenwald said with a bow to each girl. "How are you enjoying Penbrose House?"

Miss Lydia started to speak, but her sister held up a hand to silence her. Miss Lydia looked affronted but allowed her sister the privilege of answering the question.

Amusement crossed her father's face at this highly irregular behavior. She herself was struggling to tamp down a smile.

Squaring her shoulders and lifting her nose, Miss Williams answered, "It is a beautiful house, indeed, and the grounds are quite lovely. It has been an age since we have been to this part of Northamptonshire, and I had quite forgotten the beauty of the country. I believe it is one of the loveliest parts of England, don't you agree, Miss Greenwald?"

The question, though innocuous enough, held a bit of a challenge. Surprised by the unseen tension emanating from the petite girl, Sybil was immediately put on her guard. She had met many ladies of her ilk back in London—those who took one's measure and decided right away if one was competition or ally. Apparently, she had been placed firmly in the competition category.

"This is my first time in Northamptonshire, Miss Williams. I am not well-acquainted with the county, but from the little I saw on our journey here, I do believe I shall like it. We passed a good many churches on our journey, and each seemed lovelier than the last. Kettering was especially charming. I should very much like to visit some of the shops there."

"Your first time, you say?" A calculating look entered Miss William's eyes. "I have been here at least twice a year for the past five. You see, we are often invited to Penbrose House for visits."

Miss Williams was clearly marking her superiority by her close relation to the family. However, if she had been coming for the past five years, the previous Lord Penbrose would have been the one giving those invitations.

"Your father must have been well-acquainted with the late Lord Penbrose to have received so many invitations. How grand for you to be able to spend so much time in such a beautiful home! You must be quite the *old* family friends." Sybil tried to smile innocently. She almost lost her composure when the Miss Williams wrinkled her nose at the word *old*.

"Well." The woman straightened her back. "Perhaps I would not have said it thus, but our acquaintance with the family is of quite a long standing."

"I am especially well-acquainted with Lord Penbrose's uncle, Mr. Thomas Fairchild," Mr. Williams interjected, "He has an estate just fifteen miles south of here. We attended Eton together and later Cambridge."

"Mr. Thomas Fairchild?" Mr. Greenwald asked. "The youngest son of the late Lord Penbrose?"

This statement was met with uncomfortable glances from Mr. and Mrs. Williams and looks of indignation from the two sisters.

"That is what they would lead you to believe," Miss Williams began, but her father cut her off.

Sybil was intrigued by the girl's statement. Either the man was the youngest son of the late earl, or he was not. How could there be any question on that score?

"It would seem so, at least according to the late Lord Penbrose's will. Are you acquainted with Mr. Fairchild?" Mr. Williams asked.

"No, I am afraid we are not," Mr. Greenwald replied.

"Ah." Mr. Williams paused, drumming his fingers nervously on his pant leg. "And how is the weather in your county? I believe you said you hailed from Durham."

*Saved by the weather.* However, Miss Williams's frustration was palpable. It was evident she had more to say but was unwilling to interrupt her father. If the girl had not been so immediately hostile against her, Sybil would have liked to ask more questions about Nicholas's rise to the earldom.

When they had known each other in London he had claimed no such right. But they had rarely spoken of such matters. From the little she could remember, his father was not in line for a title. She knew he was somehow related to the Marquess of something and the Earl of blank. Penbrose had obviously been the name of the latter.

Curse her poor memory. She did recall one piece of information, however. Some discord existed between Nicholas's father and the uncle to which the Williamses were acquainted. Which made the late Lord Penbrose his grandfather. Why had he not touted that relationship?

Another gentleman joined their circle, and Mr. Greenwald was obliged to step back to allow the newcomer's entrance. Turning, Sybil smiled in welcome to the man and two women. Did every man who had been invited have a set of unmarried daughters? Sybil battled back a grin as she imagined Lady Julia combing through a list until she had found every gentleman with exactly two daughters of marriageable age.

"Lord Brock," her father said, "might I present my daughter, Miss Greenwald."

The tall man with the slightly rounded middle stared down his nose at her. Sybil was caught off guard by that nose, long and angular with a distinct crook in the middle. She had never seen the likes of it. Perhaps it had been broken and not set quite right. Other than the unsightly nose, the older man was not terrible to look at, with his light blond hair and hazel eyes. He was dressed in the first stare of fashion from his form fitting jacket to his highly polished Hessians.

"A pleasure to meet you." Sybil dipped into a proper curtsy. The older gentleman, however, barely acknowledged her presence with a dip of his head.

"Yes, yes," he said with some annoyance. "And this is my daughter, Miss Cattering," indicating the young woman standing directly to his right. Sybil dipped a smaller curtsy to the tall, full-figured blonde.

Miss Cattering, like her father, barely acknowledged them with the slightest of curtsies. The self-important manner with which she held herself, glancing about the room as if they were beneath her notice, left Sybil in no doubt that Miss Cattering considered herself the most important woman in the room.

Sybil glanced to the right of Miss Cattering at the second young woman, but Lord Brock had already entered into conversation with Mr. Williams. His oversight was not even noticed by the Williamses, but her father had noticed. He met her questioning gaze.

She hoped Miss Cattering might rectify the oversight, but the woman subtly motioned to the two sisters, and without a word, the three girls left the group and crossed the room to a pair of gentlemen standing by the pianoforte. The smaller woman watched them go but did not seem inclined to follow, nor did she seem interested in stepping any closer into the group to stand by her father.

Finally, Sybil took pity on the young woman and decided to introduce herself. Clearing her throat, she was stunned into silence when the woman lifted her gaze from the floor. She had never seen eyes like hers before. Green circled her pupils, but as the color moved to the outer edge of her iris, it faded into blue, making them appear almost turquoise. They reminded Sybil of the ocean on a sunny day.

"Hello," she said tentatively, finally finding her voice. "Please forgive me for forwarding my own acquaintance, but it seems your father did not notice you were standing near the group. I am Miss Greenwald."

The young woman smiled slightly. "I am Miss Diana Cattering, and Lord Brock is not my father. He is my uncle. I am sure he knew I was here, but I thank you all the same."

Not her father, then. But the slight distance in relationship did not merit the lack of attention. Sybil was even more affronted on behalf of the young miss.

Sybil smiled brightly at Miss Diana. "Has anyone ever told you that you have the most exquisite eyes? I was quite taken aback by their beauty when I first saw you."

Miss Diana blushed prettily. "My mother often tells me so. She says they are the best mix between her blue eyes and my father's green ones."

"I must agree with your mother. They are quite striking."

"Thank you, Miss Greenwald," she said, ducking her head.

"You are quite welcome."

Seeing Lord Penbrose enter and begin making his way in her direction, Sybil quickly devised a plan. As much as her traitorous heart was drawn to him, she had a promise to keep. Hopefully, in only a few more hours, she would be safely away from Penbrose House. No need to break her vow if she did not have to.

"Well, Miss Diana"—she cast the girl a conspiratorial grin— "would you like to take a turn about the room with me? I see someone coming this way I should very much like to avoid, and you have presented the perfect excuse."

"Anything I might do to help," the petite woman said.

Taking hold of Miss Diana's arm, she steered her toward one of the unoccupied sofas. However, just as they sat, Mr. Lenning took up the other remaining space. Miss Diana appeared surprised to be sandwiched between Sybil and Mr. Lenning but did not scoot away.

"My apologies," he said. "There are so few places to sit in the room, and I had not realized we were destined for the same seats until we all began to sit."

Sybil doubted his words; there was too much of a roguish glint in his eyes to believe him completely innocent, but she did not press him.

"Mr. Lenning, are you acquainted with Miss Diana Cattering?"

"I am not," he said all too innocently. This, then, had been his design. Sybil could not blame him. Visually, Miss Diana was as her Roman name suggested, a goddess among women.

"Miss Diana, this is Mr. Lenning, from..." Sybil suddenly realized she did not know where Mr. Lenning hailed from.

"Venworth," he supplied. "It is a small village just outside of Oxford. My family owns a small estate there. Have you heard of Fallow Hall?"

"No," Sybil said, "but I am unfamiliar with much of the country. Living so far north and not being tolerant of long journeys, I do not travel often."

"I have heard of Venworth," Miss Diana as she stared intently at her hands, "but I have not heard of Fallow Hall. I have family in that area. Have you heard of the Marrols?"

"At Foxcroft Grange, why, yes, I am well acquainted with the family."

"Mrs. Marrol is my mother's cousin."

"I see. Have you ever been to visit?"

"I visited twice as a child," she said, "before my father's passing. It is a very beautiful place. I have many fond memories of playing with my cousins there."

"Oh, I am glad to hear it," Mr. Lenning said, smiling. Miss Diana finally raised her eyes enough to look directly at Mr. Lenning. The moment his eyes met Miss Diana's, his breath hitched. Miss Diana self-consciously dropped her gaze back to her lap, and Mr. Lenning resumed breathing. An uncomfortable moment of silence followed.

Sybil finally cut through it. "If you do not mind me asking, how long has it been since your father's passing?" She directed the inquiry at Miss Diana. Not the most cheerful of subjects, she knew, but lately, death was never far from her mind.

"Five years this September," she said quietly. "I was fifteen at the time."

This surprised Sybil. She would have guessed the girl barely beyond the schoolroom. It must be owing to her slight frame. She was not particularly short, but everything else seemed petite on her, from her small pert nose to the tiny fingers she was now interweaving in her skirts. The only thing not small were those impressive eyes. They seemed bigger than all her other proportions, lending her a look of wide-eyed innocence.

"What a difficult time to lose a parent," Mr. Lenning said. "My father passed two years ago, but I was three and twenty at the time. It is much different as an adult."

Sybil struggled with the direction of their conversation. Why had she so foolishly brought it up? Her grief, while it had faded, would crop up at the most inopportune times. She was nearly twenty when Mama had quietly slipped away. Even though she was technically an adult, she still felt like a little girl in her loss.

Miss Diana and Mr. Lenning continued speaking on the topic in quiet tones as Sybil scanned the room. Perhaps by blocking out the particulars of their discussion she could regain the composure she was sure was slipping.

The gold-trimmed room with cream papered walls was quite full. There must be nearly thirty people, and as she had noted before, ladies outnumbered gentlemen.

A slight touch to her arm brought Sybil back into the conversation. Miss Diana was looking at her expectantly, and she realized she must have missed something. "Pardon me. My mind must have wandered."

"'Tis no matter. I only observed your gray gown. If you do not mind my forwardness, I wondered if you are in mourning."

Sybil did not mind that Miss Diana had asked, but she did mind that she was now obligated to speak on the subject. "Yes, for my mother," she said slowly, endeavoring to keep her feelings in check.

"Oh, I am sorry. How long has it been?" Miss Diana's doe eyes softened. Her compassion almost undid the last bits of Sybil's composure, but at that very moment Lord Penbrose began making his way in their direction again. She could not break down now.

"A year and a month," Sybil said simply. "If you will please excuse me for a moment, my father is beckoning me, and I must attend to him." It was a lie, but the only way she could possibly keep from having to speak to Lord Penbrose was to not be caught in conversation with him. So if he was bound for his friend, she would be bound for anywhere else.

As she stood, she noticed Miss Diana's distressed face. "You are welcome to join me, Miss Diana, if you wish."

The young woman appeared relieved as she joined Sybil and they made their escape. Just in time too, as Lord Penbrose was almost to the sofa.

Glancing briefly over her shoulder, she saw confusion register on his far too attractive face. His hazel eyes swept the room. Perhaps he had not seen their removal as he'd weaved his way through the other guests.

Sybil rejoiced at outwitting him yet again. In an odd way, this impromptu game of cat and mouse was quite thrilling. Of course, she had always enjoyed being pursued by Nicholas.

Frantically, she pushed the thought back down. By morning she would be gone. She could not let him draw her in again.

# Chapter Six

Where had they gone? Nicholas was sure Miss Diana had been sitting here just moments before. The young woman had seemed so fragile and friendless when the Catterings had arrived this morning. He wanted to put her at ease in his home, but it appeared Sybil was determined to keep her from him.

He caught sight of Sybil's dark tresses as she wove her way among the guests, Miss Diana firmly in tow. Not wanting to appear as if in avid pursuit, he stopped for a moment to speak with Bradley.

"It would seem you have met the younger Miss Cattering," he said, his eyes flitting from the blonde beauty to the tall slender temptress at her side.

"I have." Amusement lit Bradley's face. "I must say, I have not met her equal in all my time in London or abroad."

"Yes, she is quite unique," Nicholas acknowledged. "Shy, too, if I have not missed the mark."

"I noticed that as well, but not so much that she can barely utter a word. We talked for upwards of ten minutes before you scared the ladies away."

"Me? What makes you think I scared them away? I would wager it was that hideous purple waistcoat you have on," Nicholas said, indicating Bradley's attire. Truthfully, the deep purple looked quite well with Bradley's black jacket and grey pantaloons, but Nicholas would never admit as much.

"Say what you must to comfort yourself, Penbrose." Bradley used Nicholas's title due to the gathered crowd of people. "But you and I both know you like my waistcoat, and you dislike Miss Greenwald. And if her hasty retreat is anything to go by, the feeling is mutual."

"Yes, and it would seem Miss Greenwald has unfortunately become acquainted with Miss Diana," Nicholas said with a huff.

"And why does that frustrate you, *my lord*? Is it not good that someone befriended the girl? Because from the looks of things, her family does not give two figs about her."

"Don't you go 'my lording' me now, Lenning," Nicholas ignored the truths Bradley spoke. And if his irritation actually stemmed from not being able to get within ten feet of Sybil, well, he would never admit it to his friend.

Bradley's smirk grew to a grin. He was nettling Nicholas, as was the custom in their friendship. He eyed the women across the room, then, turned to Nicholas.

"You are dodging. Why are you not pleased with Miss Greenwald's acquaintance with Miss Diana?"

"Because Miss Greenwald will corrupt the poor girl, that is why."

Bradley coughed in an attempt to cover his laugh. "Miss Greenwald is not all that bad, Penbrose. She has been nothing but polite when in my company. Honestly, with all you have told me of her, I am somewhat shocked."

"Why is that?"

"Well, I guess I expected to see the young lady sporting horns and carrying a trident after your impassioned descriptions of her treachery."

"You do not see them?" Nicholas asked with a raised eyebrow. "Ah, well, it must be all that dark hair piled on her head. It hides her horns well."

He tried not to let his eyes stray to those luscious locks. Memories of an errant curl wrapped around his finger assailed him and he shook his head.

"Well, if that is the case," Bradley said, "it is no wonder that Miss Greenwald is keeping company with Miss Diana Cattering, for Miss Diana is a veritable angel."

"An angel and a devil, how is that not a wonder?"

"Opposites attract."

"They do not," Nicholas said emphatically. "At least not in terms of angels and devils. In this case, I am afraid Miss Greenwald has been sent to tempt Miss Diana."

"Or Miss Diana has been sent to redeem Miss Greenwald from her wicked ways. Either way, I believe they shall be good for one another as one in our estimations is far too good for this world, and the other too bad. Best to make a mix of devil and angel, for then they will be as we are."

"And what is that, pray tell?"

"Human." Bradley grinned.

"Touché, my friend." Nicholas felt his lips twitch. Bradley, usually the clown of his close group of friends from Eton, had bested him at wits.

His gaze again strayed to Sybil. She was trying to smother a laugh, and he could see that all too familiar sparkle of amusement in her eye. Something tugged at his heart and his lips pulled into a small smile of their own accord.

The doors opened, and the servants entered the room carrying trays laden with small cakes and sandwiches, large tea pots of hot water, tea leaves, cream and sugar.

His mother approached the laden tables, two matronly ladies flanking her sides. With deft hands, the three ladies prepared cup after cup of tea for the gathered group. Soon everyone present was enjoying the afternoon repast.

Taking his own teacup to a seat at the edge of the room, Nicholas was pleased to find himself in company with Mr. Martin. He had been acquainted with the man most of his life, as their estates were but seven miles from one another. They had not claimed a close relationship, however, until after Nicholas's father's death. Mr. Martin had become a sort of mentor, helping him learn the responsibilities of running an estate.

"Martin, how was your journey?" Nicholas asked before taking a sip of his tea.

"Quite pleasant. The weather was fine, the journey not too long, and I was happy to get away from the London crush."

"Yes, the countryside is a fair bit more enjoyable than London this time of year."

"Most definitely, and the company is good, too," Mr. Martin said, tipping his head toward Nicholas.

Nicholas smiled. "Did you stop by Martin's Lodge on your way from London?"

"We did. I had some business—"

"Lord Penbrose, there you are," a high sickeningly sweet voice broke in. Nicholas tried not to groan.

"It has been an age since we were last in company together," Miss Cattering said, batting her eyelashes at him.

Rising out of duty, Nicholas acknowledged Miss Cattering and the Williams sisters.

"Has it?" he questioned. Had he not welcomed her and her father and cousin just this morning upon their arrival?

"Why, yes, I believe the last time we have been able to spend more than a moment's greeting was two years ago at the Wilmoth's ball."

Nicholas was surprised she would even bring up that unfortunate encounter. Perhaps they remembered the event differently, but he doubted it.

At the ball of which she spoke, Miss Cattering had barely even acknowledged his presence. Halfway through the ball, however, Nicholas had noticed she was in want of a partner. Thinking to show her some kindness, he had offered to lead her to the floor. To his surprise, she had refused him, claiming she needed rest, but instead of sitting down she made her way to a different part of the ballroom. Only a few moments later, Nicholas had seen her being led to the floor by another gentleman whom he knew to be in expectation of a title. Her slight had not gone unnoticed.

With the barrage of smiles and glances she had cast his way since her arrival, however, Nicholas was quite sure she had recently had a change of heart. What a difference a title made in the minds of Society.

"Was it?" Nicholas asked, all too innocently. "Were you in attendance at the Wilmoth's ball?" It certainly was not gentlemanly of him to imply he had forgotten her, but he could not help himself now that the tables had turned.

"Oh... well," Miss Cattering said as a blush rose to her cheeks.

Nicholas was sure she remembered clearly, but if she tried to bring up their interaction to jostle his memory, she would be forced to acknowledge her own rudeness. He had her backed into a proverbial corner, and he could not say he was sorry for it in the least.

After a moment, she chose to abandon the subject all together. "You have quite the gathering here. This house party is bound to be a pleasant experience with so many *interesting* people in attendance." Miss Cattering's words seemed to indicate she thought them odd and assorted rather than actually of interest.

"I hope it is a success for my mother's sake," he said, trying to remind Miss Cattering who had made the guest list. "She has taken great care to plan this gathering. I would hate for anything to go amiss."

"Lady Julia is an exceptionally talented hostess," Mr. Martin complimented. "I am sure anything in her care could not possibly go awry."

Miss Cattering took in Mr. Martin a moment before apparently deciding an introduction was not necessary. Turning her body to somewhat exclude the gentleman, she directed her comments to Nicholas and the Williams sisters.

"I am sure she has planned plenty of diverting activities for us to partake in. Can you tell us about them?"

Miss Cattering's behavior toward Mr. Martin rankled Nicholas. How dare she mistreat his friend. He decided an introduction would be made whether she liked it or not.

With some unholy pleasure, he said, "Please forgive my negligence, Miss Cattering. May I introduce Mr. Martin? His estate borders Fairfield Manor on the south. We use his road as a shortcut when we travel to Harlow." Turning to his long-time neighbor, he said, "Mr. Martin, this is the honorable Miss Cattering, daughter of Lord Brock."

Miss Cattering seemed unimpressed but gave a perfunctory curtsy anyway. Mr. Martin gave a very proper bow in response.

"And these," Nicholas indicated the other two women, "are the Williams sisters. Miss Williams and Miss Lydia Williams. They hail from the town of Whitney in Oxford."

Both ladies curtsied, and Miss Lydia, who seemed less disgusted with the introduction than Miss Cattering, said, "I am unfamiliar with Harlow. Where, pray tell, is it?"

"About thirty miles northeast of London in Essex County," Mr. Martin answered with a polite smile.

"You must be often in London, then," Miss Williams responded.

"I am, indeed. My business brings me to London a good majority of the year."

"Do you often go for the season?" Miss Lydia's tone held a bit of excitement.

"Yes. I usually spend a good deal of the spring in London."

"Do you keep rooms or have you a home of your own there?" she pressed.

Had the girl taken a special interest in his friend, Nicholas wondered? The honey blonde leaned closer toward Mr. Martin with each question.

"I have a London residence," Mr. Martin said slowly. He eyed the young women, misgiving evident in the expression.

Miss Cattering perked up at this revelation, finally gaining interest in conversing with the gentleman. She appraised Mr. Martin from his head of neatly styled dark hair down to his polished boots. No doubt she was probably calculating his monetary worth. Apparently, the idea of speaking with a mere mister was not quite so distasteful if he could keep a London townhome.

"And where is this residence in London?" she asked doubtfully.

Nicholas saw the dilemma Mr. Martin was facing. Telling the arrogant miss would put her squarely in her place but would possibly lose him his peace and enjoyment for the rest of the house party.

Mr. Martin, while fairly unassuming in appearance, was as rich as king Midas. The man held more properties than most duchies. Some from family inheritance, but many acquired through sound investments.

However, he went to great lengths to hide his wealth for two important reasons. The first was for his own safety as lord and highwayman alike would both love a chance to empty his pockets. And the second of those was standing right before him. Mr. Martin could not stand grasping misses and their meddling mamas.

Nicholas did not blame him. In his estimation, grasping women were no different than highwaymen. Both were only after Mr. Martin's money and would stop at nothing to get a portion. At least with the highwayman, he might be rid of him shortly, but a lady would suck him dry for rest of his life.

For Mr. Martin's sake, Nicholas hoped he would keep his peace. Unfortunately, Mr. Martin either felt the need to exert a little influence or was much more forthcoming than he would have been, for he answered simply, "Maddox Street."

The ladies took a collective breath at the fashionable address.

As smiles began to spread on each of their faces, Mr. Martin turned to Nicholas and asked, "Did I just see Lady Olivia enter?"

Nicholas's head whipped around, surprised to see his cousin, Lady Olivia Burtrum, daughter of his Aunt Evelyn, walk toward his mother. The look on his mother's face was every bit as shocked as his. She sprang from her chair, greeting Olivia with both enthusiasm and alarm.

If Lady Olivia had arrived, then so had his aunt. Nicholas's cousin Edward Burtrum, Marquess of Caraway, was to escort the family here, but they had not been expected until tomorrow.

Seeing his mother's distress and subsequent departure from the room, Nicholas said, "Please do excuse me. I must attend to my cousin."

"I shall accompany you," Mr. Martin insisted. "Ladies," he said with a bow.

As they made their way across the room, Mr. Martin whispered, "Bless Lady Olivia for her timely entrance. I owe her for giving me a much-needed excuse to extricate myself from the grasping gleam I saw in Miss Lydia Williams's eye."

"Miss Lydia! I should say that Miss Cattering had the far more predatory look."

"You may be right; however, I believe her attentions are focused elsewhere." He gave Nicholas a sidelong glance. Nicholas caught the hint but was unwilling to discuss the subject.

When his mother had made plans for this house party, he had hoped for three weeks of relaxing entertainment. His mother had not been far from the truth when she had said he worked too hard. The strain of the long hours was wearing on him. While he *now* had competent stewards, they all still required oversight to make sure things ran efficiently and honestly.

Already he had been required to replace the Penbrose House steward as he had not been honest in his accounts and was now sitting in the gaol in Kettering. It would seem, though, that the rest he had planned for himself would be hard-won if all the ladies invited were as tiring as Miss Cattering.

Stopping in front of Lady Olivia, both men bowed. She bobbed a curtsy much like a cork in water. Nicolas smiled at his enthusiastic cousin.

"Good afternoon, Olivia. You made quite the entrance."

"You know me, Nickie. I cannot help taking advantage of a moment of surprise."

Mr. Martin's left eyebrow arched, casting an amused look at Nicholas. Apparently her use of his childhood nickname had been quite amusing to his old neighbor. Leave it to Olivia to bring a man down a peg with her impetuous use of the moniker. He really should have expected it, though. She always had enjoyed defying propriety every now and then, and apparently now seemed as good a time as any.

"And this was a prime opportunity to cause a stir," he said indulgently. "Why didn't your mother and brother come in?"

"Oh, Mama was far too tired after the journey and decided to retire for the evening. Edward and Caroline are helping her get settled upstairs."

"And Caroline's husband?"

A sour expression crossed Lady Olivia's face. "He could not be imposed upon to attend. You know how he is."

Nicholas did know. His cousin's husband did not care for large crowds. Caroline, on the other hand, adored socializing and flitted about the countryside enough for the both of them. He would have worried more about her relationship had not Caroline adored her husband. Truthfully, he was a bit envious.

"Well, I am glad you have arrived safely. I hope we will see Edward and Caroline at dinner."

"Thank you. I am sure they will be down by then. Now, where is Mary?" Olivia's eyes flitted about the room as if she had no patience to wait for Nicholas's reply. Of course Olivia's first thought would be for his sister Mary. The two were as thick as thieves every time they were in company with one another.

"I am afraid she has not arrived yet from her stay with the Claptons."

"That is unfortunate. I would have thought your mother would have wanted her here to help greet all the guests. It is her duty as the eldest daughter, is it not?"

"That had been the plan; however, she took ill at the Claptons a few days back, and they chose to delay their journey in order for her to recover."

"Oh, I do hope it is nothing serious." Real concern and alarm laced her voice.

"Nothing to fret over, dear cousin. An illness of the stomach is all. Mrs. Clapton wrote us day before yesterday to say that Mary was much recovered, and they would be about their journey today. They planned to spend one evening at an inn and be here early upon the morrow."

"I am glad of it. I have been so looking forward to these weeks with Mary." Recollecting her manners, Olivia turned to Mr. Martin. "And how are you this afternoon, Mr. Martin? It has been at least a twelve month since I saw you last."

"It has at that." A genuine smile curved on Mr. Martin's lips. "And somehow in that year you have grown even lovelier than I remember."

"That, sir, is because you have a faulty memory," she said cheekily. The teasing smile on her lips and the hint of a blush on her cheeks had Nicholas glancing between the two.

"I do not believe so." Mr. Martin's smile widened to a grin. "But who am I to correct a lady? It is good to see you, Lady Olivia. How was your journey?"

The question led into a very animated retelling. Apparently, his aunt and her family had been in Bristol finalizing some details before Edward's marriage to Lady Agatha Easton. The first set of banns were to be read this Sunday.

Nicholas realized he was only half listening to the current conversation as he surveyed the room, but Olivia could talk for a full quarter-hour without needing a single response in return. His mother had reentered the room. Thankfully, she seemed less harried and far more composed. All must be well with the rest of the Burtrum family.

*Good.* It would not do to have something go wrong in their first endeavor to show the world he was capable of this title. Heavens knew there were many naysayers, Uncle Fairchild and his sons in particular. They were hoping, if not praying, for his failure as the earl.

Nicholas felt his congenial mask slipping. The thought of his Uncle Fairchild and his two cousins never failed to dampen his mood. That they had been angry when he rose to the title was a complete understatement. Livid would be a better descriptor. Over the last six months they had exhausted every avenue of the law, except petitioning the Prince Regent, to disprove the testimonies given in the late Lord Penbrose's will; but in the end, the will was deemed solid, and they had reached a sort of ceasefire. If only Society would do the same.

When Nicholas crossed paths with his uncle and cousins Tom and John, they were civil to him, but no more than that. He, in turn, tried to be civil to them, but at times he could not help wishing there was a way to divorce one's family because he was quite sick to death of not only their rudeness to him, his mother, and sisters, but also of the constant reports of Tom's unscrupulous behavior.

He had learned from the best, Nicholas thought darkly. It was no secret Uncle Fairchild had kept a mistress for years. He had, in fact, fathered a son and two daughters by her. How he was able to remain in polite society, Nicholas still could not fathom. Perhaps his constant claims of being the older son had helped. Why in heaven's name had his grandfather not corrected Uncle

Fairchild before his passing? Then again, Grandfather had not been right ever since his oldest son's death the year before.

Olivia's voice suddenly reached through the perturbation of Nicholas's mind.

"Oh, please do excuse me." Nicholas tried to reestablish his company smile. "What were we speaking of?"

"Are you quite all right, Nicholas?" Olivia asked. "You looked as if you were ready to go to war, or perhaps call someone out." She glanced around the room trying to identify his target.

Bradley's voice responded from near Nicholas's left shoulder, catching him by surprise. When had he joined their circle?

"Oh, I am sure he is. Did you not know, Lady Olivia, Nicholas's archenemy has reappeared, and he must assemble his armor and troops forthwith."

Nicholas rolled his eyes at Bradley's melodramatic speech. "Well, then I should probably inform you that I plan on putting you on the front lines. Hopefully, it will keep you busy enough that you will stop running your mouth."

"Do tell," Lady Olivia said, a gleam in her eye at being able to receive such juicy gossip. Covertly, she redoubled her efforts to scan the room for the objective. "Who is this archenemy? You say he is actually here?"

"Not *he*, Lady Olivia. *She*." Jubilation lit Bradley's face when Olivia's eyes shot to his.

"You mean to say Miss Greenwald is *here*?" she asked in an excited whisper.

Nicholas decided a hasty retreat was necessary to save his own composure. He had guests to see to and wished to be spared his friends' and family's speculation.

"Well, I believe this is my time to move on and mingle with the other guests," he said dryly. "That way you all may gossip properly."

"Properly?" Bradley asked.

"Yes," Nicholas replied. "Behind my back, like the good old tabbies of the Ton do." Bowing, he extricated himself from the group. The devious smile on

Bradley's face let him know he was not far from the mark. By the time they all retired for the night, Olivia would be completely caught up on the Fairchild family gossip.

# Chapter Seven

Sybil had hoped to speak with her father after tea, but he was always in company with someone. Unable to relay a message to him without causing a disturbance, she found herself waiting for him to leave the drawing room after dinner. She was exhausted after a morning of travel and an evening of socializing. Her bed was calling, but she refused to stay more than one night in this horrible place.

It was bad enough to be trapped in a home with Lord Penbrose, but during tea she had overheard Mr. Lenning speaking with a gentleman and lady, and, to her horror, she had been the subject of the conversation. Did all of Lord Penbrose's family and friends know of their past? It was London all over again.

Immediately her anger had ignited, adding starch to her spine and fire to her soul. Sybil knew in order to contain herself, she would need to retreat. But not without a little retribution. She had approached Mr. Lenning from behind. Unaware of her presence, he had prattled on, but the lady and gentleman he was speaking to had not been so oblivious. The various throat clearings and eye movements would have been hilarious if she had not been so mortified.

She had made a pretense of searching for someone and quickly shifted course, but not before walking close enough that her skirts brushed the back of Mr. Lenning's legs. It had been quite rewarding to see his chagrin as she passed by.

It had taken all her courage to attend dinner after her embarrassment at tea. The only way to silence rumors, though, was to make a good show. So she pushed forward when she would have rather stayed in her room for the night.

The rest of the evening had gone smoothly, except for the part that had her now waiting in a small alcove just down the hall from her father's bedchambers. The window in the alcove looked out over the gardens of the estate. Surely the view would have been beautiful if it were not full dark out. There was no moon tonight and only stars dotted the sky.

It truly was a shame they would be leaving in the morning. A walk through the gardens would be lovely.

Did Penbrose House have a rose garden? She was quite partial to roses especially if they had a strong scent. Around the east side of Tave Hall, there was an entire garden devoted to her roses. Mama had commissioned it when Sybil was ten, all because she had declared roses her favorite flower.

Oh, how she loved that patch of earth. Every spring it came alive with vibrant reds, yellows, pinks, and oranges. Her personal favorites were the white and orange roses with red tips. The colors spoke to her soul. Her own life, no matter the color, was always tinged with fiery red. Fire was in her blood. Seeing the representation on a flower soothed her. She was not the only one of God's creations with fire in their soul.

Hearing the low timbre of her father's voice, she stepped from the alcove ready to greet him. But to her dismay, she saw he was in company with Lord Penbrose. Both gentlemen stopped when they noticed her.

Her father peered at Lord Penbrose, but the man's eyes were locked on her. Her breath hitched and she quickly glanced down at her hands. Heat crept up her neck and warmed her cheeks.

Was she blushing? She hoped not. Not wanting Lord Penbrose to get the wrong idea, she straightened her shoulders and raised her head to look at him, but he had turned back to her father.

"Well, Mr. Greenwald," he said, "this is where I bid you goodnight. The family wing is down that corridor." He motioned with a slight movement of his head in the opposite direction from the guest rooms. "It has been good to see you again. I do hope you enjoy your stay. My mother has looked forward to your visit. I believe it has been the highlight of this house party for her."

"I would not have missed a party hosted by your mother for a kingdom. She has been a dear friend to me, and I am in her debt for helping me see my way back into Society."

What was this? As far as Sybil knew, her father had only received the one missive from Lady Julia containing the invitation to this party. But apparently there was more to their correspondence than her father had let on. What else was he not telling her?

"She will be glad to hear it. Good evening." Lord Penbrose bowed, then turned to her. "Miss Greenwald." After another bow, he turned and made his way down the hall.

"I thought you had gone to bed an hour past," her father said once they were alone.

"I needed to speak with you, Father."

"Father! I really must be in the suds if you have reverted to such a formal address. Come. There is a small parlor just off the hall before the guest chambers where we can have a private moment to speak. I am quite sure by the set of your chin, you would rather not have an audience as you filet my hide," he said with a smirk.

His light manner of speaking took a little of the starch out of her spine. Sybil tried to formulate the best argument to extricate herself from Penbrose House as they made their way into the small room.

The space was dark save for a few coals burning in the grate. A maid must have lit a fire when the sun went down, for most of the grates in the house were empty of flame. Sybil was about to borrow one of candelabras from the hall when her father moved to the fireplace and took up the poker. Moving the coals about, he was able to produce a small flame that lit the room enough to give it a comforting glow.

"That is a bit better," he said.

They sat in the chairs facing the fire and Sybil began her inquiry. "Why did you not tell me Mr. Fairchild was the new Earl of Penbrose? Porter already admitted you swore her to silence."

"Because you would not have come." A look of contemplation crossed his face as he turned to her.

"So you tricked me." Her neck and face grew hot with anger.

"No. You never asked."

"Yes, I did." Her voice became strained as she tried to keep her tone even. "In the carriage, remember? You said that Lady Julia was to act as hostess for this party and I asked for a surname."

"And I gave you one."

"But not the correct one, Papa. And when I pressed for more, you acted as though you did not know her married name."

His look of contemplation now seemed calculated. "I suppose you did, but you did not ask before you agreed to attend the house party."

"It was deceptive of you, Papa!" She almost shouted, but at the last moment hushed her voice so as not to alert anyone. "I have never known you to be thus."

He heaved a great sigh before turning fully to face her. "Sybil, would you have come if I had told you one of my dearest friends would be here?"

His strong words and desperate tone caught her off guard. The winding tale of how he knew Lady Julia and his childhood friend Lady Evelyn came to her mind. Apparently the story had been more important than she had given it credit. She searched his eyes for a moment but was still unsure how to answer. Would she have? Sybil was not completely sure. But at this moment, she was desperate to avoid any further embarrassment.

"Could you not have seen Lady Evelyn at another place or another time? Some place where Lord Penbrose was not?"

"Perhaps," he said slowly, "but when would that occasion arise? If there is one thing I have learned from losing your mother, it is not to let life's opportunities pass you by. We never know when the next will be, Sybil, or even if we will get another chance. I saw this chance, and I took it. I knew you would not be happy with the situation, but I think you need this opportunity as much as I do. You, my girl, have been too withdrawn, too solemn, too alone."

"But here?" she squeaked.

"Here is as good a place as any," he said. "I think it high time you admit to yourself that you need to speak to Mr.—erm, Lord Penbrose. From the small amount you told me of your last conversation, I believe you both left things unsaid."

"I cannot!" An unseen tightness clawed at her throat.

"Why ever not?"

"Because, Papa, the last thing I ever said to him was that I would never speak with him again, and I will not go back on my word."

"Do you think you are the first woman to ever utter those words in anger? Perhaps, my dear child, this stay will be a good lesson in humility."

She shot to her feet. "I do not wish to stay, Papa. I wish to leave! First thing in the morning."

"I am not leaving, Sybil." He rubbed his temples.

"Then send me and my maid home. We shall be fine at Tave Hall without you for a few weeks."

"No, Sybil," he said firmly.

The stern tone caught her by surprise. She had always been able to persuade him into her way of thinking. She could count on two hands the times in her life he had actually said no outright. It was usually a *not today* or *maybe another time* but hardly ever an actual no.

"But, Papa, you cannot think to subject me to this humiliation. It is not just Lord Penbrose I cannot face. I overheard some of the other guests talking about me and my history with him. How can you want me to relive that hurt? Do you want my reputation to be further maligned by this house party?"

"So a few guests know your history. It is not likely to cause any more of a stir than the small conversation you already overheard. It was years ago, Sybil. It cannot hurt you now. This is your chance to show Society that strong backbone of yours."

"You are determined to see me suffer, then?" Heaving a sigh, he said, "The amount you suffer is entirely up to you. Make of this house party what you will, but I will not be persuaded to leave. I know you will view me as cruel, but you'd best reconcile yourself to our original plans. We will leave three weeks hence and not a day earlier."

Sybil wanted to scream or throw something. Taking a deep breath and counting backwards from one hundred, she searched her mind for any other argument she could give to change her father's mind.

"You might as well switch your counting to French," he said, "for what I have to say next will probably anger you more." There was a hardness to his voice that surprised her. A slight fissure of fear ran down her spine. "Your mother and I did our best by you. We loved you, taught you to be a lady, and gave you everything a girl could ever desire. However, I now see we did not do enough. I am quite ashamed to say it, but lately you have been quite selfish."

His words stung, more than any other word he had ever uttered. Words from another man in her past echoed in her ears. *"You are selfish, Sybil."*

How could her father, of all people, say such a thing? Had she not nursed her mother? Was she not willing to give up her life to care for him? Tears pricked the back of her eyes. Her Papa had always been gentle and kind. How could he say such things?

He stood. "We are not leaving, no matter your protest, so you might as well consign yourself to our stay. I hope you will make the best of our time here, but even if you do not, I shall make the best of mine. Good night."

Sybil knew he was angry, and somewhere in the back of her mind she realized he was probably hurt, but his words kept washing over her again and again like waves lapping at the shore. *Selfish. Selfish. Selfish.* With each wave, bits and pieces of her anger washed out into a sea of guilt. She could see now how desperate her father was to have this time, and what had been her response?

She had begged him to give it up. No, not begged, basically demanded. She had thought only of her discomfort at being face to face with Nicholas once again. She had demanded her comfort over her Papa's happiness.

Wiping away the  tears that had trickled down her cheeks, she thought through all the times her father had stopped what he was doing to give into her demands. Each memory was more painful than the last as the truth sank into the recesses of her heart. Her selfishness had not been purposeful. At least she did not think so.

She simply felt her way was best, and if someone did not agree, she would press them until they saw the right of it.

She let out a short bitter laugh. Was that not the nature of selfishness, trying to make everything and everyone act in your favor? How had she not recognized it before? It was thoughtless on her part, but her thoughtlessness was not malicious.

Was it her fault if he thought her cruel? She had never meant it to be. Besides, he had been the one to lie to her. Was that not just as unkind? Either way, she would have to stay here.

Going back on her own promise galled her, but she could not very well keep silent for three whole weeks, especially after her father's accusation. She would show him. She was not as selfish as he might think.

Tomorrow she would talk to Lord Penbrose. It would not be so terrible. How hard could a few greetings possibly be?

# Chapter Eight

G reeting Nicholas, it turns out, was quite possibly the hardest greeting Sybil would ever be required to give. She was quite sure it might be the death of her. Nervousness drove her from bed early so she rang for Porter to help her dress for the day. It was her routine to take Tempest out for a ride every morning, but today especially, it was a necessity. A nice bruising ride would be just the thing to clear her head.

After dressing in her riding habit, she slipped down to the breakfast parlor. Not yet ready to face Lord Penbrose, she listened at the door for movement. When no sound came, she slowly peeked in, breathing out a sigh of relief when the long narrow room was blessedly empty. Hopefully, the others would be in bed for quite some time. She was in no mood for company.

She quickly breakfasted on tea and toast, not wanting to take time to eat much else, lest any of the other guests should arrive. Having not slept well due to the hard cry she had indulged in at bedtime, her face was unusually puffy, which probably did not do anything for her appearance. The cool morning air would hopefully help remove the evidence of her fretful night.

Tempest was saddled when Sybil reached the stable, the Tave Hall groom waiting by his own mount. As she approached, he started toward her mare, but she waved him away. She was no helpless miss, and Cormac knew it. Tempest began to prance at her side as she led her toward the mounting block. Sybil smiled to herself at the spirited animal's antics and was grateful Tempest's current mood matched her own. They were two springs tightly coiled, ready to be sprung.

Mounting the mare used to take some time with her constant motion, but Tempest had learned very quickly. The sooner she settled next to the mounting block, the sooner she could run. Sybil swiftly seated herself, wrapping her right leg around the fixed head of the saddle, then quickly squeezing her left under the leaping head before Tempest set to prancing beneath her again.

She held Tempest back as they crossed the fields behind Penbrose House. She needed to get some distance from the house before letting Tempest have her head. When they reached the top of the rise, she turned the mare to face the estate.

Penbrose House sat imposingly in the distance. Sybil scoffed at the name of the place. Could the past proprietors not have named the monstrous edifice something more fitting? The grey stone building was far more than a house, but not quite a castle. It had three levels above ground and boasted more than forty bedrooms, at least according to the housekeeper's words. Who knew how many more were in the servants' domain which lay below stairs.

Tempest snorted, obviously frustrated with her mistress's woolgathering. They had made their way to this point at an antsy trot, Tempest being far too excited for her run to maintain anything decorous. As it was, she was only standing marginally still because Sybil was keeping her tightly reigned in.

Sybil turned and nodded to the groom, their well-known signal that she was letting her horse go. Cormac would do his best to keep up, but he would be lucky if he stayed within twenty paces of her on a good day. She turned Tempest toward the open fields and let the mare loose. With a large leap, the mare shot out, reaching a full run within seconds. The cool air held a bit of a bite as it hit her face. Not only would it help her swollen eyes, but perhaps put a bit of color back into her cheeks. It was so refreshing.

These early morning runs were by far Sybil's favorite time of day. She never felt more confident or accomplished than when she was in the saddle. While she was marginally good at all the lady-like pursuits, riding was her true talent.

The sound of hooves thundering to the left pulled her attention from the view of the lush fields in front of her. Glancing over her shoulder, she saw a horse and rider heading perpendicular to her own course. Had the rider been closer, she might have been worried they would collide, but Tempest would be long out of the way by time their paths crossed. Facing forward again she urged the mare on. Tempest gladly complied.

However, the sound of hooves still grew louder as a large black horse pulled up to the side of them, the rider shouting something unintelligible in the wind. How were the horse and rider keeping pace with Tempest? Papa had specifically acquired the ex-racer because of her speed. The mare had outrun almost every horse she had ever been matched against.

Out of the corner of her eye, Sybil could see the rider edge even closer. He was yelling so hard his face was red from the effort. Recognition dawned. Nicholas was riding low over his horse's saddle, trying desperately to tell her something. The frustration she saw in his face fed her natural defensive anger. She looked away from him, pulling her horse's head gently to the right hoping to redirect her course and take them away from him.

Her father's word of the night before chose that moment to assail her. *Selfish. Selfish. Selfish.* It repeated over and over again. The angry fire that licked at her heart dampened. Reigning Tempest back, the mare slowed for the wide turn—away from his lordship.

Sybil still was not ready to speak with Nicholas—Lord Penbrose yet. Hopefully, he would continue on to the house and stables.

Unfortunately, he did not. Cutting his horse in a tighter turn than hers, he brought them up on the right side of Tempest. After a few minutes of galloping side by side, Sybil pulled her horse to a stop. There was no help for it. Her vow would end here. Realizing she would probably never be ready for this encounter, she tried to steady her nerves.

She wished she had taken some time to prepare what she would say. Perhaps if they had met in a room full of people, this would not be so awkward. On second thought, she was grateful they were not in hearing of anyone else. At least here she would not be subjected to the scrutiny of the other guests. For that, she had to give begrudging thanks to Lord Penbrose for providing this circumstance.

Nicholas's heart had been in his throat as he saw the bay mare bolt from the hilltop. The small woman on top would never make it, even with her groom in hot pursuit. He had to intercept them before it was too late. He urged Rogue faster as the pair approached the stand of trees. Nicholas did not even want to imagine what would happen when the woman's horse reached the creek hiding among the tall grasses beyond the trees.

As he came abreast of the rider and horse, it struck him how well she kept her seat. She did not look concerned at all. In fact, her face appeared almost joyful. The woman glanced his way and recognition dawned. Sybil! He should have known. She had once told him how accomplished she was, but never had he imagined her this well-seated. He could not, however, let her travel in this direct course. No matter how good of a rider she was, the mud and water near the creek could break her horse's legs—and possibly Sybil's neck—in the process.

Shouting at her as loud as he could, he tried to warn her. To his dismay she turned away from him and urged her horse faster. Stubborn, reckless woman. She was going to kill herself.

Urging Rogue to match the bay's speed, he shouted until his throat grew raw. She must have heard him, for the horse slowly turned away from its current path. He sighed with relief as the horse took a wide turn to the right.

Following her movements, he pulled his horse up next to hers. When she finally stopped, a mutinous look was on her face, but he could see the moment she tried to rein in her emotions. The wrinkles in her forehead softened and the pinch at the edge of her flashing green eyes disappeared.

The mare still danced beneath her. It would seem the animal had not yet exhausted its energy.

Sybil peered expectantly at him. He tried to decide whether speaking was in his best interest while she was still trying to gain her composure. Perhaps he should wait and allow her to speak first.

After several minutes of silence, it became apparent that she had no intention of going first.

"Shall we walk them, so they might get a proper cool down?" he asked.

She dipped her head, letting her horse begin a walk that looked a little more like a sideways dance. The mare obviously would rather trot, but Rogue was spent. Nicholas felt bad for pushing him so hard but was grateful the faithful beast had given his all.

"Miss Greenwald, I am unsure if you are aware, but the stand of trees you were racing toward hides a very boggy creek beyond it." Her quick glance over her shoulder told him she did not know. He had done right, then.

"In the future, I would warn you from running this particular field. We have other fields, much drier ones that are more conducive to such speeds." Still, she said nothing.

Birds chirped in the distance and somewhere a cow lowed, but Sybil stayed quiet. The steady clop of their horses' hooves filled Nicholas's ears, making Sybil's silence even more unnerving. Suddenly he blurted out, "If you are amenable, I could show them to you on the morrow." His words caught up with his brain and he found himself confused. Why would he offer such a thing? He was still angry with her, wasn't he? Besides, Miss Sybil Greenwald wanted nothing to do with him. Why was he offering to be her personal escort?

The same surprise he felt was evident on her face. She did not look upset, though, so that was a step in the right direction.

He scanned her familiar face and with it his own heart. He expected to find anger still hidden there, but sometime in the last twenty-four hours, the coals of his indignation had begun to sputter, and instead, a different warmth filled his chest. How was it after all these years just the sight of her could still affect him so? They continued in silence for a few moments. Just when he was about to retract his words, she cleared her throat.

"If you recall, I said I would never speak to you again." Her words were tight, her expression strained.

He remembered very clearly, but somewhere deep inside he had always hoped she had not meant it. "I do."

His first instinct was to lighten the moment with a teasing remark, but a warning voice inside stopped him. For reasons he could not quite explain, he wanted the silence between them to end, and he did not believe goading her would help. If she was willing to break her promise, he would give her the time she needed to express whatever she was thinking.

Sybil sighed. "You might as well crow over me now, Mr.—I mean, Lord Penbrose. I know how much I would want to do the same."

"Miss Greenwald, I do not want to make your stay here anymore upsetting than it already has been. I do not find you weak or doubt your word because you did not hold through with your promise. I must admit myself relieved."

"Relieved?"

"Yes, I would hate for you to have to resort to pantomimes in every conversation because speaking was strictly forbidden."

Nicholas was rewarded with a broad, genuine smile, the first he had seen since she had arrived yesterday.

"Well, since we both know I am quite terrible at charades," she said, "we shall both be spared the embarrassment by my speaking."

More silence followed, but it was not the uncomfortable silence of moments before. Her mount had finally settled into a steady walk, and they rode amicably for a few moments before he recollected his earlier question.

"So," he said carefully, "might I show you the far west field tomorrow morning? You do plan to ride, do you not? If I recall, it is something you enjoy every morning, unless, of course, it is raining."

She seemed taken aback that he had remembered. Little did she know there was not much he had forgotten. How could he when the memories of their time together played through his head almost daily, no matter if he wanted them to or not?

He noticed the way her dark brows furrowed. She was debating something. Her green eyes focused on nothing but the path in front of her horse. In her contemplation, she sucked one side of her bottom lip into her mouth.

Something twisted in his middle, and he realized how much he had missed that exact expression: Sybil deep in thought, worrying the inside of her lip. It was a common enough look, but to him it had been one of his favorites. It showed how deeply her thoughts ran. She was no mindless deb.

Their angry conversation in Hyde Park came crashing to the forefront of his mind. She had been mindless that day. Mindless, flippant, and arrogant. Completely different from the Sybil he had come to know. Nicholas waited for the pain of the conversation to envelop him again, but it did not. Not with her riding beside him almost close enough to touch. Instead, he found himself confused, his mind filled with questions.

Sybil finally spoke. "I think I would enjoy that very much, Lord Penbrose."

Her use of his title felt foreign. He was both relieved and nervous about her acceptance. The conflicting emotions led his response to be slightly delayed, but he finally managed to say, "Good. Do you usually ride this early every morning?"

"No, I am usually not out until eight or nine, but I needed to clear my mind this morning. An earlier ride seemed just the thing."

"Hmm... we must have been suffering from the same malady. I am also not so early a riser, but the morning air beckoned me today."

Looking at Sybil out of the corner of his eye, he could see the slight quirk of her lips on the right side. The smirk said she understood all too well his turmoil.

He tried to think of another, safer, topic of conversation. "How have you been enjoying the house party?"

The raise of a single brow let him know his question was completely ridiculous. Of course, she had not been enjoying the party, especially after she had basically admitted to a poor night's sleep.

"I believe the polite answer is, 'Why, Lord Penbrose, it has been the most marvelous party I have ever attended.'" The last half of her sentence was said with such an obnoxiously high and nasally voice that he could not help but chuckle.

"I am unsure why I asked such an inane question," he said sheepishly. Again, she rewarded him with a smile, then faced forward.

"This is a lovely estate. I do not believe I have seen its equal." The sincerity of her compliment touched him.

"Thank you. I would like to take credit for its condition, but it is mostly my late grandfather's doing. He was nothing if not thorough in his care of the Penbrose estates."

"Well, then you have much to live up to, it would seem. Are you up to the challenge?"

"I surely hope so, as it is too late to change things now." However, he would not put it past his uncle to petition all the way to the Prince Regent. Things had been quiet on that front this last month, so he hoped the whole debacle was finally over.

More silence followed as they rounded one of the hedges. The sun was just starting to break through the clouds and bathe the green countryside in its warm light.

Not knowing what else to say, he finally asked, "Should we settle on nine tomorrow for our ride? That will give us ample time to breakfast before setting out."

"Oh, I ate before coming out this morning." She grinned.

"Good for you," he answered sardonically. "I, on the other hand, am starving even as we speak."

"Perhaps it would be best if we made our way back to the stables, then. I would hate for you to swoon in the saddle. I do not believe I am capable of playing the rescuer as effortlessly as you did this morning."

"You mean you do not hold massive amounts of strength in those slender limbs of yours?"

"Not enough to catch you, your lordship. You would find yourself kissing the ground if left to my rescue."

"We best hurry, then. I would hate to, as you say, 'kiss the ground.' I am sure it would be a very gritty affair."

He was rewarded with the tinkle of her light laugh as they turned their horses toward the house and sped into a trot, and suddenly the day seemed just a bit brighter.

# Chapter Nine

The morning ride and subsequent conversation had lifted some of Nicholas's apprehension. He hoped Sybil's acceptance of his offer meant a cessation of hostilities. Dinner had gone well other than the fact that he had been obliged to sit next to Miss Cattering. Her less than sincere compliments and overtly flirtatious tone had made the whole affair quite unappealing.

Card tables had been assembled when the men reached the drawing room, but he made his way to his mother, not particularly in the mood for cards.

"Mother, I thought Mary was to arrive early this morning."

"She was, however, I received a message from the Rose and Crown in Oriwick that they were delayed due to a problem with their equipage. I am sure they will be here soon, for Mrs. Clapton assured me it should take no more than a few hours. She had high hopes of being back on the road shortly after midday."

"That is a relief, for I am sure Olivia would combust if she was required to wait one more day for her cohort in crime."

"Crime?" a female voice said from behind him. "What crime? Do not tell me you have gone off and murdered Miss Greenwald already, cousin." Olivia stepped up next to him.

"Not my crimes. I was speaking of yours." Then, lowering his voice so only his mother and cousin might hear, he said, "And the first is not knowing when to hold your tongue with so much company around."

"I thought you raised him to be a gentleman, Aunt Jules." Olivia indicated Nicholas with a tip of her head.

"I did my best, Olivia," his mother said with a smile, "but he is a grown man now. One can hardly tell an earl what is proper. Whatever his address, I would ask you, both of you"—she took in Nicholas with her eyes— "to remember your manners. You are ladies and gentlemen now. You may banter as much as you like in private, but please do watch yourselves in public. Especially when one of our guests is the subject of your verbal spar."

Olivia nodded knowingly and then in a fabricated lower-class accent whispered, "No speakin' of the deceased before the guests. Got it." She punctuated the statement with an uncouth wink.

His mother quickly put her hand to mouth as she tried to cover her laugh with a cough. Olivia always had been able to break through her "social face," as they called it.

"Are you quite all right, Lady Julia?" Mr. Greenwald asked as he approached with Aunt Evelyn on his arm.

Nicholas was glad to see his aunt looking so well. He had worried when she had not come down for breakfast, but she had joined them for luncheon and seemed none the worse for wear. She was, however, thinner than he recalled. Trim, even after birthing four children, three of whom were still living, he could now see where her dress was too big for her frame, and her cheeks had taken on a bit of a sunken appearance.

Her coloring was good, though. In fact, she had a bit more of a rosy hue to her cheeks now than prior to dinner. Perhaps a few good meals and good company was all she needed to recover herself.

"I am quite all right, Mr. Greenwald. Just a bit of a tickle in my throat." His mother shot Olivia a quick accusatory glace, to which the lady merely smiled innocently. "How are you faring this evening? Are you planning to join a game of whist or casino?"

"I believe I shall leave the cards to the younger set," he said. "It has been an age since I have had a good chat with you and Lady Evelyn. I was hoping you might oblige me."

"Of course, Mr. Greenwald. I would love to." Looking at Nicholas and Olivia, she said with a twinkle in her eye, "Run along you two, but remember to play nice."

"You would think as the Earl of Penbrose, I would have earned a little respect," Nicholas said in a loud enough aside to Olivia that his mother, aunt, and Mr. Greenwald could hear him.

"Perhaps when you are king, it will finally be enough," she responded, matching his tone. "For now, though, let us go find some ginger biscuits like good little boys and girls."

With that, they walked away from their elders, listening to the sounds of their collective chuckles.

"By the by, where is Miss Greenwald if you have not dispatched of her?" Olivia asked as he led her to one of the card tables.

"I do not rightly know. She attended dinner. Perhaps she is only in the ladies' retiring room."

"I highly doubt that." Olivia sniffed. "When the ladies removed from dinner, she did not enter the drawing room with us, and that was a full half hour ago."

A footman entered the room a few feet from where they had stopped. When the man's eyes fell on Nicholas, he came forward.

"Mrs. Phillips sent me to inform you that Miss Fairchild has arrived."

"About time!" Olivia exclaimed, promptly dropping his arm, and leaving the drawing room without a backwards glance. No doubt to accost Mary in her room, where the two would spend the rest of the evening catching up on everything from their favorite fashions to their newest beaus. But first Olivia would undoubtedly share with her all the current gossip concerning he and Miss Greenwald.

Nodding his thanks to the footman, Nicholas made his way back to his mother to relay the news. She would be grateful to hear of Mary's safe arrival.

After delivering the message, he was cajoled into joining a pair of ladies and Mr. Martin at a game of whist. And so the evening went, Nicholas being volleyed between one set of women to another, either to play a hand of cards, listen to a piece on the piano, or to be regaled with indulgent compliments.

The whole experience was quite nauseating. He felt like a horse on display at Newmarket, and each young lady was casting her finest bid. As a gentleman of some means he had received a fair bit of attention before gaining a title, but that was nothing compared to how these ladies fawned over him. Why, he was unsure, as he was not the only single titled gentleman in the room.

Glancing about, he could see there was another man being accosted with the attentions of several young women. The Viscount Ansley, a man he had hoped to win over to his cause in the House of Lords, appeared as miserable as Nicholas felt. Twice already Lord Ansley had pinched the bridge of his angular nose while listening to the tittering ladies around him.

Bradley, on the other hand, sat at the edge of the room talking quietly with Miss Diana. Lucky chap. What he would not give for some quiet conversation.

When the clock chimed eight, Nicholas rose to stretch his legs. He was desperate for some peace and quiet. Excusing himself from the current gathering of young women, he made his way to the tea service at the edge of the room. The tea was lukewarm at best, but Nicholas did not care, so long as it got him a moment by himself.

Most of the older guests had retired for the night; his mother, aunt, and Mr. Greenwald were the only three still remaining. Nicholas wished to retire as well, but he needed to play the good host.

He could not stomach another inane conversation with the Williams sisters or Miss Cattering. While they were all tolerably well-looking, there was not an ounce of wit between them. What they lacked in wit, they made up for with arrogance and conceit, especially Miss Cattering. He could not count how many times that young miss had extolled her own virtues while cunningly displaying the other girls' insufficiencies with dual-edged compliments.

He was quite sure she had made one of the other young ladies cry after saying that her dress had been quite the fashion three seasons ago. Shaking his head in disgust, he decided to take his chances with the mysterious Miss Bawden. She was the only young woman not seated near everyone else, and as far as Nicholas could tell, had hardly interacted with anyone all night.

The young woman sat in the corner with a book in her lap. If it were not for the flick of her eyes over the pages, he would have assumed her a statue. Briefly he wondered why gentlemen were not vying for her attention. She was quite pretty, with her chestnut curls framing a well-proportioned face.

Taking a seat in the chair adjacent to hers, he noticed the moment his movements caught her attention. Raising her eyes to his, she sat expectantly. Odd. She had offered no greeting, but no censure in her look either, just expectation of his purpose in seeking her out.

"Have you enjoyed the evening, Miss Bawden?"

"I have, Lord Penbrose."

"Was the meal to your liking?"

"It was."

"I see you have a book. Is reading a favorite past time of yours?"

"It is."

"Do you often spend your evenings reading?"

"I do."

"What is your favorite book?"

Miss Bawden contemplated this for a moment, then shrugged one shoulder. Nicholas ran out of things to ask after so many short answers. There was only so much a man could do by way of conversation with a lady who was either unwilling or unable to give an answer longer than two syllables.

They lapsed into silence. Miss Bawden must have concluded her participation was no longer needed, and she went back to reading her book. So, Nicholas quietly stared out the window into the darkness.

Unbidden memories of his lively conversations with Sybil arose in his mind. She had always had something to say—not just *something*, but things of interest. While she was versed in small talk as much as the next debutante, she excelled in keeping a conversation going past the typical polite topics of conversation. He was sure some men, and women, probably found her conversation off-putting, but most of *his* acquaintances relished it.

Sybil had been in high demand among the young men of the ton—and some of the old men, too. Yet somehow she had always made time to talk to him. While her looks were pleasing, it was her mind and heart that had captured him. If he was truly honest with himself, they held his heart captive still. No matter how hard he had tried, his feelings still beat strong.

He had tried casting her the villain in his thoughts and sometimes even in his conversations. He had tried relegating her to the past. He had even tried to pretend she'd never existed, and those few months had been only a figment of imagination. Juvenile as the latter was, it was his preferred way of coping. It allowed him to move throughout his day-to-day tasks with at least a modicum of peace.

And it had worked— until yesterday, that is. One glimpse of her dark hair, flashing green eyes, and graceful curves, and those tender feelings flared to life again.

As much as he wanted answers to his questions, he knew asking her to ride this morning had probably been a bad idea. It would only feed that hope and desire in him. Her lack of participation in today's activities and her disappearance after dinner indicated her feelings did not tend in the same direction as his.

Maybe she would not show in the morning at all. Perhaps her acceptance was merely a polite way of extricating herself from this morning's awkwardness.

That did not sit well with him. Sybil was not deceitful, at least he had not thought her so, until...

Their last conversation in London had felt like a lie from beginning to end. So which Sybil had shown up to his house party? The one who had laughed, danced, and bantered with him for three full months, or the Sybil of that fateful day two years ago?

Perhaps neither had shown themselves. It had been two years, after all, since they had last spoken. A person could change quite drastically in two years. He should know since he had gone from a mere mister supporting his widowed mother and sisters off a small estate, to the Earl of Penbrose with multiple properties at his disposal and the much-needed power his father had only dreamed of wielding in the House of Lords.

Yes, time could enact a great deal of change in one's life and subsequently in oneself. So what had time changed in Miss Sybil Greenwald? He was not ready to admit it, but the prospect of finding out provided more excitement than had experienced in a long time.

# Chapter Ten

Although Sybil had retired early the previous evening, it had been another restless night. She could not help revisiting her conversation with Lord Penbrose. During their ride, the irritation that had exuded from him on the day of her arrival seemed to have blown away with the wind leaving only Nicholas—the confident, witty, handsome man she had met in London.

It surprised her how easily they had conversed, even bantered as they used to. By the time they'd returned to the stables, she had been quite at ease, but upon entering the house, reality had come crashing back down.

Lord Penbrose's cousins, Lady Caroline and Lady Olivia, had been making their way to the breakfast room, heads bent together tittering like schoolgirls. The previous day's gossip, still fresh in Sybil's mind, had pushed her into a state of confusion.

Just because she and Nicholas had spent a few enjoyable moments together did not make their past disappear—Hurtful words had still been said, and gossip had still ensued— gossip that Sybil had hoped would die after her swift departure from London. But, from the looks of things, it had not.

Consumed with fear and humiliation, Sybil spent most of the day in the only respectable way she knew—hiding in her room.

The only time she had left was to find a book. It was during her wandering that she had come across Mr. Lenning. Wanting nothing to do with the reprobate, she had tried to slip into a nearby room when he'd called out to her.

Not knowing what else to do, she had stopped and let the gentleman come to her. To her great astonishment, he had apologized for his poor behavior, admitting it was not his place to pass along stories that had been told to him in confidence.

The shock of his humility still surprised Sybil, even now. She had not known how to answer. Eventually, she had stammered out an acceptance, and he had been kind enough to show her the direction to the library.

The interaction had given her even more to contemplate. Had Nicholas confronted his friend, or had Mr. Lenning acted on his own? None of it really made sense. Sybil had analyzed and reanalyzed both conversations late into the night before she finally fell into a fitful sleep.

Unfortunately, she had also risen well before dawn. Ringing the bell, she waited for her maid, hoping Porter would forgive her for the early morning call.

Her maid entered and went straight to the wardrobe, unsuccessfully covering her yawn. Saying nothing, she removed the black riding habit. Sybil wished it were the grey one, but she'd worn that yesterday. The white lace at her throat and wrists relieved some of the darkness of the color, but it did not elevate her mood.

Perhaps she should not go. She could claim a headache from a bad night's rest. It was not really a lie since her eyes burned and her muscles were sore from lack of sleep, but she needed this ride to clear her head.

Not only had she avoided Nicholas yesterday, but her father as well. While she had taken his words to heart, they still stung. Plus, there was the matter of his lie. He may have meant well, but it was still a falsehood. She would have to face him at some point, just like she would have to face Nicholas. But did it have to be today?

A new idea struck. Perhaps she could go early and avoid a meeting with Nicholas—Lord Penbrose, she corrected herself. Goodness! She really needed to stop thinking of him informally if she was going to keep space between them.

It could not be much past six, and he would not be expecting her until nine. It was a full hour earlier than when they had met yesterday, so she should be blessedly alone.

Papa would be a bit harder to avoid, but she did not think she could face him today without losing her composure and embarrassing herself.

Pulling her dark tresses into a simple bun at the back of her head, Porter asked, "Which dress should I set out for your return, miss?"

"The light lavender muslin with the short sleeves will do. I will be spending a good deal of time out of doors this afternoon, and I wish to be as cool as possible."

"Very good. Your father asked me to keep watch for the new riding habit we ordered before leaving Tave Hall," Porter said conversationally. "Apparently, he gave the seamstress the address and paid extra to have it delivered here."

"That's a two-day journey! Why would he go to such expense for a mere habit? I can get along fine with the two I already have."

"I don't know, miss. I was just instructed to let him know when the package arrived."

"Well, if you ask me, it is silly." Rising from her seat, she gave Porter some last-minute instructions, then made her way downstairs.

The aroma of fresh baked bread wafted through the lower level of the house, and her stomach growled. The reminder of her hunger pulled her to the breakfast parlor, grateful they had food ready this early in the morning.

Lost in her thoughts, she was surprised to find Lord Penbrose already seated at the head of the table, a plate of food in front of him. Seeing her enter, he swiftly rose from his seat.

"Good morning, Miss Greenwald. I had not expected to see you this early."

Flustered, her reply was not as deliberate as she would have liked. "Yes, well... I could not stay in bed—that is, I was struggling to sleep, and I thought I might start out earlier. I mean—to have my breakfast earlier. Since I was already up." Anger heated her cheeks at his knowing smile. Embarrassment, she reminded herself, was emotion hidden under the anger.

She ducked her head, hurried to the sideboard and started her backwards count from one hundred—this time in German. Since that language was particularly hard for her, she hoped it would give her enough time to collect herself.

Slowly, she selected a piece of toast, preserves, and a boiled egg. Pausing, she decided to add two rashers of bacon. Not yet having made it past *dreiundsiebzig*, seventy-three, she looked over the rest of the selection. She added a sweet roll even though she knew she would never eat it. Too much food before a ride often left her sick, so she always ate with caution at breakfast.

She stared at the food on the sideboard, stalling as long as possible as she continued counting. But when she reached *einundfünfzig*, Lord Penbrose's voice broke her concentration.

"I know there is not much to choose from. This early in the morning, only a few dishes are added. When we return from our ride, there will be a more substantial selection."

Turning herself about, she saw him still standing. Of course he would still be standing. He was a gentleman, after all. Giving up on her count altogether, she slowly made her way to the table.

"This shall do quite nicely; I need nothing fancy," she said evenly. "At home, I usually only have toast and preserves before a ride. If I am hungry upon my return, Cook sends up some eggs and sausage. Otherwise, I do not eat again until luncheon."

Not wanting to cause offense by seating herself as far away as possible—which was the safer option if she wanted to guard her heart—she chose the seat to his left. At her approach, he waved the footman away, swiftly pulled out her chair, and helped her to sit. When they were both situated, Sybil looked about for the cups. Lord Penbrose saw her quick glance about the table and asked, "What might I get you? Tea, coffee, chocolate?"

"I know this might sound odd, but might I have a cup of chocolate with a dash of coffee in it? I once made the mistake of adding chocolate to the remnants of a cup of coffee. In the name of adventure, I drank the cup anyway. It was actually quite delicious."

"Really?" he asked, picking up his own mostly finished cup of coffee. "I think I might try this adventure as well." The footman in the corner stepped forward again to assist, but Lord Penbrose motioned for him to stay.

Sybil was grateful for Lord Penbrose's short absence from the table. It gave her a moment's time to think of a safe topic of conversation. As she cut her food, she recalled his mount from the day before. The horse had been large and black, quite a fine animal.

A well-defined masculine hand set a cup of steaming chocolate in front of her. Sybil glanced up as Lord Penbrose sat and began lightly blowing on the surface of his own.

"Lord Penbrose," Sybil began. He grimaced. Odd. He had not yet tried her suggested beverage, so it could not have been because of the taste. "The animal you were riding yesterday—is that, perhaps, the famed Friesian stallion for which Penbrose stables are known?"

"Rogue? I am afraid not. He is, however, one of his offspring. Mirage is the stallion of which you speak."

"Ah, yes, that is the name Mr. Lenning mentioned."

"While Mirage is a stunning animal, he could never pull off the incredible feat of catching your fleet-footed mare as Rogue did."

"Why is that?"

"Because while Friesians are quite beautiful, they are not particularly fast. Their large muscular build is for strength, not speed. How much do you know of the breed?"

"Very little, I am afraid."

"Ah, well, they are war horses. Used for centuries on the field of battle because they could carry a man in full armor with ease. However, even *if* they were particularly fast, Mirage is twenty years old, well past his prime."

"I see." Sybil took a bite of her food, hoping to save herself from having to say any more.

"Rogue, on the other hand, has a much better capacity for speed. His dame was a thoroughbred who retired from the races at Tattersall's a decade ago. Rogue was her first foal. If memory serves, he is around eight years old."

"Tempest is a retired racehorse as well."

"I remember you mentioning as much when we were in London. A gift from your parents, if I recall."

Again, Sybil was caught off guard by his good memory. "Yes, upon my seventeenth birthday. I believe they were trying to make up for not taking me to London for the season."

"Oh?"

"Yes, Papa believed it best to wait a year for my coming out as he felt I was not quite ready."

"And why was that?" He glanced down at his cooling chocolate-coffee mixture.

"I am unsure, but I believe the real reason for the delay was Papa's reticence," she said with a small smile. "I think he was unprepared to see his little girl all grown up. He probably would have pushed to wait for several more seasons, but Mama was determined to see me out the very next year. She was quite the force to be reckoned with when she set her mind to something."

Sybil tried to hold her smile, but it felt a bit forced. Remembering her mother's unrelenting insistence, she wondered now how long she had been sick. Was that why she had been so determined that Sybil should marry? Frustration enveloped her and her smile slipped. If Mama had known her days were short, why had she not said something?

Lord Penbrose seemed to notice her shift in mood. "I am truly sorry for your loss, Miss Greenwald. I know how it is to lose a parent. No amount of time can erase the pain of their absence."

She was touched by his concern and at the same time relieved that he could not discern her thoughts. She doubted his words would have been quite so consoling if he knew of her irritation with her mother.

Why, when Mama had been so determined she should marry, had she insisted on a man with a title? If she had hoped to see her well-settled before she died, why had she not encouraged Sybil to marry the first available man who offered? Shouldn't she have encouraged her to follow her heart and find a man as loving and kind as Papa? If she had, perhaps Sybil would not be sitting here as a guest, but one of the family.

The irony of the situation hit her. If she had married Nicholas when he had offered, she would now be a countess. She would have the title Mama had insisted she deserved.

Glancing up at Lord Penbrose, she saw him appraising her with a look of concern. She had forgotten to respond entirely.

"Thank you, my lord. Your words are too kind. It has been a difficult year. However, I believe we have veered from our original topic. We were speaking of Rogue. I meant to ask why your grandfather chose to cross bloodlines with a thoroughbred?"

"Rogue was an experiment. Grandfather wanted to see what would happen if he crossed power with speed. It worked adequately well. However, Rogue does not have a great amount of endurance and cannot maintain ample speed for any great length of time. We were only able to keep pace yesterday because you ran right into our path."

Sybil nodded. Hopefully he would continue talking so she would not have to, but he took that moment to sip the cup of chocolate in front of him. His eyebrows shot up as he swallowed the drink. Whether good or bad, she could not quite tell, but when he took a second sip, she assumed he must have enjoyed it.

"Well, I must say I have never really cared for chocolate as much as my sisters, but I do believe you may have changed my mind. This is quite good."

Sybil took a sip of her own chocolate to wash down her bite of food. "I am glad you enjoyed it, your lordship."

Again, that grimace crossed his face. She could not dismiss it this time. "Are you feeling unwell? You seem to be in a spot of pain."

"Only when you 'lord' me?" he said. "I have yet to grow accustomed to the title, and it always feels rather odd to have family and friends address me as such. I feel as if I am putting on airs."

Sybil did not miss the reference. Did he consider her a friend? "You did not seem to mind so much last night at dinner."

"The people at table with us were mostly new acquaintances. For some reason, the address does not strike the same coming from them."

"Miss Cattering was seated right next to you. Her use did not appear to bother you, and I have it on good authority that you have been acquainted these five years at least."

The look of mischief that enveloped his face made Sybil smile. Eyebrows arched, one side of his mouth slightly higher than the other, hazel eyes dancing as if they held a great secret. Good heavens, it was his lark face. Memories of their misdeeds in London came rushing back, pushing the corners of her mouth up even higher.

One particular memory surfaced, and she found herself hard pressed not to laugh. Frustrated at Mrs. Darling for humiliating her in front of all the other guests, their group of friends had decided to take turns sneaking lumps of sugar into the matronly woman's tea when she set her cup down. Everyone knew she hated sugar. It had been the perfect revenge after the older woman had most ungraciously mentioned how thin Sybil was. Her observation had hurt as she was not the first woman to disparage Sybil's figure.

A small, quiet chuckle brought her back to the present.

"I must admit," he scanned the room as if he were searching for listening ears. Only the footman stood by the door. "I may feel a little bit of satisfaction at taking that particular miss down a peg or two. She slighted me a few years back, and now, thinks we should be on intimate terms. I am sure the only reason for her attentions is the Penbrose title, something she has been itching after for years."

The small amount of food Sybil had eaten felt like lead in her stomach. She too had once sought after a title.

Lord Penbrose suddenly sat back and the twinkle in his eyes vanished completely. Lifting his napkin, he wiped any traces of breakfast, as well as good humor, from his mouth. He cleared his throat and rose from his seat.

"Are you quite finished?" Their previous camaraderie was completely absent from his voice.

The feeling in the room shifted with it. While Sybil had not wanted to speak with him, his kindness and ease had drawn her in, reminding her of all they had shared. The memories of conversations and larks past had warmed her, but now the coolness was palpable.

"I am. Thank you." She rose as he moved her seat out for her.

"If you are not opposed, might we begin our ride now as we are both ready?"

"Yes, I believe that would be best." Sybil glanced at the floor. The tip of her black riding boot poked out from under the edge of her skirt, and she slid it back as she waited for him to say more. Would he offer to lead her out of the room, or should she exit first?

She breathed an inward sigh of relief when Mr. Lenning entered the breakfast room dressed in his riding togs. "Are you both to ride this morning?"

"Yes," Nicholas visibly relaxed at his friend's question. Was he as nervous as she was regarding their tête-à-tête situation? Perhaps, if Mr. Lenning were amenable, they could all ride out together.

"Might I join you? I just came to fetch a cup of coffee, but if the two of you are going now, I can forgo."

"We would love to have your company," Sybil responded before realizing she should have deferred to Lord Penbrose. It was his house, after all.

"Yes, but please go ahead and drink your coffee, Lenning." Lord Penbrose gestured to the coffee pot. "We can wait."

"Capital!" Mr. Lenning said in an overly exaggerated tone. He made his way to the sideboard, took up a cup, and poured a generous amount of the steaming black liquid.

To Sybil's astonishment, he quickly drained the whole cup in several large gulps. No cream, no sugar, not even giving it time to cool. She was dumbfounded. Coffee such as that would have scalded her throat the whole way down, but he seemed to think nothing of it.

"Thank you." He set down the cup, "Now." He stepped up to Sybil and extended his elbow. "May I?"

Sybil took his arm and smiled. Just like that, she was whisked outside to the cool air, the smell of earth in the morning, and the relief of being able to avoid yet another embarrassing situation with Lord Penbrose.

# Chapter Eleven

Nicholas should have felt upset when Bradley inserted himself into their morning ride, but he was too relieved. Things had become entirely too confusing in the breakfast room. For just a moment, he and Sybil had leaned toward each other in the same way they used to when they were conspiring about some lark. Then the imaginary band that had drawn them together snapped with just a few words.

Thankfully, Bradley kept up a constant stream of polite conversation with Sybil, giving Nicholas time to settle his mind. The pair talked almost exclusively the entire ride. They even arranged a race of sorts. No prizes were agreed upon, only the opportunity of boasting over the loser.

When asked if he would join, Nicholas declined and opted instead to be the judge. Sybil's mount easily bested Bradley's by ten to fifteen strides, and she jubilantly crowed her win.

"It would seem that beast of yours has quite the knack for speed, Miss Greenwald."

"Beast! Did you hear that, Tempest? Calling you a beast. It seems we did not beat him soundly enough, or perhaps Mr. Lenning is just a sore loser."

"Loser? Hardly. The sun was in my eyes."

"Riding due west in the morning?" Nicholas interjected. "That would be a feat indeed."

Sybil cast a conspiratorial grin in his direction that made his insides do somersaults. He had not meant to involve himself in their banter, but Bradley's claim had been completely ridiculous. Trying to gather his wits as his friend insisted on a rematch, Nicholas let his mind wander back to breakfast.

He had almost laughed out loud when Sybil had entered the breakfast parlor. She *had* planned to dodge the excursion, it would seem. His talent at reading her had not completely fled him since that day in London.

However, over breakfast he'd started to wonder. While initially silent, she'd warmed to him quite quickly, something he had not expected. He could feel himself being drawn in to that certain something Sybil possessed that no other lady of his acquaintance seemed to have.

Over the last two years, he had met plenty of young women. His mother had practically thrown several at him last season when Mary had ventured out. He had seen many beautiful faces and figures, scores of entertaining personalities, and even stumbled upon a few kind and thoughtful young ladies, but none had possessed whatever it was that drew him to Sybil.

That certain something had been in full force during the course of their meal until he had mentioned Miss Cattering and her grasping behavior. While Sybil had tried to put up a good show, he'd seen her stiffen. The tightness of her expression and the way she'd moved back in her chair had him on his guard. Too late, he'd realized his example of Miss Cattering had touched upon the same subject that had built barriers between them.

After they returned to the stables, Bradley offered to escort Sybil to the house. Nicholas followed the pair, noting how similar in height they were. Two inches was probably all that separated them.

In the entry, Bradley stopped. "Might I have the pleasure of being your partner at lawn bowls this afternoon, Miss Greenwald?"

Nicholas, not wanting to hear the end of their discussion, excused himself.

They both looked at him oddly, but he quickly made his way to his private study. The party would not be assembled until one, so he had time to enjoy some solitude and examine the feelings that had been dogging him all morning.

Entering the study, he poured himself a glass of brandy and sat behind his desk. It was odd how chummy his best friend had become with Sybil. An easy camaraderie had erupted between them in the scant two days since they had met, but he could not think when they would have had time to form such an easy accord.

She had avoided people all day yesterday, had she not? Or perhaps it had just been him she had avoided. To his knowledge, she had conversed very little with Bradley since her arrival. Yet this morning he would have thought the two had been friends for ages.

Swirling the brandy in his glass, he stared at the amber liquid. Why again had he poured the drink? It was far too early to imbibe, he thought, as he turned to stare out the window. Ah, yes, his mind. It had been in turmoil ever since breakfast. Questions plagued him, and no matter how he approached them, no answer was satisfactory.

First, why were Sybil and Bradley able to get along so well in such a short amount of time? Was there a preference there? Second, why in the world did it bother him? It should please him that her attention was focused on his friend—it would answer his third question quite easily. That elusive question that had taken their conversation at breakfast from easy to intensely uncomfortable.

A knock sounded upon the door just seconds before Bradley let himself in.

"Ah, I see you have hied yourself off to sulk."

"What?" Nicholas asked curtly.

"Sulk. You know, like when a dog goes off to the corner to lick his wounds."

"I thought we agreed you were the dog in this relationship."

"Only when spirits are involved," Bradley shot back. "But seriously, Nicholas, what has you so blue-deviled?"

"I am not blue-deviled. Simply pondering. Something which is best done *alone.*"

"Alone, aye? You truly want me to leave?" The sudden seriousness in Bradley's tone pulled Nicholas's attention from the window. The concern he saw on Bradley's face gave him pause.

"Actually, you might be just the person I need to speak with," he amended. There was no use beating about the bush. If anyone could give him insight into the morning, it would be Bradley.

Bradley sat. "Should I be nervous about this conversation? You look as though I stepped on your toes one too many times while dancing."

"It was five times, mind you, and that is why I have never trusted you to teach me a dance again."

Bradley laughed at the childhood memory. Nicholas could not help smiling a bit himself. Their days at Eton had been some of his favorites.

"What are your plans, Bradley? I mean, for the future—for a profession."

Bradley leaned back. Nicholas knew his friend had contemplated taking orders, but not feeling particularly called to the church was putting off any decision for the time being. While he could not really see Bradley in the role of vicar, he did not think it was beyond his scope of abilities. The man was kind to a fault and seemed to know what people needed long before Nicholas ever noticed their distress. Case in point, his mother on the first day of the house party.

"I... well, I still am unsure," Bradley answered hesitantly. "I know I have talked of the church, but I still feel rather off in that regard. You are one of the only people I think I can admit that to. Those who are not as devout see no reason for my hesitancy. It is an honest living, and so there should not be much more thought, but Nicholas, I cannot take on a role that I don't feel suited to."

Nicholas nodded. He understood completely. His own religious convictions would lead him to make the same conclusion if he had been in Bradley's position. He despised men who took up a position in the clergy, only to go against all the principles they were meant to teach. Not that Bradley would do such a thing, but many did.

"I understand, and I commend you for your convictions. You still have time, I assume, until your allowance runs out?"

"Yes. Father's will stipulated I be allowed income until my twenty-sixth year."

"That is only four months away."

Bradley stared at his hands. Nicholas noted the tightness forming around his friend's eyes. Perhaps they should change subjects. Bradley had never been comfortable talking about his finances.

"I will still have interest from the two thousand pounds left to me," Bradley said. "But without my quarterly allowance, I do not think I'll be able to keep up without an occupation."

"Are there any other avenues you are considering?"

"I could always fill the position of your steward." He smirked.

"Please do not remind me." Nicholas set his untasted glass of brandy down on the desk. "I still cannot believe Mr. Gates was so dishonest. I have known the man since childhood."

"It does seem odd, does it not, that people we admired in our youth are not who we thought them to be."

Somehow, Nicholas did not think they were still talking about the steward, as Bradley studiously examined the bookshelves behind Nicholas.

"So, why are you hiding from Miss Greenwald, Nicholas?"

He leaned forward in his chair. "How did we get from talking about my steward to Miss Greenwald? Perhaps you need a lesson in the rules of conversation, my friend."

"Hardly. We had just been discussing people we admired in our youth, and it was a simple jump from the steward to the woman. And do not say you were not hiding. I know that is your next line of defense. I have known you far too long to fall for that."

Yes. Far too smart for the man's own good. Nicholas steepled his fingers together and took several slow deep breaths.

"I am not hiding, only taking my time to regroup. There are many people in my home at present. You cannot fault me for needing some space."

"No, but you seemed…" Bradley tapped his chin, "*tense* while we took our ride. Even with me. I found it odd."

"I am only confused." Nicholas furrowed his brows. "You were quite comfortable with Miss Greenwald. I had not realized you were so well acquainted."

"Jealous?"

"I beg your pardon?" Nicholas shifted in his chair.

"You heard me. The woman has only been here three days, and already you're storming about the castle. Looks like jealousy to me."

"I am not storming, and this is not a castle."

"Could have fooled me. Listen, Nicholas, if you are worried about the nature of my relationship with your—"

Nicholas held up his hands to stem any words that might come from his mouth. "Not mine. She made sure of that two years ago."

"All right." Bradley paused. "I am not interested in *Miss Greenwald*. I simply wanted to make her feel comfortable. Not many have, you know. Besides, you both seemed quite at odds this morning when I entered the breakfast parlor, and I wanted to dissipate some of the tension. While you insist there is nothing between the two of you, I must say I am somewhat appalled you think I would take my chances with the girl you have been pining over for the last two years."

Heat rose up Nicholas's neck. He had not been pining. But he had questioned his friend's loyalty. Shifting forward in the large wingback chair, he placed his forearms on the desk and clasped his hands.

"I am sorry, Bradley. I should not have doubted you."

"No. You should not." Bradley grinned, then rose from his seat. "Now, you have a half hour to get yourself together before you are required out of doors."

Picking up the glass Nicholas had set down, Bradley drained the contents in two large gulps. "There, now you will not be tempted to drink that stuff. Can't have you tipsy around the guests."

Nicholas smiled as Bradley left the room. The conversation had answered his first two questions nicely, leaving only his last question.

Was Sybil's sudden change in demeanor part of a scheme to gain a title? Was she as calculating and conceited as Miss Cattering whose only desire was a title and money?

He had fully expected Sybil to leave at the first chance. She would either beg her father for a complete and immediate removal or spend the remainder of her stay upstairs. Nicholas knew her to be dedicated enough to carry through with both. And her father... well, the man was so indulgent he would give in to whatever she asked of him.

What other answer was there for her continuance if not a pointed hunt?

But was she really that shallow? Many women were, but he had thought better of her. He still could not reconcile her words in Hyde Park with the woman he had come to know. She was kind, generous, and respectful even to those below her station.

He had witnessed firsthand her kindness to children selling their wares in the park. She had always brought a purse full of coin on their walks, and he saw the compassion in her eyes as she looked upon their plight and did what little she could for them.

And what of her maid? He had never seen a woman so upset over her maid's health. When Porter had fallen ill with fever, Sybil had demanded only the best physicians.

He had been there the morning news had come of Porter's improvement. Sybil had literally jumped from her chair and rushed off to see her maid without even excusing herself. What well-bred lady did that? Especially one who insisted she was only climbing the social ladder. No, he could not seem to fit the two sides of Sybil together.

But he was not naïve. He knew the ways of society. Men and women of every birth married to improve their positions. The fishmonger's daughter tried to reach for the shopkeepers' son, just as the baron's daughter tried for the duke. It was cold and calculating, but his father's brothers had chosen their unions for that exact reason. They had married to raise the family standing and add money to the family coffers.

Nicholas did not think he could ever bear to live in a cold, detached marriage as his uncle had. It was well known that after fathering his first two sons with his wife, Uncle Fairchild had preferred the bed of his mistress.

Sad was the day Nicholas had happened upon Aunt Fairchild sobbing to his mother about the state of her marriage. He would never forget the stricken look on her face as he'd peered in at her from the slightly ajar door. Tears trickled down her cheeks as she'd asked his mother what she had done to lose her husband's affection.

Two years later, the poor woman had died while Nicholas and his cousins were away at school. A bad case of influenza, they had been told, but he was sure it had been exacerbated by a broken heart. It was too bad his cousins had turned out so much like their father. Aunt Fairchild had been a kind and gentle woman. She was probably rolling over in her grave at her sons' reprobate ways.

Lord Hepton, his father's eldest brother, had at least had mutual respect in his marriage, but it was much colder than Nicholas' parents' union. Theirs had been a love match filled with warmth and true admiration. His father had told the story of their first meeting hundreds of times. It was one of his sisters' favorites, and while Nicholas's boyish pride had kept him from admitting it, the story was his favorite as well.

Perhaps that is why the idea of a woman only marrying him for his title made Nicholas so sick. He wanted friendship. He wanted affection. In truth, he wanted love. The type of devoted love his parents had shared.

The addition of his new title, however, made divining a lady's intent that much harder. While some women were quite obvious, like Miss Cattering, others were far more shrewd. How was he to know where a lady's heart truly lay?

Nicholas rose and walked to the empty hearth. Leaning an elbow on the mantel, he picked up a small white statue of the lighthouse at Dover. It had been a gift from his father after one of his many trips. Father had been gone so long that time that Nicholas had feared he would not return from the dangerous voyage.

As an apology for his absence, his father had brought him the small trinket. Nicholas still remembered the day his father had placed the white marble figure in his hand.

"Sometimes life can be full of stormy seas," his father had said, "but the good Lord has anchored lighthouses to light your way and lead you safe to harbor. When you are troubled, look for lighthouses, Nicholas. They will guide you safely to shore."

Right now, he could really use a metaphoric lighthouse. Lately life had tossed him about and he was worried he would crash into the sharp rocks of the shore, or more likely the sharp claws of grasping females. He was caught between one woman he knew to be scheming for him, and another who might be— but he could not exactly tell.

Fate was a cruel mistress. With his title, he could now have the only woman he had ever loved. There were no other barriers. But if she only wanted him for his title, did he still want her?

As he set the figurine down, he realized he could not live with doubt. Perhaps his lighthouse today had come in the form of a good friend who had given him time to slow down and think about the consequences of his actions. It would not be wise to rush headlong into the rocks that had damaged his vessel once before. He felt himself again pulled to Sybil far more than he should. She was still just as intoxicating as she had been two years ago, but he could not enter a marriage based on status alone.

He wanted love—no, he *needed* love. Nicholas could not live his life without it. But he was not sure Sybil could ever return it. It would be best to avoid further tête-à-tête interactions with Sybil—Miss Greenwald, he corrected himself. If he was ever going to heal, he had to start there first. She could no longer be Sybil. He must distance himself from her. Miss Greenwald it would have to be. Now if only his traitorous heart would listen to his head.

# Chapter Twelve

Joining Mr. Lenning, Miss Diana, and Mr. Martin for a game of lawn bowls had actually been quite enjoyable. Sybil would have loved to play another game with that arrangement of guests, but at the completion of their game, Mr. Martin had been set upon by Miss Cattering and the Williams sisters.

Adamant that Sybil and Miss Diana not monopolize all of his attention, they had begged him to play a game with them. Mr. Martin looked like a hunted fox who found himself with no place to hide. Poor man.

In the end, however, Sybil had not been able to come up with a single idea to save him, and so he had been swept away with the swirls of pastel-colored skirts.

Mr. Lenning peered after the other gentleman. "Well, what shall we do now?"

His eyes strayed to Miss Diana. Sybil realized it would be awkward to have the three of them matched.

"I am feeling quite fatigued." She patted her forehead with a square of linen. "I believe I need some refreshment."

"Would you like me to attend you?" he asked.

"No, no. Please stay. Besides, I need to speak with someone. Good day."

Sybil ducked her head and smiled as she walked away. Mr. Lenning appeared to be quite taken with Miss Diana. After all, the man could hardly keep his eyes off her. And while Sybil did not know Miss Diana very well, her pretty blushes and covert glances indicated she might be just as interested in Mr. Lenning.

Glancing at a group of trees, Sybil saw her father happily situated in the shade. A battle warred within her. She *could* stop and greet him, then again, he had not even bothered to acknowledge her today. Besides, he seemed happy enough as he sat in conversation with Lady Evelyn, Lady Caroline, and several of the other guests. Why intrude?

Lord Hamdon passed her as he led his very expectant wife to the seat next to Lady Caroline. Stepping up to a table laden with refreshments, Sybil watched as the two women began an animated discussion. By the way they leaned into each other as they spoke, she assumed they were close friends.

A moment later, Lord Hamdon joined her at the table. "Good afternoon, Miss Greenwald."

"Good afternoon."

"I wondered if you might join me for a game."

"I thank you, but I am feeling fatigued. I believe I will retire to the house."

She set her drink on the table and turned to leave, only to find Lord Hamdon's elbow at her side.

"May I?" he asked.

Sybil looked at his arm in confusion.

He smiled impishly. "It is an arm, Miss Greenwald. You are supposed to take it."

She heard Lady Hamdon chuckle from where she sat several paces away. Glancing her way, Sybil saw the lady's startlingly blue eyes on her, a smile gracing her pert lips. Then the woman's eyes flicked to her husband and some unspoken message passed between the pair causing Lady Hamdon's cheeks to flush before she turned back to her friend.

Sybil turned back to Lord Hamdon. "Yes. I can see that, but for what purpose, my lord?"

"I plan to escort you back to the house."

She was unsure how to answer. Sybil did not know Lord Hamdon well. He seemed personable enough, and his teasing words led her to believe she would enjoy his company.

Not wanting to offend, she finally decided to take the proffered escort.

"I must admit, Miss Greenwald, I have been curious to make your acquaintance for quite some time," he said as they walked toward the house.

"Have you? And why is that, for I had not heard of you until we were introduced on our first evening here."

"You had not? Are you sure?"

"Quite. I am sorry to say I have only heard of your father, Lord Lincolnhurst."

"I believe you have."

The smirk on his face was beginning to irritate her. She was sure she had never heard of a Lord Hamdon in her life, and yet this gentleman acted as if she should know quite a bit about him. His arrogance was quite astounding.

"Let me enlighten you, Miss Greenwald. My Christian name is Anthony Kempton, but sometimes I am called Hood."

Realization dawned and she was mortified. This was one of Nicholas's closest friends. He had spoken often of his good friend Anthony, even mentioned Lord Hamdon's title and nickname. But in conversation he had simply been referred to as Anthony. All of Nicholas's Eton chums were referred to by first names or nicknames. Anthony, Bradley, and Fredrick— Hood, Tuck, and Scarlett respectively—were names that had been just as commonly mentioned in Nicholas's conversations as the weather.

Heat crept up her neck. Clenching her teeth, she tried to control her irritation at being put in such an embarrassing situation.

"You are correct, my lord. I have heard of you," she said, tightly. "Have you been sent to spy on me for your friend? I assure you I have not defaced any of the portraits in the gallery and have only stolen a few pieces of silverware, which I shall forthwith return with my next tea tray."

Lord Hamdon's bark of laughter startled her. She had meant her statement as a rebuke, but thinking back on it, it was humorous.

"Penbrose said you were witty; I should have been prepared for that. I did not mean to make you uneasy, Miss Greenwald. I only wish to make the acquaintance of the woman I have heard so much about."

"Considering the source, my lord, I am astonished you should want to know anything of me. More likely you should want to throttle me or send me packing."

"Do you think Nicholas's accounts are all bad?"

"I do, my lord, for I know who I am and what I have done."

"You do not give yourself enough credit."

Sybil stopped and turned to face him. Lord Hamdon was shorter than Nicholas, but still taller than her own father. His curly light brown hair seemed to sweep forward in a devil-may-care style. It was similar to the fashions of the times but with less structure. Unlike most men, Lord Hamdon apparently did not wrestle his hair into submission with ample amounts of pomade.

Searching his face, she was surprised to see sincerity in his deep blue eyes. She looked down at the green summer grass. "The only credit I can give myself, is that of being incredibly foolish."

The pricking sensation behind her eyes let her know her flash of frustration was gone. She needed to extricate herself from this situation as soon as possible. She had not meant to admit so much to Lord Hamdon, but now that the words were out, she could not retract them.

Lord Hamdon gently took her hand and placed it back upon his arm. They walked in silence the rest of the way to the house.

When they reached the terrace doors, he said, "We all make mistakes, Miss Greenwald. I believe all turns out as it should in the end. As for what I have heard of you, foolishness was not one of them. Witty, spirited, lovely, talented, kind, and thoughtful are all the adjectives that were used to describe you. Take heart, Miss Greenwald. You are not despised as much as you think you are."

His kind words made the tears behind her eyes brim to the surface. "I thank you, Lord Hamdon, for both the escort and your kind words. Good day."

"Good day, Miss Greenwald."

Freed from Lord Hamdon's perceptive gaze, she made her way to the library. She needed the comfort of a good book to rid herself of the thoughts racing around her head.

Walking along the rows of books, she read each title. Most in this section were educational tomes in mathematics, Latin, and geography. Not in the mood to stretch her mind, she scanned the shelves for the novel section she had happened upon yesterday. Having finished her re-reading of *Sense and Sensibility*, she was in need of a new book.

While the book had been a good distraction, it had not completely drowned out the tumult in her brain.

Not only had her father's words been echoing in her head, but now she was quite sure Lord Penbrose thought her nothing more than a grasping, ladder-climbing female, no matter what Lord Hamdon had said.

She had seen his expression change in the breakfast room, knew the thoughts that must have swirled in his head. Now her words from two years ago had come back to haunt her.

Lord Penbrose had physically and mentally pulled away from her after that. She had not only seen it in his actions, but she had felt it deep within herself. It was disconcerting. It was as if an old connection had reformed and then broken within a matter of minutes. She should not care, but her heart cried that it did.

She desperately needed a book good enough to distract her, or she might actually scream aloud from the confusion and pain. Hopefully she had at least two hours before she would be required to dress for dinner.

Riffling through the novels, she could not find one that fit her current mood, so she crossed to a shelf on the adjacent wall next to the desk and searched its contents. The books here did not match most of the books in the library. The late Lord Penbrose must have commissioned his books to be specially bound to match one another. These books, however, varied in shape, size, and color.

Haphazardly placed, many of the books looked as if they had only recently been stuffed back on the shelf and the maid had yet to see to their careful rearrangement.

Sybil's interest piqued as she scanned the titles. She had not seen a single one of these books in any other library, to her knowledge. She did, however, recognize one of the titles. While she had not seen it in any personal or circulating library, she had seen it in a bookstore.

She picked up the book. The cover clearly read *Letters of the Late Ignatius Sancho, an African.* Flipping through its pages, she was intrigued. She had only seen a few people of African descent in her entire life. This man, the foreword indicated, had actually been raised in England, owned his own shop, and even had the right to vote.

Taking the book to one of the large blue upholstered armchairs, she began reading.

Sometime later, a distant chime in the house alerted her to the change of the hour. Sybil reached into her pocket and produced her timepiece, only to be met with unmoving hands. A very unladylike snort escaped her as thoughts of Porter's laughing eyes mentally assailed her. She had forgotten to wind her timepiece— again.

A small clock rested on the mantelpiece, and as she approached it, she was dismayed to find it was nearing five already. She would be expected in the drawing room in a half hour to await dinner. The thought of food caused her stomach to gurgle.

Tucking the book under her arm, she rushed out of the library and up the stairs. When she entered her room, Porter rose from her seat near the window. A dark lavender gown already lay on the bed ready for her to dress.

"I am sorry, Porter. I lost track of time. What will you be able to do with my hair in twenty minutes?"

The maid examined her from several angles. "I had expected to work with windblown hair, not hair that looks as if you slept on one side all night."

Sybil reached up and felt her hair. Sure enough, one side was almost completely flat, with strands sticking up in a peak on one side and tendrils of hair smashed against her ear and face. She smiled sheepishly at her maid.

"Reading again?" Porter's question was more of a statement.

"Guilty." Sybil had a habit of leaning the side of her head on the edge of the overstuffed wingback chairs at home. It would seem today was no different. However, the chairs in the Penbrose library were far taller than those her father had commissioned for Tave Hall. The large chairs here had fairly engulfed her when she'd sat in one.

Porter nodded with a knowing smile and began removing Sybil's day dress. "I am also guessing you forgot to wind your timepiece." Porter's smirk said she knew as much.

"Nosy servants," Sybil said with no bite in her words.

Porter chuckled at the oft-mumbled statement. "Just remember how much you enjoy nosy servants the next time you need a bit of information from below stairs."

"In that case, they happen to be my absolute favorite."

The maid chuckled and motioned for her to sit at the dressing table. After unpinning and combing her hair, Porter cleared her throat.

Sybil realized she had been woolgathering. Glancing up through the mirror, she said, "Yes, Porter?"

"Tomorrow is my half-day, and I wondered if you would rather I take it in the morning or evening? At Tave Hall I would usually take the last half of the day, but I was unsure if you would feel more comfortable having me dress you for dinner rather than your usual morning ride. Either way, I could have one of the house maids attend you in my absence."

Sybil deliberated for a moment. "I believe I will need your help for dinner, as I will be seeing more people at that time."

She did not want to leave her appearance to a random house maid, not with so many unknown people about.

"That is what I thought you might say. There is a young maid below stairs who I have come to know quite well. She is a wonder with hair. I believe you will get on well, at least for the morning."

"Thank you, Porter. Your thoughtfulness does you credit."

"I plan to walk into Kettering with a couple other maids. Is there anything I might get for you while I am there?"

Sybil smiled ruefully. "If I send you with coin, could you get me some anise candy?"

"Yes, miss, I would be happy to."

"As usual, you may get a few pieces for yourself as payment," Sybil reminded her. Porter smiled to herself.

Over the years, their candy routine had been the same. It was one of the many ways Sybil had found she could care for her maid without the young woman feeling like it was charity. She knew Porter was saving every bit of income she had and would not spend so much as a half penny on a frivolity like candy. Since Sybil would never want for money, it was the least she could do.

They had not spoken often of Porter's dreams, but Sybil knew she had hopes of a home of her own someday. One day she would leave. The thought was not new, but for some reason, today it made Sybil sad to think that there would be a day when they would part ways.

Glancing at Porter again, Sybil noticed for the first time how pretty she had become. The rounder cheeks of her teen years had given way to the more angled features of adulthood. While Porter most often kept her caramel-colored hair back in a tightly braided bun, Sybil had seen it loose on occasion.

She envied Porter's natural curl. Sybil's dark tresses were unforgivably straight. If it were not for ample use of the curling tongs, she would never have been able to sport the most recent styles.

With a small sigh, she consigned herself to the fact that Porter would one day catch some man's fancy, and if he was lucky enough, she would return his regard.

Porter looked at Sybil through the mirror. "Are you quite all right, miss?"

"I am just borrowing troubles."

"Not enough current ones to keep you occupied?"

"Enough and to spare." Sybil laughed. "But I always was a glutton for punishment, so I thought I would take on a few from our futures."

"Our?"

"Have you ever thought about marrying, Porter?"

Porter's cheeks suffused with color. That was a new sight for Sybil. While Porter had blushed a time or two over the years, Sybil had never seen her face go so terribly red.

"Forgive me, Porter. I did not mean to make you uncomfortable."

"Not at all, miss." She busily put away the extra pins.

Sybil did not think she would get an answer, but Porter surprised her.

"I would like to marry. I think of it quite often, in fact. It is only me and my aunt in this world, and she is more than busy as housekeeper at Grenwich Hall. We see each other but twice a year, and then for only a few days at a time. I should like to…" Her words died away as her cheeks pinked again.

"Please continue, Porter. I promise not to think less of you."

"I should like to belong somewhere. To have a family."

"I can understand that. I cannot imagine how lonely you must be. At least I have my father with me."

Porter looked up and Sybil gazed into her soft brown eyes. "I am sure, you shall find a good match someday. You are pretty, educated, and kind. Perhaps some merchant or solicitor will take notice of you and give you the life you deserve."

"My, you do think highly of me, if you think I could marry someone of that station. I would be lucky to catch the eye of a footman, let alone a man of business."

"Nonsense, Porter! Your father was a shopkeeper, was he not?"

"Yes, miss."

"Did he own the shop, or was it to let?"

"Owned it, miss," she said proudly. "It and the shop connected to it. He let that one out to a printer."

"Then it is not too much of a stretch to think you might have something of that life, as well."

"But miss..." Porter's shoulders sagged as if someone had placed a large boulder on them. "I was not raised to that life."

Sybil had not forgotten why Porter was in service. Tragedy had brought her to this place. Mr. Porter, his shop, and the rest of the Porter family consisting of his wife, son, and daughter had perished in a fire when Porter was fourteen. She was the only one spared as she was away at school, a fact that often caused the young woman great amounts of grief and guilt.

"Porter." She quietly turned in her seat. Assessing the woman's pain-filled eyes, Sybil took some liberties. "Maria. It was not your fault. And even though you have spent the last several years in service, you were meant for that life. It is what your parents would have wanted for you."

A tear slipped down Porter's cheek and splashed on the front of her dress. Rising from her seat, Sybil awkwardly gathered the smaller woman in her arms. Porter tensed at first and then relaxed as the silent tears fell, wetting both their dresses. After a few moments, Porter pulled back.

"Oh, dear, miss. I am sorry. Your dress. Let me find you a new one."

Sybil waved away the concern. "I shall just throw a light shawl over my shoulders. It is not so warm that it would seem out of place. Besides, I have been dying to wear that silver gauzy creation Papa gave me for my birthday."

Moving to the closet, Porter retrieved the shawl. "I think the silver will look particularly well with that shade of lavender." Placing the shawl on Sybil's shoulders, Porter asked, "Would you like the locket to match?"

"Yes, please."

After fastening the locket and handing Sybil her gloves, Porter declared her ready. "Have a wonderful evening, miss." Then just as Sybil was exiting, "And miss?"

Sybil turned to face her.

"Thank you."

Smiling back at Porter, she dipped her head in acknowledgement. If only *every* relationship was as easy as the one she shared with her maid.

# Chapter Thirteen

Nicholas walked about the drawing room, greeting his guests as they waited on dinner. A flash of blue caught his eye seconds before his mother latched onto his arm. Blue really was his mother's color. The heavenly hue offset her brown curls in a most becoming way.

"Almost everyone seems to be assembled," she said, sotto voce. "I believe we are only missing a few of the neighborhood gentlemen I invited to round out our numbers. Once they arrive, we should be ready to go into dinner."

. Taking another sweeping glance of the room, he noticed they were not the only ones not yet in attendance.

"Miss Greenwald," Nicholas responded in an equally low tone.

His mother looked at him, a question in her eyes.

"Miss Greenwald is not here yet either." He tried to elicit a mask of unconcern.

"Ah, yes. I see." His mother glanced about the room then back at him. The polite smile slowly slipped from her face as she assessed him. Her cheeks relaxed and the middle of her eyebrows dipped.

Nicholas tried not to view his mother's sad expression and motioned to a couple sitting across the room. "Mr. Greenwald is here, I see. He is just there, speaking with Aunt Evelyn."

"Yes." A full smile returned to her face at the scene.

Nicholas's forehead creased. It seemed his aunt and Mr. Greenwald had been spending a lot of time in one another's company. Come to think of it, he had seldom seen the older man without his aunt over the past couple of days. Not only had Nicholas come upon them talking in the parlor when he returned from his ride, but they had spent the whole of the afternoon ensconced in the shade while the younger people played lawn games.

"It is nice to see the light returning to Evelyn's eyes." His mother's eyes shimmered as she looked at her sister. "It has been so long since I have seen her this happy. Hopefully..."

The implication crashed down upon Nicholas, and his eyes shot back to where the couple sat. He could tell they were quite fond of each other, but was there really more?

He would never begrudge his aunt her share of happiness, but the thought of who was connected to Mr. Greenwald made him frown. What would Syb—Miss Greenwald think? Would she be happy for her father? Would she be angry?

Most likely. Anger was to Sybil as water was to a fish. She had once claimed it was her first reaction to most everything disagreeable.

Was Mr. Greenwald as grasping as his daughter? There was no title connected to his aunt, but she would bring a fair amount of money into a marriage.

Nicholas began walking toward the two. He should intervene until Mr. Greenwald's intentions could be assessed. The doors opened, and he stopped as several gentlemen were announced. As host, it would be his responsibility to aid his mother in facilitating introductions.

He glanced at his mother who stood a few paces away and caught the reprimand in her stare.

Walking back to where he had left her, she hissed, "Not your place, Penbrose. Leave them be."

She was right, of course. But how could he? The last thing any of them wanted was for Aunt Evelyn to suffer another heartache.

He directed his mother toward the newcomers. "We must at least advise Caraway."

"It was his idea, Nicholas. Do not go charging off and ruin things. I know it is uncomfortable to think of a closer connection with Miss Greenwald, but you must step out of your own troubles for a bit and think of other. Let her be happy for once."

The barb hit its mark. Was he really just concerned for his own peace of mind?

Their conversation halted as they stepped up to the three tall handsome men near the door. Their presence caused quite a stir among the young ladies. Nicholas knew his duty. Stepping forward, he began the introductions.

Somewhere in the whirl of feminine excitement, Miss Greenwald entered. Nicholas had not seen her, but when the butler announced dinner, she was among the crowd. The shimmering silver shawl around her shoulders seemed to catch the light and direct his attention right on her.

He tore his gaze from the lovely picture she made and offered his arm to Lady Evelyn to escort her into dinner. Couples fell in behind them, and out of the corner of his eye, he saw Mr. Martin offer his arm to Miss Greenwald. A burning rose in his chest. He pushed the feeling away and reminded himself of his resolve. He needed to focus on the enormous formal dining room ahead of them.

Throughout the meal, Nicholas tried to focus on his aunt's conversation, but eventually she began speaking with Lord Brock on her left. Turning to his right, he thought to engage Lord Ansley in a discussion, only to find him already speaking with his cousin Caroline. With nothing else to do he placed a bite of roasted partridge in his mouth.

The fairy-like sound of Miss Diana's voice mixed with the lower richer tones of Miss Greenwald's and carried over the chatter. Mr. Martin's deep timbre punctuated different moments of the conversation. Halfway down the table, they were discussing horses. His horses in particular. Leaning forward, he tried to catch more of their words.

"We would love to ride with you, Mr. Martin, wouldn't we Miss Diana?" he heard Miss Greenwald say.

The other girl's cheeks pinked at the question. Nicholas could not make out Miss Diana's quiet answer, but by the nodding of her head, he guessed it to be an agreement.

Realizing numbers would be uneven, he briefly wondered if they would welcome his company.

Miss Diana then turned to Mr. Lenning on her right. His hearty, "I would be delighted!" silenced Nicholas before the words even formed on his tongue. Disappointment settled over him as he applied himself to the dessert that had just been placed before him. While rice pudding was not his favorite, the soothing flavors of vanilla and cinnamon seemed to calm his mind. Collecting his thoughts, Nicholas gave himself a reminder of his course. It was a bad omen, indeed, if he could not keep his distance from Miss Greenwald for one whole day.

After-dinner entertainment was to be music. Each lady and a few of the gentlemen performed a variety of music. Some played while others sang. A trio of siblings favored them with a splendid piece. The sister played the pianoforte and sang while her two brothers accompanied her soprano with their tenor and bass voices. Nicholas was impressed by their talent. He did not believe he had seen any piece executed as flawlessly, even on the stages of London. The applause of the guests seemed to echo his sentiments.

Only two other young women had yet to exhibit. Miss Cattering approached the piano. Her air of self-importance nearly made Nicholas laugh. Did that young woman know how ridiculous she looked? She was the daughter of a mere baron, but she comported herself as if she were a duchess gracing the lowly audience with her presence.

The piece she played was actually quite well done. The lively tune must have taken a great deal of practice to learn. In the end, he could not fault her performance. She did have a talent, he had to admit. Perhaps she had a right to take pride in herself.

Nicholas glanced at Miss Greenwald, knowing she was the last of the ladies. It was not required of them all to exhibit, but he knew she possessed great skill at the instrument. Would she play?

As the applause for Miss Cattering died away, the room went silent in anticipation. His mother rose, appearing somewhat concerned. Perhaps she had forgotten to inform Miss Greenwald, but a subtle movement caught his eye. Miss Greenwald had nodded ever so slightly to her.

Standing before the group, his mother announced, "Miss Greenwald will be our last performer of the evening. Before she takes her place, however, I would like to thank all of you for sharing your wonderful talents with us. I do not believe I have ever before seen so much skill exhibited in one evening. Bravo to all of you."

Here, she started a round of applause. When the room quieted again, she said, "And now, Miss Greenwald."

Nicholas felt a pang as Miss Greenwald rose and took her seat at the pianoforte. It was not the first time he had listened to her perform. Memories assailed him. Not sure if his heart could endure the pummeling Sybil's melodic voice would give it, he braced himself for the first strains.

As the first few chords filled the room, his heart leaped into his throat. Not this song. Anything but *this* song. Sybil's rich alto voice filled the room as she sang the haunting ballad.

Did this woman know what she was doing to him? She had to. He had told her once how this song moved him.

Now, however, the story of love and loss drew his heart out in a way he had not experienced before. The dips and swells of the melody brought emotions to the surface that he did not want to face. An emptiness within him burned, begging for the wholeness only the woman before him had filled. As Sybil's voice rose in crescendo, he shot from his seat, exiting the room as quickly as he dared.

He could not bear to hear the words of the last refrain, but like a siren's call, it followed him into the hall.

*Perhaps with the dawn a new love*
*Faithful, true, and strong.*

Nicholas hurried away from the music room, hoping no one had noticed his exit. He had been seated near the back, but he did not delude himself. Someone would have noticed him. He just hoped it had not caused a stir and given slight to the beautiful performer. It was not her fault his heart would not stay restrained as his head told the disobedient organ it should.

Sybil sat at the pianoforte, trying to gather her emotions. While every performance drew out her soul, this one had laid it bare before her. She stared at it there in her mind, lonely, cold, hopeful, scared, longing. Gone was the anger she'd used to protect herself.

Lord Hamdon's words of praise filled her mind in that moment. Had Nicholas really said those things about her? Did he still care? Was it possible? The clear, honest picture scared her. Things she had pushed away for far too long became exceedingly apparent, and she almost broke down right there in front of the crowd.

She loved Nicholas, had probably always loved him, but Mama's wishes had superseded her own. Why?

Honestly, it did not matter now. Mama was gone, and Sybil was yet living. And her living, beating heart told her she would never be the same if she did not fix her foolish mistake. Taking several deep breaths, she steadied herself.

When she had gained adequate possession of herself, she stood to accept her accolades. Pasting a smile on her face, she caught sight of an empty chair. One that had not been empty when her performance began. Lord Penbrose—Nicholas—had left. She was not sure when, but he had been there when she'd begun, and now he was not. Her heart sank to her toes.

Why had he left? Had her performance been that upsetting? She did not think she had played or sang poorly. Why now, of all times? Why when she had just come to know herself so clearly?

Lord Ansley stood in front of her. "Just splendid, Miss Greenwald. Absolutely splendid."

Sybil tried to respond with the correct words, but the tumult of her mind was making it difficult to even think. A movement to the right caught her attention as Lady Julia stepped up and threaded her hand through Sybil's arm.

"Might I steal this beautiful young lady away from you, Lord Ansley?" she asked sweetly.

"Of course, Lady Julia." Bowing to each lady, he bade them good evening and made his way to congratulate Miss Cattering.

"Come," Lady Julia commanded softly. It took some maneuvering on Lady Julia's part as others were intent on congratulating her, but suddenly Sybil found herself escorted out the double doors of the music room to the veranda beyond.

The stars had just begun to dot the evening sky, and a faint bit of light still lingered over the horizon. Bless the long summer days, for she was not sure she could have handled pitch black darkness at the moment. The cool breeze in the air cleared some of the fog swirling in her mind.

"Are you all right, my dear?" Lady Julia murmured softly, still holding gently onto her arm.

"I think so."

"You appeared awfully pale in there, and I thought perhaps some fresh air would do you good."

"Thank you, Lady Julia. I think the room may have been a bit too warm for me." It was not the complete truth, but also not an utter lie. The room had been quite stifling with all those bodies packed in; the abundance of westward facing windows were most likely not helping the temperatures.

"Is that all?" Lady Julia asked.

From the corner of her eye, Sybil saw the older woman studying her. Uncomfortable under her scrutiny, she gently removed her arm from Lady Julia's and walked to the stairs leading down into the gardens. There she stopped to look up into the clear evening sky.

"The stars are quite beautiful here."

"They are, indeed. We did not see them quite this clearly living in Essex. Too close to the city, I suppose. While our part of the county was much cleaner, bits of smoke still found its way to our neighborhood, especially during the winters. As much as I love Fairfield Manor and the memories held there, I find I am quite content at Penbrose House."

"You are glad to be farther away from London, then?"

"I am," Lady Julia responded. "I find I like the country far better than town. While I like people, I also enjoy wide open spaces and moments when I can be by myself."

"I have found myself to be the same. Solitude has become a special treasure over this last year."

"Yes, mourning often requires a great deal of solitude, but it should never be done alone."

The comment confused Sybil. Were not solitude and being alone the very same thing?

"Forgive me, I do not follow." She turned to face Lady Julia.

"When my husband died, I craved solitude. I did not want to see anyone. However, the longer I remained alone, the worse I felt. I did not heal, but only became a victim of my melancholy. Eventually my sister Evelyn, who had lost her husband several years previous, convinced me to sit with her each day. She did not talk, nor did I. In essence, she gave me my solitude, but made sure I knew she was there when I needed her."

"I see." Sybil contemplated the words.

"Miss Greenwald, I would like to provide the same for you."

Sybil's gaze shot to Lady Julia's.

"I know it is presumptuous of me to put myself forward like this. You do not know me well, but I cannot bear to let you face whatever you are grieving alone. I know too well how it feels."

The kindness was so unexpected, Sybil did not know how to respond. Of all the people here at the house party, this woman had every right to hate her. But, somehow, she did not. How could that be?

"I...I thank you, Lady Julia." Sybil stumbled through her words. "It is exceedingly kind of you to offer your support. I must admit I am taken aback. You of all people must know my... my history with... your family."

Lady Julia nodded, a small smile on her lips. "That does not mean I hold it against you. We all have our reasons, Miss Greenwald."

Finally, Sybil felt the tug of a genuine smile lift her lips. "Thank you. It is a great relief to me; you can be sure. As for your offer, I believe I am all right. It has been over a year since Mama's passing, and I am adjusting. I would not say I am well, but I do not feel the pain as acutely as I used to."

"I am not just speaking of death, Miss Greenwald. There are many things in life we might grieve." An all too knowing expression entered her eyes.

Sybil felt completely bare, as if Lady Julia could see right through to her inner thoughts. Wondering what had given her away, she wrapped her arms around her middle in a futile effort to cover her exposed parts.

Looking at the stars, she was grateful the few minutes they had spent outside had darkened the sky significantly. The darkness, which a few moments ago had seemed like a burden, was now a comfort. She hoped it would hide her from Nicholas's mother's searching eyes.

"I have made you uncomfortable. I am sorry. It was not my intention. Quite the opposite. I wanted you to feel you were welcome here."

"I do feel welcome, Lady Julia," Sybil said quietly. "I thank you. I must admit your words have surprised me. And if I find myself in need, I will seek you out."

A beat of silence passed between them, and she could still feel Lady Julia's assessing gaze. Eventually the older woman broke the silence.

"I am glad," she said cheerfully. "Now, I really should be getting back to my duties as hostess. Shall we join the others? I do believe tea and coffee are being served even as we speak. I have also ordered the most divine strawberry cakes you have ever tasted."

"Divine?" Sybil asked with a smile.

"Most assuredly!" she answered, returning the gesture.

"Well then, I must not miss out on the experience."

Taking Lady Julia's arm, they walked companionably to the double doors and entered the music room. Sybil glanced about the space hoping Nicholas had returned, but he had not. Perhaps he had become ill or sudden business had come up. But deep in her heart she worried his absence was completely her fault. What had possessed her to play his favorite song?

# Chapter Fourteen

Sybil woke to the sound of birds singing and sunlight streaming in through the window. Apparently, she had slept late enough for people to be hard at work in the stables—if the sounds filtering in through the window were any indication.

She bolted upright. What time was it? She was supposed to go riding with Miss Diana and the others at nine o'clock. Throwing back the bed covers, she quickly crossed to the dressing table, picked up her timepiece, and was relieved to find it working. Bless Porter for winding the piece after Sybil had carelessly tossed it onto the dressing table last evening.

It was a quarter past eight. Why had Porter not woken her? She knew Sybil was to ride with company this morning. Then realization hit—it was Porter's half-day.

With a sigh of frustration, she rang the bell pull. Rummaging through her wardrobe, she found her gray habit and threw it onto the bed. She knew they had agreed upon Porter taking the morning off, but now she was not so sure it had been the best plan. Who knew when the downstairs maid would be free to tend to her?

Untying the ribbon that held her plait, she began brushing her hair in long, even strokes. When she finished, she pulled her stays out of the bureau drawer and set them next to the habit.

A light knock sounded on the door. "Enter," she called, relieved that the maid had been so swift.

Turning to face the door, Sybil froze. The brown face that stared back at her was so unexpected that she gave a start of surprise.

"Mornin', miss," the girl said, a comfortable smile blossoming over her face. She had not seemed to notice Sybil's shock, or if she had, she was trying to ignore it.

"Good morning," Sybil finally said.

"My name's Aida. Miss Porter asked me to see to you on her half-day."

Sybil nodded and tried not to stare again as the girl helped her into her habit. The maid was taller than Porter but not quite as tall as Sybil herself. While she was not the first African Sybil had seen, she was by far the loveliest. Her bronze skin glowed in the early morning sunlight. Little dark brown ringlets lay intricately piled on her head. Her most stunning feature, however, were her eyes. They were an unusual shade of hazel. Brown centers faded to green with dark rings around the perimeters.

After the gray habit was in place, Aida rummaged through the closet, bringing out Sybil's boots.

"Are these the ones you'll be wantin' miss?"

"The very ones," Sybil said with a soft smile.

Sybil pulled her stockings on, then allowed Aida to help her with her boots. She faced forward on the dressing table bench and looked at the young woman through the mirror's reflection.

"Aida," she said as the girl began braiding and pinning her dark locks, "how long have you been employed here at Penbrose House?"

The girl glanced up in surprise. Perhaps she was not used to conversing with the women she helped. "I've been here about five months, miss. 'Tis my first post."

Now it was Sybil's turn to be surprised. The maid appeared to be in her late teens. Most girls her age had been employed for a few years by now, usually starting out in the kitchens as scullery maids. To be given the job of a house maid before lower jobs was highly unusual. Perhaps this girl was new to England, and she had acquired experience elsewhere, but her speech was too good. She must have been here some time to speak English so well.

"And how long have you been in England?"

A confused expression crossed the girl's face. "My whole life, miss. I was born here."

Sybil glanced at Aida, feeling ridiculous. Somehow she had not even considered that there were people of color who lived their whole lives in England.

"You were? Here on the estate?"

"No, miss. At Fairfield."

Sybil knew the estate to be the one Nicholas had inherited from his father. He must have brought the girl over when he'd inherited Penbrose.

"And your family, are they still at Fairfield?"

"My mah and dah are, along with my brothers 'n sisters. My dah is the stable master there. My nana is here at Penbrose House, though. She's the cook." Aida smiled. "Lord Penbrose says we couldn't do without her cooking. Personally, I agree. There isn't anyone who cooks like my nana. So he moved her here to Penbrose with him."

"I see. And do you like it here?"

"I do. I like having my own bed. Back home I had to share with my sisters. It can be a trial to have to sleep next to little girls who keep wiggling and squirming during the night." She clamped her mouth shut looking chagrined. "My apologies, miss. You don't need to be hearing me go on. Sometimes I forget to keep my peace."

"I do not mind, Aida. I am used to having some conversation with Porter in the morning. I think I would like having my own bed, as well, if I had ever had to share."

"Did you never, miss? Share a bed, that is." Awe covered her face.

"No, I am my parents' only child."

"That's too bad. Its right fun having brothers 'n sisters. Even if ya have to share a bed."

"I think I would have liked it very much, but my parents were blessed with only one baby that made it past birth."

"I see." Pity passed over Aida's expressive face. She placed the last pin in Sybil's hair, then picked up the curling tongs and proceeded to curl the small hairs around her face. The sheer concentration on the girl's face kept Sybil quiet. She did not want the maid to accidentally burn her. It was times like these she cursed her completely straight hair. What she would not give for some of the beautiful curls Aida possessed in spades.

Finally finished, Aida stepped back to inspect her work. "What do ya think, miss?"

Sybil turned her head from side-to-side and marveled at the elegant coiffure. While it was styled adequately for her riding bonnet, it seemed too beautiful to be covered. Curls framed her face while tiny perfectly arranged braids swept back and into the hair piled on top of her head. The detail was far more intricate than what Porter did, even when preparing Sybil for a ball.

"Porter was not wrong when she said you were a wonder with hair, Aida. This is exquisite!"

The girl ducked her head, a pleased smile on her face. "Thank ya, miss."

"I might need to make use of your abilities more often."

"I'd be happy to help."

Sybil rose and placed her timepiece in the pocket of her habit as Aida tidied the dressing table. Taking one last look at the room, she made sure she was completely prepared. "I believe I am ready. I should like my light grey silk with the white lace trim when I return."

"Very good, miss." Aida quickly stepped to open the door. Sybil smiled her thanks as she entered the hall and made her way to the breakfast parlor.

The prospect of having a different maid to help her dress in the mornings had always made her nervous. Usually, she left her room feeling oddly out of place after not having had Porter's ministrations.

This morning, however, she was happy and excited for the day. Aida had been quick and precise, and Sybil was sure she had not felt quite so pretty before.

The maid had been a bright spot that she had not expected, making her feel well turned out and ready to face whatever came her way.

Apparently, whatever came her way was a whole lot of mud. The ride with Miss Diana, Mr. Martin, and Mr. Lenning had gone quite smoothly—until their return. Tempest had slipped on the wet ground of the meadow, going down on her side and tossing Sybil face-first into the marshy ground, leaving her covered from head to toe in mud.

Sybil was grateful, at least, that neither she nor Tempest were any worse for the wear. A fall such as the one this morning could have broken both their necks.

Aida and the footmen carried bucket after bucket to her room, filling the copper tub that had been brought in for her use. After a thorough scrubbing, she had finally rid herself of the sticky grit.

Wrapped in a dressing gown, she sat before the fire and patiently waited as Aida combed and dried her hair. She regretted that the beautiful style the girl had worked so hard to create had not lasted more than a couple of hours.

When she was redressed, her hair mostly dry, Aida began working her magic. As before, the girl produced a veritable masterpiece.

Sybil thanked Aida again for her ministrations, then made her way to the library. She had finished *Letters of the Late Ignatius Sancho, an African*. It had been sad and eye opening.

In the library, she walked to the disheveled shelf behind the desk and replaced the book upon it. She picked up another book and found it had also been written by an African. Moving the books around she realized they were all written by or about people of color. Intrigued, she took a book of poetry to one of the two chairs by the fireplace.

A sound to her left made her jump. Looking up, she saw Miss Bawden occupying the seat next to hers, a small table with a display of flowers being the only thing that separated them.

"Oh, hello," Sybil said brightly. "I did not see you there. I thought the library was unoccupied."

"It is no matter," Miss Bawden answered, an open book in her hands.

Having been introduced to the woman on their first night, Sybil had yet to hear her speak more than a sentence at a time. Should she attempt a conversation?

"I think you will like Francis Williams's poems." Miss Bawden surprised Sybil. "They are quite well done. I am glad to see someone else reading them as many shun his works due to his color."

"I have not read anything by this author before. I am glad to hear your praise, for I do so like a good poem."

"He is no Byron, mind you. His works are not about love and fluff, but rather the injustices of man."

"I see. It is good, then, that I was not hoping for love and *fluff*." Sybil was entertained by Miss Bawden's use of the word fluff. Whatever did she mean by it?

Miss Bawden gave a cheeky smile. The small exchange seemed to open a floodgate of words from her. Soon, she and Sybil were discussing anything from the current fashions, to politics, to their shared view of the other house guests. Sybil was halfway through the conversation before she realized how relaxed she had become. It was not often she found someone whose ideas and views mirrored her own.

All too soon, though, the clock signaled it was time for tea with the other guests.

"Back to silence," Miss Bawden mumbled as she rose from her seat.

"Why is that?"

Miss Bawden appeared surprised that Sybil had heard her.

"That is a story for another day, Miss Greenwald." She grinned. "It is a long tale and will take some time to explain, but I promise it is a good one."

"Then I look forward to hearing it."

They walked toward the door when Sybil realized she had left her book of poems behind.

"Oh, dear, I seem to have forgotten the book I was going to take with me. Please go on ahead. I will be right behind you."

Sybil paced back to the table and reached for the book, but it slipped from her grasp and fell open on the floor. Picking it up, she noted that it was opened to a poem entitled, "An Ode to George Haldane." What an interesting name. She scanned the verses and found someone had made notes in the margins.

Perusing the page as she exited the library, a movement in front of her brought her up short. Her eyes fell on Lord Penbrose stumbling backwards to keep from running into her.

Surprised at his closeness, she realized her error and was about to apologize when the man gave a curt nod and mumbled, "Good day."

Then he stepped around her and entered into the library.

Why did she get the feeling Lord Penbrose was worried she might bite him if he got too close?

Shaking her head, she closed the book. After depositing the book in her room, Sybil continued to the drawing room for tea. Would Lord Penbrose join them today or did he plan to hide out in the library as she had often done?

His absence last evening when she had completed her song still stung. She'd tried to justify his behavior and pretend it had naught to do with her, but her heart screamed otherwise. She wished she knew what was going on in that head of his. He remained as cold today as he had been yesterday.

Perhaps Lord Hamdon was wrong after all, or maybe he had not been speaking of Lord Penbrose. Perhaps he had been referring to Lady Julia. She had been extremely kind to Sybil.

That did not sit well either. Lady Julia had just met Sybil and could not have told Lord Hamdon more than he could have already assessed for himself.

She and Lord Penbrose needed to talk, but for now she would just bide her time. An opportunity to speak with him would surely arise. They could not be in the same house without finding themselves together at some point. Perhaps she should have followed him into the library since she knew the space to be empty.

She grimaced. It would do no good to make the man feel trapped. Nor would she want to compromise either of their reputations. No, she would just have to be patient.

After dinner entertainment was cards again, something Miss Fairchild had insisted upon since she had missed the first night of activities.

Sybil could not help but feel sorry for Miss Bawden this evening, as she sat again by herself, a book completely neglected in her lap. The longing in her eyes as she looked toward the card tables pricked at Sybil's heart.

It would seem Miss Bawden's abbreviated conversations had alienated her from the other ladies and gentlemen of the party. Knowing she was being held either to some internal rule or a dictate by her parents, Sybil decided to give up her seat at Vingt-et-un to sit with her.

Sybil sat in the chair facing Miss Bawden. "I do not see why you could not join a game of cards," she said, sotto voce. "Most games require little conversation if you do not wish to speak."

"True," Miss Bawden said. But she still kept to her seat.

Sybil studied this paradox of a woman. She appeared to be a year or two younger than herself with a fine figure and an abundance of chestnut curls that framed a most becoming face. Sweet round cheeks and a pert nose sporting a handful of freckles gave Miss Bawden an impression of approachableness. In all, this woman would have garnered far more attention than she was getting were it not for her stilted conversation.

Miss Bawden looked at the tables. "I am far too competitive," she said quietly. "My father has forbidden me to participate unless I am specifically asked by a gentleman. Even then, I must not play to my full potential because it is often *offensive to men*," she said in an obvious imitation of her father. "As most of the gentlemen are occupied at the moment, I cannot very well join in."

That *was* a difficulty. Sybil searched her mind for a way to remedy the situation. Mr. Lenning was standing at Lord Penbrose's right arm observing the game, having just finished a game of whist with Miss Cattering and Miss Lydia Williams.

Mr. Lenning happened to glance her way at that moment, so she made direct eye contact with him and raised her brows. He mumbled something to his friend and made his way directly to them.

When he stopped in front of the ladies, he asked, "And why are two lovely ladies such as yourselves not in on the play?"

Bless Mr. Lenning for being so perceptive! His question made it far easier to accomplish her goal. Now she would not need to cajole him into asking Miss Bawden to play.

"We have not partners, as you can see, Mr. Lenning."

"Might I offer myself to partner one of you, and I will take the liberty of offering Penbrose to partner the other."

"That is quite the liberty," Sybil said with a smirk, "Do you think Lord Penbrose will bend so easily to your will?"

"I do, indeed, for he owes me a favor."

"And you plan to call in his debts for a card game?"

"That and a great many other things until he finally remembers he has already paid back the favor. It is quite a luxury to have a friend with such a short memory."

Both ladies held their hands over their mouths to smoother their laughs. Sybil knew Lord Penbrose to have an excellent memory, but perhaps she had found its weakness.

Mr. Lenning made a motion to Lord Penbrose, who looked very reluctant to approach. Upon a second motion he walked toward them, back ramrod straight.

"Penbrose," Mr. Lenning said, "we are needed on a rescue mission."

"A rescue mission, Lenning?" He glanced between the two women and settled his eyes on Miss Bawden. "I do not see anyone in distress."

"That is because you are blind, my friend. An unfortunate circumstance I have to face whenever I am in company with you. Never you fear. I shall interpret what has been said for you."

"I believe you are confusing blind with deaf, Lenning. Blind people can hear perfectly well. It is the deaf who need an interpreter."

"Then you, my friend, are both blind and deaf if you cannot see the beauty before you and hear the sounds of enjoyment all around us that they are unable to join for want of partners."

"I see. In that case, Miss Bawden, would you mind partnering a blind deaf lord at a game of whist?"

Miss Bawden had struggled to keep her composure throughout the banter between the friends, but upon Lord Penbrose pronouncing himself blind and deaf, she let out a snort of laughter. Her face immediately colored at the unladylike sound. Sybil found herself hard-pressed not to repeat Miss Bawden and add an unladylike snort of her own.

Lord Penbrose's shoulders relaxed and a smile of triumph lit his face. He held out his hand to Miss Bawden, and she took it.

Sybil and Mr. Lenning followed the pair to an empty table, where they took up the game with some amount of ease. Miss Bawden even broke her own rule and spoke more than two words together, but no more than a sentence at a time.

When Sybil retired for the night, she found she had enjoyed the evening far more than she had expected. It was a step in the right direction.

# Chapter Fifteen

Two days had passed since the night Sybil and Miss Bawden had played at whist. Sybil had hoped the positive interaction with Nicholas would be a new beginning for them, but in the days following he had not spoken above ten words to her. His continued coldness had significantly dampened her optimism.

She tried to distract herself from the ache in her heart by riding out with Miss Bawden both mornings. The few hours away from the house in such delightful company, went a long way toward easing her distress. After their morning rides, they joined Miss Diana for a stroll of the gardens.

Today, instead of a stroll, all the ladies were gathered in the west parlor at Lady Julia's request. Not sure what the meeting would entail, Sybil entered the gathering with some trepidation. The thought of spending several hours with *all* the ladies of the party was unsettling.

Of the single ladies, only Miss Diana and Miss Bawden did not seem to view her as some sort of competition, or, even worse, an enemy.

Miss Cattering and the Williams sisters had taken a firm disliking to her. In the moments they were not launching sly underhanded aspersions on her character, they occupied themselves with criticizing and maligning anyone who showed Sybil any form of friendship. For her part, she did not care for them either. They were shallow and deceitful.

Having glimpsed a bit of Lady Julia's character, Sybil was curious why she had chosen to add them to the guest list. Perhaps it was out of obligation due to the long-standing closeness between their fathers and the previous earl.

Her eyes were drawn to Miss Fairchild as she observed the other ladies. The young woman closely resembled her brother, albeit in a more feminine way. Her hair was a few shades lighter than Nicholas's, but her eyes were the exact same shade of hazel.

The lady's firm dislike of Sybil had been evident from their very first introduction. She had not spoken above three words to Sybil since. While Miss Fairchild and her cousin, Lady Olivia, did not openly attack her, they also did not include her either.

Sybil was sure the conversation she had overheard the first night in the drawing room was the basis for their treatment. It seemed she was firmly an enemy in their books—the evil miss who had beguiled Miss Fairchild's brother and then left him for naught.

Even though it was frustrating, she had to respect Miss Fairchild for wanting to protect her brother. Had she been granted a sibling, she would probably have done the same. It did not, however, make a meeting in the parlor particularly desirable.

Ultimately, it had been for Lady Julia's sake that she had decided to attend this gathering instead of claiming a headache. She would not for the world risk offending her hostess after the kindness the sweet woman had shown her.

A sudden hush fell over the room as Lady Julia stood in front of all the ladies.

"I have an announcement." She eyed the occupants of the room. "I have convinced Lord Penbrose to allow me to throw a ball at the conclusion of our house party, one which many of the surrounding neighbors will be invited to attend."

The murmurs of delight from all in attendance seemed to please Lady Julia. Sybil was happy for her but felt none of the excitement that otherwise ran rampant through the room. Since she was still in half-mourning, she would not be required to participate in the ball.

"As this is my first time planning a ball of this magnitude," Lady Julia continued, "I thought it might be enjoyable to have your help." Discussions of colors and themes popped up around the room, with little groups chattering about previous balls they had attended.

Sybil found the discussion dull. So for the majority of the meeting, she sat uninterested and unconcerned.

Halfway through the discussion of decorations and dances, Miss Cattering could be heard above the din.

"It is a shame Miss Greenwald will not be able to join in the dancing," she said in a faux whisper.

"Yes," Miss Williams agreed, "but perhaps it is for the best. It has been a very long time since her last dance. We would not want to endanger anyone's toes."

A chorus of giggles followed this pronouncement.

"Exactly." Miss Cattering puffed her ample bosom out and raising her nose just a fraction. "Best to leave the entertainment of the gentlemen to more refined ladies."

Irritation bubbled in Sybil's chest. Miss Cattering did not know it, but she had just issued a challenge. If she thought Sybil would sit back and allow the woman to trample all over her blossoming hopes, she was sorely mistaken.

For the last half hour of the discussions, all Sybil could think of was stuffing that overdressed lady's words down her overconfident throat. Her anger was fully engaged by the time everyone was dismissed and she determined to put off her mourning clothes just to spite Miss Cattering.

It was not the most mature reason for stepping out of her lavenders and grays, but she hoped her mama would understand. She could no longer sit back and allow Miss Cattering to run rough shod over her.

Luncheon was to be a picnic in the gardens. Sybil was not sure if she could stand two more hours in Miss Cattering's presence, but the introduction of the gentlemen into their midst eased the tension.

Stepping out of doors, she was met by Lord Caraway. "Might I attend you for this meal, Miss Greenwald?"

"I would be delighted." She graciously accepted and rejoiced when he led her far away from the other ladies.

Sybil knew him to be a well-read gentleman, forward thinking as well, if his choice of subject matter with her was any indication.

"Have you read the recent news about the Royal Army's movements against Napoleon?" he asked.

"I have not."

Sybil smiled. Lord Caraway may not know it, but he had won a small piece of her heart with just that one sentence. Not many men respected a woman's interest in matters of state, but he seemed to be one of them. In fact, she could only think of one other. Considering their relationship, it was no wonder both allowed for a woman to have interest in politics.

"Tell me, have Napoleon's troops reached—"

"Might we join you?" Mr. Lenning said, interrupting Sybil's question.

"By all means," Lord Caraway said, accepting for the both of them.

Miss Diana smiled at them as Mr. Lenning helped her take her seat. Miss Bawden and Lord Ansley soon approached the table set up in the shade of a fine oak tree. The men retrieved plates for the ladies, and conversation started with the usual pleasantries.

"The shade is quite refreshing; do not you agree?" Mr. Lenning said.

Everyone gave hearty agreement.

"While the day is warm, it is not stifling," Lord Caraway added.

"Yes, much better than the last ball I attended. Balls in June can be quite taxing due to the heat, but at least by then the young debutantes know to take more care for your toes."

The mention of toes drew Sybil's mind back to the conversation with the ladies in the parlor. The anger she thought she had sufficiently tamped down rose back to the surface, heating her face.

"I am afraid," Miss Diana said quietly, "that many gentlemen's toes were sacrificed at my first ball. But I am grateful for their sacrifice. My dancing education would have suffered without them."

Grins lit the gentlemen's faces at Diana's soft witty remark. Mr. Lenning, in particular, seemed quite intrigued.

"I look forward to testing your education at the upcoming ball," he said, tipping his head forward to more fully view Diana's downturned eyes. She lifted her head a fraction and smiled at him.

"Are you sure you trust me with your toes after my confession?" She turned her head slightly to face him.

"I think it is I who should be asking you if you trust your toes in my presence, for just this last assembly I trod on one young woman's foot so forcefully, she was obligated to sit out the next three dances, at least," Mr. Lenning admitted to the smiles and chuckles of the whole table.

Not long after everyone finished their meals, it was agreed that a walk through the gardens would be just the thing before some of the ladies retired for an afternoon rest.

Lord Caraway was a fine escort, but today he seemed particularly distracted as most of his conversation was filled with details of his betrothed. It was very evident to Sybil that the man was excited for his upcoming nuptials to Lady Agatha Easton, fourth daughter of the Duke of Landry.

"And she is so gentle and kind, Miss Greenwald. And did I mention her elegance..." he prattled on.

His obvious love for the lady was so sweet, and Sybil tried to be happy for him, but her heart stung with a bit of envy. The feeling was new. She had never wanted something so badly as she now wanted to have a love like Lord Caraway's.

Eyes straying to Lord Penbrose, her chest tightened. She could not even get him to look at her today. He was determined to stay as far away as possible, as was evidenced by the fact he had chosen the far opposite side of the garden to lead Miss Cattering.

On further examination, Sybil amended her assumption. It would seem Miss Cattering was the one leading Lord Penbrose about, if his lagging steps were any indication.

She smiled at his predicament.

"Oh dear, I am boring you?" Lord Caraway said. "I am sorry. It seems the closer my wedding approaches, the more I am unable to focus on those around me."

"No, Lord Caraway, it is I who should ask your forgiveness for my woolgathering. Might I ask if Lady Agatha will be attending the house party at any time?"

"Yes!" he said, beaming. "She is to arrive the last week of the party, which for my part is the best week as it will close with the ball. I do so love standing up with Agatha. She is an exquisite dancer. She is poised and graceful…" and with that, he was off again, talking of his betrothed.

Only when they neared the house did he switch topics to one Sybil could engage in.

"Are not the roses here lovely?" he asked. "I think they may be the finest in England."

"I must politely disagree. Tave Hall has an exquisite collection, far superior to those at Penbrose House."

"Impossible," he countered. "Penbrose House roses have been cultivated for the past century. The late Lady Penbrose went to great lengths to have the most exotic roses brought in for her collection."

"Just because they are exotic does not mean they are the best. A plain red rose that is well-formed and contains the purest of scents can outshine a rosa chinensis with ease. It is not the exotic that makes them superior, but the care and nurturing of the plant, and my mother's roses are grown with love."

"Love, you say? Does love really grow roses?"

"It does if you want ones as beautiful as those found at Tave Hall."

They were almost to the terrace doors when Lord Penbrose arrived leading Miss Bawden. Sybil was surprised to see her friend on Nicholas's arm and not Miss Cattering.

"Excuse me, Caraway, Miss Greenwald, but would you mind escorting Miss Bawden into the house? I fear she is unwell. I would go myself, but I must attend to my duties as *host*."

Sybil noticed how he referenced his host duties as if he was pronouncing his own demise. She really should feel sorry for him, but a tiny smile cracked her lips at his discomfort.

It would seem he was not as enamored with the lovely Miss Cattering as she was with him. And if Miss Bawden's overblown dramatics, which Sybil had detected the moment the woman stopped in front of them, were any indication, Lord Penbrose was indebted to the woman for saving him for a time from Miss Cattering's machinations.

"We would be delighted to have Miss Bawden's company," Sybil said with a sly grin.

# Chapter Sixteen

Sybil and Miss Bawden excused themselves from Lord Caraway and acted as if they would walk to their rooms. But as soon as the gentleman was out of sight, the two ladies grinned at each other and changed direction toward the library.

"I must ask how you did it?"

"Did what?" Miss Bawden asked, far too innocently.

"How did you unlatch Miss Cattering's claws from Lord Penbrose?"

"Miss Cattering? Claws?" A bark of laughter echoed through the hall before Miss Bawden was able to clamp a hand over her mouth.

"What?" Sybil asked.

"Miss *Cat*tering," Miss Bawden enunciated.

Sybil giggled. "I think from now on when it is just the two of us, we should just refer to her as the Cat. The name definitely fits the taciturn creature."

"I believe you are right. It is the perfect *pet* name." Miss Bawden snickered. "Honestly, I have never met someone with sharper claws. She is a mean one, that Miss Cattering. Plus, I do not like the way she plays with her prey."

They both giggled as they entered the library and took up the spots they had assumed the day before. The high plush wingback chairs were just the comfort Sybil needed after spending most of the past hour on her feet.

Sybil glanced about the room as Miss Bawden settled into her chair. It was a beautiful space. High shelves made of dark mahogany were filled with similar sized books. A tall ladder attached to the far wall made it possible to access the highest shelves.

"I do so envy this library," Miss Bawden said, scanning the room as well.

"As do I. We have a nice library at Tave Hall, but it is half this size and is used as both my father's study and the family library."

"Perhaps Lord Penbrose uses this one the same way. I assume that is what the desk is for."

Sybil leaned over to peer behind her at the desk that sat next to the messy section of books. "Perhaps," she said, "but I do not think so. The second day I was here, Lord Penbrose excused himself to go to his study after our morning ride. He ascended the stairs, so it is probably on the second or third floor. I believe this desk is one for the entire family's use."

When she sat back and turned to Miss Bawden, a gleam shone in the woman's eyes.

"You went riding with Lord Penbrose?" She wiggled her eyebrows.

"Hush, you," Sybil said through a laugh.

"I believe there is more to your story with Lord Penbrose than you let on. I see the way he looks at you."

"What, with derision?"

"No, with longing."

"Longing?" Sybil was completely serious now.

"Yes, whenever you are not looking, I see his eyes stray to you. Almost as if he is a child who longs for a biscuit he's forbidden to have."

"I am a biscuit, then?" Sybil tried to steer the conversation another direction. She was not ready to discuss such a painful topic. At least not yet.

"You know what I mean." Miss Bawden laughed. "You must forgive me. I am terrible with my analogies."

"No. I quite like it. It suits you."

"Thank you, but I do not believe everyone would agree with you."

"Yes, you hinted at that yesterday. I am quite ready for the story you promised me."

"You are?" she said, wiggling her eyebrows again.

"However do you do that?" Sybil was awestruck.

"Do what?"

"Your eyebrows. They move in waves like the ocean."

"Oh, that. Our steward's son often accompanied his father to our estate when I was a child. One afternoon I made a cheeky remark to him as we were playing in the apple orchard, and he wiggled his eyebrows at me. Fascinated, I begged him to teach me. He insisted it was not ladylike but gave in when I promised him one of my dog's puppies. Sadly, he moved before I mastered it."

"Did he not get his puppy after all?"

"Oh, no, I gave him the puppy when he taught me. It was not his fault I was a slow study."

"Oh, good. Some day you will have to teach me, as well. I would like to implement that skill as a distraction measure."

"Upon whom, pray tell?"

"Why, you, of course, for you have almost completely distracted me from my purpose in coming here today, which is to hear your story."

Miss Bawden laughed. "I had not meant to distract you, only to add to the silliness of my story. As you may have figured out, I am quite a silly woman."

"You are not." Sybil said indignantly. "I find you intelligent, well-read, and easy to converse with."

"All right, how about amusing?"

"That I can concur with." Sybil relaxed into her chair. "Now, story master, out with your tale."

"All right, but I have a request if I am to recite my tale of woe."

"What might that be?"

"Might we dispense with surnames and call each other by our given names? I believe if we are to share our darkest secrets, we should at least drop the formality between us."

"I agree. You may call me Sybil."

"And you may call me Eliza."

"Well, then, Eliza, what is this *tale of woe*?" Sybil said dramatically as if she was quoting the title of a ghost story.

Eliza smiled. "About a year after my come out, I attended a dinner party at the Earl of Mansfield's townhome. It was a lavish affair. My parents had warned me to be on my best behavior. You see, at that time I was not one to hold my tongue. I still am not, but I was even more prone to speak my mind then."

"How old were you?" Sybil asked.

"Eighteen. Mind you, I did try. But every so often I could not help myself. I would go on about subjects that were not quite proper for young ladies, much to my parents embarrassment. Most of my previous infractions were of small consequence as I was not often in company with such esteemed members of the Ton.

"I had been warned by my father time and again to check my tongue, but that organ seems to have a mind of its own. So it was that I sat at dinner, Mr. Glover on my right and Lord Burton of Shropshire on my left."

"I am acquainted with Lord Burton," Sybil interjected. "He has very fine stables."

"He does. Which is why when we were in the middle of the third course of a five-course meal I brought up the topic of horses. I am quite familiar with horse husbandry, and I happened to ask about the animals he kept. He mentioned a few and then went on to give an account of his prized stallion.

"Apparently, he keeps a fine thoroughbred racer whose colts have been known to win the races at Ascot. I, trying to be conversant, asked if all the colts were born on his estate. He answered they were not, and I said, 'So, you let out your stallion for stud services?'"

"You did not!" Sybil covered her mouth as her eyes danced with merriment.

"I did, but it does not stop there. Several people around us had gone silent, and I looked at him, patiently awaiting his answer. He finally responded that he did, and I said, 'Well, for my part, I am glad I am not a horse. I would hate to have my services out for let.'"

Sybil could not help herself as she doubled over in laughter. Eliza began laughing as well. Soon they were laughing so hard that they both held their sides.

"I am guessing your father was none too pleased with that display." Sybil tried to catch her breath.

"Most definitely. He was seated just down the table on the other side from me and heard the entire exchange. It is the reason he has forbidden me to speak more than is necessary."

"I am sorry for that," Sybil said, still chuckling. "But does he mean only two syllables?"

"Oh, no! That is my own way of getting even with him. My father is very strict and enforces some of the most ridiculous rules. There are several, you see. He is very eager to have me married off, and this is the perfect deterrent. Thankfully, my reputation combined with my near silence scares off many suitors."

"Is one of those not being able to play card games with gentlemen unless expressly asked?"

"That and not allowing me to walk out with anyone unless I take my tattletale governess along."

"But you are too old for a governess."

"Now you see the rub of it. She is my younger sister's governess now, and she is a dragon of a woman. It is no surprise that she never married. She is passably pretty, mind you, but she is the most cantankerous woman I have ever met."

"Why not allow your maid to escort you? That would be more appropriate, would it not?"

"Because Harper would not utter a word about my behavior to my father. She's a good sort, and probably the best maid a wild-hearted woman like me could have."

"It is nice to have a loyal servant."

"Yes, indeed, but my father would not bring anymore servants on this trip than necessary, so only my mother's lady's maid came along for this journey. For my part, I am grateful. That means I am not followed around like a young child about to get into mischief."

A clock in the room chimed the hour, and Eliza rose from her seat. "Is it time for tea already? It feels as though we just sat down."

"It does at that," Sybil said. "However, all this laughing has left me quite parched. I could use some tea."

"I as well," Eliza said, and they both made their way to the door of the library. "Next, time, Sybil, you will have to tell me your story."

"Mine?" Sybil was confused. The mischief in Eliza's hazel eyes made her squirm. She couldn't be talking about—

"Yes, the one with Lord Penbrose."

# Chapter Seventeen

When Nicholas had first decided to avoid Miss Greenwald at all costs, he'd thought the endeavor would be quite simple. After all, the vastness of Penbrose House and the surrounding estate would provide plenty of room for two people to avoid one another for days.

He should know. His sister Mary and cousin Olivia were never where he expected them to be. He had been trying to run them to ground for three days, hoping to have a private moment to speak with them. In those same three days, however, he had stumbled upon Miss Greenwald no less than ten times. Ten! Possibly even more.

At breakfast, in the stables, and even the hall. Nicholas had even thought to avoid people by hiding in the library only to almost run Miss Greenwald over, quite literally, as she was exiting.

They would have met again in the hall at dinnertime had he not seen her walking down the corridor and decided to duck into a window alcove. After dinner, he could not avoid her so easily as Bradley had called upon him to play a game of whist with her and Miss Bawden.

Nicholas had noticed she seemed more at ease during the card game than she'd been since her arrival. Her easy manner with the others had been far too intoxicating and his gaze had continuously strayed from his cards to her enchanting face. Her various looks of enjoyment had drawn him in, and he'd found himself fighting the urge to obtain some of that attention for himself.

Yesterday he'd seen her ride out with Miss Bawden and been shocked by the yearning that had filled him. It had taken all his restraint not to rush after them and beg to be included in their party.

Nicholas was quite sure he had seen Sybil—Miss Greenwald, he corrected himself—more than any other guest. After a moment, he had to amend the thought. She was actually the second most.

Miss Cattering claimed the right of most seen. Also, the most heard. As well as the most avoided. It seemed Nicholas could go nowhere these past three days without her somehow converging on him at the most inopportune moments.

Curse chivalry and all the gentleman's code, for he had been forced to keep company with her on so many occasions just to satisfy social propriety.

She and Miss Williams had twice ambushed him before his morning ride. At the first encounter, he had felt it his duty as host to invite them along. Miss Cattering had agreed most readily, but Miss Williams had insisted she was not up to a ride and excused herself to return to the house.

Nicholas had the sinking feeling he had been outwitted into spending time alone with Miss Cattering. Not one to be outfoxed, he'd asked a groom to attend them. He would never forget the disappointment that crossed Miss Cattering's face when they rode out with the groom not three paces behind them. In an effort to spend as little time as possible with the scheming woman, he had also cut his usual hour ride in half.

He had been ready for her the next time, however. Having secured Bradley as a companion for his morning ride, Miss Williams had been obligated to make up one of their party in order to even out their numbers.

Nicholas knew Miss Cattering and Miss Williams held no affinity for Mr. Lenning, but in the name of civility and perhaps to appease him, they'd conversed easily with him as they rode out. Bradley did his best to carry a good majority of the conversation with both ladies. At one point, though, Miss

Cattering claimed her horse had thrown a shoe. Slipping from the mare's back, she'd made a pretense of looking for the offending hoof.

Miss Williams continued riding on, acting as if she was unaware her friend had dismounted. Bradley, deep in a conversation with her about men's waistcoats, truly did not notice he had left Nicholas behind to stare down at the now unmounted lady. Knowing her aim, he was tempted to also continue riding, but his mother's training had been too thorough.

After dismounting and assuring her all four shoes remained attached, he offered to help her remount. Stepping to the side of the horse, Miss Cattering raised her hands to place them on Nicholas's shoulders.

Nicholas chuckled to himself, remembering her shock and disappointment when instead of wrapping his hands around her waist to place her on her mount, he had dropped into a crouch, avoiding her touch and cupped his hands for her to step into.

He was not only averse to the intimacy, but unsure his own strength could lift the muscular woman onto her horse without assistance. Miss Cattering was not a small woman. She stood just a few inches shy of his own six feet. Along with her height, she had an abundance of curves that were all the rage in London but by no means made a woman easy to carry. In the end, it had taken a great deal of Nicholas's strength to help her mount by foot.

However, some of the difficulty might have been caused by her continual effort to throw herself off-balance. Whether she was doing so out of spite or the hopes of throwing them both into a compromising position, he was not sure, but it was not as subtly done as she may have believed.

In addition to their two disastrous rides, there had been two entreaties to play parlor games, three nights of her stalking him around the drawing room, and five hallway meetings, one of which she had feigned tripping into him.

The fates had smiled upon him, however, for her aim had been off and she'd landed in Mr. Martin's arms instead of his.

Today had been the most blatant of her attacks. The second the women exited to join the men for their afternoon picnic, she had latched onto his arm before he was even aware that she stood at his side. Not wanting to make a scene, he had seen no other option but to invite her to be his partner in the alfresco meal.

Now, as he navigated the halls on his way to the library, he tried to push away the feeling that he was sneaking around his own house. He was not. He was just determined to walk slowly, and if he happened to peek around the corner of a room or hallway, it was just to make sure he did not accidentally run into someone. He would hate to be the cause of injury.

Upon slinking up to the third corner, he noticed the footman give him an odd look. The corner of the man's lips twitched into a smirk. Nicholas straightened, brushed at his coat, and gave a curt nod to the man before he walked around the corner. Thankfully, the hall was empty.

Nicholas froze when he neared the library. Peals of feminine laughter came from within. He strained to decipher its occupants lest he be walk into another encounter with Miss Cattering.

Miss Greenwald's rich tones floated through the closed door and he turned to leave. While Sybil was a far cry better than Miss Cattering, he was not at all in possession of himself enough to spend time with her. Her beautiful song still haunted his every waking hour.

When he heard Miss Bawden's voice, however, he turned back in surprise. Not only was the woman speaking, an oddity in and of itself, but she seemed to be telling a story of a dinner encounter gone wrong. Nicholas could not help himself. He leaned into the door a bit to hear the sordid tale.

It was such a shock to hear the woman use so many words and at such a great speed that he did not hear Lord Ansley and Lord Caraway's approach. A throat cleared and he glanced up. Both gentlemen were looking askance at him. He straightened quickly and took a step back.

"Ansley, Caraway." He tried to appear as though he had not just been caught eavesdropping.

"Are you for the library?" Ansley glanced at the door and tipped his head.

"I am."

"Might we join you? Caraway was telling me of a most fascinating collection you have of, um…"

Nicholas knew what collection he meant with the nervous clearing of the man's throat. The word abolition did not always carry the best connotations in Society. But it would be good to have another lord on their side when votes were cast this next spring. Nicholas knew the bill he and Caraway had proposed would probably take more than one session to pass at Parliament, but hope welled up in him at Ansley's interest.

He raised a questioning brow at his cousin. The man nodded, a measure of assurance in the motion. "Ansley has heard the rumors of our cause, Penbrose. He will be a good ally."

"Very well, but I am only paused here because there are two ladies already ensconced in my library with whom I do not particularly want to share our business."

A knowing expression crossed Caraway's face followed by a teasing grin. His cousin had read between the words and knew exactly which lady Nicholas wished to avoid.

"Perhaps we can return later when the library is empty," Ansley suggested.

Movement from the other side of the door belatedly alerted them that the ladies were approaching. Looking to one another, they scrambled to step away but were unable to take more than a step before the door was thrown open and Miss Greenwald and Miss Bawden stood before them.

The guilt on the trio of lords' faces was priceless in its appearance. Sybil would have laughed had she not been so surprised to see them all standing so close to the door looking as if they had been caught stealing biscuits from the pantry. Eliza, who stood a step behind her, did snicker.

The sound seemed to break the tension as all three men began talking at once, trying to explain their presence. Upon hearing each other speak they all went silent again. Finally, Nicholas spoke up.

"We were on our way to the library in search of a particular book. Where are you ladies off to?" He appeared, oddly, the guiltiest of the three as his eyes flitted between the interior of the library and both ladies' faces.

"Tea," Sybil said. "Are we to have the pleasure of your company today?"

"Ah, yes, it is that time. Yes, yes, we shall be along shortly."

Sybil took her cue and stepped out of the library. The gentlemen stepped back to make room for her and Eliza's exit. Linking arms with her friend, she told herself not to look back as they walked away, but her heart did not listen to her head.

Glancing ever so covertly over her shoulder, the sight she saw made her heart pick up speed. While the other men had already entered the library, Nicholas watched her retreat. The longing in his eyes gave her a glimmer of hope, but as quickly as the look had come, it was gone again, and he followed his companions into the library.

"I had not thought those three gentlemen to be bugs on the wall," Eliza said.

"Bugs on the wall?"

"Yes," she said peevishly. "They were eavesdropping at the door. I hope they do not add gossiping to their list of bad habits, for while I do not mind telling my story, I do not want others to go around telling it for me. Gossipmongers can never get the story quite right, you know."

Sybil spluttered. "Are you not more worried that it shall be told at all? I, for one, would be quite humiliated if it were my tale being bandied about."

"Oh, no, Sybil. Perhaps you have not noticed. While my poor parents get embarrassed at a mere sneeze out of place, I am rarely embarrassed. I am sure they see me as a great trial, but I refuse to let Society make me feel bad for my blunders. I just sally through them and have a good laugh along the way."

"I wish I could be as brave as you."

"Brave or idiotic, they are the same thing. It just depends on your point of view. I am sure there are many who find me quite imprudent. But I would rather be imprudent than insipid. No one having met me will ever forget I was there."

"You are definitely unforgettable." Sybil grinned.

Eliza's smile briefly flattened, and pain flashed across her face, but as they entered the drawing room it was quickly replaced with a polite smile. It was such a strange reaction, but Sybil did not have time to question her with all the other guests around.

A quarter hour into tea, the three lords joined the rest of the party. While Sybil did not see them enter, she knew exactly when they arrived by the way the rest of the ladies fixed their posture. Putting on their most alluring smiles, they began talking a bit more animatedly. Only a trio of lords could cause such a stir.

In contrast, she acted as if she had not noticed. Through her months in London she had studied the people around her with great care. She had made a great discovery not long into her season. Gentlemen were often drawn to a woman who did not let their presence change the course of her own enjoyment.

Sybil had seen it time and again. The women who paid no mind to the men in the room but stayed confident in their own abilities gathered the most admirers, and so it was today. Not more than five minutes after arriving in the room, all three men, with the addition of Mr. Lenning and Mr. Martin, were seated near herself, Eliza, and Miss Diana.

As Sybil talked with the men, she happened to glance around the room at large. Miss Cattering was glaring, as usual, in their direction. However, instead of her gaze being directed toward Sybil, the lady's ire was firmly pinned on her cousin.

What reason had she to be angry with Miss Diana? She was not monopolizing any of Miss Cattering's prospects. The only person to whom Miss Diana paid much attention was Mr. Lenning, and Sybil knew Miss Cattering would not give that gentleman a second thought.

Sybil scanned the room and noticed that her father was again seated with Lady Evelyn. While she was excited to see him so happy, she was frustrated with his lack of attention. Over the last few days, he had not taken a single opportunity to talk to her. Of course, she had avoided him as well. Only short greetings had been offered when they passed one another, and half the time he did not even acknowledge those.

She had tried to appear happy whenever he was near, hoping he would recognize that she had taken his words to heart. Had he even noticed?

A movement at her right caught her attention as Lord Penbrose rose from his seat. He had not said more than a handful of words since coming to sit with the group. The dark look upon his face now made her wonder if she had somehow angered him, but suddenly multiple people in the room were standing, and before she could rise from her seat to see why, she heard the butler's announcement.

"Mr. Thomas Fairchild of Downing Way."

# Chapter Eighteen

The butler's announcement left Nicholas feeling first cold with dread, then hot with anger. The last time that man had dared enter Penbrose House had been five months ago. The volatile nature of the conversation had made Nicholas fume for months. Just the thought of his uncle could ruin an entire day.

He had never really liked Uncle Fairchild. The man had been dismissive at best in Nicholas's youth. At his worst, he had been downright mean. Being civil to his relations in public was one thing but having them in his home was quite another.

Uncle Fairchild bowed over his mother's hand, his grey-streaked blond hair staying perfectly in place as he moved. Protectiveness surged through Nicholas at the sight of the unscrupulous man touching his mother and his feet made their way to her side of their own accord. He wanted to reach out and hit his uncle's hand away, but good sense prevailed at the last moment. Nicholas clenched his fists and tried to smooth his face into a façade of nonchalance.

"Always a pleasure to see you, Julia," Mr. Fairchild said smoothly as he rose from his bow. Nicholas could not help but notice how the cad's eyes raked over his mother's figure as he rose from his position. The scoundrel! Why had he come?

"Thomas," she said with a nod of her head. "What a surprise to see you. I had thought you to be in London. Margaret was sure you planned to remain another month, at least."

"And how is our dear sister-in-law?" Mr. Fairchild asked, no doubt trying to infuse his question with charm, but Nicholas caught the note of irritation in his voice. Lady Margaret, Lord Hepton's widow, had never gotten along well with Mr. Fairchild.

"She is well, if her last letter is to be believed. She wrote to announce the birth of her new grandson."

"She has a grandson now, does she? A generation too late, but I am sure she is happy to finally have a boy in the family. And which of her four daughters does she have to thank for this little...*miracle*?" Mr. Fairchild's double meaning was not so veiled this time.

It was, however, a miracle that he had been able to have such a civil, although condescending, conversation thus far.

"Her second, Isabelle. Sir Blakeney is overjoyed to have an heir after two daughters."

"I am sure he is," he said dismissively while eyeing Nicholas. His eyes flicked from one part of Nicholas's person to another. Finally, he broke the short tense silence.

"Well, as you can see, I am returned from London for your wonderful house party. I am sure you sent me an invitation, but somehow it was misdirected. Please forgive my tardiness. I only heard of the gathering two days ago."

His mother's slight grimace would not be evident to the room at large, but Nicholas had seen it before she was able to cover her unease. He, on the other hand, knew his disgust was still evident on his face.

No invitation had been sent, and he was sure his uncle knew as much. He had not been welcomed in this house since their argument in February. Ever the lady, however, his mother seemed to gather her wits and courage.

"You are welcome to come any day and join in our activities. Whenever it is convenient for you to leave your estate, of course. I know you have been away quite some time. I am sure you have much business to see to."

The message was clear. She wished him to see to his own matters.

"I have been to my holdings already and have everything well enough in order that I might enjoy a few weeks' respite. Wilson has already directed our things to be taken to our usual rooms in the family wing."

His mother's wide-eyed stare at the man's audacity mirrored Nicholas's own feelings. Not only had he not been invited, but he and his sons had arrived ready to stay for the duration of the house party!

That he had already had the servants' ready rooms and deliver his things spoke of another problem Nicholas would have to address. Many of the current staff had been employed at Penbrose House for years. They had taken orders from Mr. Fairchild through those years, but Nicholas could not have them bowing to this man's demands every time he entered his home. No, he would need to speak with them as soon as the man was removed.

He stepped forward to give his uncle a firm dismissal, but his mother's hand shot out and touched his sleeve. The contact, however brief, let him know she intended to handle the situation. But Mr. Fairchild spoke first.

"As we are family, there is no need to stand on ceremony. We feel adequately welcomed and wish everyone to return to their tea," he said to the room at large.

The majority of the guests took their cue and sat, returning to their conversations and tea.

Several, however, remained standing. Nicholas was not surprised to see his sister Mary take a step behind Bradley and Anthony. The two men created a sort of shield for her. Caraway was also still standing, as well as Lord Brock, Mr. Williams, Mr. Greenwald, Lady Evelyn, and Miss Greenwald. Even though his cousins Olivia and Caroline had taken their seats, Nicholas could tell both they were still engaged in listening to the conversation.

His eyes fell for the first time on his cousins, who stood back awaiting their turn to greet his mother. Nicholas did not remember them being announced. Had he missed it in his haste to be by his mother's side?

His younger cousin, John, looked about the room with some interest, inspecting the occupants. While the man had a penchant for gambling and drink, he was more of a nuisance than anything. Even though Nicholas did not care for his company he was not a true threat.

His cousin, Tom, on the other hand—well, he was the devil incarnate as far as Nicholas was concerned. He knew of at least one young woman of genteel birth who had been ruined by the man, and gossip had surfaced of a half-dozen others of the working class. If rumors were to be believed, he had several illegitimate children already, but Nicholas had never been able to verify any of the claims. Behind Tom's debonair smile and charming manners lay a snake ready to strike.

The thought of hosting these three men for a fortnight—fourteen whole days—set Nicholas on edge. He would never allow it. He had a mother and sisters to protect. He especially feared for Mary.

He had no proof, but he was sure one of his cousins had done something untoward to her last season. Her current place behind Bradley and Anthony was proof enough that his assumptions had been right. And if either of his cousins was to blame, it would be Tom.

He needed to get them out of this house, and soon.

"Of course, we are happy to have you, Thomas," his mother said. "With the addition of you and your sons, our numbers should be rounded out quite nicely."

Shock reverberated through Nicholas. How could she stand there and calmly accept these Judases into their midst? Not only had his uncle most thoroughly tried to steal his current title as earl, but he was by no means good company. Even if the man and his sons did not do true damage, his reputation was sure to tarnish everyone in the room by association. Looking to his mother for explanation, her eyes seemed to say, *I will explain later.*

"Thank you, Julia. Always the gracious hostess. A most admirable lady."

Uncle Fairchild gave a short bow and turned to where Nicholas stood stunned.

"Fairchild," he greeted with a nod, then walked away to join Lord Brock.

Soft gasps from those still standing echoed in Nicholas's ears. To call him by his former address after his uncle had been graciously accepted into the home was the height of impropriety. Some may have viewed it as a momentary lapse in memory, but Nicholas knew otherwise. It was a blatant slight. As always, his uncle refused to acknowledge him as the rightful heir.

Tom stepped up and kissed his mother's cheek. "Aunt Julia, it is such a pleasure to see you again. You are as beautiful as ever. However do you do it? I believe every woman in the room is quite green with envy."

"Good to see you too, Tom. I see you have yet to lose that silver tongue of yours. Still lavishing the ladies with compliments?"

"Naturally." He cast her a debonair smile. "How can I not compliment beauty when I see it?"

Nicholas knew his mother was too well-acquainted with Tom's ways to be swayed by a little flattery, but she held a soft spot for both these boys. She and Aunt Fairchild had been particularly close. The fond feelings the women had shared seemed to have transferred to her children.

"I hope your health has been well?" Tom shifted from one foot to the other.

"It has, thank you. And how have you fared?"

"Quite well, I thank you." His eyes strayed to the side. "And how about the rest of your family? I see *Lord Penbrose* is in the pink of health, and if my eyes do not deceive me, Mary also seems to be doing *quite* well."

"Yes," his mother said with reserve. "All of my children are well. As you have already recognized Nicholas and Mary, I will tell you that my other two girls, Anna and Eva, are in good health. Unfortunately, they will not be joining us as they are on holiday at my brother's estate."

"Ah, I see." Tom's gaze darted to the side.

Nicholas stepped forward, then noticed the mischief on his mother's face.

"Tell me, Tom, will you be joining us for church, tomorrow?" she asked.

Nicholas did not miss the disdain on Tom's too handsome face. Apparently, the thought of church brought the devil a bit of unease. Good—perhaps a day in church would go a long way to change the man's ways. He knew better, however. His cousin was sure to find some excuse for not attending. He always did.

"Perhaps," Tom said evasively, then turned his attention to Nicholas.

"Nicholas, you seem to be as tall as ever," he said with a smirk. The childhood jab about his unusual height was strange in this situation. He had reached his full height at an early age, and his cousin's had enjoyed teasing him about being a giant. But he could see at least two other men in the room who were around his same height. In fact, Lord Brock was probably two inches taller.

"Yes, it seems I have not shrunk even one bit. You appear to be in good health, Tom. I do hope your journey was uneventful." Nicholas tried his best to not cause a stir.

"It was, I thank you." His eyes strayed again to the side. Nicholas followed the man's line of sight. When it landed on Miss Greenwald, his heart leapt into his throat, then sank to the pit of his stomach. Looking back at his cousin, he could see the man's interest.

"I see you have several uncommonly pretty guests. Might I ask for an introduction to the emerald-eyed Venus standing near Lady Evelyn?"

Nicholas flicked his eyes back to Sybil, all formality in his brain chased away by protectiveness.

"I am afraid I cannot do that, Tom," he said, knowing his tone was far too hard, but unwilling to soften it even the smallest bit.

The low chuckle that rumbled in his cousin's throat made the hair on the back of his neck stand on end.

"Worried you are not enough for her, are you? Maybe—" Nicholas's hand shot out and grabbed the man's shoulder, pulling him closer.

Leaning forward, he whispered, "You will conduct yourself as a true gentleman while in my home? If I hear even one whisper about unsavory conduct,

I will have you thrown out without ceremony, and you shall never be allowed back to Penbrose House for the remainder of your days. Am I clear?"

Tom jerked back from the close contact and straightened his jacket sleeve. "Yes, *my lord*."

Turning on his heels, he joined his father near Lord Brock. Confusion crossed Miss Cattering's face as she looked between the new arrivals and Nicholas. He knew her father and Mr. Fairchild had been friends for quite some time. At one point he had thought Miss Cattering and his cousin Tom would make a match of it, but no betrothal had ever been announced.

Nicholas took up his previous seat near Bradley after a brief greeting with his cousin, John. When he glanced at the chairs opposite, he was met by Miss Diana's nearly colorless face.

Sybil leaned over and whispered something to Miss Diana. She nodded, and Miss Bawden and Miss Greenwald escorted her from the room. As the group left, Tom's eyes followed them all the way to the door. It made Nicholas want to retch. How in the world could his mother have invited such a man into their midst?

# Chapter Nineteen

Compassion welled in Sybil's chest as she watched the whole distressing scene play out. While she could not remember the particulars, she knew Nicholas had never liked his uncle's family. He claimed they were not the type of people one would wish to associate with, but in town they were quite popular.

Her attention, however, was stolen away when she saw Miss Diana's ashen face. Sybil sat as long as her nerves would allow, then decided it was time to extricate the girl from the situation.

Excusing herself and Miss Diana, she made her way to the door. Eliza quickly took up a position on Diana's other side. Once in the hall, Sybil locked eyes with Eliza and they simultaneously said, "to the library."

Miss Diana gained back some color as they walked, but upon entering the library, she took a huge breath of air and burst into tears. Eliza stared at Sybil, fear and confusion in her eyes. Sybil reached forward and gathered Diana into her arms. It would seem another of her dresses would have tear stains to decorate the shoulder.

When the dainty body in her arms stopped wracking with sobs, Sybil asked, "Would you like to talk about it?"

Diana shook her head at first, but then nodded into Sybil's shoulder. Pulling away, Sybil kept one arm around her shoulders as she led her away from the desk at the entrance, past the tall wingback chairs before the fire, and to one of the small tables that sat by the tall windows near the far wall.

As the three girls sat, both Sybil and Eliza produced squares of linen. Being presented with not one, but two pieces of cloth, Miss Diana gave a short, mirthless chuckle.

"Is it really all that bad?"

"Yes," Sybil and Eliza said in unison. They all giggled.

After giving Diana time to repair some of the damage the tears had caused, Sybil prompted her to explain.

"I am not sure I can," she said, wringing one of the linen squares in her hands. "I do not want to burden you, and we are not all that well-acquainted."

"Diana," Sybil said, "may I call you Diana?"

The pretty blonde locked eyes with her and searched her face. "I suppose, if I might call you Sybil."

"I believe," Eliza said, "we are all far past standing upon ceremony and are now quite firmly in Christian-name territory. Perhaps even to the point of pet names." Eliza grinned at her own wit. "You must call me Eliza after sharing such an intimate moment of distress. You have seen how silent I can be, Diana, and I promise you I shall not share a single detail with another soul, if that is what you are afraid of."

"Nor I," Sybil agreed.

"I have not had friends since I was a little girl," Diana said. "If I might be so bold, it seems odd to have found two at one house party."

"Agreed," Sybil and Eliza said in unison. They peered at one another with almost identical smirks and laughed again.

"It would also seem that Sybil and I are beginning to think with the same mind if our synchronous language is any indication," Eliza quipped.

"And now, Eliza," Sybil added, "we shall use your half of our brain to lead us into all sorts of mischief, and I shall be bound to use my half to help fight our way out of it."

Eliza looked comically affronted. "Me? Mischief? Very well, it is probably true. But mark my words, one day you shall be the damsel in distress, Miss Sybil, and then I shall be forced to be your knight in shining armor."

Sybil grinned at her incorrigible friend. "I look forward to it."

"Well, you both have quite thoroughly played my knights in shining armor today, and for that, I must thank you." A slight quaver to Diana's voice sobered them.

"You are most welcome," Eliza said, reaching across the table and patting Diana's hand. "Now, enough with our theatrics. What is your story? I am sure it must be something ghastly. Your face appeared paler than my coming out gown."

"It is ghastly. I must give you fair warning," she said, dabbing under her eye, "My story may shock your tender sensibilities."

"Tender sensibilities?" Eliza said. "What are those? I do not believe I have ever been afflicted with such a malady."

Diana giggled. "Then perhaps you are just the person for this tale."

"Indeed." Eliza leaned back in her chair and waved her hand regally in the air for Diana to continue.

"I suppose you should know that I have been a ward of my uncle for the past four years."

"What has that got to do with the story?" Eliza interrupted.

"Hush," Sybil reprimanded. "Let her speak."

Eliza looked chagrined. "I shall hold my peace and let you do the telling."

"As I was saying, I have been my uncle's ward these past four years. In truth, the last five as he was appointed guardian after my father's death. The law, you see, does not allow a woman to be guardian of her own children. At first my uncle was more than happy to leave me and my two brothers in my mother's care. But after my mother...rejected his advances"—a deep blush colored her cheeks— "he removed myself and my brothers from our home. I think he hoped that she would relent with the loss of her children, but my mother has strong morals, and she refused to compromise them."

"Let me get this straight. Your uncle asked his sister-in-law to be his mistress?" Eliza said bluntly.

Diana's red cheeks flamed brighter, but she nodded.

"The rake! Why did your mother not expose him?"

"And risk her children's well-being?" Sybil pointed out.

"Ah. I see. Men are such bothers," Eliza mumbled.

Diana hesitantly glanced between them. Sybil signaled her to continue.

"My brothers were promptly sent back to school in the fall. Honestly, they spend no more than a few weeks in the summer at Lord Brock's estate. As for me, I have been secured as a sort of companion for my cousin. Not a real companion, mind you. I am not paid, nor do I constantly wait upon her. I am just another person to add propriety in social interactions. Since then, I have been obligated to travel about with my uncle and cousin."

Looking down at her hands, Diana took a deep breath. "I first met the elder Mr. Fairchild and his sons three years ago when they came for a visit to my uncle's estate. It was the summer before my first season, and I was still quite slender."

"You are even yet quite slender," Eliza said.

"Yes, but back then, I had not acquired, umm, a more... womanly form."

"I see."

"Mr. Thomas Fairchild the younger and Mr. John Fairchild did not take much notice of me. The next summer, however, I'd acquired my... charms," she said, a bit of a blush returning to her pale cheeks. "Mr. Tom Fairchild took a liking to me and began finding moments to talk and flirt. At first, I was thrilled at the idea of attracting a gentleman's attention. But Kitty was so angry, I thought she would claw my eyes out."

Eliza snickered. "Your cousin's first name is Kitty?"

"Not exactly. It is Kathryn, but most people call her Kitty."

Eliza full-on guffawed. Sybil was hard-pressed to hold back her laughter, as well.

Diana seemed confused. "Why is this so funny?"

Eliza could not gather her wits about her, so Sybil illuminated the joke.

"Forgive us, but we have often commented on how your cousin seems to have many mannerisms that resemble a cat."

Diana continued to appear confused.

"Currently she is trying to sink her claws into the earl and prowls about Penbrose House like a cat ready to pounce at the first opportunity. It seemed very fitting, considering her last name is *Cat*tering."

Diana burst into laughter. "Kitty Cat!"

Sybil laughed along with her friends.

After a few moments, Eliza's chuckles subsided and she wiped her eyes. "I am sorry I interrupted yet again, but it could not be helped. Please continue, Diana."

Diana's smile softened. "Please do not apologize. I shall cherish that bit of knowledge. It will make dealing with her tempers much less wounding if I view her as a spitting cat."

"In that case, you are welcome," Eliza said with a self-satisfied smirk.

"As I was saying," Diana continued, "Kitty had heard rumors that Mr. Fairchild was the heir presumptive. As such, his son Mr. Tom Fairchild would be next in line and she was determined to be a countess."

"Wait. I thought the current Lord Penbrose was the heir presumptive?" Sybil asked.

"You do not know?" Eliza stared at her with wide eyes.

"Know what?"

"There was a huge to do when the late earl's will was read. You see, the earl's second and third son were twins, but no one knew who was older."

"Truly?"

"Yes, apparently the late Lady Penbrose did not want her sons fighting over who was older since she already had an heir, so she swore the midwife and her lady's maid to secrecy on who was older."

"Smart woman," Sybil said. "Children squabble enough as it is."

"I agree," Eliza concurred.

"How did they know who was oldest, then?" Sybil asked.

"I can answer that," Diana interjected. "The only other person Lady Penbrose told was her husband. Upon his death it was revealed in the will that Mr. Jonas Fairchild was the elder twin, much to Mr. Thomas Fairchild's dismay."

"Yes," Eliza added, "it seems Mr. Thomas Fairchild had started claiming he was the elder son in his early twenties. And with each successive daughter Lord Hepton fathered, Mr. Fairchild increased his claims. It opened a lot of doors for the man, and I am sure he did not appreciate losing his place in Society when his claims were proven false."

Diana nodded her head. "That is why Mr. Fairchild fought so hard to have the will dismissed. He claimed it to be the delusions of an old man, the late Lord Penbrose having been sick for quite some time before his death. But enclosed with the will were signed testimonies from Lady Penbrose and the two women who attended the birth."

"No wonder Lord Penbrose looked so angry at his uncle's arrival." Sybil shook her head.

"Yes," Eliza said. "But we have wandered from your tale again, Diana. Might I point out, though, that I was not the cause this time."

Sybil scoffed at her friend's words, then grinned. "Very well, I take full blame, but at least mine was for a good purpose."

"And what was that?" Eliza smirked.

"Clarification."

"That is a fair excuse," she conceded.

"Yes, well," Diana began again, "Assuming that the younger Mr. Fairchild would someday be heir, Kitty tried everything to obtain a proposal from him. His attentions to me during that season made her green with envy. In retaliation, she sabotaged every event I attended and one night, in a fit of jealousy, she spilled ratafia all over my cream gown in the middle of a ball. I can only assume she hoped my uncle would send me home."

"I never did like that woman," Eliza muttered under her breath.

"Unfortunately, Mr. Tom Fairchild offered to escort me home. I thought for sure my uncle would refuse due to the impropriety of a single man escorting a young lady home, especially since he had just as many hopes of his daughter obtaining a proposal from Mr. Tom Fairchild as I believe Kitty did. To my shock, however, he readily agreed, and I was escorted out of the home and into a waiting carriage, leaving me alone with... that man," she said with a shudder. The color that had flamed in her cheeks moments before seemed to fade entirely as she went completely silent.

Sybil and Eliza waited patiently as Diana took a few slow breaths, obviously fighting for her composure.

"I should have refused, perhaps made a scene, but I was young and naive. I thought perhaps Mr. Fairchild meant to declare himself..."

Sybil waited until the silence became too unnerving. "I assume that was not his intention?"

"No, it was not. But I did not find that out until much later. I realized too late that he was as deep in his cups as my uncle had been. He began saying things to me, scandalous things. But I, like a fool, thought he was just bungling his proposal. About two streets from my uncle's townhome he—he..."

Tears pooled in the ocean-blue depths of Diana's eyes. "He told me it was far too cold to be in such a wet dress, and he should help me out of it. I was so shocked, I could not even form words. Moving to my side of the carriage, he began kissing my neck and pulling at the sleeves of my dress. I was so frightened; I did the only thing I could think of—I lunged for the door handle and flung it open. But before I could jump out, he threw me back against the seat. He tried to grab the handle to shut the swinging door, but we hit a bump just at the moment he leaned out. It sent him off balance, and as he tipped forward, I sort of helped him along with my foot, sending him sprawling onto the pavement."

Eliza snorted and covered her mouth, laughter dancing in her eyes.

"With the city being so loud," Diana continued, "the driver did not even notice, and the door snapped back shut as we took the next bend."

"Bravo!" Eliza gave Diana a standing ovation. Diana smiled through her tears.

"I did do that quite well, I suppose."

Sybil was surprised at such humility. It had been an amazing bit of genius on Diana's part.

"Later that night, I overheard my uncle and cousin when they returned from the ball. Kitty was in the biggest fit of temper I have ever experienced. Her screams could be heard through the entire house. I can only attribute Lord Brock's lapse in judgement to the amount of liquor he'd consumed at cards."

"Or just plain idiocy," Eliza interjected. "Men are not necessarily the wisest of creatures."

Diana appeared taken aback by Eliza's assessment, but Sybil had spent enough time with her this last week to not be shocked by the statement.

"What about rumors?" Sybil asked, "Did anyone see you leave with Mr. Fairchild?"

"No. Luckily, no one of importance saw us enter my uncle's carriage together, so I was saved from social ruin, but Kitty has been furious ever since. She made it her goal to make my life more miserable than it already was. She found every excuse after that for me not to attend any more activities that season. Eventually, I was sent home early with a maid, which honestly was a complete relief to me. Anything to be free of Mr. Tom Fairchild's looming presence. Somehow, I think I became a challenge to him after our encounter in the carriage. I have been frightened of him ever since."

"How could your uncle be so negligent?" Irritation creeped up Sybil's spine, lighting a fire within.

"I believe, upon sobering, he realized his mistake. It was ultimately his decree that sent me home. I was too much competition for his daughter, and he did not want me in the way."

"Well, I, for one, am grateful for the modicum of good sense daylight brought," Eliza muttered, "for what good it did him."

After pacing the full length of the room to calm herself, Eliza finally said, "Well, ladies, I believe we have a mission on our hands." After viewing her friends' quizzical looks, she continued, "We must not let Diana be caught alone with Mr. Tom Fairchild if she fears a repeat of his advances."

"Yes!" Sybil agreed. "I propose that none of us let you go anywhere unattended."

"How shall you do that?" Diana queried.

The library door opened, causing all three ladies to jump. Three sets of wide eyes flew to the man in the doorway. Lord Penbrose entered, and they let out a collective breath of relief. He seemed surprised to see the three ladies ensconced as they were by the window. Straightening his cravat, he crossed the room to the edge of the table.

"Good afternoon."

"And to you, Lord Penbrose," Eliza responded. Nicholas stared a moment at Eliza, no doubt trying to puzzle the woman out.

Turning, he said, "Miss Diana, I could not help but notice you seemed to be in some distress this afternoon at tea."

She looked down at her hands in her lap. "I was, my lord, but I am feeling quite recovered."

"Very good. Is there anything I might do to alleviate any remaining distress you might feel?" The way he evaluated Diana with care and concern warmed Sybil's heart.

Diana glanced up at him, her gaze flitting between Eliza and Sybil. "I am unsure there is anything to be done, my lord, but I thank you for your kindness."

"Very well. Please know that I will do my utmost to help all my guests have a safe and enjoyable stay at Penbrose House. If you—any of you," he said, observing all three women, "should have any concerns with your stay, I sincerely hope you will not feel at all discomfited to come to me."

Sybil studied her companions. "Thank you, Lord Penbrose. I assure you we all feel your kindness. You have been a most attentive host."

To her surprise, his gaze locked with hers for the first time in days. The thrill of his full attention brought a small smile to her lips. She could tell by his expression he was trying to convey something he had not said. What was it? Perhaps he wished to talk with her privately.

She wanted—no, needed—to talk with him, but with the current company, she knew he would not wish to discuss any particulars. His distressed expression faded.

He inhaled deeply and broke eye contact. "Well, I shall leave you ladies for the time being, but I hope to see you all at dinner."

Sybil's followed Nicholas's movements as he walked to the door to leave, but he stopped and looked at the shelves. Stepping to the disorganized area, he began leafing through the books. Confusion passed over his face as he moved a few volumes around. Finally, he picked one up and exited the room.

Sybil turned back to the other ladies. Eliza's eyes danced with merriment. Even Diana looked a little mischievous.

"I do believe, Miss Sybil, it is your turn to be the storyteller," Eliza said, wiggling her eyebrows.

"Me?" Sybil tried to elicit a show of innocence.

"Yes, you. You minx. I know there is a story between you and Lord Penbrose, so you might as well spill it."

Sybil smiled. She did not have to tell them everything, but perhaps a little story would soothe Diana's distress.

"Very well," she relented.

# Chapter Twenty

Nicholas tried not to fidget on the pew as the vicar droned on. The church on the southern end of Kettering was one of several in the area, Northamptonshire having an abundance of the beautiful structures.

He wondered, however, if all the other parishes had a vicar as uninspiring as the one who happened to be in possession of this living. He knew the man to be a kindly old gentleman, but he did seem to ramble—a lot.

How was the vicar to inspire the congregation to live good principles if he could not even maintain the subject of religion? Already, he had rambled on about sheep husbandry for twenty minutes. Nicholas was sure he had meant to speak on the story of the Savior leaving the ninety and nine to save the one, but at the moment, the man was describing a tick he'd seen when observing the shearing of a sheep.

Nicholas's gaze flitted about the old stone building, taking in the expressions of those in attendance. Several of the ladies in his party looked sickly as the vicar droned on. Perhaps it was time to speak to the vicar about retirement.

His eyes continued to wander. It was no surprise that his uncle and cousins were not in attendance. He could not remember the last time he had seen either of them in a church. Too condemning for their taste, perhaps.

Mary sat on his right; her brown curls accented by her smart yellow dress. On his left was his cousin, Olivia. Bless her, for she had provided just the space he needed from his pursuer.

Miss Cattering sat on the other side of Olivia, scowling down at the smaller woman when she was not looking. Either she was irritated by Olivia's constant movements as she tried to stay comfortable on the hard benches, or Miss Cattering was jealous of her position.

Olivia deserved his gratitude and he planned to thank her after church for being so insistent she sit by him. He was quite sick of Miss Cattering's attentions. Somehow he needed to make it clear to the woman he was not at all interested, but he had yet to figure out a suitable method. They still had two full weeks of the house party. A confrontation would either cause things to be entirely too awkward for the rest of the party or cause a scandal worthy of any newspaper in London.

A movement out of the corner of his eye caught his attention. Aunt Evelyn sat immediately to Mr. Greenwald's right. The last two days, little whispers of a budding romance had started to circulate among the house party. Even though he had suspected as much, to hear the rumors bandied about the room had made him uneasy.

He still could not place Mr. Greenwald. The indifference with which the man had received Nicholas in London was no more. He was all warmth and ease now.

They had enjoyed several after dinner discussions, as well as a few when they'd both retired for the evening. It was in those talks that Nicholas had discovered the man was as adept at business ventures as Mr. Martin.

While not nearly as deep in the pockets, Mr. Greenwald was by no means hurting for finances. Nor did it seem he lacked connections. The man had quite the network of acquaintances. Needing neither finances nor connections, Nicholas had been forced to concede that Sybil's father was indeed sincere in his attentions to Lady Evelyn.

The thought had made him squirm. Mary cast him a look of reprimand that could have rivaled their mother's and Nicholas was hard-pressed not to laugh at its effectiveness. She would make a fine mother someday.

He continued to scan the party. Lord Brock was also not in attendance. Why had the man not escorted his daughter?

Nicholas frowned. Where was Miss Greenwald? Quickly he scanned the party again and reaffirmed she was not there. A sick feeling settled into the pit of his stomach when his mind conjured up his cousin's apparent admiration from the evening before.

Why had Sybil stayed home?

The thought of her alone in his home when Tom was about made his skin crawl. He wished he could tell the man to be gone, but his mother's rationale had been sound on the subject.

For the sake of family relations and social dignity, they needed to at least try to heal the breach between the two families. While he was the Earl of Penbrose, they were still on shaky footing in Society. Uncle Fairchild had a large network of acquaintances, and a fair amount of them still believed the title had been stolen from him.

It was his mother's belief that if Nicholas and Uncle Fairchild could amicably spend some time together, many of the rumors would be put to rest. While he thought his mother's hopes were fanciful at best, he could not go back on her invitation without making a scene.

Not that he would mind making a scene. He would be more than happy to bodily throw his cousin out the door and down the front steps. But he knew such behavior would only make things harder for himself and especially for Mary.

This past season had been difficult on her as various rumors had been bandied about London—the most prominent one being the validity of *his* inheritance. The rumors had caused the decent men of the Ton to be hesitant in paying her court.

Unfortunately, the fortune hunters and rakes had been all too willing to try their hand at landing an heiress. When word had somehow broken that Mary's dowry was not the gold mine many had thought it was, most of her admirers had left the playing field. And good riddance, too, he thought. If money was their only inducement to marry, they were not good enough for his sister.

However, Nicholas would not hurt Mary's chances at happiness. He could not help but feel some resentment with Society. Why did they let his uncle's hideous behavior slide while Mary was ostracized for something completely out of her control? Society was a fickle thing, spouting morality at every turn, while courting lasciviousness in its dark corners.

Unable to remove the gentleman as he wished, he had no other choice but to make provisions for his stay.

He had warned his staff of the potential danger Tom's presence posed for the household. Expressions of confusion from the newer staff were followed by knowing looks from his housekeeper and butler. They, it seemed, were well-aware of his cousin's character. While he could not throw his uncle and cousins out, he could reduce the chance that any of his maids were ill-used by them.

The thought that Sybil was, at this very moment, in the house quite alone with that very cousin made him sick.

Was she well? Had she fallen ill? Did she keep her door locked? Was her maid with her? The last thought sent his eyes roving about the room.

Searching the upper balcony as the final psalm was being sung, Nicholas was dismayed to find Porter sitting among the Penbrose House servants. Sybil could not be sick or Porter would not have left her side. He knew enough of their relationship to be sure of that.

When the final prayer was completed, he quickly excused himself, slipping past his cousin, Miss Cattering, and Miss Diana. Other parishioners greeted him as he passed, but he only nodded as he made his way quickly out of the church. His mother was still in the pew, looking as if she would like to lecture him for his rudeness, but he could not stop to explain. She would have to ride home in one of the other Penbrose House carriages.

He gave a quick thank you to the vicar as he passed through the door, then dashed down the steps of the church.

Several people cast him curious glances, and he slowed his pace to a brisk walk. From behind him, Nicholas thought he heard Miss Cattering calling to him. Glancing briefly over his shoulder, he saw the young woman scurrying down the steps of the church. The last thing he wanted was to get caught in another of her traps, so he pretended not to hear her. Jumping into the carriage, he slammed the door and rapped on the roof.

On the road headed to Penbrose House, he leaned back into the squabs, willing his mind to calm. What in the world could have possessed Sybil to stay back without her maid, her father, or any other protection to speak of?

She was not obligated to attend services, but he'd assumed she would. She always had when they were in London.

Perhaps she was fatigued or overwhelmed with all the people. Anything could have kept her home. He tried to come up with excuses for her absence, but all of them led him back to the same fear. She did not know the full extent of his cousins' poor character, and she was unprotected. He knew he was being unreasonable, but the fear remained.

Sybil curled up in the chair by the fire. The rain from the night before had lent a bit of a chill to the late June day, so to help combat it, the maids had lit several of the fires about the house.

While she did not usually care for rain, the overcast sky out the window was a welcome relief. Her soul felt particularly heavy today, and sunny days always seemed a burden when the melancholy hit.

Of course, Sundays had become the most difficult this past year. The thought that perhaps she should have attended church with the others flitted through her mind before she banished it. Why should she give God her time when he had taken so much from her?

Trying to find some peace from her uncomfortable thoughts, she sat in the small upstairs sitting room with her most recent acquisition from the library. It was the same room she and her father had ducked into the first night at Penbrose House, but by the light of day the room appeared completely different.

Red velvet drapes flanked both sides of two large windows that let in an abundance of light despite the overcast sky. For some reason, she had not noticed the desk the night they had entered the room, but there it sat against the left wall opposite the chairs and fireplace.

Bookshelves seemed to have been added to the room of late, for the wood was of a darker shade than most of the trim in the house. The smell of fresh-cut lumber and varnish still clung to the room, further hinting at the newness of the addition. Odd that someone should add the large masculine desk into a room that was obviously meant to be a sitting room.

Ensconced as she was now in the overstuffed leather wingback chair, she thought it the most comfortable room in the house. The pop of the crackling fire in the grate drew her attention away from the collection of abolitionist tracts she had been reading. Perhaps it was not the wisest choice for someone who felt blue-deviled, but it had kept her interest.

She had never thought much on the plight of the Africans. Truthfully, she had not known much either. But with each book she read, her curiosity grew.

Twice she had come upon Aida tidying her guest room, and just as many times, Aida had come to light her fire in the evening. While pale skin was all the rage in England, Sybil found Aida's rich brown complexion strikingly beautiful.

Sybil had learned quickly that the girl loved to talk, which was wonderful because she had been a fount of useful information. Aida had surprised her when she'd admitted she was only fourteen, her height and build being much larger than most girls her age. Apparently both her parents were quite tall.

Most surprising, however, was her description of her family. She was the daughter of former slaves, an African mother and an Irish father, the latter of which was now the stable master at Fairfield Manor.

It seemed Fairfield had employed many Africans and a handful of Irish for the past decade. Aida claimed the late Mr. Jonas Fairchild had been particularly zealous in forwarding the plight of the oppressed.

Odd that Nicholas had never mentioned as much to her. They had talked of many things in London, and she'd thought she knew him quite well.

Looking back down at the tracts, she was shocked by the gruesome accounts. How could anyone be so heartless and cruel to any human being? In each line, she imagined Aida as the victim of such abuse. It was heart rending.

Roused after a few minutes of reading by heavy footsteps, her gaze quickly flitted to the closed door.

It would seem the rest of the party were returned from church. She studied the clock on the mantel next to the white figure of a lighthouse. Were they early? Carefully closing the loosely bound book, she tried to decide whether she should quickly return to her room or wait in the parlor until the hall was clear. She was in no mood to speak with anyone.

The sound of a loud knock on a door down the hall surprised her. Who would be knocking so insistently upon a bedroom door? The hair on her arm prickled. From the direction of the sound, it was quite possibly her bedroom door. Or maybe it was Diana's.

Had Mr. Tom Fairfield come searching for Diana? He would not find her. She had gone with the rest of the party to attend services.

Mr. Fairchild perplexed her. He had been all affability and good manners last night when Lady Julia had introduced him. She could see no hint of the scoundrel of which Diana had spoken. Of course, it was possible he was quite different when not under the influence of drink; many men were. Whatever the case, she would keep her distance if only for the sake of Diana's comfort.

The loud knock came again along with a muttered curse. Whomever it was, they were awfully angry. Heavy footfalls approached the sitting room door. Her heart hammered in her chest. Pulling her feet up into the chair, she tried to make herself as small as possible. Hopefully, whomever it was would not come in and find her alone.

Just as she gathered the length of her dress around her, the door flew open, and someone entered. The distinct click of the bellpull echoed in the room. Whomever it was intended on staying if they had summoned a servant. A few moments later, she heard the butler's voice.

"Yes, Lord Penbrose?"

Nicholas? Her mind reeled at the revelation. Why in the world would Nicholas be pounding upon a guest's door? Whose door had it been?

"Wilson, please have Miss Greenwald located immediately."

"Yes, my lord," he said. His footsteps retreated down the hall and the room was left in complete silence.

It had been *her* door he had been pounding on. What reason could he have to be angry with her? She could think of nothing she had done to earn his ire. Well, at least not recently.

Her own irritation began to rise. She wanted him to leave. They could talk later, maybe when he had calmed down. Trying to keep her skirts tucked up around herself, she moved her hand the slightest bit to gather more of the slippery material.

Something slithered down the side of her hip and leg. It took her a moment to realize what the feeling was, but by time the sensation registered in her mind, it was too late. A resounding clunk filled the room as the book she had been reading fell to the floor.

# Chapter Twenty-One

Nicholas's head shot up from where he had been senselessly staring at some papers. A moment before the thud reverberated through the room, he had been trying to convince himself not to continue his rampage through the house. His taut nerves nearly snapped at the loud sound, and he was instantly ready to defend himself.

Staring at the spot where the sound had originated, a book lay on the floor before one of his favorite chairs. He recognized the green cover of the book he had been trying to locate the day before in the library. He must have brought it to his study.

Walking toward the fire to retrieve the book from the rug, Nicholas noticed a piece of lavender satin hanging over the arm of the chair. As he got closer, a head of dark hair came into view.

He would have laughed if he had not been so intensely angry and relieved all at the same time. Sybil sat curled up in the chair, trying for all the world to hide. When she realized she had been found out, her feet fell to the floor and she straightened her skirts.

He was overcome with the urge to either throttle her or kiss her. The conflicting feelings warred within him until he finally said the first thing that came to mind.

"What in the world were you thinking, Sybil? Do you know what kind of danger you put yourself in today?"

His words seemed to galvanize her and she sat up straight.

"I do not know what you mean, *your lordship*," she said with sarcastic emphasis on his title, flashes of anger brightening her eyes. "I have done nothing but spend the morning in some light reading. In no way have I done anything dangerous, as you say."

Knowing the contents of the bound volume, he almost snorted at the thought of it being light.

He knew he was being ridiculous. It was not as if she knew all of his cousin's past deeds. Indeed, he hoped she never would. Such sordid details were hardly proper for men to talk about, let alone ladies.

"You stayed behind at Penbrose House without either your maid or your father."

"I am not a child, Lord Penbrose. I can care for myself."

"I did not say you were," he said with exasperation. "However, there were men of no relation to you who remained home from services as well. What if you had been caught in a compromising position without a maid or a chaperone?"

Her belligerent expression dimmed slightly. She looked down at her gloveless hands. "I am sure there were other ladies who stayed behind as well. Not everyone feels a need toward piety."

It was true. The majority of Society did not, but the statement was rather odd coming from her, knowing she carried quite strong religious convictions. It was one of the things that had attracted him to her.

At the small shake of his head, her mouth formed a silent *oh*.

She tried another avenue of defense. "There are servants about. I am sure I could have called upon one of them if I'd found myself in need of assistance."

"Most of my servants attend church with us, Miss Greenwald. I only have a minimal staff of a footman and my cook here while I am gone." With his pronouncement, her shoulders sagged.

"Miss Greenwald, you cannot be completely ignorant of my uncle and cousin's characters. I distinctly remember telling you in London that they were not the most upright of men and cannot be trusted."

He had never given specific details, of course, but he was sure she must have heard at least a small bit of town gossip to fill in any spaces his explanation had left. Then again, Sybil had never been one for gossip. But she nodded her acknowledgement.

"Do you think they would ever darken the doors of a church?"

"I suppose not. I had not thought on the precariousness of the situation before deciding to take the morning for myself."

His own irritation slipped away in an instant, replaced instead with a fair amount of curiosity. Bending down, he retrieved the book that had fallen, then took the seat next to hers. Her eyes followed him as he sat.

"Next time, please have a care," he said gently, casting her a small smile.

She nodded, her eyes studying his face.

He was relieved they had not come to harsh words again. He did not want to repeat their Hyde Park exchange. He turned the book over in his hands. Holding it up, he raised a brow. "A bit of *light* reading?"

She laughed softly. "The better wording would have been a bit of *heavy* reading, as nothing in those tracts are light or happy."

"It would seem I have found the person who has been pilfering my private collection of abolitionist materials."

"Private?" Her eyes widened. "But it was in the house library. It was in no way hidden or out of the way. I happened upon them the third day of my stay. If you do not want your guests to read them, my lord, you should keep them in your private study."

"Well, that most definitely would not have worked, as you seem to have invaded that space as well."

Utter confusion crossed her face. "Me? I would never think of imposing upon your private space, I assure you."

Nicholas looked about the room pointedly. She followed his lead and her face flushed bright red. He could not help but smile at her embarrassment. As she took a deep breath to calm her frustration, Nicholas thought of all the times he had seen her perform that exact exercise. Even now, she was probably counting backwards from a hundred. Off-handedly, he wondered which language she had chosen this time.

In the back of his mind, it registered that, somehow, he had missed little things like this. Why, he could not say, as it was evidence of the fiery temper she kept in check. In this moment, though, he found the action endearing.

"This is not a parlor for guests?" she asked quietly.

"No, it is not."

"But its placement in the house? The lay of the room?"

"It had been a parlor before I came to live here, but I enjoyed the view from the windows so much I had it converted into my private study."

"Oh." She deflated into her chair.

Just then, Wilson entered the room. Upon seeing Miss Greenwald in the chair opposite Nicholas, the man simply nodded and exited the room again, leaving the door open as it had been when he entered.

"I am so very sorry for invading your private rooms, Lord Penbrose." She leaned forward as if to rise.

"Please." He put his hand out to stall her motions. "Do not go quite yet. I do not believe you entered with any malice."

She sat back, curiosity spreading over her face. For some reason, he was desperate to keep her here. He knew he probably should not, but with the tumult of his feelings fading, he realized how much he had feared for her safety.

Seeing her unharmed and so cozily situated in his study had done something to his senses he did not yet wish to examine. He glanced down at the book in his hands again.

"Did you like the book?" he asked.

"I must confess I have a morbid fascination with the idea that anyone could do what these papers outline. I am shocked, saddened, and disgusted with many of the accounts. How could people be so... so... cruel?"

"It *is* most shocking. It is perhaps not the most delicate of reading materials, however."

She actually snorted. "When have you known me to shy away from reading something because it was deemed inappropriate for ladies?"

"True," he said with a smile.

"I cannot help but wonder how you came to have such a collection."

"It was started by my father more than a decade ago. He collected a fair amount of reading materials on the subject during his lifetime."

How much could he tell her? Not everyone held the same views on human freedom that his father had.

"And are you following in his footsteps?" Her words were not condemning in the least. In fact, to Nicholas's surprise, she sounded impressed.

"I suppose you could say that. You know, there are not many people who would take time to read this literature, let alone sympathize with the plight of oppressed people."

"Well, as you can see, I am not like other people."

"You never were." He heard his own wistful tone and a small piece of him thawed. Sybil had *always* had a caring nature. She had been a bit of rebel in that aspect. In the cold, calculating drawing rooms of London, she had been a ray of light.

She was not a zealot; she did not flaunt her opinions to gain attention. But she did not let the dictates of Society control her, either. Instead, she chose quiet ways to stand for what she believed in and caring for those in need.

Would this become one of those convictions? Could she possibly have the compassion and drive for the cause? Most ladies of his acquaintance turned their nose up at even the mention of anything to do with slavery. They were all far too busy with their own entertainment, town gossip, and increasing their families' coffers to care for the abused and neglected people who held neither title nor money. But Sybil? She had always cared. The thought gave him a thrill he could not explain.

Looking up at the mantel, he caught sight of the lighthouse. The alabaster cylinder seemed to glow against the dim interior of the room.

*Is this a lighthouse, Father? If so, which way are the rocks? Do I need to be cautious about proceeding toward or away from Sybil?* Such an insight into her character should surely mean toward, but what if this was just another way she was trying to lure him in? A way she could obtain the coveted title.

He regarded her. She was gazing into the fire, seemingly lost in her thoughts. There was no pandering, no praising, no façade. She was just Sybil in this moment.

Her dark hair was styled in a loose chignon, a few stray hairs falling about her face. It was the first time since her arrival that her hair had not been done up in tight curls, and he found he preferred it. The more natural style was more in keeping with the person who existed within. No pomp. No frills.

She must have sensed his gaze, for she turned toward him. The pain in her eyes made him want to reach out and hold her. Was it sadness, hopelessness, remorse? He could not decipher the myriad of emotions that swam in their brilliant green depths.

What had caused her so much distress? Glancing down at her person, the lavender gown reminded him that she was still in mourning. Her thoughts must have turned to her mother. What else could cause such anguish? It had been over a year, but it seemed her grief still ran deep.

She'd loved her mother. He had yet to see a mother and daughter as devoted to one another as the Greenwald women had been. Even with their close bond, it still surprised Nicholas that Sybil remained in mourning.

From the little he knew of Mrs. Greenwald, she would not have wanted Sybil to conceal herself away from the enjoyments of Society. Her father had quite fully put off his mourning. For a woman who eschewed many of Society's dictates, it seemed odd she would hold to this one.

"At the risk of being presumptuous, might I ask why you still wear half-mourning?"

She glanced down upon herself and her apparel with some confusion. Maybe she'd forgotten her current mode of dress. It was possible she had just become accustomed to the colors, maybe even enjoyed them.

"At first, I did not want to put off my mourning because it seemed a disservice to Mama's memory. So many moved on so quickly after her passing, as if she had never been here at all. I did not want to forget, or have others forget, I suppose." She stared at the fire. "But now... now I do not put it off because I have yet to order new gowns."

The sheepish smile that lit her face was at odds with the earlier despair he had seen. Whatever had weighed her down must not have concerned her mother.

Mining his thoughts, he tried to think of what he had said moments before she had become so morose. *"You never were."* They had been speaking of how she was different from other women of her age. How could that have made her sad?

"Do you," she said tentatively, "do you fight for the cause of the Africans?"

The shift in topic back to their earlier discussion surprised him. Was she still pondering on the collection of tracts? Perhaps this had been the cause her grief all along. But the look on her face had been too personal, like she was revisiting ghosts of the past.

How to answer? He did not want to expose too much of his life. Experience had taught him to be careful as ridicule was the usual response to his position. He could not handle scorn from Sybil on this subject, so he decided the question deserved a question of its own.

"Why do you ask?"

"I have made the acquaintance of a most intriguing young maid," she said with a hint of a smile. "Let me just say she has been most enlightening."

"Aida, I presume?" He grinned.

"Yes. She did a masterful job with my hair on Porter's half-day. Since then, she has been assigned to tend to my rooms, and I must admit, I enjoy being there when she is at work. She has a way of spinning a tale that draws a person in."

"That is her dah's blarney. He can charm the gloomiest person into a good mood. Of course, her mah can tell a fine story as well. The animation in that woman's face is enough to hold anyone's attention. I suppose Aida gets it from both."

"Whatever it is, I have enjoyed her tales. She says you have many more Africans back at Fairfield. I just assumed that with so many in your employ, you must be an abolitionist."

Nicholas felt himself leaning toward Sybil. Her frank and honest curiosity was intoxicating. When he had asked her to marry him years ago, he had hoped to gradually introduce her to the convictions his father had fought so hard for, knowing it would take time. But to have her independently take a personal interest, to seemingly come to the same feelings as he held... well, it was completely exhilarating.

The excitement began to build. What a story he had to tell. One that had changed his life forever. Just as he opened his mouth, however, noise erupted in the entryway downstairs.

His excitement immediately deflated. He looked at the door, then cast a glance around his study... his very secluded study. It struck him how this tête-à-tête would appear to the other guests. He had been alone with Sybil in a nearly empty house for a full half hour. Best to wait.

"It would seem the others have arrived. Could we perhaps take up this conversation another time?" he asked hopefully.

"I would like that very much."

"Would you be amenable to riding out with me in the morning?"

"I would have to cancel my usual companion. Miss Bawden and I have been riding together most of this week."

"I should not like to displace her."

"No, I believe she will welcome the reprieve." Sybil reached up and tucked a strand of dark hair behind her ear. The movement was simple, but as Nicholas's eyes followed the action his senses snapped to attention. It took a great deal of effort to pull his gaze away from the contours of her jaw line.

"She did mention yesterday," Sybil continued, "that she is not used to riding every day. She was probably exceedingly relieved that today was Sunday, and, since Mama never countenanced excessive activity on the Sabbath, I do not ride."

"Yes, you read."

"As you have witnessed." Merriment lit her eyes.

"Tomorrow, then?" he said softly.

"Tomorrow." There was wistfulness in her voice and eyes. Nicholas wanted to continue peering into those inviting deep green pools, but the sound of footsteps on the stairs sent him scuttling out the door before anyone caught them alone together.

Tomorrow, he repeated quietly to himself. Tomorrow.

# Chapter Twenty-Two

T he next morning when Sybil awoke, Porter stood just inside her room, several large packages in her arms.

"These came this morning, miss. I believe they are the garments you had commissioned before we left Tave Hall."

Sybil remembered the riding habit her father had paid to have sent by post to Penbrose House. Originally, she had thought it a ridiculous expenditure, but to be able to wear something new on this day of new beginnings made her feel giddy, even if the drab blue she had ordered was not very interesting.

"Do you want to unwrap them, miss, or would you like me to?" Porter asked, standing at the foot of the bed.

"Oh! Please go ahead, Porter," she said, throwing back the covers.

She had yet to share more than a moment's greeting with her father, and it was beginning to wear on her. She had never gone so long avoiding anyone. *Except perhaps Nicholas*, she thought ruefully. She was no longer angry with Papa, but she just could not bring herself to have the discussion. Did he feel the same way? Was that why he had not approached her?

A gasp from Porter drew her attention. Her maid stared down at the most beautiful red riding habit Sybil had ever seen. Slipping to the floor, she walked to the edge of the bed and gently fingered the thick material.

There must be some mistake. She knew she had ordered blue.

The excitement of wearing such a beautiful garment overtook her confusion. It did not matter what the mix-up had been. The habit was here now, and she could not wait to see how she looked in it.

As soon as Porter had her arrayed in the outfit, she examined herself in the mirror. The image that stared back made her smile. It was incredible how much the red changed her complexion.

No longer did she appear pale and sallow. Her cheeks and lips now reflected the rosy hue of the ensemble.

Seated at the dressing table, she could not help smiling so big that her cheeks hurt. Her excitement must have been contagious, for Porter smiled just as broadly as she arranged Sybil's hair.

The next quarter-hour was filled with their excited chatter. Placing one last pin in Sybil's locks, Porter said, "I'll be going back into town for my half-day, miss. Is there anything I might get you?"

Sybil sat momentarily surprised. It was only Monday. Why were they discussing Porter's half-day on Wednesday?

"I would enjoy some peppermints." What would draw Porter to town a second week in a row? At home she went to town no more than once every three weeks. "I have a couple of coins in my extra coin purse. Please take the money from there."

"Yes, miss." Porter's smile was wistful, almost secretive. Sybil was instantly suspicious. But when the last curl was finished, thoughts of Porter were swept away. Yesterday's conversation with Nicholas played over in her mind. Something had changed. She could not identify when or why, but Nicholas had warmed to her. Had been attentive to her. Even invited her to ride with him.

Grabbing her gloves, hat, and riding crop, she exited her room with a bit of bounce in her step.

At the breakfast room door, she noticed Nicholas and Mr. Lenning already enjoying their meal at the far end of the table. Nicholas lifted a bite of food to his mouth just as she entered the beautifully furnished room. His eyes fell on her, and his fork paused midair.

Mr. Lenning turned to see what held his friend's attention. When he saw Sybil, he grinned. Glancing between the two of them, Mr. Lenning's grin settled into a smirk as he slowly rose to his feet.

His movements must have shaken Nicholas out of his stupor because he shot to his feet, mouth slightly agape, fork still in hand. Sybil had to bite her lip to keep from laughing.

"Good morning, Miss Greenwald," Mr. Lenning said. "You are looking resplendent this morning."

"Thank you, Mr. Lenning." Then because she could not resist basking in Nicholas's admiring gaze, she made a slow twirl. "My new habit arrived this morning. Is it not the loveliest?"

Mr. Lenning heartily agreed. Considering the man's own attention to fashion, Sybil found his words high praise indeed. However, the dark expression Nicholas cast his friend was the highest praise of all.

He was jealous! Whether it was because he now saw Mr. Lenning as competition, or simply because his friend was still looking at her appraisingly, Sybil did not know, and honestly, she did not care. It was such a heady feeling knowing she had his interest.

"You look very well, Miss Greenwald," Nicholas finally stammered out. "Might I get you a plate?"

She waved off his offer, disappointed by his lackluster praise. She placed her usual toast and bacon on her plate. Turning, she was surprised to see him pour a cup of chocolate and coffee for her. Taking the seat to his right, she began spreading strawberry preserves on her toast.

"Might we assume, Miss Greenwald, that you have completely put off your mourning?" Mr. Lenning asked.

"Yes, Mr. Lenning. I have been meaning to do so for some time now." Truthfully, the plan had only come about in the last few days, but she need not divulge all the details. "I have not, however, commissioned any new gowns to be made. This particular piece was supposed to be in a dark blue, but a mistake was made, and well, I was blessed with this magnificent creation."

"What a marvelous mistake for us all," Nicholas interjected. "When shall you be able to acquire more new dresses?" The eager way he asked the question released a swarm of butterflies in her heart.

"I hope to go into Kettering sometime this week and order a few new gowns from a dressmaker. I have heard there are two there who do exquisite work. I would at least like to commission a gown to be made for your mother's ball."

"You might ask my sister Mary which dressmaker she prefers. I know she has one in particular that has made a fair amount of her dresses." Nicholas picked up his fork. "Kettering is not that far. I am unsure of the activities my mother has planned for the day, but perhaps the others of the party might enjoy an excursion into town today as well. I myself have several matters of business I must attend to there."

The thought of applying to Mary for suggestions was laughable. Sybil did not believe Nicholas's sister would offer any such help. The young woman had made it amply clear that she wanted nothing to do with her.

That he would reorganize his day just so she might order new gowns was flattering. She saw no need to rush the change, but if he insisted—

"That would be lovely, Lord Penbrose."

"Very good," he said, setting his fork back down and removing the napkin from his lap. "I shall consult with my mother before we ride out this morning."

Sybil was going to suggest he finish his breakfast first, but he was already out the door before she could finish swallowing her own bite of food. She shared an amused smile with Mr. Lenning.

A few minutes after Nicholas's departure, she was surprised to see her father enter the breakfast parlor. He was not by nature an early riser, and even when he did, he usually ordered a tray to be brought to his rooms.

His presence in the room dampened her excitement. There was really no way of avoiding a discussion now. It would be odd if she ignored him.

Papa glanced at her when he took his seat on the other side of the table. His eyes lit up. "So it has finally come. I had wondered when your wardrobe would arrive. Is it not a fine piece? I knew that shade would be particularly fetching on you."

"It was you who had the color changed?" she asked in astonishment.

"Yes, I must admit I took some liberties with your order. Please, do not be cross with me. I just knew when I saw the red wool it would look splendid with your dark hair. I believe it even brings out the hints of red your hair naturally possesses. I could not resist changing the order. Do you like it, poppet?"

He was definitely pandering for her approval if he was bringing out her childhood pet name. Why did his use of it always cause her to soften?

She was a little affronted that he had gone against her wishes to remain in half- mourning, but in light of her recent decision, it seemed fortuitous. It was time to let go of her frustration with him. While his words still pained her and his lie still stung, he had not been wrong.

Mr. Lenning took in the two of them, then excused himself. Sybil watched him go, grateful for his intuitive nature.

"It is lovely, Papa," she said softly. "Thank you."

His light green eyes warmed. "And the other dresses? Do you like them, as well?"

"Other dresses? I had only ordered this one."

"Yes, well, Mrs. Piper already had your measurements, so I requested she make a couple more in case you changed your mind about half-mourning."

Sybil eyed her father, trying to decide whether to laugh or cry at his perceptiveness. How did he do it? She had not expected to step out of her mourning attire one week ago, and yet it seemed three weeks ago he had known she would.

"This was the only one I saw this morning. However, I did notice Porter carrying several other packages. I was so distracted by this one that I did not think to ask what was in the others."

"Let me know what you think when you have seen them all. It is not enough, mind you, to replace all your wardrobe, but it is a start."

"Actually, just this morning I have made plans to go into Kettering for the express purpose of having several pieces made up," Sybil said. The surprise that spread across his face at her pronouncement made her smile.

"Well, then I believe my orders came just in time."

"Yes, Papa." She dabbed her mouth and rose. "I am for the fields this morning."

"Excellent. Do have a good ride, my dear."

Sybil stepped around the table to his side and gave him a quick kiss on his weathered cheek.

"Thank you again, Papa," she whispered. "I really do love the riding habit."

He reached up and patted the hand she had placed on his shoulder. Sybil saw the barest sheen of moisture in his eyes. "You are most welcome, my girl."

Nicholas was glad his mother had agreed to a change of plans for the day. He did not particularly like parlor games, and the game of charades planned for the afternoon's activities was by far his least favorite. It was a relief to be able to put off the activity for at least one more day.

After collecting his horse, he and Sybil rode for the back pasture, her groom riding a respectable distance behind.

Sybil's mount was up to her usual antics, prancing sideways in her excitement. It appeared they would have no semblance of a conversation until the energetic animal had expended her pent-up energy.

"How about a race?" Nicholas suggested.

"And what shall be the prize?" Sybil asked, a smug smile on her lips. Nicholas knew she would win, so he decided to name a prize that did not cost him too much.

"Winner gets to ask the first question, for I know we both have many."

"Yes, but is the loser bound to answer said question?"

Was he ready to answer any question she could pose? Perhaps not, but what good was a question if the loser did not answer? Finally, he nodded. She grinned in triumph.

And, of course, she did win, by quite a distance. Rogue had given it his best, but the lighter mare had outstripped him before they even reached the trees. He heard Sybil's laugh as she doubled back and passed him. When he and Rogue finally passed the agreed-upon finish, she had already lapped Tempest in a circle twice.

Taking up his position next to her, he walked his mount along the path that wound by several of the estate's fields. Poor Rogue was quite winded, while Tempest looked as though she could run again. But by the time Rogue's breaths slowed, Sybil's mount had finally dropped into a sedate walk.

He turned in his saddle, expectantly waiting for the question she would ask as her prize. She glanced briefly over her shoulder at the groom, who followed at a far distance behind them.

Bless him, Nicholas thought. He was nervous enough to share his past with Sybil, let alone have a servant as an audience. Turning back in her saddle, Sybil cleared her throat, but did not say anything.

Nicholas finally broke the silence. "I believe you are most firmly the winner. What is your question?"

"I have been asking myself that same thing for the last several minutes. I have so many that I do not believe one question will be quite sufficient."

"Well then, perhaps we can come to an agreement. You shall ask the first question, and for any additional questions, I shall be permitted to ask one of my own."

She smiled ruefully. "Shall I be required to answer all of your questions?"

"You seem quite concerned with whether answers are to be given. Whatever are you hiding, Miss Greenwald?"

"Far too much," she laughed. "But no more than the next person."

"You shall have nothing to fear from me. I will keep your confidences if you will keep mine." He locked eyes with her. The look that passed between them warmed him to his toes. It was equal parts camaraderie and part something else. Did she still hold some affection for him after all that had transpired?

He knew her feelings were most likely just those of the friendship they had shared in London, but his traitorous heart was determined to hope for more. Of course, that had been the problem in the beginning—he had wanted more than she was willing to give. Two years ago, he had been sure that she felt as he did. Her looks, the occasional tender touches, the way she had gravitated toward him in a room full of people.

"Was Aida's father really a slave?"

The question intruded upon his thoughts. Of all the things she could have asked, this was not the one he had expected.

"Yes, he was. My father purchased his freedom over a decade ago on our trip to the Caribbean."

"You have been to the Caribbean?" She appeared both surprised and excited.

"I have, and while it is a beautiful place, it is not as exciting as you might assume. It is hot and muggy, and the insects there are insufferable."

"You do not sound like you enjoyed it in the least. How old were you?"

"I began the voyage at twelve, and please, do not get me wrong. There were many things that I enjoyed about the trip. It is just that through the years, so many people have been excessively excited to hear of my adventure, and I believe the actual tale disappoints them."

"You are asking me to temper my expectations, then?"

"Precisely."

"Noted. How did a boy of twelve come to embark on a trip to the Caribbean?"

"That is a tightly held secret." He cast her a flirtatious look.

"Oh, really? Am I going to be required to enter into some sort of pact in order to hear it?"

"Yes. You will have to promise me a dance at my mother's ball."

Sybil's eyes widened a bit before a becoming smile spread slowly over her face.

"Agreed."

Exultation rose from within him. "Are you sure you are up for the tale? We could always save this for another day."

"You are stalling." She laughed lightly. "Now, out with it."

# Chapter Twenty-Three

He paused, searching his mind for the best place to begin.

"My father's first encounter with a woman of African heritage was actually in London. Sometime in 1801 or 1802," he began, but when Sybil gave him a confused look, he said, "Just wait. It will make sense in a moment."

"I do hope so," she teased.

Nicholas smiled at her easy manner, wishing it could always be this way between them.

"He was invited to a small gathering hosted by a friend. When my father arrived, he met a man by the name of Davinier, who was a Frenchman by birth. He had a most unusual wife. Mrs. Davinier was born the daughter of a gentleman, but her mother had been enslaved. Freed by her father, she had eventually come to England to live with her great uncle, the first Earl of Mansfield. She intrigued my father with her refined manners and pleasing conversation.

"Over the course of that season, he met several more times with the Daviniers, striking up a sort of friendship with the couple. The stories Mrs. Davinier told of her early days in the Caribbean caused my father great distress."

"I can imagine they did. The stories I read from your library were horrifying," she said.

"They are. And they were of special interest to my father because of the property he had inherited there from my great uncle, the profits of which had allowed him to buy Fairfield Manor. Having never gone to inspect the plantation himself, he was unaware if his steward and foremen exacted the same punishments Mrs. Davinier described.

"My father returned home that summer determined to visit his holdings in the Caribbean. He wanted to make sure his own plantation was not being run in the same manner as the others."

"And so he set sail for the Caribbean?"

"Yes. I begged to go with him, and he, believing the experience would be good for me, agreed to remove me from Eton for that year. We waited until fall to travel, as the weather in the tropics is sweltering during the summer months. I celebrated my thirteenth birthday aboard the ship bound for the islands and we made port on the first of January.

"The sights and sounds thrilled my young adventurous heart. After months on the boring ocean, we were finally going to get to explore. However, the experience soon left something to be desired. While the white sandy beaches and clear blue water were inspiring, the excessive sun and heat soon caused my skin to turn red and blister. I spent a great deal of my time searching out shade and applying ointments to help cool my skin."

"You poor thing."

"Do not feel too bad for me," he protested. "My lot was nothing compared to that of the men, women and children I saw laboring in the fields."

"Was it as bad as your father had feared?"

"Worse than anything I had ever seen up to that point in my young life. It was so bad my father eventually asked that I remain in the house until his business was completed. He learned that while his plantation was one of the most lucrative on the island, the methods used to keep the African and occasional Irish slaves working were indeed hideous."

"I have to admit I did not know Irish people were also sold as slaves." She looked back to her groom in the distance. Nicholas had detected the man's Irish brogue and understood her concern.

"I believe most are called indentured servants, but when a person is indentured for more years than they are expected to live, it is nothing short of slavery. Any children born during that time were also indentured. They worked their whole lives for a debt they could never pay because the owners placed the cost of freedom too high. Aida's father was one of those, and she would have fallen to the same state if my father had not purchased the family's freedom. In fact, her plight would have been worse, as children of African women are enslaved themselves unless someone buys their freedom."

"How awful!"

"Indeed. My father released several foremen in hopes of reversing some of the methods used by his steward, but to no avail. He started to incur the wrath of other owners and managers on the island and eventually grew sick of the constant violence he saw around him."

"What did he do?" She leaned forward in the saddle, her attention rapt.

"Nothing at first. But then he saw the foreman of another plantation whip a young boy nearly to death."

"Why would someone whip a child?" she exclaimed, revulsion obvious in the lines about her eyes and mouth.

"Because he fell and broke an earthen jar filled with rum. It is not sensible at all, but nothing really is on the island. Unfortunately, things only got worse after that, so my father deemed it necessary to make a hasty removal.

"Rumors of his behavior spread like wildfire, causing a great deal of indignation to be directed toward us. So my father located a buyer for the land and loaded all his goods on a boat headed for England. But he refused to sell the slaves with the property, claiming they were needed for another of his ventures."

"And that is how Aida's family came to England?"

"Nearly. Aida's mother had been sold to another estate. So my father bartered with the estate's steward in an effort to keep the family together. It took a great deal of money and rum, but he was finally able to make the purchase. Upon her release, we boarded the ship hired for the express purpose of transporting my father's *property*," he spat out. Using that word in reference to people always felt like a curse word to him. It was a nasty idea that people could claim other people as property.

"When we returned to England, my father immediately set the entire group free. He offered jobs to any who would care to work for him, but several chose to make their own way elsewhere. Some even returned to Africa to see if they could find any of the families from whom they had been stolen.

"Aba, Aida's nana, and her husband Bakari chose to take up employment at Fairfield. Their daughter Becka is Aida's mother."

Sybil sat for some time staring at him. He was unsure when both horses had stopped, but they now stood in the shade of an elm tree. Tempest flicked her tail, and Rogue bobbed his head in rest.

"I apologize. I believe my story was more than you were prepared for."

"No," she said adamantly. "I am just trying to... to let it all soak in. Thank you for entrusting me with such a tale."

Silence stretched between them for a few moments before she said softly, "I believe I would have enjoyed meeting your father. He sounds like an extraordinary gentleman."

"He was," Nicholas said quietly.

"It is no wonder you have such a collection of literature in your library. I must now wonder why you do not have more, for you seem quite passionate about your experience."

"I do not have more because there is no more to be had. It is not a popular position to take. And up until six months ago, I had little else I could do other than read about it.

"My father used to take trips in an effort to assist in the cause in whatever way he could. He joined forces with a man named William Wilberforce and several others shortly after his first return and provided as much financial backing as was fiscally responsible. While my father never stood forth publicly, it was their combined efforts in Parliament that ended England's participation in the Transatlantic slave trade. So as you can see, I have done very little compared to my father and others."

"That is quite the accomplishment, but I do not believe your efforts have been as little as you portray them to be."

"I disagree. Many have given so much more. I have done nothing compared to men like Toussaint Louverture who helped free the Haitians, or Olaudah Equiano whose narrative was the real catalyst in bringing about change in the slave trade. You may have seen his book among my collection in the library."

"I did. And I know there are many who have fought valiantly for their freedom. I only mean to say that while your part may be small, you have put your convictions into action. Aida says good employment and fair wages are hard to come by, and yet you provide both for many freed people at Penbrose House and Fairfield Manor. Doesn't that prove you have done far more than just read?"

"Yes, but there is far more to be done."

"And that, I believe you will help do. You hold a seat in the House of Lords now, do you not?'

He smiled to himself. That had been the sweetest thing about inheriting all of this. He would now be able to enact change where he could not have before. While he had no desire for money, property, and prestige, the ability to finally have a say in the laws was too enticing to give up. It was the *entire* reason he had fought so hard to keep the Penbrose title. He needed that seat in the House of Lords. It was his only key to fulfilling the dream his father had instilled in him after they had grown to love the people aboard the ship bound for the shores of England.

That Sybil understood and believed he could enact change made him giddy with delight. She had not scoffed at him for his ideals, nor had she ridiculed him for being a dreamer. She had simply offered her support.

"Thank you, Miss Greenwald."

"For what?" Confusion clouded her face.

"For believing in me."

Her expression cleared and her lips lifted in acknowledgement. "You are welcome."

After a short silence, Nicholas motioned his head in the direction of the house, and they urged their horses into motion again. Sybil was still digesting his words when his voice interrupted her thoughts.

"Now, I believe I counted eleven extra questions. Actually, twelve if we count, 'For what?' So, it is my turn."

"What?" she protested. "You play unfair, my lord. Those questions were just for clarification."

"A question is a question, Miss Greenwald, and you did agree to the terms."

She laughed. "I absolutely refuse to count 'For what?' as a full question. Perhaps next time, we shall need to employ a solicitor to ensure all terms are in writing and that both parties understand the definition of a question."

"Perhaps, but it is too late now. However, I will be generous and allow your last question without asking for payment. Now, for my first question," he said, tapping his chin. "If you were a horse, what color would you wish to be?"

The absurdity of the question made her sputter. "A horse? Why ever would I want to be horse?"

"I did not say you wanted to be. I said if you were."

"And of any question you could ask, you chose that one?"

"Yes, and now I anxiously await your answer," he said, a confident, almost smug look upon his face.

She shook her head at the ridiculousness of it but responded. "I can honestly say I have never thought of what color I would wish to be. However, I do enjoy Tempest's coloring."

"What is it you like about her coloring?"

"Is that your second question?"

"Yes and no. It is the second question of the fourteen questions I may now ask you."

"Fourteen!"

"Actually thirteen, since we both asked a question."

"But it was twelve earlier. Or have you already forgotten?"

"I had not forgotten, but then you asked three more questions about my first question. Then I asked about coloring, and you distinctly asked if that was my second question. Which, in and of itself, is a question. Bringing the grand total to thirteen questions."

She stared forward, revisiting their conversation in her mind. Drat, the man was right. She had asked more questions. "You, sir, are sneaky and underhanded."

"I disagree. I am, in fact, wily."

"They are the same."

"No, they are quite different. One is using one's intelligence to bring a certain outcome to pass, while the other..." He paused for a moment, and Sybil used the opportunity to cut him off.

"And the other is using one's intelligence to bring a certain outcome to pass. Both usually through deceitful ways," she finished with an arched eyebrow.

He chuckled. "Nevertheless, you did ask four more questions, and a question is a question."

Sybil smiled at his restatement of his earlier excuse. She had to give him credit; he was indeed wily. Thinking about the innocuous nature of his first two questions, she did not mind answering several more.

"Fine." She relented with her own theatrical look of defeat. "I enjoy the way Tempest's color goes from ebony upon her back, mane, and tail and slowly transforms into the fiery red bay upon her sides and belly to change yet again to black upon her legs. However, I also enjoy black horses. The gloss and shine of their coats in the sunshine is most pleasing."

Nicholas reached forward, giving the neck of his own mount a pat. "Did you hear that, Rogue? She likes you."

Sybil shook her head. Rogue was not the only one.

"Have you had a chance to visit Mirage?" Nicholas asked.

"I have. On my third morning here, a groom led Miss Diana and me on a tour of the stables, along with Mr. Lenning and Mr. Martin. He is a magnificent animal. I have not seen another like him."

"I agree. I must admit he scared me as a child. To a small boy, Mirage is a gigantic animal. He is still large to me, but time has taught me that he is as gentle as a lamb. He is so calm I have even seen the barn cats jump upon his back and curl up for a nap when the weather turns cold."

"Tempest would never stand for such a thing. The poor cat would find itself thrown into the next stall before it had completely landed upon her back."

"Yes, I believe most horses would not be so patient. Do you like cats, Miss Greenwald?" She raised her eyebrows at him, and he chuckled. "Yes, I realize that is my fourth question."

"Good, because I will not fall prey to your *wily* ways anymore. I do like cats. I find their taciturn dispositions suit me much better than the adoring affections of dogs. I do not like to always be followed about and slobbered on. However, Mama would never countenance any animals inside, so I have never had a particular pet of my own. Our stable manager has always kept several cats to control mice, though. As a child, I would spend time everyday playing with the new litters of kittens. I think kittens the sweetest of babies, next to humans and horses, that is."

"That is good to know. Did you know my youngest sister has a calico named Demi who had a litter of kittens about five weeks ago?"

"I did not."

"They are in the stable. You are welcome to hold them if you would like. They are all extremely friendly, at least, they should be with all the time my sister spends mauling the poor animals."

"I remember my own papa saying the same of my love. It is hard, however, as an eight-year-old to conceptualize that the little animals might not like so much attention. I was convinced they would be lonely if I left."

Nicholas smiled at this, but his expression was distracted. Perhaps she had bored him with her talk of kittens. It was his question, though.

Shifting in his saddle, he faced her. "Are you ready for my next question?"

His complete change from lighthearted to serious was ominous. Sybil clenched the reigns. What did he intend on asking?

"As long as you realize you just asked a question," she dodged.

"You are correct." Then after a pause, he said, "Why did you choose to remain home from services on Sunday? If I recall, your mother was quite devout. I assumed you were the same."

"She was." A pang shot through her heart. "As for your question. I have found that I enjoy a quiet morning reading. It is the only time I get completely to myself at home when my father is out." It was a half-truth at best. She did love to read, but she did not like being alone, at least not as much as she had been this last year. Sybil did not care to admit the real reason for not attending services. Would he accept her answer and move on to the last question?

"Reading is a fine activity," he said thoughtfully. "It enriches the mind. I have noticed you spend a good deal of time in my library. I also remember you read a great deal in London. Many of those times I noticed you were, indeed, alone. With you and your father being the only two people in residence at Tave Hall, I cannot think you were always in one another's company. Surely you would have had many other opportunities for solitude."

She had not fooled him, it would seem. His sideways glance and raised eyebrow let her know he had seen right through her. Why could he not just be a gentleman and take her statement at face value? She fidgeted, causing Tempest to sidestep and toss her head.

"I suppose," she slowly ground out, irritation growing from within, "it is because I am not on speaking terms with God right now."

"And why is that?"

"Because he took my mother," she said coldly, fire filling her chest.

"I know it is not fashionable to bring talk of God and religion into a conversation, but as you said yesterday, you are not like other people."

She rolled her lips inward, not wanting to have this conversation.

"I have lost a parent, too, Sybil," he said quietly. "I am not at all naive to the feelings such a loss brings to one's heart. I, too, was angry at God."

She could feel his eyes on her even if she was not looking at him. She had to batten down her irritation at being caught in such an uncomfortable conversation.

"It will not bring your mother back, you know. Nor will it change who God is. Holding on to the anger will only make you bitter and disenchanted with life. I should know. I cursed God the day my father was taken so suddenly. He did not deserve to die when he did. He was doing so much good in this world. Why would God take him when other much more corrupt people continued to impose their cruelty upon humanity? Why did a man like my uncle, who was unfaithful to his wife, hated his brother for his position on slavery and the good he did, and who held contempt for the world in general unless it afforded him a fortune, continue to live and breathe when my father, who would have given anything for another, lay cold in the ground?

"I battled with that question for months. One day, I realized my anger would never change who God was but instead was eating me alive. I was easily upset, I did not want to spend time with my family, and friends were a burden. I was no longer living, just existing. I had no gratitude, no hope, no joy, and I had become almost as hard as my uncle. I found myself wishing for his demise if only to free myself of his distasteful presence in my life."

The anger that had welled up in Sybil suddenly burst like a bubble, leaving her feeling raw. She was astonished at how much Nicholas's feelings mirrored her own.

"I was on my way to London the day of my revelation," he continued. "Along the journey, I realized I had a choice. I could let go of my anger, which would allow me to grasp on to love and forgiveness, or I could hold on to my hate and allow it to destroy me. In essence, I could let my father's death make me bitter, or I could let it make me better."

Pulling Tempest to a stop, she stared at him, his words reverberating in her head. She had been angry so long that she had not thought of how it affected those around her. She had spent an entire year cursing God, and it had made her miserable. She could see now that some of her father's distance had not been all his doing. Her anger had spilled over into every aspect of her life. She had pushed him away just like she had pushed friends and neighbors away. The thought made her ache inside.

"I am unsure I can get better," she finally murmured. "How does one surmount such a large obstacle?"

"One step at a time," he replied. "Make the conscious choice every morning that you will no longer hold onto your anger. One day, you will wake up and find it no longer exists."

She let out an unbecoming snort. "Anger is part of who I am."

"Yes, but bitterness is not, and that is what you will find under the anger."

She wanted to protest, but his words had dumbfounded her. Silence settled between them as she stared out at the green pasture.

He was right. It *was* bitterness. The aching realization burned deep in her heart. She turned her head away to hide the tears that gathered in her eyes. All this time, she had stewed in her anger, letting bitterness canker her soul. Could a conscious choice really change that?

Pondering, she realized she had made a conscious choice to be kind to Porter, and that had completely changed their relationship. She had made a conscious choice to enjoy this house party.

Could she choose to let go of her bitterness against God? Against her mother? Against her father?

Seeing the stables looming ever closer, she was both relieved and saddened her time alone with Nicholas was coming to a close. She covertly dabbed at her eyes with the back of her glove. She did not want their ride to end so somber.

"You have given me a lot to think about, but it looks like we are nearing the end of the path. I guess you will have to forgo asking any more questions." She cast him a sidelong smirk.

"Do not be too sure. We did not put an end date for my questions. Ride with me tomorrow?"

"That is another question."

"I will risk it. Will you come?"

She raised her eyebrows and he laughed. If she kept going, she might be able to use up all his questions on this one request, but deep down she knew she did not want to.

"I will."

# Chapter Twenty-Four

Sybil was no longer sure inviting the whole party on an excursion into town had been the best idea. The long line of carriages stood ready to carry the party a scant few miles into town. Ladies and gentlemen, drivers, footmen, and maids were scattered among them, creating such a cacophony, she could barely hear herself think. The commotion gave her a headache.

She was grateful for Porter's calming presence next to her. Intending to visit the dressmaker's, Sybil had asked Porter to come along, trusting the maid's sense of fashion more than she trusted her own.

Most of the older ladies and gentlemen, including Sybil's father, had decided to forgo the trip, leaving the younger set to make up the majority of the party. However, Lady Caroline and Lady Hamdon had offered to act as chaperones for the rest of the ladies, much to the disapproval of the latter lady's husband.

Lord Hamdon tried in vain to persuade his very expectant wife to remain at the house, but she would not be dissuaded. Sybil had found the disagreement between the couple the most entertaining part of the morning. Lady Hamdon was a master with words and somehow seemed to lead her husband into her way of thinking without him even knowing he was agreeing to her wishes. Sybil had not been able to contain her grin at the little look of triumph Lady Hamdon shot Lady Caroline when Lord Hamdon had capitulated. In the end, both Lord and Lady Hamdon had joined the party headed into town.

Sybil watched as Nicholas walked between groups of ladies and gentlemen, assigning them to various carriages. When there was only Miss Cattering, Diana, Sybil, and Porter remaining, Nicholas approached the waiting ladies and pointed to the last two carriages in the line.

"Miss Cattering, you will be riding in the second to last carriage with Lady Caroline, Lord Ansley, and Mr. Tom Fairchild."

Sybil did not miss the disappointment that passed over Miss Cattering's face as she looked at the last carriage. Apparently, Nicholas had placed his carriage at the end of the line so he might get everyone situated before leaving himself.

Miss Cattering compressed her lips, inhaling deeply through her nose. Sybil was sure she was about to protest, but the arrival of Lord Ansley stopped the words before they could escape. At his proffered arm, Miss Cattering seemed slightly pacified and walked with the gentleman to the waiting carriage.

That Nicholas had chosen to have Sybil placed in his own carriage showed how much the situation between them had changed these last few days. A thrill shot through Sybil at the thought, one that even Miss Cattering's scathing glare could not chase away.

Once inside, Sybil realized the awkwardness of the situation. With Porter's addition, there would be three ladies and only Nicholas. One of them would be required to ride on the backward-facing seat.

As the maid, it fell to Porter to be that person. And Nicholas, being a gentleman, would take up the space next to Porter. After a moment's indecision, Sybil finally sat beside Diana on the forward-facing seat. Propriety really was a nuisance sometimes.

Nicholas stepped into the carriage and immediately took the seat next to Porter. Signaling the driver with a rap of his knuckles, the carriage immediately sprang into motion.

He turned to Porter and smiled. "Well, Miss Porter, it has been an age since I have been able to be in company with you. How have you been? I do hope your health has been good."

A momentary look of surprise crossed her face, then Porter straightened under his gaze. Sybil could see the formal training the young woman had received coming into play.

"I have been quite well, I thank you, Lord Penbrose. My health has been as good as ever, and I have not suffered another relapse of the illness that kept me abed so long in London."

"Good, good. I am glad to hear it, for I know how much Miss Greenwald depends upon your service."

Porter agreed, and the conversation turned to a discussion of England's favorite topic— the weather.

When their carriage stopped in Kettering, Sybil found they were parked in front of several shops. On one side of the street stood a dry goods store, a printer, a grocer, and down the way, a dressmaker's shop.

Stepping out of the carriage, she could see on the other side was a haberdashery and a mercantile. The candy jars in the window of the mercantile caught her attention, and she placed another item on her mental list of things to purchase.

Several other members of their party were already making their way among the shops. The Williams sisters were standing in front of a large window display talking animatedly as Mr. Tom Fairchild listened. His eyes strayed in their direction. Sybil felt a hand at her elbow and looked down to see Diana standing very close, her eyes cast down. Sybil knew she had seen Mr. Fairchild's gaze. How was she to extricate herself for her errand? Perhaps she should just take Diana with her.

Nicholas must have understood her hesitation. Offering his arm to Diana, he said, "Miss Diana, shall we join Miss Bawden and Mr. Lenning? I believe they are perusing some fine hats and ribbons across the street."

Diana's shoulders relaxed. A shy smile crept over her face as she took Nicholas's arm.

"At what time should we expect to meet up with you, Miss Greenwald?" he inquired.

"I shall only need an hour, I believe. We can meet at the mercantile if that is agreeable."

Nicholas nodded, touched the brim of his hat, and bid her farewell.

The woman who greeted Sybil when she entered the tidy dressmaker's shop was kind, helpful, and efficient. After taking Sybil's measurements, asking about fabrics, and discussing current fashions, they set about making plans for several day dresses and a few evening gowns.

They were nearly finished when the woman brought out the most beautiful peach concoction Sybil had ever seen. Another lady had ordered the dress, but when the gown was finished, she'd decided the color did not suit her complexion. Since Sybil was of a size with the other woman, the dressmaker said it would be no trouble to quickly take in the waist a touch if Sybil was interested in the dress.

"I'll take it," Sybil said, rather excited at the prospect of wearing such a beautiful creation.

"Very good, miss. It won't take me much time to alter it. Would you like me to have the gown delivered to Penbrose House tomorrow?"

"Yes, that would be lovely," Sybil agreed.

With the addition of the peach dress to the cream and blue day dresses her father had gifted her, Sybil would have at least one piece per day for the rest of the week that did not reflect grief.

The dressmaker agreed to have two of her other dresses finished by Friday. The rest, however, would take another week, but the dressmaker assured Sybil that her ball gown would be ready in plenty of time for the Penbrose ball.

As they exited the shop, Sybil noticed Porter's eyes flit up the street to the mercantile. They still had some time, but she was too excited to examine the candies to wait any longer.

It was quite childish, but she still loved the sugary confections. As a little girl, Papa had always let her pick out a candy on their trips into town. Mama always insisted the treats would upset her tummy, but Papa had equally insisted that every child deserved to have something sweet in their life every now and then.

As they entered the mercantile, Sybil noticed Porter's face appeared a bit sun kissed. Odd, she thought. They had not walked that far, but the day was warm, and perhaps the heat was affecting Porter far more than herself.

Approaching the counter, Sybil began perusing the various flavors of sweets.

"Miss Porter, I had not thought to see you again until Wednesday," a male voice said from somewhere down the counter.

Sybil's eyes shot up, assessing first the clerk and then her maid. The flush she had seen on Porter's face was now rosy-red, and a shy smile accompanied it. Sybil could not help a slight smile of her own. Porter's flushed face, it would appear, had not been caused by the heat but by the prospect of seeing a certain clerk.

"I had not thought to be in town, Mr. Brown," Porter answered, "but my duties required I visit today." Then ducking her head, she said, "This is my mistress, Miss Greenwald."

"A pleasure to meet you, Miss Greenwald. What can I do for you this fine day?" he said. His eyes strayed back to Porter for a moment before he looked at Sybil for instructions.

"Some clove candies, if you please."

The man nodded and retrieved a square of paper in which to place the candy. As he scooped out some of the pieces from the jar and placed it on the brown paper, Sybil raised an eyebrow at Porter, sending a taunting smile. Porter responded with a deep blush. The sight almost made her laugh, but she did not want to embarrass Porter more than she already had. Then she had an idea.

"Porter, please stay here with my purchase. I see some lovely blue ribbon I want to examine."

Porter glanced at her in confusion but nodded in agreement.

Sybil was far too curious to actually wander far. Walking to a table several feet away, she admired the ribbon while keeping one ear toward the counter. Sure enough, the moment she left, Mr. Brown began speaking to Porter in low tones.

Sybil peeked in their direction. Both Porter and Mr. Brown were leaning toward each other as they spoke, oblivious to the world about them. The sight both warmed her and caused a pang of sadness. Porter had lost so much. If not for the fire, she might be here in the shop of her own choice, perhaps even be mistress of a shop herself.

Walking to another spot in the store, Sybil heard the front door open and saw Nicholas step in by himself. Briefly, she wondered where Diana might be, but then Porter let out a quiet giggle, and her thoughts were pulled back to what was happening at the counter.

"I promise, I will be in town again on Wednesday," Porter was saying.

"Then I will get Henry to watch the shop that morning. I am sure you would like—"

"Are you in need of a new razor or some shaving soap?" Nicholas asked from behind her. Sybil jumped. A look of devilment was in his eyes, and she knew he suspected she was up to something.

"Hush." She glanced about herself. It would seem she had wandered into the men's supplies. Smiling at her own distracted state, she whispered, "I am trying to eavesdrop from a respectable distance."

Nicholas grinned, casting a look over his shoulder at the two people near the counter. They were so engrossed in conversation that Sybil was sure they would stay thus as long as she browsed.

"Ah, I see. You are aspiring to the position of matchmaker?"

"Position? Heavens, no! I had just thought to give them time. As you can see, my maid seems quite enamored with the fellow, and I cannot help but wish the best for her."

"And that requires your listening ear?"

"Of course, for how else am I to help her along if I do not know what is transpiring?"

"I believe, Miss Greenwald, you have given the description of a matchmaker's duties."

Sybil paused in confusion and then laughed at herself. The sound startled Mr. Brown into recollecting his job, and he moved down the counter to help another woman who had just entered the shop.

Leaning in, Nicholas said in a low voice, "Well, it appears their tête-à-tête has unfortunately come to an end."

The smell of leather and cinnamon washed over her at his closeness. She wanted to draw closer, to feast her senses on his nearness, but just as she shifted her position, Nicholas straightened and offered his arm to her.

"Shall we be on our way? That is, unless you have other purchases to make." He pointedly eyed the men's wares.

Sybil laughed softly. Taking his arm, she felt the warmth of the contact even through his sleeve and her gloves. It was comforting and familiar. She gave into the temptation and stepped closer to him as they made their way to the counter to pay for her sweets.

Exiting the store, Sybil was keenly aware of Nicholas. His closeness did strange things to her senses. Had he always made her feel this way, even in London? Perhaps, but she did not think it had been so strong.

Maybe absence really did make the heart grow fonder, as the saying went. It was no surprise to Sybil that she cared deeply for Nicholas. She had known that almost immediately after his departure two years ago. The beautiful ache in her heart now, though...

Did Nicholas feel the same pulsing awareness? It was so palpable; how could he be ignorant of its existence? It drew her to him with a power that at times almost overwhelmed her senses. For at this moment in time, she wanted nothing more than to place the arm her hand now rested upon around herself so she might fully step into his embrace.

The urgent calling of Nicholas's title shook Sybil from her delicious imaginings. A small, portly man with wispy gray hair was hurriedly making his way along the walk toward them, waving his hand in an effort to attract Nicholas's attention.

Nicholas stopped their progress to wait as the man approached. When he was but five paces from them, they were joined by Mr. Lenning, Diana, Eliza, and several of the other young ladies, who had appeared from the opposite direction.

"Is that Mr. Nile?" Mr. Lenning asked quizzically.

"It is," Nicholas confirmed, a look of consternation upon his face.

When the small man arrived, he was quite out of breath. Taking a few deep gulps of air, he said, "Lord Penbrose, I am so glad you are about town. I was just on my way to the livery with the express purpose of making a call at Penbrose House. I have some urgent business I wish to discuss with you."

Then, glancing about the gathering of ladies and gentlemen which had now increased by the addition of Mr. Martin and Lady Olivia, the man seemed to rethink his next words for he paused before asking, "Might we have a private word in my office, my lord?"

Nicholas nodded, begging they all excuse him, and promised to be home in time for dinner. Then he followed the gentleman down the street in the direction he had come.

His sudden departure left Sybil feeling adrift. One moment, she'd been imagining snuggling into his embrace, and the next he was walking away. It was ridiculous, she knew. Nicholas obviously had important business to attend to, but she could not help but wish the man of business had waited at least until their outing was finished.

From behind her, she heard Diana ask Mr. Lenning about the odd little man. Realizing she was still staring after Nicholas like a dolt, she turned to hear Mr. Lenning's reply.

"Mr. Nile is Penbrose's solicitor." Then he turned to Mr. Martin. "It would seem we are now tasked with escorting two more lovely ladies home."

"The more the merrier, I say." Mr. Martin responded with a smile.

A fleeting look passed over Lady Olivia's face that Sybil could not quite decipher, but she thought the lady appeared disappointed at Mr. Martin's trite words. Perhaps it was due to Sybil's inclusion into the party. If that were the case, the ride home would prove to be an uncomfortable one.

# Chapter Twenty-Five

Nicholas stared out the window of his study at the gardens below. The morning rain had finally stopped, and shafts of light were starting to break through the clouds, illuminating various parts of the garden. Colorful dots where different flowers bloomed covered the landscape. The sight was magnificent, but it was lost on him.

His mind churned with turmoil as he tried to make sense of all the information he had obtained the day before.

A knock on the study door caused him to turn from the window and stare in the direction of the offending sound. It was probably childish of him, but he did not wish to answer. He did not have time to talk of balls, or young women, or attend to his servants' concerns at the moment. Nicholas needed his whole brain to puzzle out a solution to his current situation.

When the knock sounded again, he finally relented. "Enter!" he growled.

When his cousin, Edward, stepped through the door, he felt a moment's regret at being so brusque.

Edward gave him a quizzical expression before saying, "I have seen that same look in the mirror a time or two, Penbrose. What has soured you today?"

"My apologies. I did not mean to be terse with you. It is just this blasted estate seems to have come with more troubles than it is worth."

"How so?"

"Yesterday, Mr. Nile waylaid me in town and asked me to meet with him at his office."

"By the by, how was town?" Edward asked, "Besides, of course, your meeting. I am sorry I could not attend. Mother was insistent we go over wedding details. With the majority of the party away to town, she felt it was the perfect opportunity to talk without distraction."

"You really did not miss much. The shops are the same as they ever have been. The company was a bit better than usual, but otherwise nothing to excite."

Edward sat back in one of the armchairs near the fire, propped his ankle on one knee and folded his arms. His expression was smug. "Might I ask which company you kept that was 'better than usual'? I am sure you do not speak of Miss Cattering."

An involuntary shiver ran over Nicholas at the thought of the woman. Being able to avoid that particular lady for the majority of the previous day had been a blessing straight from heaven. He was growing increasingly tired of her overt gestures. He had tried in vain to convey his disinterest, but she was determined.

Just this morning, he had entered the breakfast parlor to find her and the Williams sisters already seated. He'd almost turned to leave, but the ladies had spotted him and began inquiring after his health.

After sitting down at the table, however, both sisters excused themselves, their plates still full, claiming a prior obligation. The intent was so obvious that Nicholas would have laughed had he not been worried about Miss Cattering's feelings. Why, he was not sure. It was not as if she was worried about his.

With their exit, Miss Cattering had readjusted her position to sit next to him. Her closeness had made his skin crawl. He'd felt hunted. Looking for a means of escape, he had been saved from her machinations by the entrance of his cousin Tom. Moments later, John and several other ladies of the party arrived to break their fast. The relief he'd felt was almost as evident as the irritation Miss Cattering exhibited.

"Your expression just now says it all." Edward chuckled.

"What? Do you not find Miss Cattering alluring enough?" Nicholas said sarcastically. He was rewarded with a full bark of laughter.

"Alluring is not exactly the term I would use to describe that particular lady. Conniving would be more her ilk."

Nicholas smiled to himself. He had often used less flattering terms in his mind. The image of compelling green eyes and dark hair replaced that of the heftier blonde. As he had left the breakfast parlor, he had seen Sybil descending the stairs. The rain outside had cancelled their plans to ride, so instead of her usual attire, she was wearing a soft cream morning dress that accentuated her dark hair and eyes perfectly. The lack of grayscale colors on her person had been refreshing, and the few words they had exchanged at the bottom of the stairs had been the highlight of his day.

"Your smile gives you away, cousin. It would seem your heart has been again affected by a certain dark-haired, emerald-eyed beauty."

"Perhaps," Nicholas said evasively, "but there were many other ladies and gentlemen in town yesterday, and their company was as good as any other of the party. Miss Diana is a delightful young lady, and Miss Bawden surprised me by carrying on a short conversation, which I take as a win, as getting that particular miss to talk is quite the challenge."

"You are trying to deceive me, but it will not work, Nicholas. I have seen the way you look at Miss Greenwald when you think no one else is watching. Your heart is as swayed by her as it was two years ago, more so, if I am not mistaken."

"Are we to have a long gab, then, about love and courtship? I do believe you have the corner on that market. Speaking of which, how is Lady Agatha?"

"Well, if her last letter is to be believed, she is very well and shall be arriving on Saturday. I must admit, the day cannot come soon enough."

"Yes, and then we shall all be made ill from watching you make a cake of yourself over her."

Edward chuckled, uncrossing his legs and sitting forward in his seat. "Perhaps we should get back to the real problem at hand. What did Mr. Nile say that has set you into this foul mood?"

"I have not been in a foul mood. Just contemplative."

"All right, what has sent you into this *contemplative* mood that makes you hide in your study, snap at your favorite cousin," he said, puffing out his chest, "and look as if someone killed your favorite hunting dog?"

"You are right. That does sound foul, indeed. Well, as I said previously, I met with Mr. Nile, and he has news of Mr. Gates."

"The swindling steward?"

"The very one. It seems my previous steward wanted to meet with me before his transportation. He claimed he had information that, although it could not clear him, would perhaps be of use to me."

"Was he trying to broker a deal for you to keep him here in England?"

"Yes, but it was the information he had that has me reeling."

"So you met with him at the gaol?"

"I did."

"What did he have to say?" Edward asked.

"Do you remember me telling you that there were some miscalculations in the Penbrose House accounts?"

"I do. Somewhere around the sum of two thousand pounds by time you caught the man."

"Yes, well it would seem that sum was a drop in the bucket compared to how much was actually taken."

"Really!" Edward leaned in. "How much did he say was actually missing?"

"It would seem he had been slowly siphoning money from the estate for the last ten years."

"Ten years!"

"Yes, the total summing up to nearly thirty thousand pounds."

"Thirty thousand—I cannot believe it. Your grandfather surely would have caught that. He was a stickler for his books."

"Yes, but if you recall," Nicholas said, "he was nearly blind for the last decade of his life, and not very reliable the last year. In truth, it would have been very easy for someone to take his money."

"I did not think of that." Edward sat back in his seat, a look of contemplation on his face.

"Yes, well someone did, and it was not Mr. Gates."

"It was not?"

"No, he was merely the pawn in all this. I should have known, though. Mr. Gates was always such a kind and thoughtful man. At least, that is the way I remember him. It was he who really took notice of us when we came to visit. My grandfather could never be bothered with children."

"Yes, but just because he was kind to you in your youth, Nicholas, does not mean he is honest. It does not take much to fool a child—just hand them a biscuit or piece of candy and send them on their merry way."

"Very true, but he claims he has proof."

"What sort of proof?"

"He says there are papers in my grandfather's study that can prove his innocence."

Nicholas looked at Edward as he absorbed the information. Edward's wrinkled nose mirrored his own feelings. He did not like the idea of entering his grandfather's dungeon of a study either, but it would need to be done, and soon, for Mr. Gates was to be taken to Newgate at the end of next week, then transported to Australia from there. They would need to work quickly. Nicholas could not stand the idea of sending the man overseas if he had truly been blackmailed.

"Why did he not come forward with this information sooner? The man has been sitting in gaol for weeks."

"His family was being threatened."

"And that has stopped?"

"No. Mr. Gates's son-in-law has taken Mrs. Gates and their daughters to Scotland in hopes of keeping them from harm."

"I see. In other words, he has nothing left to lose and everything to gain if he can prove his part in all this."

"That seems to be the case."

"So who is our actual culprit?" Edward leaned forward, his eyes bright with anticipation.

"Take one guess."

Sybil perused the books on the shelf as Eliza recounted the story of when she'd quite literally launched a quail across Lord Sumter's dining table during a dinner party. Sybil chuckled at the imagery her friend created. Eliza, she had quickly realized, was a master storyteller.

After finding the book she was looking for, she turned to Eliza, who sat in their favorite place in front of the fire.

"Then the footman picked up the unfortunate fowl from Lady Sumter's lap and carted it off to the kitchens, probably to be thrown in the slop bucket for the pigs. Poor thing. No one shall ever know it was the first bird who managed to fly after being roasted with rosemary and thyme," Eliza finished with a flourish.

Sybil laughed at the self-pleased manner with which Eliza imparted the tale, as if the misfortune had been one of her greatest accomplishments.

She opened her mouth to ask a question, but it lodged in her throat when the library door flew open, and Miss Cattering stalked in.

Eliza sank against the high-backed chair, effectively hiding herself from Miss Cattering's view. The expression on Miss Cattering's face as she came within a few paces of Sybil alerted her that this was not to be a polite gab.

"Well, I see you are holed up in the library again, Miss Greenwald. You seem to spend an inordinate amount of time is this location, don't you think? You must either have an avid passion for reading," she said, gesturing to the library with her hand, "or clandestine designs that keep you hidden away in this place."

"Pardon?" Sybil was not quite sure what Miss Cattering was referring to. Had she learned that she and Eliza met in the library every day? In a way, she supposed that was clandestine, but there was hardly anything about the meetings that was not proper, let alone illicit.

"Everyone can see you are trying to lure the earl into your bed, Miss Greenwald, for it is the only way a person like you could possibly obtain his recognition."

Sybil's face flamed red, both from anger at the accusation and embarrassment at the vulgar speech. Such language coming from a woman of genteel breeding was beyond the pale, but before she could gather her wits to respond, Miss Cattering continued.

"It will not work, you know. Even if you do manage to bed him, he would be a fool to marry you. You have no title to recommend you, and your connections are paltry at best. Why marry an insignificant and relatively poor woman with little figure to speak of when he could have someone who brings a title, fortune, and womanly curves to the table?" She indicated her own person with a flourish of her hand.

Sybil's face heated further at having her figure disparaged. She knew her tall willowy frame was not fashionable, buxom women being the order of the day, but she was not lacking in "womanly curves."

As for fortune, it appeared Miss Cattering was as clueless as the rest of Society, thank the heavens. At least Sybil would not have fortune hunters knocking down her door. In fact, she would not be surprised if her own inheritance actually exceeded Miss Cattering's dowry tenfold.

Sybil could not refute the title, however. She was not a Lady or Right Honorable. She was simply a miss. The same as many a young woman in England.

Gathering her words, she finally said, "I wonder at your audacity in making such an accusation, Miss Cattering. It is my observation that if anyone is trying to be as crude as you outlined, it would be you. I have seen the way you stalk Lord Penbrose about the house. The man cannot get a moment's peace from your attentions."

Miss Cattering let out an offended squeak. "How dare you. I do not stalk him about the house."

"What would you call your behavior, then?"

"I will have you know we are to be married, and it is perfectly normal for an engaged couple to spend ample amounts of time together, but you are trying to step in and take him from me with your arts and allurements."

Sybil almost laughed at the woman's lie. She was not so naïve as to believe Miss Cattering's claim. She had seen Nicholas in love once and knew he would never settle for anything less.

"When, may I ask, did he make this offer of marriage you claim? I have heard of no such occasion."

"Why would you? It is not as if you are privy to all our private affairs."

"No, but my father has been associated with this family since childhood. Lady Julia would have alerted us immediately had such a *happy* event taken place." Sybil was not completely sure Lady Julia would have let them know, but she needed Miss Cattering to realize that she had just as much claim on this family as anyone else.

Miss Cattering stumbled through her words. "We have not... made it public... as of yet, but we will very soon. I strongly suggest you stop your pursuit of my betrothed."

"My pursuit? Come now, Miss Cattering. We are both grown women. Let us be honest. I am well aware that your claims lack substantiation. You wish for the earl to return your affections in hopes of one day becoming the countess of this fine estate, but it is out of both of our hands. You can no more make Lord Penbrose love you than you could turn back the moon. It is up to the man himself, and as a fair warning, he does not particularly enjoy clingy, overzealous women. If he was, in fact, interested in your company, you would not have to hunt him as you do. He would seek you out."

"How dare you call me a liar!" Miss Cattering shrieked, coming toe to toe with Sybil. Sybil's fists clenched, and the temper she had been trying desperately to contain flew into her throat at the woman's nearness. Miss Cattering's indecent and irritating accusations could not be left unrewarded, but just as Sybil opened her mouth to give Miss Cattering a tongue-lashing the woman would never forget, a hissing sound came from behind one of the tall chairs by the fire.

Miss Cattering suddenly jumped back, grabbing at her skirts and wrapping them around herself. Sybil had quite forgotten about Eliza's presence until the catlike sound filled the air.

Eyes wide with terror, Miss Cattering asked quietly, "Did you hear that?"

"Hear what?" Sybil tried desperately to sound innocent, her irritation of moments before faded to the back of her thoughts at the entertaining sight. Miss Cattering looked for all the world as if wolves were at her door ready to devour her.

"The... the cat. I heard it hiss."

"Cat?"

"Yes, cat!" she snapped. "Miserable nasty creatures with claws like razors and evil eyes. If you ask me, they are the devil's own creation." Her eyes never stopped canvassing the room. Taking a step toward one of the chairs, she bent to glance under the nearby table.

"You do not like cats, Miss Cattering?" Sybil tried to smother the laugh that so desperately wanted to break through.

She straightened. "Of course not. I cannot see how any well-bred lady could."

Sybil could not agree more; however, the cat she was thinking of was more of the human variety. The ones with fur were quite charming. She would take their sharp little claws any day over the scathing tongue and conniving ways of the *Cat* in front of her.

"I am sorry. Perhaps you'd best leave, and I will see if I can locate the creature and have one of the servants remove it. I am sure it just wandered up from the kitchens."

"They keep cats in the kitchen here?" Miss Cattering's eyes were as round as saucers. "Why would anyone do such a thing?"

"To control the mice, of course."

"Well, that shall be the first thing I change when I am mistress of this place. I cannot abide cats. Drown them all, I say."

A small hiss again sounded from behind the chair. Miss Cattering yanked up her skirts, higher than was decent, and quite literally dashed out the door. When the sound of her hurried steps finally dissipated, Eliza erupted into guffaws of laughter, bending forward, her arms wrapped around her middle.

"Oh, how I wish I could have seen her face," she said between laughs.

Sybil was not sure which was making her laugh more, Miss Cattering's entertaining display or Eliza's infectious laugh.

"Her expression *was* quite comical," Sybil supplied. "Did you see the way she gathered her skirts up so high you could almost see her knees?"

"No, I did not," Eliza gasped out between peals of laughter. When she had calmed herself enough to draw breath, she said, "I was so worried Miss Cattering would see me that I pressed myself as far back in the chair as was possible. I did not dare look for fear the ruse would be up."

"Well, it was masterfully done. I shall never forget the horror on her face at the simple thought of a cat in the room."

"I'm sorry I missed it. I wish I had known this bit of information sooner. It will come in handy."

"I see your mischievous brain working, and I am unsure if I should ask what you have in mind."

"Oh, nothing yet, but I shall, count upon it. Especially if that crude lady makes any more unfounded accusations. I have never heard such unprincipled drivel coming from a lady of quality, and I have known a fair share of ridiculous women, mind you."

"I was quite astounded myself," Sybil said, sobering. She had never had someone say something so lewd to her in all her days. It gave an insight into Miss Cattering's character that was very unflattering.

Only a woman who had contemplated such extremes herself could possibly accuse another of stooping to that level of moral degradation.

"If I was any match for her," Eliza went on, "I would have clawed her eyes out on your behalf, but she is an entire head taller and at least four stone larger than me."

"I think your method of fighting far more effective. I must admit I wanted to punch her squarely in the nose. Can you believe she claimed a connection with Lord Penbrose? How could someone lie so completely?"

"Apparently, she can quite easily. She will never get away with it, though. Anyone can see her claims are unfounded. Lord Penbrose cares for her about as much as she cares for cats."

"Indeed."

Silence filled the room for a moment before Eliza asked, "What do you plan to do?"

"Do? With what?"

"Come, Sybil, you cannot possibly let Miss Cattering have her way. Lord Penbrose will be miserable if she corners him and forces a proposal, which is, of course, her intent."

"What can I do? It is not as if I have any sway."

"Do you not? Just tell him of her lies. That should be enough to have her removed."

"Yes, but it will remove Diana as well, and I would not even think of bringing any more hardship on her."

"I see your point. Perhaps just a warning? Something that will put Lord Penbrose on his guard."

"I suppose that is possible, but I doubt it will make any difference. He's an intelligent man, and I am sure he has already figured Miss Cattering out."

"An intelligent man?" Eliza blurted out with a snort. "Never seen one, Sybil. I am pretty sure they only exist in fairy tales."

# Chapter Twenty-Six

Half an hour later when the door to the library opened again, Sybil leaned forward in her chair to see Lady Evelyn enter with her daughter. They seemed to be in some sort of tense discussion, their voices low and their demeanors serious. She heard a few words here and there as the women made their way toward where she and Eliza sat in the high-backed chairs.

Sybil caught her father's name before they rose to greet the women. The two ladies immediately stopped talking. Lady Evelyn looked chagrined, and Lady Olivia appeared downright guilty.

Whatever the topic of discussion, Sybil realized her father had been at the center of it. She had hardly seen him the last week and a half, but it appeared the Burtrum ladies had spent a good deal of time in his presence.

What was he doing that could have caused these two women to be at such odds with each other?

Sybil broke the silence. Pasting on her polite smile, she said, "Lady Evelyn, Lady Olivia, I do hope you are both well today."

"Yes, we are well," Lady Olivia answered.

After an awkward pause, she went to one of the shelves and busied herself looking through the collection. Sybil was about to suggest they move to the table by the window, since there were not three chairs by the fire, when Eliza excused herself, claiming fatigue.

Awkwardness permeated the air between Sybil and Lady Evelyn as they took up the two chairs by the fire. In an effort to break the silence between them, Sybil said the first thing that came to her mind.

"My grandmama used to tell me stories of you when I was a little girl."

Lady Evelyn's eyebrows shot up, "She did, did she?"

"Yes. She would tell me funny stories about the larks you and my father had. I had thought you were a boy," Sybil said sheepishly. "It wasn't until the journey here that my father mentioned you were the Lyn she was referring to."

Lady Evelyn ducked her head, a small smile on her face. "Yes. As a young girl I insisted on going by the name. Evelyn was far too fancy for my taste."

"I used to listen with rapt attention to Grandmama's tales of stolen biscuits, loose pigs, muddy dogs, and naughty children."

"Your grandmother could tell a story better than anyone I know," Lady Evelyn said with a wistful sigh. "I still remember how she would pitch her voice high or low depending on who she was imitating. I miss her. She was like a mother to me."

"I miss her, too. Life has not been near so bright without her."

The shared connection seemed to build a small bridge between the ladies, dissipating the awkwardness as they each shared their favorite stories. Lady Evelyn laughed often, and Sybil realized how much she enjoyed the tinkling sound of it. After a time, Lady Olivia was also drawn in by the stories.

When the clock on the mantel chimed five o'clock, Sybil was shocked to realize they had spent almost an hour together. Lady Olivia, who had entered the room so sour, was now smiling and conversing as easily with Sybil as she did with her own mother.

Sybil found she actually liked the bubbly young lady, and she hoped today's interaction would alleviate Lady Olivia's distrust. The days would be easier with one less enemy in the house.

The ladies rose, needing to dress for dinner. At the foot of the stairs, Lady Olivia pulled Sybil aside.

"Thank you," she said quietly.

"You are welcome, I am sure, but I must admit I do not understand for what I am being thanked."

"For making my mother smile and laugh. She needs all the happiness she can get in life right now, and I was worried you would make things difficult for her."

"Why would I make things difficult? Lady Evelyn seems to be a kind, amiable sort of person. I am not wholly bad, no matter what others might say."

"Please, forgive me. I did not mean to imply that you would do so out of malice. It is just I feared her relationship with your father would... well, it is just so soon after your mother's passing, and I know it was difficult for me when my father died."

Sybil was confused. Why should her father's friendship with Lady Evelyn be a problem? Now that Mama was gone, he needed friends. They both did. She had not realized how much until she had gained Eliza and Diana's friendship. They had both needed to get out, to live again.

"Losing a parent is hard," Sybil said cautiously, "but I would not deny my father his friendships for the world. He too has suffered much this last year. I am sure he draws great comfort from reminiscing and renewing his connection with your mother."

Lady Olivia studied her face. Her closeness made Sybil feel suddenly awkward. "They do have a close connection, Miss Greenwald, a *very close* connection."

It took Sybil several moments before she realized what the lady was implying. When the revelation came, she inhaled sharply. The burning sensation that filled her chest made it hard to draw another breath.

Lady Olivia took a step back, worry crossing her features. Undoubtedly, she was well aware of Sybil's fault of temper. How could she not, knowing Nicholas's past so well? Lady Olivia looked as if she were deciding whether to explain or run.

Sybil held out her hand to stay her. "I thank you for your concern. I will think upon what you have just expressed, but I must excuse myself now. I am suddenly not feeling well."

It was awful the way her voice cracked on the last word. Sympathy filled Lady Olivia's eyes, and the tears Sybil had been trying to hold at bay spilled over. It would seem this time she would jump right over anger and go directly to hurt.

She tried to step around the lady, but a small hand grasped her arm before she could leave.

"I am sorry for the pain this causes you, but please, please, do not make this harder for my mother. She has had a lifetime of hurt, and she deserves some joy."

The embarrassment from Lady Olivia seeing her so emotional finally ignited her anger, and she almost lashed out at the woman, but her father's words reverberated through her mind the moment her mouth formed the words.

She dropped her head in defeat, the pain enveloping her fully. Papa was right again; she needed to think of others. She could not stand in the way of Lady Evelyn's happiness any more than she could stand in the way of her father's. But, oh, how it hurt. Her world seemed to be tipping on edge at the very thought.

The small hand on her arm pulled her into a sitting room off the vestibule. Without realizing much of what was happening, she found herself sitting on a sofa wrapped in Lady Olivia's arms. If she had not been so devastated, she would have been surprised. But the tears that choked her just kept coming. She prayed her sobs could not be heard throughout the entire house.

How long she cried, she was unsure, but it felt as though she had lost her mother all over again. She was angry at the thought of anyone stepping into her place, and yet she was also aware that her father was lonely and needed companionship. She had heard his story of Lady Evelyn's sacrifice of love and knew she had borne years of hurt as well. Who was she to take another love away from her?

Gently pulling away from Lady Olivia's embrace, she tried in vain to retrieve the linen she carried. A square appeared before her face as Lady Olivia offered her own. Sybil mopped at her face, knowing there was probably far more damage than one handkerchief could handle.

Through a stuffy nose and choked voice, she finally said, "Thank you, Lady Olivia."

"You are quite welcome, Miss Greenwald. No one should ever be alone, even in moments of solitude."

Lady Julia's words rang back to Sybil. But the words were not Lady Julia's; they had actually been Lady Evelyn's. It would seem Lady Olivia had learned well from her mother.

"I will do my best to not be a burden on either of our parents," Sybil said, tears still choking her voice.

"As will I." Sympathy etched across Lady Olivia's brow. "Heaven knows I have experienced some of the same feelings you are feeling now. It would seem, however, that I was not as caught off guard by all this as you have been."

Silence stretched between them, filling the space of the room. It was not an awkward silence, just that of two people who needed time to absorb the moment.

Finally, Lady Olivia said, "We should probably dress for dinner."

Sybil did not see how she could possibly attend the meal in this state. "Would you mind giving my excuses? I need to retire early tonight."

"I can understand. Yes, I shall inform Aunt Julia of your absence. I hope you are able to get some rest. My mother always says things look much better after a good night's sleep."

Sybil wished she could have gotten that good night's sleep, but her dreams had been so filled with loss and heartache that she woke even more tired than before. In her mind's eye, she could still see her mother's retreating figure in her dream. The image played over and over again as she sat quietly at the dressing table allowing Porter to style her hair.

For the first time in ages, she had decided not to take her morning ride, even though the sun was shining. Tempest would not be happy with her, but Sybil could not muster the energy for the exercise. She was tired, oh so tired, both in her body and spirit.

A throat cleared behind her and she lifted her gaze. "Yes, Porter?"

"Are you all right, miss? You seem a bit downtrodden today."

Sybil wanted to lie and say she was fine, but another idea came into her mind. "Porter, have you heard any rumors below stairs about my father paying particular attention to any one lady?"

"Yes, miss," she said with a soft smile. Apparently, the thought did not cause Porter any distress. "They say he is quite smitten with Lady Evelyn. From what I have heard, the servants think her a fine lady, kind and such." Porter glanced up from her work and took in Sybil's face again. "I would not worry about his heart, miss, for I believe the lady truly cares for him as well. If her maid is to be believed, that is."

Sybil slowly blew out the breath in her lungs. It was not that she doubted her father and Lady Evelyn could make each other happy. She just did not know if she could be happy for them.

It felt too much like a betrayal to her mother this soon. Had her father completely forgotten the year he'd spent in deep mourning? And what about all the happy years when Mama had been alive? How could he move forward so quickly?

She knew she was getting ahead of herself. Her father had not even informed her of his intentions. Perhaps this was just a moment's infatuation, but deep in her heart she knew it was not. All evening she had revisited the different times she had seen the pair together since coming to Penbrose House. By the time sleep had finally overtaken her, she'd recognized what Lady Olivia had already known.

It had been a long time since her father had appeared so relaxed and happy. If she was really going to adhere to her own resolution, she must forget herself and wish only for his happiness, but where did that leave her? How was she to stand seeing Lady Evelyn take her mother's place in her home? This was far more complicated than simply making the decision to be happy for her father.

Nicholas's words from days before floated through her mind. One day at a time, he had said. Make the conscious choice one day at a time. Today she would need to make the decision to be happy for Lady Evelyn and her father, and perhaps in time, her own happiness would follow.

Porter completed her hair and retrieved Sybil's locket to accent the soft blue day dress. Draping a light shawl about her shoulders, Sybil examined herself in the mirror. She looked as tired as she felt. Hopefully, breakfast would add a bit of color back to her face.

Nicholas did not appear in the breakfast room while Sybil ate, something she was grateful for and yet regretted. She did not want him to see her appearing so poorly, but she could also use a bit of comfort right now. Halfway through her meal, Eliza appeared in the doorway dressed in her riding habit. More guilt flooded her when she realized she had not sent word to her friend that she did not intend to ride this morning.

Come to think of it, she had also agreed to ride with Nicholas since their ride yesterday had been rained out. She would need to find him and explain.

After Eliza filled her plate at the sideboard, she sat next to Sybil and appraised her. "You look terrible!"

"Good morning to you too, Eliza."

"No, really. You look as though you need a week's worth of sleep. Are you feeling well?"

"Well enough," Sybil finally mustered.

"Are you sure? You do remember we are having another ladies' meeting today to plan for the ball?"

Sybil had, in fact, not remembered. The thought of a morning with the other ladies was even more draining.

After finishing her breakfast, Eliza excused herself to go change out of her riding habit, but Sybil stopped her.

"Might I accompany you?"

Eliza raised an eyebrow, then, taking a quick look at the other occupants of the room, said, "Of course."

They made their way to the second floor in silence, Sybil wondering why she had even asked to go along with Eliza.

"Spill your budget," Eliza declared almost on the instant they entered her bedchamber. Sybil was surprised at the cant but complied most readily. At the end of a half-hour's confession and more tears, Sybil noticed Eliza's eyes studying the ceiling, the floor, and finally landing on the folds of her dress.

After the incident in the library with Diana, she should not have been surprised that Eliza would be at odds with her tears. Tears and Eliza, it seemed, did not mix well.

Eventually, Eliza finally asked, "Did you know, Sybil, that Lady Bawden is actually my stepmother?"

She had not, but she should have guessed. The woman was much fairer in coloring than Eliza, and where Eliza's eyes were hazel, Lady Bawden's eyes were a light blue.

"She married my father when I was six. I have very few memories of my own mother, but I remember being angry when Ingrid came to live with us. My brother and I did not treat her well. However, I believe Charles would not have been so troublesome, being only four, had I not been set against our new stepmother. I made her life miserable for the first year, but no matter how much I rejected her, she still remained patient and kind.

"It was not overnight, mind you, but over time, I began to realize how much I liked Ingrid, even loved her, and eventually I began to call her Mother. She has never replaced my mama, but she has formed her own place in my heart."

Sybil sat quietly thinking about her words when Eliza blurted, "I do not know if what I am saying is helping any. I know our situations are different. I am just not very good with comforting or saying the right thing."

"No, you are doing just fine, Eliza. I am honored you shared your experience. I needed to hear it. I suppose the lesson here is that one's heart can make room for others. "

Eliza began to nod, but a commotion from the next room over caused her to stop and scowl. Muffled shrieks were coming through the wall. Sybil began to fear for whoever was in such distress.

"It is only Miss Cattering," Eliza grumbled. "Our rooms share a wall, and she is always going off on the servants. I feel sorry for anyone who has to wait on that feral feline. She is sure to bite them and give them rabies."

Sybil was shocked to hear a few curse words filter through the walls. It would seem Miss Cattering's fits of temper were not limited only to her cousin and competition.

Eventually a door to the hall opened and shut, and scurrying feet headed down the hall. Peeking her head out Eliza's door, she was surprised to see Aida's retreating form.

How could anyone not be happy with Aida? She was so sweet and very precise in all her work.

Shutting the door, Eliza asked from behind her, "Who was the victim this time?"

"It was Aida."

"Aida! That girl is nothing but kindness," Eliza exclaimed. Her brow furrowed and her eyes darkened. "Whatever could Miss Cattering have to complain about her?"

# Chapter Twenty-Seven

The room was only half full when Eliza and Sybil arrived for the meeting. From the doorway, they could see Miss Cattering holding court in a corner with the Williams sisters, their mother, and several other women.

"Can you believe they sent me a darky for a maid this morning?" she was saying. "I was quite astounded, I assure you. It is bad enough that she touches our beds, let alone our hair."

Sybil was instantly angry. How dare this self-absorbed, arrogant woman speak about Aida like that. It would appear, however, her complaints had not kept Aida from working her magic, for Miss Cattering's hair was piled exquisitely upon her head.

She stalked toward Miss Cattering, ready to give her a piece of her mind, when a small meow sounded from somewhere behind her.

Miss Cattering jumped and pivoted completely around to face them, and just as she had done before, she began gathering her skirts about her person. The sight made Sybil smile through her anger. She couldn't help feeling vindicated when Miss Cattering's eyes flitted about the room in horror.

From the doorway, Lady Caroline exclaimed, "What on earth? Miss Cattering, do put your skirts down."

"But there is a cat in the room. It must have escaped from the kitchens."

"A cat?" Lady Julia asked. "There are no cats in Penbrose House."

"Not even in the kitchens?" Miss Cattering questioned, allowing her skirts to drop to the floor.

"Not usually," Lady Julia assured her. "But even if we happen to get one below stairs, they never venture into the main house."

Miss Cattering absorbed this information, then turned to glare at Sybil. Apparently, she blamed Sybil for all this, and frankly, she was not far from the truth. It was, after all, she who had claimed they kept cats in the kitchen. Sybil tried her best to look as innocent as possible as she took her seat, but she was afraid her bemused smile still showed on her face.

"Well!" Miss Cattering huffed as she took her seat, and the meeting began.

The next hour's discussion almost put Sybil to sleep. If she had only had the discussion of drapes, lace, and flowers as background noise last evening, she would have had a much better night.

When they finally adjourned for luncheon, she excused herself to her chambers. She needed rest, and no amount of food could induce her to change her plans.

The moment her head hit the pillow, Sybil slipped into a deep, dreamless sleep.

At the door of his grandfather's study, Nicholas inserted the key and turned the squeaky lock. It was much harder to turn than he remembered. The squeal it made grated on Nicholas's ears and set his nerves on end. No one within a hundred feet of the room could have missed the loud sound.

The room was dark, other than the light squeezing in from around the black drapes. Nicholas walked the length of the room and pulled the coverings open to let the light in through the too small windows. The dust that cascaded down caused him to sneeze several times.

"How long has it been since you last used this room?" Anthony asked as he closed the door behind Bradley and Edward.

"Five months, at least. Not since my argument with my uncle."

"And you have not let your servants in to clean it? I hear they are pretty good at dispelling dust," Bradley said, running his finger along the desk.

Nicholas ignored Bradley's jab. "We might as well get to work. Anthony, Bradley, you search the bookshelf for the safe. Edward and I will search the desk."

The safe ended up being the easiest place to find. Anthony and Bradley went directly to the spot behind the books that Mr. Gates had described. Unfortunately, it was locked, and the key was not in the vase where the imprisoned steward had claimed it would be. Frustrated, Nicholas and the others looked through the drawers in the desk.

On his visit to the gaol, Mr. Gates had handed Nicholas a small key, claiming it would open a lock box in the false bottom of the desk drawer. However, Nicholas had forgotten to ask which drawer had the false bottom. After inspecting the desk, he realized they all did. Apparently, his grandfather had many things to hide, for they found pocket watches, jewelry, and even two small miniatures of women.

Finally, in the third drawer, they found the box they had been searching for. Being protected from the dust and humidity by the false bottom, this lock was much easier to turn. Inside he found the accounting and bank draft records just as Mr. Gates had said he would.

To his surprise, underneath the ledgers and papers he found another key. Holding it up to the light, Bradley snatched it from his hand with a quiet exclamation of triumph, then marched over to the bookshelf. The sound of the turning lock was the reward.

"They are here." Bradley exclaimed.

"Should we take them back to your study?" Anthony asked.

"No," Nicholas replied, "I think we should inspect the documents here to make sure we have the information we need, then lock them back up. If no one has found them thus far, this seems to be the safest place for them."

Bradley walked to the window to inspect the records under better light. "Unfortunately, some of the ink has faded, and some of these receipts are quite difficult to decipher."

"That will complicate things," Nicholas said. "We will just have to do our best to find all the information we can and hope we do not need the faded ones."

"Actually, I do not think we will need to look any further." A grin spread across Bradley's face when he held out one of the papers. "This bank draft alone is damaging enough."

Nicholas stepped closer to examine the paper. It reflected the same amount Nicholas had calculated to be missing each quarter of the past year. Thankfully this draft had not been taken to the bank. Nicholas had assumed control over the financial accounts, the books, and ledgers just a day after it had been written.

The numbers of the secondary account were exactly as Mr. Gates had said they would be. The scheme really had been brilliant, so good no one had even questioned when the old earl had moved money from one of his accounts to another, they both supposedly being under his control.

"Why did no one question the extra account, especially when withdrawals were made by another man?" Bradley asked.

"It is not completely unusual," Edward said, "especially if a man has multiple inheritances at his disposal. Each estate's income must be kept separate for inheritance purposes."

"But how would they accomplish it? Mr. Gates would not have had access to the primary account," Bradley countered.

"Yes, but my grandfather's solicitor did," Nicholas responded coolly.

"Mr. Nile?"

"No. I hired Mr. Nile when I became the earl. The previous solicitor was an elderly man who retired shortly after the reading of my grandfather's will. His apprentice was supposed to take over in his stead, but he moved to Surrey a fortnight prior to my arrival."

"More like *escaped* to Surrey," Anthony grumbled.

"Exactly," Nicholas agreed. "It seems the man was not as honest as his predecessor."

After another half hour checking numbers and receipts, they had a pretty good indication of how the deed had been accomplished.

When they finished, Nicholas gathered up all the ledgers and papers and secured them back in the safe. Taking out a handkerchief, he began wiping down the desk.

Bradley looked at him strangely. "What exactly are you doing? Have you decided to take up a new position as a maid?"

"No," Nicholas said. "But I think this would go a lot faster if I hired all of you to assist in cleaning."

"Us?" Anthony protested.

"Yes. I do not know who has keys to this room, but I have a suspicion there are more than the ones I have. If anyone should enter, I do not want them to be led directly to the safe and desk simply by following our fingerprints in the dust."

The other three took a brief look about the room before they pulled out their own linens and wiped dust off of surfaces. When a good many places were cleared, Nicholas declared the room ready to leave.

Stepping into the hallway, they were surprised by Wilson rushing toward them, a silver salver in his hand.

"What is this, Wilson?" Nicholas asked.

"An express, my lord. Just delivered. However, it has taken me a quarter-hour to locate you, so I suppose it is not just."

"I wonder who could be sending me an express," Nicholas mused aloud. He picked up the letter.

"It is not for you, my lord, but Mr. Lenning."

Nicholas scanned the directions to find it was indeed addressed to Bradley. Handing the folded piece of foolscap to his friend, Nicholas watched Bradley as he slowly opened the letter. The longer Bradley's eyes scanned the page, the paler his face became. Nicholas noticed when Bradley's eyes shot back to the top of the page, and he read the words a second time.

Finally glancing up, Bradley simply said, "I must go." He raced down the corridor, calling back to Wilson to send a message to the stables to have his horse ready. Nicholas could do nothing but stare after his friend as he disappeared around the bend.

"It must be something truly dire for him to race off like that without a 'by your leave,'" Edward mumbled.

"Indeed," Nicholas said, still confused. Pulling his watch from his pocket, he checked the time. He was not sure where Bradley was going, but he would only have five hours of daylight before he would have to either procure a lantern or stop for the night.

For Nicholas's part, he hoped it was Fallow Hall. Bradley might make it there shortly after dark if he hurried. His family's London rooms, however, would be far too great a distance to travel in such a short time.

Of course, it could be from some other person entirely, though he could not imagine Bradley running off so quickly for anyone else. Just one more mystery to add to the stack, Nicholas thought ruefully.

Sybil awoke to loud voices echoing through the house. It sounded like someone was calling orders downstairs. The commotion of the house was so foreign from its usual calm that fear crawled up her throat. Pulling herself out of bed, she rang for Porter.

She tried to calm herself with routine as the bleariness of sleep faded. Checking her timepiece, she noted that it was a quarter past four. Plenty of time to dress for dinner. Perhaps she should even have some tea sent to her room to help tide her over for the evening's meal.

Loud pounding footfalls ascended the stairs and then retreated down another corridor.  Sybil's unease flared back to life. It was so intense that when Porter entered the room, she actually jumped at the maid's sudden appearance.

"What is going on out there?" Sybil demanded. "It sounds as if the whole house is in an uproar."

"An express has come, miss."

"From where?"

"I do not know."

"Then for whom?"

"I am sorry. I do not know that, either. I just heard a footman asking a groom to ready a horse in the stable."

Sybil was intrigued. What would cause such a fuss? Had something happened at Fairfield? Was Nicholas, even now, preparing to leave? She dearly hoped not since she had not been afforded the opportunity to speak to him since Tuesday. She still needed to warn him of Miss Cattering's intentions. However, if he were gone, that would stop any more attempts on his person. But where would that leave her?

She needed to speak to him, not only to relay her information, but to settle her own heart. She needed the friend she had come to rely on in London. The one who had ultimately stolen her heart. The only person who knew her well enough to piece back together the parts of that tender organ.

# Chapter Twenty-Eight

"What do you mean the magistrate is unavailable?" Nicholas spluttered.

"Just that," Edward said. "It seems he was called away on urgent family business."

Nicholas could not believe this day could get any worse. First had been Bradley's quick departure two days ago, then yesterday, a deluge of rain had delayed them from gathering the needed help. Those things had been bad enough, but an express had come just an hour ago from London informing them that Mr. Reginald Lenning, Bradley's older brother, had died.

Bradley's mad dash had been for naught as his brother had died by the time of his arrival. He had never been particularly close to his eldest sibling, but they were family, and although his older brother's behavior of late had left something to be desired, Bradley must still feel great sorrow at his passing.

"We shall just have to wait until the magistrate returns," Edward was saying, interrupting Nicholas's thoughts. "Once all is in place, you can hire a few men to help your bailiff collect the guilty parties."

Nicholas knew he could not proceed without help, but it frustrated him that he must wait. Who knew what could happen in the meantime?

"Nicholas," Anthony said from where he sat by the fire, "do not forget that I am to leave on the morrow. Emma is getting very close to her confinement, and I do not want her to travel too late in her"—he cleared his throat— "delicate state of health." Nicholas almost laughed at his friend's discomfort when alluding to his and Emma's expectation.

"Is there no way you might put off for another week? I understand your concern, but you said the doctor thought she had several more weeks yet. I could use your support here, and it is not as if you live a great distance away. You could easily get to Blackwell Manor within the day if you wish. It is less than fifty miles of good roads."

"Yes, but I would not want my wife to suffer from a hasty journey. She already feels every jolt of the carriage as it is."

Nicholas could see the determination in his friend's eyes, and truthfully, he could not blame the man for his concern. He would probably do the same if the roles had been reversed.

Sybil's image floated into his mind at the thought of a wife and children. Nicholas had tried to banish such images whenever they had intruded in the past. Today, however, they called to him. So much had changed. The thought that he might have his dreams if he stepped carefully was tantalizing.

"You do not need me here to save the day, Little." Anthony said, using the nickname Nicholas had been given at Eton.

Nicholas balked at the idea. Their group of Merry Men had always been a great comfort to him. And Anthony, their Robin Hood-like leader, had always led them in righting wrongs.

Looking at Anthony's firm visage, Nicholas realized Hood would not be leading the charge this time. No, he would just have to right this wrong without him.

"I suppose so," Nicholas finally conceded. "I should like you here all the same, but you have a wife and child to think of now. Good heavens, that feels odd to say."

"It feels odd for me too, and I am the married one." Anthony grinned.

Silence prevailed for half a minute while they all digested the changes that were happening in their lives, then Edward finally spoke.

"Nicholas, I was examining your ledgers this morning, trying to match some of the numbers we found, and I noticed a gap between the years eighteen ten and eighteen eleven. Are you missing a ledger?"

"I do not believe so," he said, standing to peruse his shelves. When he did not find the volume, he turned to his cousin. "It might still be in the library downstairs. My grandfather only kept the most recent ledgers in his study. I moved all of those up here. All the older ones are kept on the shelves behind the desk in the family library."

"Shall we go have a look, then?" Anthony rose from his chair.

Descending the stairs to the lower floor, Nicholas saw Wilson carrying the newest copy of the London Gazette. Instead of having him climb the stairs to place it on his desk, Nicholas took the sheets, intending to read them after he had procured the ledger.

In the corridor that led to the library, Mrs. Phillips motioned for his attention. Nicholas begged Anthony and Edward carry on without him, promising to meet them when his business with the housekeeper was finished.

After seeing to Mrs. Phillips' concerns, he again pointed his steps toward the library. He glanced down at the front page of the newspaper in his hand. Briefly scanning the page, he picked up his pace.

Bursting through the door of the library, he exclaimed, "It is over! They have had a complete success at Waterloo."

Both men shot to their feet where they had been shuffling through various books on the table.

"Are you sure?" Edward asked.

Anthony followed up with, "Where did you hear it?"

"When did it happen?"

"Is there a list of casualties?"

The last question was at the top of Nicholas's list, too. It was not as if their dear friend Fredrick would have been on land for the battle. He was, after all, a navy man, but it had still crossed Nicholas's mind. It was not completely unusual for naval men to be asked to fight on land, but he hoped that with the battle being so far inland Lieutenant Fredrick Marshall would not have been called upon to fight.

Nicholas handed pieces of the paper to each man as he exclaimed his ignorance. A feminine voice came from behind him, and he whirled around to see both Sybil and Miss Bawden peeking around edges of the high wingback chairs.

"Is it really true?" Sybil asked. "Has Napoleon been bested at last?"

"It says so in the morning post," Nicholas answered with a smile. Approaching the chair as Sybil rose out of it, he continued, "Of course, I must admit, my newspapers from London are a few days later than print. I suppose that means it is Wednesday's post."

In his excitement, he wanted to sweep her in his arms and swing her around, but the presence of his cousin and friend, along with Miss Bawden, stayed his enthusiasm. Instead, he settled for clasping her fingers as they spoke of the things he had read before he entered the library. The battle had been fought the previous Sunday, and it was expected that troops would march to Paris within the next few weeks.

"This is cause for celebration." Anthony said excitedly. "I must tell Emma." Nicholas smiled as his friend rushed from the room, the missing ledger completely forgotten. Miss Bawden had picked up Anthony's forgotten sheets of paper and was reading through the casualty list, her face falling by time she finished.

"So many men lost," she said mournfully. Then her brows lowered and her face hardened. "War is such a stupid thing. If men would just hand over the running of countries to women, I am sure we could come up with better ways to settle our disagreements than bashing each other's brains out."

Nicholas's mouth fell open at her proclamation. It was by far the most words he had ever heard the woman speak. The bend of her thoughts was radical, to be sure, but having grown up with a mother and three sisters, they were not wholly surprising. They had often lamented men's control in their lives.

But to hear them from Miss Bawden, who hardly spoke, and in such vulgar terms—his laughter broke through the stunned silence of the others. It was entirely irreverent, but Nicholas could not help himself.

"I am sure, Miss Bawden, my mother would agree with you. She is far better at running things than I am."

"A man of sense," she declared. "You are a rarity, Lord Penbrose. I approve."

Nicholas was not sure what she meant by the statement, but a look passed between Sybil and Miss Bawden that led him to believe she had not been speaking entirely to him. Nicholas realized he still held Sybil's fingers in his grasp. Slowly releasing them, he turned to his cousin.

"What say you, Caraway? Shall we inform the rest of the house and prepare for a feast this evening?"

"I believe a feast is definitely in order," he agreed.

That night, the mood of the whole party could only be described as festive. Everyone talked and conjectured on the wonderful news.

Dinner was a lavish affair, Aba having prepared an ample amount of food in her enthusiasm. Nicholas was praised more than once for his cook's fine offerings, especially by Miss Cattering.

A mischievous smile curled his lips when she went on for a full five minutes about the meal. Nicholas was not ignorant of her tirade against Aida, nor her cruel words in the parlor.

Mary, having overheard Miss Cattering's derogatory statements, had reported back to him of the woman's dislike for African people. If she was so opposed to them touching her hair, he thought, how would she feel to know the very food she now praised was made by the hands of one?

Nicholas would be sure to add a couple extra pounds to Aba's pay this year for the trouble he was sure this house party had caused her. He needed to do something for Aida as well.

He wished he could refuse Aida's service to Miss Cattering, but her maid was still ill, and Aida was the only other maid qualified enough to act as lady's maid. She would have to put up with Miss Cattering until the other maid was well again.

Nicholas was contemplating how he might address Miss Cattering's maltreatment of his hired help when Mr. Martin rose from his seat, holding up his glass.

"A toast," he said, "to all who fought, so we might have peace."

"Hear! Hear!" echoed about the table.

After Mr. Martin sat, Lord Ansley rose. "May Napoleon never gain power ever again!" he declared, raising his glass.

Again, everyone readily agreed, with toasts to their neighbors. Several others toasted England's good fortune. With each toast, Nicholas's eyes strayed more and more to Sybil, who was smiling and chatting with those around her.

The last few days he had seen a strain about her, as if something were on her mind, but he had never been afforded any time alone with her to inquire after her distress. Tonight, however, her tension seemed to have vanished.

To his surprise, he realized both Mary and Olivia were including Sybil in their conversation. He had seen the tension between the women these last two weeks. What had changed? His cousin Olivia was especially attentive, enthusiastically talking and laughing with Sybil and Mr. Martin.

The moment seemed too perfect. Not only had a peace been brokered between Sybil, his sister, and cousin, but his Aunt Evelyn was happier than he had ever seen her. His mother radiated joy, he was surrounded by many of his dearest friends, and the country would finally know some peace.

Even the presence of John, Tom, and Uncle Fairchild could not dampen the mood. The only thing that would make the evening more perfect was if Sybil could have taken up the place beside him at the table. He would have to content himself, however, with a conversation in the drawing room.

When the ladies left the men to their port, Nicholas was anxious to be done with the after-dinner ritual. The men, however, seemed happy to linger and consume far more drink than was best. After a second sip from his glass, Nicholas put it away from himself, watching until the clock ticked off thirty minutes. Then he rose from his seat, signaling that their time to linger was done.

Tom grumbled his complaint at the shortened time, as did Mr. Williams, but Nicholas ignored them, watching as several of the men hurriedly gulped down the rest of their third and even fourth servings of drink. Alcohol and the Fairfields was never a good combination, but Nicholas tried to push the thought to the back of his mind as he hurried from the room.

When he entered the drawing room, Sybil sat with Olivia on the sofa, his aunt on a nearby chair. Sybil's father took up a place not far from the trio.

All three ladies had hands over their mouths, trying to contain their giggles. The sight warmed Nicholas. He hoped to see many more times with them ensconced thus in the sofas and chairs at Penbrose House.

The spot to the left of Sybil was open, and he took the opportunity to claim it. She glanced up in surprise as he sat. Nicholas smiled at her, leaning back into the cushions and draping his arm along its back. The position was perhaps far too relaxed for the current party, but he could not help himself. He desperately wanted to be as close to Sybil as possible.

"And what are you three beautiful ladies so entertained by this evening?"

"Mother was just sharing the story of when she and Mr. Greenwald tried to ride the pigs at Radley Manor." Olivia erupted into another fit of giggles.

"You did not," he said in astonishment.

"We did. Do not look so shocked, Nicholas. I still remember when you and Edward decided to make a horse out of our old nanny goat."

Olivia and Sybil simultaneously turned to him with expressions of surprise and laughter. His aunt was intelligent, deflecting attention off her own misdeeds and placing it squarely on him.

"Now this I must hear," Olivia demanded.

"It is not a terribly interesting tale," he hedged.

"Let us be the judge of that," she countered.

"Very well. Edward and I decided since we were not allowed ponies of our own that the next best thing would be a goat. We managed to corner the old girl and slip a rope over her head as a makeshift bridle, but when we mounted, she refused to move no matter how much we urged her. Eventually, she lay down, trapping one of Edward's legs underneath her."

Edward, having heard, wandered near and continued the tale. "Yes, then Nicholas tried to make the stubborn animal rise, but she only glared back at him. Eventually, he had to alert a stable hand who helped lift the lazy animal off me."

"What a noble steed you had, Edward," Olivia teased, to which Edward gave his sister a scathing yet playful glare.

The majority of the evening was spent thus, with others coming and sitting in chairs about them. Nicholas knew it was rude that he did not pay as much attention to his other guests by strolling about the room, but the company was too tantalizing.

Sybil gifted him with smiles and laughs every so often, brushing against his arm and side a time or two, making it hard for him to resist wrapping his arm about her and pulling her close.

Eventually, several members of the party made their way to the music room so they might enjoy the ladies' talents. He was then required to rise if he wanted to remain in the same room as Sybil, she having been applied to by Miss Diana and Mary to come play with them.

However, just after exiting the drawing room, his attention was pulled back by the sound of raised voices. He motioned the ladies to continue without him and turned back to assess the situation.

His cousin John was making a ruckus about some horse race or such. The man was clearly very inebriated, but Nicholas's uncle was trying to shush him, saying he needed to lie down. His words only seemed to make John even more irritated.

Nicholas noticed several other ladies and gentlemen leaving the room, Tom among them. Apparently, he did not want to get involved in the family drama.

Making his way over, Nicholas heard his cousin's slurred voice say, "Those horses are mine. You promised them to me when we took over the estate, but you lied. You always lie to me. If you had left me an inheritance—"

"That is enough," Uncle Fairchild barked.

Nicholas was unsure what estate John spoke of, but he was not surprised his uncle had lied to his own son. He had certainly been lying to a good many people over the last several years.

"Get control over yourself, boy," Uncle Fairchild said, shaking his son by the shoulders. John yanked himself away and began clumsily making his way toward the door.

Just as he was about to pass Nicholas, however, he took a sluggish swing in his direction. Several of the ladies gasped as Nicholas easily sidestepped his cousin's punch.

"You took everything from me." His voice broke on the words. "How will I ever make my way now?" Tears began to stream down the grown man's cheeks.

Nicholas pieced together John's comments. Had Uncle Fairchild promised stock from the Penbrose stables to John so he could make a living?

Nicholas stepped close to his cousin, draping the crying man's arm over his shoulder. Of the two brothers, he had liked John the best when they were younger. Compassion built in his chest at the younger man's distress. All the fight seemed to have left John when the tears began, and he allowed Nicholas to escort him to his room.

"I know it is not your fault you inherited the title," John said, surprising him as they entered the guest room. "None of us had control over who was oldest."

Nicholas took in his cousin's words and current state. Maybe the man would not have admitted as much when he was sober, but maybe he would have. Perhaps it was time to get to know his cousin a bit better. It was quite possible some of Aunt Fairchild's tender heart had passed on to one of her children after all.

"Get some sleep, John. In the morning I would like to propose a business venture to you."

John's face brightened. Nicholas did not know if John would remember this conversation in the morning, but *he* would not forget. Apparently, he was not the only one who had been hurt by his uncle's underhanded dealings, and he would probably not be the last.

# Chapter Twenty-Nine

The morning sun spilled through the breakfast room window as Nicholas ate the eggs and thick sliced of ham before him. The light that filled the room illuminated the beauty around him. Never in all his years of visiting Penbrose House had he envisioned himself taking possession of it one day, yet here he sat at the head of the table.

Nicholas took in a deep breath, relishing the ability to do so without anyone else crowding around him. While the evening's festivities had been pleasant, there really was nothing like having a few moments to oneself.

Of course, he would not mind having one other person with him. Visions of Sybil smiling and laughing with his sister and cousin surfaced in his mind. The images were so homey and comforting that contentment spread to every part of him.

Last night, he had been required to share her with all the other members of the house party, but this morning… This morning, the skies were clear and the ground was dry, which meant he would have her all to himself for a morning ride.

Nicholas smiled at the thought. He still had seven more questions he could ask, and he could not wait to begin.

"Good morning," a soft alto voice sounded from the door. A smile pulled at his lips before he even looked up.

"Good morning, S—Miss Greenwald," he said, grateful he had caught himself before her name slipped out. The sparkle in Sybil's eyes held a note of mischief, and he was sure she had not missed his mental lapse. Did that mean she approved?

Retrieving a plate from the sideboard, she said, "I am glad it is not raining this morning. Tempest never does well when we miss too many days of riding. She is probably causing all sorts of chaos in the stables about now."

"I can imagine," he said. Warmth sunk deep into his soul at the easy way their conversation flowed.

They continued to talk of horses and the weather and whatever other subjects suited them until both had finished their breakfast. Nicholas decided fate must have smiled down on him to have Sybil's undivided attention, because not a single guest had entered while they'd eaten their meal.

At the stables, they laughed at Tempest's antics as she pranced about her lead when she caught sight of Sybil. It was quite evident that the mare loved her mistress as much as Sybil loved her mare. And it was equally evident that Tempest was ready for a run.

After another rousing race, on which they did not wager, Nicholas and Sybil set their mounts in the direction of an old, abandoned church that sat on the edge of the Penbrose property.

"Are you ready for my next question?" Nicholas glanced at Sybil to see her reaction.

"I see my hope was in vain. I had hoped you had forgotten, but your memory is as good as ever," she said with a cheeky smile. "But that was a question, so now you are down to six."

"I call foul," Nicholas protested. "You cannot count that as a question."

"Oh, I can count it. Remember, we have no solicitor to set the rules."

He laughed at her wit. "Very well. I suppose it will have to stand." It took him a moment to gather his courage. "What were your hopes for your first season in Town?"

Sybil's sharp intake of breath made him nervous. *Please*, he prayed, *do not shut me out again. Not in the way you did in London.*

They rode for nearly a minute before she finally answered. "I believe it was the same as any other girl upon her come out. I was meant to make a splendid match."

He did not miss the way she said *meant* rather than wanted. She was not speaking of *her* hopes but rather her duties. While it did answer his question, it was not what he had asked.

"I asked what your hopes were, Sybil. Not what you were meant to do."

Her eyes flew to his, and too late, he realized his mistake. So much for keeping distance through formal address.

"My apologies," he mumbled. "I did not mean to take such liberties."

The edges of Sybil's eyes pinched a bit as she studied him, the corner of her mouth sucking in as she worried her bottom lip. Something in her gaze changed, and he almost wondered if she were going to cry. Then, she straightened, looked forward, inhaled deeply, and let it out slowly.

"I do not mind, Nicholas," she said so quietly he almost wondered if he had heard her correctly. Had she truly used his given name as well?

But before he could inquire, she rushed on. "My hope was to make my parents proud. I was their only hope for the future. I *am* their only hope."

Nicholas let her words sink in as he relaxed into Rogue's easy walking gait. Of course Sybil would think of others before herself. When had she not thought of others first? Well, perhaps that day in Hyde Park. She had not thought of him first.

He suddenly realized how childish he sounded. All these years, Sybil had been trying to do what was best for her family and all he could think was *what about me?*

"I had other hopes as well." She looked away from him at the trees on their left.

"And what were those hopes?"

Turning toward him, she smirked. Blast, she had got him to ask another question.

"I guess that puts me down to five."

"It does indeed." She straightened in her saddle.

When they'd ridden for a while without talking, Nicholas wondered if she intended to answer his question. "You do remember the rules state that the recipient of a question must answer it."

"I do, but I was hoping you'd ask another if I was quiet long enough," she said.

"Very clever, but no more free questions, Miss Sybil Greenwald."

"Very well, then." She cast him a disarming grin. Then sobering, she continued. "I had hopes of meeting someone who would make me as happy as my father made my mother."

The words, while benign in nature, pricked at Nicholas's heart. Had he not made her happy?

"I see," he finally said. Perhaps this line of questioning was not the best for his wellbeing. He desperately wanted to know why things had exploded between them, but he was not sure he could handle the answer.

The walls of the church came into view in front of them.

"Oh, how lovely," Sybil exclaimed.

The stone walls and caved-in roof did make for an intriguing sight. One stained glass window still remained intact, the light of the early morning sun illuminating the red flower held in its green depths.

"Interesting," she said. "Why a rose for the entrance window?"

He had also found it odd that a church would have the image of a rose in its window, but there it stood just the same.

"I am unsure." Secretly, he was pleased that she had asked another question. "From what I understand, this church has been here for two centuries, but it has not been used since my grandfather took possession of Penbrose fifty years ago."

"He preferred the church in town?"

"I do not believe he preferred church at all," Nicholas said, adding another tally mark in his mind.

"I see."

"The church at the edge of Kettering, however, is the living that rests under the Penbrose legacy."

They stopped their horses in front of the small structure.

"Would you like to get down and have a look around?" he asked.

"No," she said grinning. "But you only have five questions left."

"Actually, seven," he quipped. Her mutinous look made him chuckle. "You asked two questions about the church."

"No, we were only counting questions asked from Monday."

"No, I do believe our rules were simply a question for a question. No stipulation of time was placed on the questions."

She opened her mouth to reply, then snapped it shut and laughed.

"Just when I think I have gotten one up on you..." She continued to giggle. "All right, ask away," she looked over her shoulder at Cormac, "or you may run out of time before we have to be back to the house."

"If I run out of time today, you will just have to ride with me tomorrow."

Sybil's grin slipped from her face as she studied him. "Won't that cause gossip? I would hate to make things uncomfortable for you for the rest of your house party."

She was worried about gossip... for him. Her concern warmed his heart. Other ladies would be all too keen on spreading gossip. They would revel in it, for it would give them social leverage to get him to offer marriage. But not Sybil. How had he not recognized this in her?

"I doubt it will cause much of a stir. No one else has needed my presence this early in the morning. In fact, I highly doubt many are up and about." He hoped his words would appease her worries, but she only seemed to frown deeper.

"Are you sure? Miss Cattering—" she said, but then seemed to think better of it.

"What about Miss Cattering?" He was a little annoyed that he could not get away from the woman even in conversation.

"Well, she seems to think there is an understanding between you." One of Sybil's dark brown eyebrows arched.

The air in Nicholas's lungs rushed out in a whoosh. "Wh-what?" he sputtered, not sure if he had heard her correctly.

"She confronted me in the library and accused me of interfering with her betrothal."

"That's preposterous. I have never—" he blurted out. Removing his hat, he ran a hand through his hair. His fingers caught in the tangles. He yanked his hand away, pulling a few strands out with the motion.

"That woman is going to be the death of me," he mumbled as he faced forward. Then, a little louder, he said, "I am not sure where she got such a notion, but I have never shown her any undue attention. To be completely honest, I have avoided her at all costs." Quickly, he turned to look at Sybil. "Do not tell my mother I said that. I would never hear the end of it if she knew I had been rude to one of her guests."

Sybil stared back at him, her eyes bright with mirth and something else that he could not place.

"I will not divulge your secret, Nicholas, but I do not think your mother would fault you for protecting yourself. I, myself, am not terribly fond of Miss Cattering."

There was no doubt Sybil had used his Christian name this time. He was equal parts pleased at her response and frustrated at Miss Cattering's audacity. There was one advantage to her presence, however. Each day Nicholas spent in Miss Cattering's self-interested company only convinced him more of Sybil's selfless intent.

"It appears we are of one accord where Miss Cattering is concerned. Tell me, was it her multitude of compliments, or her constant nearness that turned you from her *delightful* company?"

"Neither," she said with a chuckle. "She does not care for my company as she does for yours, and her compliments leave something to be desired where I am concerned. No, it is her talent at demeaning me in front of the other ladies that won her a position on my least-liked list."

Her words were lighthearted, but the tension around her eyes and the way she avoided eye contact with him hinted at her true feelings. Miss Cattering, it seemed, had not made life easy for either one of them over the last two weeks.

When Tempest began tossing her head about, Sybil turned her horse in the direction of the house. Taking the cue, Nicholas turned his mount to follow.

"I believe we are back to six questions."

Nicholas had been so surprised at Sybil's revelation that he had lost count, but he would not let her know that. "What do you think of Miss Diana Cattering?"

"She is an angel," Sybil said with a soft smile.

"That is exactly what Mr. Lenning said the first day he met her."

"Really? That explains so much."

"How is that?" he asked.

"His eyes and feet seem to stray toward her more than any other lady at the house party."

"I believe you are right. I have come across them walking about the gardens at least twice."

"As have I," she acknowledged with a grin. "But perhaps they just have a propensity toward botany."

"Yes, of course." He tried not to snicker. "The tender looks they were giving were only for the plants."

"Why not?" Sybil said with a giggle. "I have given several rose bushes tender looks in my day."

Her words stung his heart, transporting him back two years. They were standing by the Thames, frustration brightening Sybil's face as she stared mutinously at him.

*"What about all the tender looks you cast my way?"* Anger built in Nicholas's chest. *"Or the times we stole out to the garden, just the two of us? Are you claiming all of that was only a lark? The product of a shallow friendship?"*

*"Maybe you misinterpreted my looks. Perhaps I was admiring the roses,"* Sybil shot back flippantly.

Shaking the memory from his mind, Nicholas glanced up. Sybil was staring at him, concern written all over her face. He realized he had completely forgotten to respond. Unclenching his teeth, he tried to relax. If he was going to have this discussion, he needed to be intelligent about it.

"I suppose," he said slowly. "I have heard a woman claim to give tender looks to the flora and fauna before."

Sybil's eyes shot to the ground directly in front of them, and he knew she understood his meaning.

"Nicholas, I—" but she did not continue, and when her bottom lip slipped into her mouth, he decided it was time. They had both let this wound fester far too long, and like a large splinter, it only seemed to get worse the longer they left it.

"Sybil. I am sorry for my anger that day in the park," he said, surprising himself and her. That was not what he had intended to say. Where were the questions, the rebuke?

Thinking back, however, he realized it was true. He had been so angry that his tongue had gotten the better of him. He had called her a self-serving social climber. And when she had shot back that she had never welcomed his attentions, that he had given them without her encouragement, he had called her an outrageous flirt.

*"And what of you?"* she screamed. *"You knew from the very beginning that my mother expected me to marry someone with a title. It was never a secret, Nicholas! And yet you kept coming. Kept seeking me out. What was I supposed to do?"*

Nicholas could still see the tears that had formed, much like the ones that were now forming in those brilliant green eyes.

"Please," Sybil said. "Please don't apologize."

Nicholas was confused. "Why not?"

"Because I am the one to blame," she said, stealing the very breath from Nicholas' lungs.

# Chapter Thirty

The anger was gone. Two years she had held onto it, hoping it would fuel her, but now she was just tired. It was not Nicholas who had been at fault that day. It was her.

Hearing his heartfelt apology had broken something inside her. She had been arrogant, thinking she could toy with his emotions. She had seen his looks, felt them in her own heart. She had encouraged their conversations, their larks, even their secretive meetings. And all the while, she had told herself she would not become attached. She'd needed to fulfill her mother's wishes.

But it had not worked. He had still touched her heart.

"I was everything you said of me. I was trying to climb the social ladder."

"Only because your parents required it of you," he said.

Sybil wished that were completely true, but she had been convinced she deserved it. That she was somehow more special than the next lady and therefore destined for greatness.

Shaking her head, she said, "No, I was a self-centered flirt, just as you said. I thought I could skirt the line with you and still have the titled man Mama had always dreamed of for me. You were not mistaken, Nicholas, when you said I misled you."

Turning away from her, he stared off into the distance. She turned in the same direction, where Penbrose House loomed above the trees.

"I am sorry, Nicholas. I can understand if you never forgive me for what I did to you. I can hardly forgive myself. But I want you to know I take full responsibility for the discord between us, and I do not hold you to blame in the least."

Nicholas continued to look forward, and Sybil was sure she had hurt him yet again. That muscle in his jaw was flexing. Was he angry? He had every right to be.

"It will not do," he said, and Sybil's heart dropped into her boots. He would not forgive her after all. A bird called in the distance. Not a happy chirp, but a long low mournful trill. The sound echoed the pain in her heart as they trudged forward.

"I refuse to allow you to take all the blame, Sybil." Nicholas finally said. "I did know your mother's expectations, and I pushed you anyway. I thought, perhaps, if you could only see how much I cared for you, how happy we could be together, that I could change your mind."

Hope, like a flickering candle, began to blossom in her chest.

"But you—" The sound of pounding hooves cut off her next words as a group of riders approached them. Tempest, excited at the prospect of a race, began prancing about.

"There you are, Penbrose," Lord Hamdon said as he pulled up his mount in front of them. "Your cousin, Tom, said you had gone out for a ride."

Odd. She had not seen Mr. Tom Fairchild before their ride. Perhaps Nicholas had informed him of his plans.

"As you can see," Nicholas responded. Sybil noticed the tension in his shoulders as he sat stiffly in the saddle. Was he as upset at being interrupted as she was?

"Wilson has a missive waiting for you," Lord Caraway said, excitement evident in his expression.

"A missive?"

"Yes, from Kettering," Lord Ansley supplied.

Nicholas's brows dipped, confusion covering his face.

"I did not think—"

"From the Honorable Mr. George Morris," Lord Hamdon added.

Nicholas's expression cleared. "Ah, yes. Well, then—" Turning to Sybil, he asked, "Care to race?"

She stared back at him, trying to decipher the intent behind his invitation. In the end, she could discern nothing.

"I suppose we should," she said, not wanting to leave their conversation as it was, but knowing they could not continue with the audience they now had.

Miss Cattering had taken several verbal jabs at Sybil during Nicholas's absence during the morning, claiming it was completely indecent for a young lady to sit so scandalously close to a man for such an extended amount of time. She had even cast out hypothetical questions of what sort of relation a woman like that could have with the man in question.

Standing near the piano in the music room, Sybil tried in vain to ignore her as she continued to spout some drivel or other. But the engrossed way some of the younger, more impressionable ladies listened to Miss Cattering, along with the embarrassment of being in mixed company, galvanized Sybil into action.

She turned to Eliza and said in a voice meant to be overheard, "I do believe there is a cat in the room."

Eliza did not disappoint. "I thought I saw one as well."

She began searching behind a few chairs.

Miss Cattering did not jump as before, but her eyes widened a bit. "Do not be ridiculous. Lady Julia herself said they do not keep cats in Penbrose House."

"Yes," Eliza said, "but we have had the door open to the veranda, and I believe the poor creature may have wandered in while none of us were looking."

Miss Cattering's hands grasped her skirts, her eyes darting from side to side. Sybil began searching about the chairs with Eliza. Eventually, the tension of the moment must have touched a nerve because Miss Cattering excused herself for a midmorning respite, claiming to be far more tired than she had previously realized. However, before she could completely leave the room, Eliza let out a quiet mewing noise.

Sybil was gratified when Miss Cattering whirled around, skirts in hand.

Unfortunately Mr. Martin, having very discerning ears, said, "That was quite a brilliant recreation of a kitten's mew, Miss Bawden."

Miss Cattering shot Eliza a scathing glare before announcing that she was not as tired as she had previously stated, and she thought she might stay a while longer.

Tired of the woman's presence and hoping to get another glimpse of Nicholas, Sybil excused herself and made her way to her room.

Porter was there, readying Sybil's dress for dinner. It really was not necessary for her maid to be prepared so early; the meal was still hours away.

"Is everything all right, Porter?"

The grin that split Porter's face was so unexpected that Sybil just stared at her.

"Everything is splendid, miss. I just thought I'd get your things ready sooner rather than later." She set about the room gathering accessories. When the smaller woman began to hum a tune, however, Sybil became instantly suspicious.

Porter. Never. Hummed.

"Anything you wish to tell me, Porter?" An idea blossomed in Sybil's mind. "Perhaps about a certain clerk?"

Porter whirled around to look at her, a blush coloring her cheeks. Sybil had guessed it, then.

"Are you angry?" the maid asked, seconds before Sybil let her face break into a huge grin of her own.

"Only if you do not share the details," she teased.

Porter obliged. Mr. Brown, it would seem, was a childhood acquaintance who had moved to Kettering several years back when he'd inherited the mercantile from his uncle. Porter had not only seen him on Wednesday, but the gentleman had stopped by with a delivery the evening before.

Somehow, he had convinced the dressmaker to let him deliver Sybil's new gowns. She was surprised at his ingenuity, as the task could have easily been done by a footman or runner. As it was, he had apparently arrived while the whole party was at dinner. Porter, being free until she was further needed, had taken a walk about the gardens with the obviously smitten man.

Porter talked more than Sybil thought she ever had in their entire acquaintance. It was obvious that Mr. Brown was not the only one who had strong feelings. Sybil's previous sadness at the thought of Porter leaving was swallowed up by the joy of seeing her so happy. Perhaps her own happiness also had some influence on the situation. Her thoughts had not strayed far from Nicholas while she listened to Porter's story.

A small knock sounded on the bedroom door. Porter opened it, and after a brief greeting, admitted Eliza into the room.

Sybil grinned at her friend. "I see you managed to free yourself from the Cat's clutches."

Eliza rolled her eyes. "Barely. I was sure she would claw my eyes out after she discovered my deception. Thankfully there were enough men still about that she chose to hold her tongue. At least as much as is possible for *that* woman. The party began to disperse a half hour past, and I decided a hasty exit was in order to escape the spitting feline."

Sybil giggled. "A very wise decision."

A loud disturbance in the hall brought their conversation up short. Eliza crossed to the door and opened it a crack to peek out at the commotion down the hall. Sybil's taller frame afforded her a view of the corridor over Eliza's head. Someone stumbled out of the room she knew to be Miss Cattering's. Before the person could catch their balance, a silver-handled hairbrush came flying out the door, striking the young woman on the cheek and bringing her to her knees.

Aida knelt and rubbed the offended spot as the door slammed behind her. Indignation burned in Sybil's chest. She tried to push past Eliza, but her friend pulled her back into the room with a surprising amount of strength and shut the door.

"What are you doing?" Sybil growled.

"What are you doing?" Eliza countered with a raise of her brow.

"I am going to give that monster down the hall a set down she won't soon forget. She cannot go about mistreat all the servants as she does."

"But if we intervene now, Miss Cattering will make it far worse for Aida."

"Do we do nothing?" Sybil hissed at her friend, trying to keep her voice low as anger surged through her veins.

"I did not say that." Devilment danced in Eliza's eyes. "I am just saying that for now, we need to let Miss Cattering cool down a bit."

Taking a few calming breaths, Sybil let Eliza's words sink in. She recognized the half-cocked smile that meant Eliza was concocting a plan. She did not know what it would be, but it would not be dull. And Sybil would definitely be in on it.

She took a deep breath to cool her anger.

"Should we see if Aida is alright?" Eliza asked.

Sybil nodded and Eliza turned and opened the door again very quietly. From the doorway they could see the maid rise from where she had sat upon the hard wood floor. Aida covertly glanced up and down the hall, then with purposed steps, moved forward, her foot landing directly on the handle of the brush. A small snap echoed off the walls as Eliza and Sybil moved out the door.

Eliza snickered and Aida's eyes shot to them. Apparently, she had not been aware of their presence.

"It is too bad," Eliza said slowly, "that Miss Cattering broke her brush when she lobbed it so carelessly into the hall."

A smirk grew on Aida's tear-stained cheeks, understanding passing between the girls. "Yes. Quite the shame." Then her hunched shoulders straightened, her chin came up, and after a brief nod, she turned and walked intentionally down the hall. Sybil admired her in that moment. She was strong, kind, intelligent and brave ... and Sybil loved her for it.

When it was just Eliza and Sybil in the hall, Eliza turned to her. "How do you feel about revenge?"

# Chapter Thirty-One

Nicholas sat in his study, the day already half gone. His note had finally reached the magistrate, and the man had assured him he would be home by Monday evening at the latest. Two days. He only needed to manage things for two more days.

If all went as planned, he would be rid of his thief by Tuesday evening. Too bad Anthony had left shortly after the arrival of the good news. He would be missing all the fun.

On second thought, it was probably best for Anthony to get his wife as far from here as possible. If Nicholas could manage it, he would do the same for the rest of his guests. The scene that was sure to play out would do no good for anyone's reputations, least of all Mary's.

A knock at the door brought his attention back to his task at hand. Straightening his waistcoat, he called for the person to enter, but instead of seeing his cousin whom he expected, Aba stood in the doorway. The older woman rarely made her way up from the kitchens, the stairs being hard on her knees. Her presence here meant something was very wrong.

"Aba, please have a seat." The woman shuffled to a chair next to his desk and sat with a very audible sigh. "What brings you all the way up here?"

"Sir, I'm come to tell you one of those fine ladies hurt my granddaughter."

"Aida?"

To this she simply nodded.

"How?"

"Pitched a brush at her."

"Is she all right?"

"Her face is a bit puffy, and she is going to have some colors about the mark. You must know I'm not going to stand by and let it go on. This is the second time that woman has lashed out at her. Only this time, it was just because Aida was making her bed."

"I had meant to have a word with Miss Cattering, but I must admit yesterday's excitement quite literally brushed it from my mind. I will attend to the matter as soon as I am able, I assure you. As for now, if Miss Cattering calls for assistance, send Meg. I will not have Aida abused again. How is the Cattering's maid faring?"

"She's sitting up and sipping broth this morning. The fever is gone out, finally."

"Good. Hopefully with the return of her old maid, she will be less irritable."

"'Scuse me, but I... well, there's marks on the maid Sally, as well."

Nicholas frowned. It would seem Miss Cattering had a *habit* of laying a hand on the staff. Unfortunately, he could do little for the poor abused servant in the Cattering's employ, other than make sure she was fully recovered. He would, however, be sure to speak with Lord Brock about his daughter's despicable behavior.

Aba must have decided she was done with the conversation, for she heaved herself up out of the chair, and after dipping her head to Nicholas, made her way to the door.

He watched her go, contemplating how he might go about addressing the issue with Miss Cattering. Nicholas was unsure if appealing to Lord Brock would do any good, but it was the best course he could think of at the moment.

Another knock sounded at the door, and he once again bade the person come in. John entered hesitantly. His eyes were red-rimmed, and he looked like he might be sporting a headache if the wince at the click of the closing door was any indication.

That the man would come when he felt so poorly spoke volumes of his desperation. Nicholas was not sure why he had not seen it before, but as John stood before him, he realized the man was hurting, and not just physically. It shone in his eyes, just as it must have shown in Nicholas's after his father's death, and again after Sybil's refusal.

"Please, have a seat, John."

The younger man nodded and took the seat Aba had vacated. Nicholas sat at his desk and pulled out a few papers, along with a ledger.

"Please, forgive me for last night, Nicholas. I... I should not have taken my anger out on you."

"You already asked my forgiveness, John, and I have freely given it."

"I am unsure why. I do not deserve it."

"None of us really deserve forgiveness, but it is a privilege we both can give and receive. It gives you and I the opportunity to start again, and for that I am truly grateful."

John ducked his head, his sandy hair falling forward to hide the emotion that was evident on his face. After a moment, he composed himself and asked, "Did you mean what you said last night? That you had a business opportunity for me?"

"I did, but may I first ask a few personal questions that might seem a bit impertinent?"

"It is the least I can do."

"Did your father truly leave you with no inheritance?" Nicholas asked.

"None. He assumed he would be earl and promised I would have the property at Bristol. It is equipped with fine stables, and I was to have two of the finest stallions from Penbrose stock, along with ten of the best brood mares. With the course of events," John said, looking down at his hands as he flexed them in and out, "well, I have nothing. I am destined to be dependent on my father forever unless I join the military or the church. You know I was never a good scholar, so

I don't have enough education for anything else. The church is obviously not for me either, for God would surely strike me with lightning if *I* were ever to be a vicar."

His self-deprecating smile punctuated the words.

Nicholas agreed. Last night's fiasco had proven that John drank far too much for such a sober office. While it was a significant failing, one the man shared with his father and brother, he could not help but wonder if John had acquired some of Uncle Fairchild's other failings. Did John keep a mistress as Uncle Fairchild had? Or was he involved in dealings of a more illicit nature? He could not in good conscience help him if he could not trust him.

John seemed to sense his unease. "I have not done anything terribly wrong, Nicholas. I only meant that I am far too irreverent to be a man of the cloth. I drink too much. I love a good game of cards, and I laugh at far too many unholy things."

Nicholas studied John a moment. His cousin's eyes were shaped the same as Aunt Fairchild's, wide near the nose and pinched at the outer corners. Taking a deep breath, he pushed on with his questions.

"So you are saying you have never done anything of an immoral or illegal nature?"

The other man's face paled a bit, and frustration welled up within Nicholas. So much for his hope of reforming at least one of his cousins.

But when his cousin whispered, "Not of my own free will." Nicholas's bubble of irritation popped. His inclination had not been completely off course. Leaning forward over his desk, he looked into his cousin's blue-grey eyes. "Tell me, and I shall help set you free."

Nicholas glanced up as Lord Brock entered his study. He had requested to meet with the man nearly three hours ago, after hearing Aba's report and speaking with John, but the baron had clearly taken his time. It was nearly time for them to dress for dinner. However, this meeting took precedence.

"Lord Brock. Thank you for coming." He indicated the cushioned seat he'd moved across from him at his desk and the man sat.

"Thank you, Penbrose," Lord Brock said a glint in his eye. It irritated Nicholas that the man had been so informal. He had never given him any indication that they were on such close terms.

Sitting when Lord Brock did, Nicholas began. "I have a matter on which I wish to speak to you."

"Of course you do, or you would not have summoned me. I have been expecting this meeting for quite some time. Kathryn is a fetching young lady, is she not?"

Nicholas's shoulders tightened. Apparently, Miss Cattering was not the only one forming unfounded expectations.

"I will not insult the lady and claim otherwise, but Lord Brock, I am concerned about your daughter's behavior."

"In what way?" The man leaned forward, his expression changing from relaxed to guarded.

"In the last few weeks, I have had several of my staff complain of mistreatment at her hands. Today, in fact, she threw a hairbrush and struck one of my maids directly in the face."

A guffaw of laughter burst from Lord Brock. "Kathryn has always had good aim," he said, leaning back in his chair. "Let me educate you on the ways of women, Penbrose. They are exceedingly particular in their dress and grooming. Best not to step in the way of their toilette. As for your servants, perhaps you are too light-handed with them if they cannot perform to your guests' expectations."

Nicholas was not amused in the slightest. He did not know much about Lord Brock other than the man's childhood acquaintance with the whole Fairchild family, but based on what he did know, he was beginning to sorely dislike him.

Standing up and placing his hands on the desk in front of him, he used his position to look down on the taller man.

"Lord Brock. This is my home, and I will thank you not to tell me how to run it. Now, if you and your daughter wish to remain guests in Penbrose House, I suggest you get her under control."

The baron's face hardened at the direct threat, but Nicholas continued to stare him down.

"Why don't you talk to the lady yourself?" he asked.

Nicholas shook his head. "A meeting of this nature with your daughter would be highly inappropriate."

"Not really," he countered. "You seem to be on good terms."

The man definitely had designs of his own on Nicholas's title if he would suggest a private meeting. That was the only way such a delicate subject could be discussed. Lord Brock would be sadly disappointed, though. Nicholas would duel at dawn before he would offer for such a malicious, unprincipled, conceited scrap of a woman as Miss Cattering.

"No, Lord Brock," he said firmly. "This is the domain of a father."

Silence hung in the air as the two men fought a silent battle with their eyes. Finally, Lord Brock conceded. "I will speak with her."

# Chapter Thirty-Two

Sybil wondered for the second time if this was the right course of action. Surely, they would be struck deaf or dumb for the act of revenge they were about to enact, especially having so recently come from the church. It was the first time she had set foot in a house of God since her mother's death. She had been sure she would feel anxious, guilty, angry, sad, any of those things, but she'd been pleasantly surprised by the warmth and comfort the old building had given her weary soul.

Now, however, the morning's service about loving thy neighbor was nearly forgotten. All she wanted to think about was not getting caught as she and Eliza tried to make their way from the stable into the house as nonchalantly as possible.

Eliza, with a satchel slung over her shoulder, a hand placed protectively on the top flap, looked at her with a grin. Sybil prayed the tiny black and white ball of fur hidden deep in the leather bag's depths would stay blessedly quiet while they made their way to a certain upstairs room.

The rest of the party were still at luncheon, but Eliza and Sybil had requested trays be brought to their rooms so they might gain time to carry out Eliza's ingenious plan. Thanks to the Cattering maid's illness, there would be no real impediment. Sybil's only regret was for the little kitten they had called into service for this afternoon lark. Their past experience with the lady made them relatively sure Miss Cattering would be too frightened of the creature to actually do it any harm.

As Eliza cautiously opened Miss Cattering's door, Sybil felt her heart thumping in her chest. What if they were caught?

Eliza quickly crossed the room, opened the satchel, and pulled the black and white kitten from its recesses. The little thing seemed excited about its new surroundings as Eliza placed it upon the pink bed covers of the enormous four poster bed.

Sybil looked about herself in surprise. Her small room had been lovely, with its pretty white furniture and accenting green décor, but Miss Cattering's—well, for starters, it was twice the size. The lavish—almost gaudy—décor seemed out of place compared to all the other rooms. Who had commissioned this particular palatial room?

Eliza noticed Sybil's perusal. "She was in a holy uproar when they first got here, claiming her accommodations were inadequate. She demanded a tour of all the other guest rooms. I felt sorry for Mrs. Phillips. I overheard her tell Lady Julia that the rooms previously set aside for you and your father had been taken by Lord Brock and his family."

Sybil was not at all surprised by Miss Cattering's actions, but she was surprised by Lady Julia's deference to her and her father. She had not realized they were so valued as guests.

However, she actually preferred the green room to which she had been assigned. It was comfortable and inviting. This room felt ostentatious and a little cold.

Eliza pet the kitten. After a couple of minutes, the little creature relaxed and snuggled itself into the warm blankets of Miss Cattering's bed. Assured that it would not wander far, Sybil and Eliza exited the room, closing the door quietly behind them.

They quickly made their way toward the stairs, but just as they reached the point where the two corridors intersected, Miss Cattering crested the stairs, a Williams sister on either side. Eliza and Sybil made way for the three ladies, knowing they would not step aside for them, but also not wanting to create any delay in Miss Cattering reaching her room.

"Oh my, what is that terrible smell?" Miss Cattering said to her friends as she passed Sybil and Eliza. "A pair of polecats must be skulking about."

The other two ladies tittered at the remark, but Sybil just smiled to herself, knowing she and Eliza would have the last laugh.

Just as they reached the stairs, Eliza grabbed her arm, halting their progress.

"Let's go back and watch," she said, a look of pure excitement in her eyes.

"That is not the wisest idea, Eliza. I already let you talk me into this lark. If we get caught..." She let her words trail off, already knowing she would give in to Eliza's pleadings. She, too, wanted to see Miss Cattering's reaction.

"All right, but we must make our returning believable. I shall say something about forgetting my shawl. That way we will be close enough to see, but far enough to not seem like the guilty parties."

Eliza readily agreed, and they turned about quickly, walking back the way they had come. When they were within earshot of the three ladies, Sybil said, "I believe I left my shawl on the chair. I'll just be a moment."

Miss Cattering and Miss Williams had stopped to talk in front of Miss Cattering's door while Miss Lydia continued down the hall to her room. Sybil barely made out a plaintive meow from Miss Cattering's room. The woman's gaze shot up the hall toward them, and she narrowed her eyes.

"You shall have to do better than that, Miss Bawden, if you think to frighten me." Then turning back to her friend, she continued on with her conversation.

Sybil opened her bedroom door and tried to look for all the world as if she was not paying attention to Miss Cattering. Eliza slipped inside the door with her, but they left it open just a crack so they might peek around the edge.

The piercing scream from down the hall did not disappoint. Neither did the sight of Miss Cattering's skirts hiked up past her knees as she stumbled out into the corridor.

"Help! Help! There is a rabid beast on my bed!" she screamed.

A harried Mrs. Phillips, followed by a footman, rushed to Miss Cattering's aid. The pair hurried into Miss Cattering's room to help banish the problem. But a moment later, Mrs. Phillips calmly walked out, a smile pulling at her lips as she snuggled the cuddly kitten close to her chest.

"It is nothing but a wee kitten, Miss Cattering," Mrs. Phillips proclaimed, holding the animal out for her to see.

Miss Cattering let out a shrill cry of dismay. "Get it away! Get that horrid creature away!" Promptly turning, she ran a few doors down and disappeared into an astonished Miss Williams's room.

The quiet chuckles from the servants as they tried to hold in their mirth over the lady's ridiculous behavior filled the hallway. It would seem Eliza and Sybil were not the only ones who could not summon compassion for the spiteful lady.

Unlike the servants, however, Eliza exploded into peals of laughter the moment the door to Sybil's room shut. Sybil smiled at her friend, but a feeling of unease settled over her. Maybe they had carried things a bit too far.

She was not sure where Miss Cattering's fear of cats had developed, but it must have been a truly traumatizing experience to have caused the kind of fear they all had witnessed.

Eliza's laughter ebbed when she realized Sybil was not as amused.

"What?" she asked.

"I cannot help but feel a little sorry for her. What do you think caused such a nonsensical fear?"

"I do not know, but, Sybil, do not forget that this same woman has left bruises on not only her own maid, but Aida and even Diana. She does not deserve our compassion. A woman like that will not be stopped unless she is forced to."

"Diana? Are you sure?"

"I heard Miss Cattering screaming at Diana the other night, and the next morning I noticed a bruise peeking out from under Diana's sleeve."

"Oh no, what if she thinks Diana was involved in this and takes out her anger on her?"

"I had not thought of that." Eliza face fell into a dark frown. "Blast!"

Sybil was surprised to hear such coarse language, but she probably should not have been. This was Eliza, after all, and she did not seem to fit any mold Society tried to place her in.

"We shall have to redirect Miss Cattering's attention toward us," Eliza offered. "You know, somehow let it slip so she knows we hold the upper hand."

"How?"

"I am unsure, but I will think of something, Sybil. Never you fear. We will not let Diana or anyone else take the blame for this. Come on." Eliza beckoned to the door. "I do my best thinking in the library."

Nicholas made his way toward the library to obtain a book on animal husbandry for John. Caught up in his thoughts, he was surprised when a feminine hand reached out and latched onto his arm. Before he even had a chance see who had accosted him, Miss Cattering's irritating voice grated in his ears.

"I missed you at breakfast this morning," she said, clinging to him like a leech.

"But you saw me at luncheon just a few hours ago," Nicholas countered.

"Yes, but it was so dull without you there, not like our pleasant breakfast earlier this week."

Nicholas shuttered at the thought of the unexpected tête-à-tête. Had they been attending different breakfasts? He did not remember the situation to be at all pleasant. He had been all too grateful to have it interrupted by his cousin Tom no more than five minutes after he had arrived. Fancy ever being grateful to see Tom.

He turned to face Miss Cattering, his face stern. "Miss Cattering, I am on my way to the library. If you would please unhand me, I would appreciate it. I have much to accomplish before I must dress for dinner."

His comments were quite rude, he realized, but he could not see how to get through to her in any other way.

"I do not wish to hold you up. I shall simply accompany you." She smiled and batted her lashes.

The action rendered her rather ridiculous. Had Nicholas not been thoroughly frustrated with her, he might have laughed, but right now he wanted nothing more than to throttle the woman.

"I wish to go *alone*."

She looked a bit crestfallen, but she released his arm and allowed him to continue on his way.

Moments after entering the library, however, she sauntered in, making her way toward where he stood by the edge of the desk. Fearing she would latch on to him again, he stepped away from her, putting the desk between them.

Facing her, he decided to broach the subject of the servants himself. Perhaps pointing out her unscrupulous behavior would be enough of a distraction to dissuade her from her obvious goal of placing him in a compromising position.

"Miss Cattering, I have been meaning to speak with you."

"You have?" she cooed.

"Yes." His voice cracked upon the word. Miss Cattering had begun making her way around the desk, and it took some quick maneuvering to keep the desk between himself and her advances. "It is about my servants."

She paused her progress, confusion flashed across her face. Good, maybe this was going to be easier than he had planned.

"Your servants?" She slowly began walking about the desk again. Miss Cattering put Nicholas in mind of a cat as she crept, carefully, ever so slowly, trying to anticipate his every move.

"Yes, my servants. It has been brought to my attention that you abuse them quite thoroughly, and I will not stand for my staff to suffer bodily harm at your hands."

"Come now, Lord Penbrose. You cannot believe everything about which servants gossip. Their lives are *terribly* tedious. They cannot help but try to invent tales to make things a bit more lively."

She switched directions so quickly that he was forced to change his path just to avoid colliding with her. Thinking his chances might be a little better if he freed himself of the desk, he began stepping toward the side that faced the doorway.

"These are not tales, Miss Cattering. I have seen the bruises myself. I also do not appreciate the aspersions you cast on the character of those in my employ."

Miss Cattering must have divined his intent, for she quickly switched directions again. Nicholas tried to escape the position he was in, caught between the desk's edge and the bookshelves. But just as he stepped past the end of the desk, his foot caught on the leg, and he stumbled forward, giving Miss Cattering the advantage. She rushed forward and wrapped her arms about him, pinning his arms to his sides.

"Come," she crooned, "let us not quarrel. We have much better things we might use our lips for."

Bile rose in Nicholas's throat as he looked down at the buxom woman. At that moment, the library door flew open, and Lord Brock and Mr. Williams strode in. They stopped, faces slightly agape at Nicholas wrapped completely in Miss Cattering's arms.

It would seem Miss Cattering had just performed a checkmate, for he knew what the men's demands would be before they even left their lips. *I guess I shall be forced to duel at dawn after all,* he thought ruefully.

Eliza and Sybil had nearly given themselves away when Nicholas first entered the room, but when Miss Cattering had followed swiftly on his heels, Sybil had motioned for Eliza to stay quiet.

These chairs were becoming increasingly useful. They sat silently listening to the interchange going on behind them. Sybil saw Eliza lean forward slowly and peek around the edge of the chair. Eliza's eyes danced with merriment, and she motioned for her to do the same. Sybil shook her head at first, but after a moment her curiosity got the better of her.

Carefully leaning over, she peeked past the side of the chair. Behind her, Nicholas and Miss Cattering were in a definite game of cat and mouse. He made his way around the desk only for her to turn and cut him off. Back and forth they went for a couple of minutes until he tried to escape toward the door. Unfortunately, something tripped him up, and he fairly fell into Miss Cattering's arms.

The sight was truly hilarious, but the entrance of Lord Brock and Mr. Williams stole the humor out of the whole situation. To Sybil's relief, she saw Lord Caraway and Lord Ansley enter behind the other two gentleman. Hopefully, their presence would lend an air of reason to the ensuing conversation.

"I demand you unhand my daughter, Lord Penbrose," Lord Brock insisted, "and you must make good by her, for you have quite thoroughly ruined her."

"If you have not noticed, Lord Brock, it is she who needs to unhand me," Nicholas said, a slight uptick to his brow.

Lord Caraway snickered behind Lord Brock. How the man could find this humorous, Sybil did not know. She, for one, was quite terrified Lord Brock might carry his point.

Lord Brock cast Lord Caraway a scathing look before he realized just who stood in the doorway. Apparently, the sight of a pair of lords who outranked him was enough to at least swipe the disdain from his face.

Appealing to the other two men, Lord Brock gestured to Miss Cattering who was still desperately clung to Lord Penbrose as he struggled to free himself from her vice-like grip. "Well, you can see the position they are in."

"Yes," Lord Ansley said, "I see your daughter accosting Lord Penbrose."

"She most assuredly would not be in this position had he not first accosted her, encouraging her to behave thus. Besides, they were found in this room completely alone and unchaperoned."

Eliza's face was firm and immovable as she rose from her chair and faced the surprised room. "Had Miss Cattering checked her surroundings before chasing Lord Penbrose into the library, she would have seen she had spectators for her disgraceful behavior."

Shaken out of her stunned condition by Eliza's words, Sybil rose from her chair, alerting the others to her presence. Eliza was right. Nicholas would not be required to marry Miss Cattering, not when they had witnessed the whole scene.

Nicholas looked shocked, then relieved as Miss Cattering finally dropped her arms.

Lord Brock appeared just as stunned as Miss Cattering. He remained rooted to the spot, staring at Sybil and Eliza. Before he could form a response to their presence, however, Nicholas took hold of the situation.

"I have spoken with you previously about your daughter's wanton behavior, Lord Brock, and you have not deemed it worth your while to check her. Notwithstanding your long acquaintance with the Fairchild family, I must ask you to remove your daughter and leave this house party."

"What?" Miss Cattering fairly shrieked at the same time her father began to sputter.

"You cannot be serious, Penbrose. Such a paltry mistake does not warrant our being cast from the premises."

"This was not a paltry mistake. It was a wanton assault upon my person. I have multiple witnesses who can attest to my innocence," he said, sending a grateful glance Sybil's way. "And I am not casting you out, but respectfully asking you to leave. If you do so, I will forget this instance happened and will not bandy it about for the gossipmongers."

Miss Cattering blanched. Nicholas now held the power; her reputation could be quite thoroughly maligned by this situation. Lord Brock looked to Lord Ansley and Lord Caraway.

"And what of you, Caraway? Ansley?"

Ansley spoke for both of them. "We shall bide our peace. There is naught to worry about in our direction."

Turning to Sybil and Eliza, his eyes held the question he had just posed to the pair of lords. Eliza answered for them. "We will keep our peace, on one condition—that you restrain your daughter from hurting both her maid and her cousin. We are not ignorant, you see, of the abuse Miss Diana suffers at the hands of your daughter."

Sybil found her voice. "We have seen the bruises with our own eyes and witnessed your daughter's fits of temper. We also know of other situations you, yourself, have placed Miss Diana in that would have been detrimental to her wellbeing."

Lord Brock's eyebrows shot up at the revelation. Good—hopefully the man knew that Sybil and Eliza meant business.

"You must guarantee Miss Diana suffers no more harm upon her person, or we shall consider our agreement of silence null and void," Eliza finished.

Looks of first confusion and then frustration passed from Nicholas to Caraway and from Caraway to Ansley as realization must have dawned.

The thought of one as sweet and kind as Diana being left to the mercy of this pair of dissolute characters left a sick feeling in Sybil's gut, but she had no choice. They could not keep Diana with them forever. The law was on Lord Brock's side, and there was nothing they might do to free her from his clutches.

Lord Brock inhaled deeply, then let it out slowly. "You have my word." Then turning to Mr. Williams, he said, "Come, Williams, we have a few matters to discuss before my daughter and I must depart."

Miss Cattering started to cry and insisted they all reconsider. Grabbing the blubbering girl's arm, Lord Brock fairly dragged her out of the room in stony silence.

"Well, that was entertaining to say the least," Lord Caraway said, a broad smile upon his face.

The tension in the room seemed to snap, and the release caused nervous chuckles and laughs among the occupants.

"Lord Penbrose, if you could have only seen yourself trying to stay one step ahead of Miss Cattering." Eliza laughed. "I almost gave us away trying to contain my mirth."

"Why did you not alert us to your presence sooner?" There was no malice in his voice, just curiosity.

"Well," she said, "we would not have wanted to embarrass you more than you already were. Had you been able to dismiss her without any harm done, you would not have wanted to know you had an audience."

"True," Nicholas agreed.

"We would have made ourselves known soon anyway," Sybil interjected. "When you tripped, I think we both realized it was time to come to your aid."

"So I was the damsel in distress?" His smile widened into a grin.

"More like the lord in lament," Ansley put forth.

"Or the earl in angst," Caraway added.

"That would make Miss Greenwald and myself the knights in shining armor," Eliza exclaimed, pride puffing out her chest. "I have always wanted to be a knight."

Another round of laughter erupted about the room.

# Chapter Thirty-Three

The only drawback of the removal of Miss Cattering from the house party was losing Diana's company. If Sybil could have packed up the Williams sisters and sent them in Diana's place, the rearrangement of guests would have been perfect.

Diana accepted her removal with grace. Sybil admired her humility and courage. If it had been her fate, she was sure she would have not been quite so calm.

Due to the lateness of the day, Nicholas had permitted Lord Brock and his family to stay until morning as long as he could keep his daughter in check.

Sybil was grateful for his generosity, for Diana's sake. After all, she had done nothing wrong. The humiliation of being dismissed from a house party was difficult enough without needing to endure travel with two very upset companions. Sybil was sure Nicholas had had Diana in mind when extending the offer. It would be much harder for Lord Brock to hold to his promise concerning Diana's safety if Miss Cattering was still distressed.

"We shall be sure to write to you," Eliza said the next morning as they said their goodbyes. "Do you think you shall take a season in London this year?"

"I am unsure," Diana said. She glanced down at her gloves. "I suppose it will depend upon my uncle. I am afraid this event may preclude Kitty from having any sort of a season until the scandal dies down."

It appeared Diana was aware of the happenings in the library, but not of the promise.

"Oh, there shall be no scandal." Sybil shared a secretive smile with Eliza. "She is free to go about ensnaring other men to her heart's content." The flippant tone might have been a bit much, but Miss Cattering's actions had landed her firmly in Sybil's black books.

She still could not rid herself of the fear she'd experienced when she thought Nicholas might be forced to marry another. It was in that moment that Sybil knew if there was to be a Lady Penbrose, it must be her. It had to be her! She could not bear to see Nicholas married to anyone else.

Did Nicholas feel the same about her? They had made great strides in building back their friendship. There had been sparks of attraction and desire between them, at least on her side. Was it enough?

"Lord Penbrose has agreed that excuses shall be made for your family," Eliza said, pulling Sybil from her own thoughts. "He will tell everyone you are needed at home and Lord Brock must leave as soon as possible. None of us who witnessed the incident shall speak of it to anyone, I assure you."

Diana looked unconvinced, but the approach of her uncle and cousin silenced any further discussion. Giving both Sybil and Eliza brief hugs, she followed her sour family members out to the waiting conveyance.

"I do hope she will be all right," Sybil said to Eliza as they waved at the departing carriage.

"As do I," Eliza agreed.

Turning to enter the house, Sybil was surprised to see Nicholas standing not three paces from them.

"Miss Greenwald," he said, bowing to her, "might I escort you on a walk about the gardens? I know it has been your habit to take a turn there after your ride every morning, and I feel personally responsible for denying you Miss Diana's company."

Diana had not been her only companion on these walks, but when she turned to Eliza, she was not there. Eliza peered over her shoulder from the front steps and cast Sybil a sly smile. Apparently, she had been abandoned for the morning.

She looked back at Nicholas. "It is not your fault. The situation could not be helped."

"Nevertheless, I would be honored if you would join me."

He offered his arm and they made their way toward the gardens. Awkward silence reigned between them for the first few minutes as they strolled among the flowers and bushes. Finally, Nicholas broke the tension.

"I want to thank you most profusely for coming to my rescue yesterday. If you and Miss Bawden had not been there, I probably would have been met with pistols at dawn."

"You would have dueled over Miss Cattering's honor?"

"No, I would have dueled over mine," he said with a smirk.

Sybil smiled at his wit. Truly, it had been *his* honor at stake, not Miss Cattering's, for what honor could a woman who shamelessly threw herself at a man hold?

"I am honored, then, to have been able to aid you in keeping your honor intact," she said.

He smiled down at her, and their conversation turned to lighter topics as they spoke of the garden, the upcoming ball, and the house party as a whole. When Nicholas brought up her father and Lady Evelyn, however, she felt the small jab of pain that always accompanied the subject. Nicholas, it seemed, had observed the budding relationship long before she had even been aware of it.

"Is it unreasonable of me to feel hurt?" she asked. "I know it is not my place to dictate what my father will or will not do, but I feel so much pain at seeing someone step into my mother's place so soon after her passing."

"No, I do not believe it is unreasonable. Your entire view of the world has always had your mother and father as the foundation. When one of those is removed, it throws everything you have ever known off kilter."

"Exactly. I feel like what I thought I knew is now somehow, well, wobbly, like a stool missing a leg. Papa and I could still balance, but it took so much more effort."

"I like the imagery in that. My world tilted when my father died, and for a time, I thought I would fall. Perhaps in the case of your father and my aunt, the addition will add stability in time, but it will be uncomfortable at first because one leg does not match the others. I think eventually, however, each of you will lengthen or shorten until the stool is stable again." Nicholas cast her a hopeful smile.

She tried to smile back, but it felt forced. "I suppose everything will just take time to get used to."

"Indeed."

A flicker of sunlight bounced between the leaves of a nearby tree as they wandered in silence for a spell. Nicholas seemed lost in his thoughts. Sybil doubted they were pleasant ones, if his stern face was any indication. Should she ask after his thoughts, or would that be too presumptions? Eventually, curiosity got the better of her.

"Is everything all right?"

Nicholas's face cleared as he looked down at her. "Other than being nearly cornered into an unwanted marriage?" He teased.

Sybil gave a short laugh. "Other than that, I mean."

Nicholas sighed. "Penbrose accounts have seen a significant amount of money go missing."

"Someone is stealing from you?"

"Not of late, but in the past. I am in the process of putting things to rights."

"You are trying to catch the culprits?" The thought of illegal activities made her nervous. Did he know who the thieves were? Was there any danger?

"Yes, I am, however, I did not bring you on a lovely walk only to discuss Penbrose estate problems."

"I do not mind," she countered, hoping for more details.

"I know, but we can leave the subject of thieves for another time."

Sybil was a little flustered that he could reveal such important information and then brush it aside so quickly.

Stopping at a bench situated below a big poplar tree, he indicated they should sit. Sybil sat upon the stone structure leaving ample room. To her surprise, Nicholas sat very close, their legs fairly touching through her skirts. The headiness of his nearness caused her to completely forget the discomfort of moments before.

"I have enjoyed having you here, Sybil," he said softly. "I must admit I was reluctant at first."

"Reluctant?" Her lips curved into a disbelieving smile. "Infuriated would be a more appropriate word choice."

He laughed. "That word choice more adequately suits my feelings toward my mother when I realized she had invited you without my knowledge."

"Yes, it seems we both had scheming parents, however, I am sure it was Lady Evelyn whom they both had in mind. We were just the impediments to their happiness."

"I am not sure that is completely true." He gently lifted the fingers of her right hand into his own. She watched him as he inspected her slender hand clad in cream-colored kid gloves.

"My mother seemed to think you and I needed time together to come to an understanding of what passed between us years ago in London. I'm starting to believe she was right."

His admission touched her. Nicholas was looking at her, a question in his eyes. Sybil ducked her head a moment, unsure how to proceed.

"I should not have said the things I did in London, Nicholas, especially my vow that I would never speak to you again."

"And I should not have called you selfish." He placed a gentle finger under her chin and lifting her gaze to his. "It is done, however, and I forgive you. Can you forgive me?"

"Yes." She gazed into Nicholas's eyes. "Truthfully, I forgave you that night I sang. But," she lowered her eyes to his cravat, "I cannot understand how you can so readily forgive me. I was so—"

"Let us not quarrel for the majority of blame, Sybil," he interrupted. "It is only important what we do from this moment forward. I would very much like to renew the friendship we enjoyed in London."

Nicholas's gentle touch on her face was achingly sweet, but her heart fell at his use of the word *friendship*. She was no longer satisfied with friendship. Not when her heart was near to bursting with love for him. She wanted so much more. But friendship, she supposed, was the most she could ask for. She could not beg him to love her, as he had once begged her. It would be unfair to expect him to return feelings which she had not reciprocated in their entirety two years ago. Maybe in time...

She became keenly aware of his eyes roaming her face. Tension filled the air. Locking her green eyes with Nicholas's hazel ones, she noted the moment his gaze flicked to her lips.

Friends did not look longingly as if they might kiss each other, did they? Hope fluttered up from deep within. She leaned slightly forward, letting her eyes travel briefly to Nicholas's full lips before locking her gaze back with his. She saw the moment he recognized her acceptance, and he began leaning in. She closed her eyes, and her heart leapt into a gallop anticipating the contact. His hand on her cheek slowly slid to the back of her neck, cradling her head. The smell of cinnamon wafted on the breeze. She inhaled deeply. A frisson of awareness raced along her skin and her lips tingled with anticipated of his touch.

The clearing of a throat made her jerk back, her eyes flying wide open as she looked at Lord Caraway, who stood not ten paces from where they sat. His eyes sparkled and his mouth quirked into an all-knowing grin. The petite woman at his side was new to the party, and she could only surmise it was Lady Agatha. She, too, had a smirk upon her lips. It would seem she was of the same humor as her betrothed.

"Penbrose," Lord Caraway said as Sybil and Nicholas rose, "I am come to introduce you to my intended, Lady Agatha Easton, daughter of his grace, the Duke of Lundry. And this, my dear, is Lord Nicholas Fairchild, Earl of Penbrose."

Nicholas bowed to Lady Agatha, and she offered a brief curtsy in return. Proper introductions were then completed between Sybil and Lady Agatha, before Lord Caraway turned to Nicholas. "I am also come to tell you that the magistrate has returned, and he awaits you in your study."

"I had not expected him so soon." Surprise was evident on Nicholas's face as he set them all in motion toward the house. "I am glad, however. The sooner the better."

Disappointment landed hard in Sybil's gut, but she supposed she could not keep Nicholas any longer from his business. As her mind replayed the moment when she was sure he was going to kiss her, a warmth filled her chest. He still felt something for her, he must.

# Chapter Thirty-Four

A missive had come earlier in the day from the dressmaker. Sybil's dresses were done ahead of schedule. She had been surprised the dressmaker had not simply sent them over until Porter had happily offered to fetch the new gowns.

Aida began braiding another section of her hair, and Sybil smiled to herself. It would seem the dressmaker was in league with the young lovers. She had to admit she was too since she had willingly given Porter a few hours off to retrieve the items.

Porter's admission of long held feelings and a secret correspondence were enough for even the coldest heart to melt. If all went well, it would mean Sybil would need to find herself a new lady's maid.

"Why the sad face, miss? Do you not like the style?" Aida asked.

"Oh, no, Aida. It is lovely. Please do not mind me. I just have a lot on my mind."

Aida nodded in acceptance and continued working. The usually chatty girl had been far too quiet since Miss Cattering's assault.

"How about you, Aida? Are you well?"

Aida's face fell and tears gathered in her eyes.

"Aida?" Sybil asked in concern, but the girl turned away, covertly wiping at her face.

"It's nothing, miss," she said before sniffling.

"Aida, you can tell me. I promise I will keep your confidences."

"It's just that... well... I am not used to being so mistreated. I suppose because my family worked for Mr. Jonas Fairchild, and me for Lord Penbrose... well, I just haven't seen so many mean people. Not that I haven't seen any, but not like my mah and dah. Not like Nana Aba. They saw awful things. I've been thinking about them... and about me. I just can't understand why people are so mean."

Tears welled up in Sybil's own eyes. "I do not know, Aida. I do not understand it either." Standing from the bench, she reached out and touched the girl on the shoulder. "You are a wonderful person, Aida, and a fine maid. I know it does not change what has happened to you and the cruelty you have suffered. But I hope you know there are people who do see you for the good person you are."

Aida spun about and buried her head in Sybil's shoulder, tears falling afresh. She wrapped her arms about the girl and held her until her weeping calmed.

She would be sporting tears stains on her shoulder once again, she thought with a wry smile. A knock sounded at the door, and Porter entered with a wide smile, carrying several packages.

Aida stepped back, wiping her nose on her sleeve. "Sorry, miss," she said quietly, "but thank you."

"It is no matter, Aida," Sybil responded.

"I am sorry. Do you need a moment?" The smile fell from Porter's face.

"No, I'm fine," Aida said, picking up the brush.

"How was your trip into town?" Sybil asked as she took up her seat before the mirror again.

Porter giggled. Porter *giggled!* She never giggled like a schoolgirl.

"Are you well, Porter?"

She giggled again. "I am well, Miss Sybil. A little rainstorm came up and I got a bit damp on my way into town, but I was able to dry myself at the mercantile." Her cheeks turned rosy.

"Ah, yes, the mercantile. And how was that fine establishment?" Sybil asked with a bit of cheek.

"Well, it had to close due to a deluge of rain that came on just after I stepped inside with the other maid, Meg. We were quite stuck for nearly an hour until things lightened up."

"Oh, that must have been awful," Sybil said dryly.

Porter laughed before responding in kind. "I endured it the best I could."

Both Aida and Sybil laughed.

Noticing the wet spot on the peach dress Sybil wore, Porter asked, "would you like a shawl to cover that up... again?"

"Again?" Aida asked.

"It seems my shoulder has become a regular gatherer of tears between you, Porter, and Diana," Sybil quipped.

Aida smiled. "Well, it does a fine job."

"It does, at that." Porter removed Sybil's silver shawl from the wardrobe and brought it to her.

Mischief danced in Aida's eyes. "I'm not sure what you had to cry about, Miss Porter, but from the smile on your face, it wasn't this beau I've been hearing of."

"Nosy servants need to learn not to gossip," Porter paraphrased Sybil's words.

"Well, they are not far from the truth," Sybil interjected. "In fact, I would not be surprised if he made you an offer."

Porter's face flamed, and she ducked her head. "He has already offered for me," she admitted quietly.

"Already?" Sybil exclaimed.

"This very afternoon." Porter still looked at the ground.

"And you accepted him, I hope?"

Porter's eyes slowly rose to hers. "I asked for time to think on it. I did not want to leave you without a lady's maid, not when we have been together so long."

Tears welled up in Sybil's eyes. That Maria Porter would possibly put aside her own happiness just to see to hers made Sybil realize what a cherished gift she had been to her all these years.

"I am sorry, miss. I did not mean to make you cry."

"Please call me Sybil, Porter. I do not know why I have not asked you to do so sooner. You most assuredly must accept him. I would not have it any other way. You deserve happiness, Por—no, Maria, for you are one of the most selfless people I know."

Maria's eyes filled with tears as well. "Thank you, Sybil," she said quietly. "It is the dearest wish of my heart to have a home of my own."

Sybil pulled her maid into a full embrace. "And so you shall. I insist you take another half-day tomorrow morning to give that poor man your answer. He is probably sick with worry over what your response might be."

Maria laughed through her tears. "Thank you, miss... Sybil. I believe I shall."

"Apparently, we have all turned into a dreadful set of watering pots," Aida said, wiping a happy tear from her eye.

Leave it to Aida to make them all laugh while their eyes were full of tears.

Nicholas returned just in time to hurriedly dress for dinner. The afternoon meeting had gone far better than he had hoped. Tomorrow the parties in question would meet in the library. If all went well, they would be joined by the magistrate, the house bailiff, and a few constables. Nicholas hoped the older men were up to the task.

They would wait until his mother gathered the rest of the party in the ballroom to observe the preparations for Saturday's ball. The only thing to do now was wait.

Nicholas hated waiting. How was he to act normal?

At dinner he tried to appear unaffected, but when Caroline had to repeat herself more than once, he knew he was not doing a very good job. Sybil seemed to notice and cast him a curious look. He could only briefly raise a shoulder in reply. She gave him a reassuring smile, which bolstered his efforts.

During after dinner port, Edward had to call his attention back to their conversation several times.

"What is the matter with you this evening, Penbrose?" Uncle Fairchild asked. "Your mind seems to be miles away."

At his uncle's assertion, fear like lightning shot through Nicholas's body. Had anyone else noticed his distraction? Did they suspect?

"I know where his mind has been," Lord Ansley teased from his end of the table, "and I believe a head of dark brown hair and a pair of pretty green eyes have something to do with it."

"I believe you are right," John agreed from where he sat, not even having filled his glass of port. Part of their agreement involved John decreasing his alcohol consumption in order to have a clearer mind for business. Nicholas was proud of his cousin. He had held true to every stipulation Nicholas had put upon him the last several days and would prove to be a good business partner if he continued on this way.

"I cannot say as I blame him," John continued, "for the miss is just as interesting as she is beautiful."

Mr. Greenwald smiled knowingly behind his glass, eyeing Nicholas with some interest. Nicholas locked eyes with him but said nothing allowing the man to take his measure before attending to the next jesting comment.

"How long before Penbrose House can expect a countess, do you think?" This question came from his cousin Tom. His lips were pulled into a sneer, but he quickly covered it with a sip of port from his glass.

"I think it time we join the ladies, gentlemen," Nicholas said.

"It must be soon," Lord Ansley quipped, "if he is so eager to join the ladies... again." A few of the men chuckled but rose reluctantly to follow Nicholas into the drawing room.

Cards had again been called for, and while Nicholas did not mind the pastime, he was too nervous to sit still for long. After a round of whist, Sybil caught his eye and indicated with a slight movement of her head toward the windows looking out over the back gardens.

"Are you well?" she asked when he joined her to gaze outside at the waning mid-summer evening.

"I have much on my mind."

"Am I to blame?" Concern creased her brow.

"No." He turned to her in surprise. Taking the fingers of her right hand covertly in his left, he peered into her eyes and noticed the contrast of her dark hair against her cream-colored skin. "It is only..." he stopped himself. What could he say? "Please just be careful during the next few days."

Her eyes lit with understanding. "You are asking me to be on my guard because something is going to happen."

"Yes," he said simply.

"I will do my best, Nicholas."

His name on her lips felt like a caress, and he would have loved to stay and enjoy it, but the Williams sisters demanded his attention for a game of loo. He, unfortunately, had no excuse to give them, so he excused himself. The prospect of cards with the Williams sisters was daunting, but somehow the few quiet moments by the window with Sybil had completely calmed his nerves.

Sybil found herself seated in a quiet conversation with Eliza, Mr. Martin, Lord Caraway, and Nicholas, as the card tables were gathered up. The subjects of male verses female intellect had drawn Eliza from her self-imposed silence to converse more than usual. The topic was one Sybil knew Eliza was passionate about, but the sparse occupants of the room also played into Eliza's openness— her father and stepmother having already excused themselves for the evening.

The lateness of the hour began to wear upon Sybil, making it hard to cover her reoccurring yawns. Noticing her fatigue, Nicholas suggested they all turn in for the night. Everyone agreed, and the five made their way to the door, leaving only Lady Julia, Lady Evelyn, and Sybil's father in quiet conversation near the evening fire.

In the hall, Nicholas stopped. Sybil, with her hand upon his elbow, was forced to stop as well. The other two men made their way up the stairs toward the guest rooms, but Eliza only moved down the hall, probably sensing Sybil and Nicholas hoped for a moment of privacy.

"I am truly sorry I had to cut our walk short this morning," he said. He gazed down on her, his hazel eyes soft with regret.

"You need not apologize. I understand estates take a fair amount of work to run smoothly, and you have several. While I missed your company the rest of the day, I do not hold any resentment for your need to attend to business."

"You missed me?" he said, lifting his eyebrows comically in surprise before a cheeky grin spread over his far too handsome face.

To Sybil's own amazement, she took a step forward and said quietly but boldly, "I always miss you when you are gone."

The playfulness immediately fell from his countenance, and she saw him swallow. Unsure whether she had done the right thing by being so bold, she searched his face, noting the rigidity of his sharp jaw and the way his dark brows furrowed.

Was he scared by her forward admission? Had he read her meaning correctly? Did he know that even after their harsh words she had missed him almost immediately after he'd abruptly left London two years ago?

Heat filled her chest as the silence stretched between them. Dropping her eyes to the floor, she began composing how she might adequately bid him goodnight when a gloved finger touched her chin and slowly pulled her head up.

"I am honored, Sybil, that you would be so honest with me." The sincerity in his eyes burrowed into her heart and her embarrassment slipped away. "I have missed you, as well." He slowly rubbed his thumb along her cheek while his other fingers still cupped her chin.

She leaned into his thumb and closed her eyes, relishing his touch. To her surprise, warm soft lips touched her own. Her eyes flew open only a moment before she relaxed into the light contact and pressed her lips more firmly to his. The kiss was brief and achingly gentle, but the sensation traveled straight to her soul and, like a healing balm, soothed the wounds of years gone by.

Nicholas pulled away and she gazed into his eyes. A small smile played upon his lips, and his head again began to dip in her direction.

Eliza chose that moment to remind them she was still there by lightly clearing her throat. Nicholas cast a long-suffering look her way, and Sybil could not help but giggle at the slight theatrics. Stepping back, he took her hand in his, and after wishing her a good evening, briefly kissed her gloved fingers, then headed in the direction of the library.

The triumph on Eliza's face along with an added eyebrow wiggle was almost enough to make Sybil laugh out loud.

They made their way up the stairs and to their rooms in silence, Eliza seeming to sense Sybil's need to bask in the moment.

At the door of Sybil's room, Eliza turned and smiled. "I suppose I should wish you good night, Lady Penbrose," she said with another eyebrow wiggle.

"Hush, Eliza."

Eliza only giggled as she made her way to her own bedchamber.

# Chapter Thirty-Five

Rain trickled down the window as Sybil sat in the library with Eliza, an open book between them.

"This is the law," Eliza said, "the one that outlawed the slave trade over the Atlantic in 1807."

Sybil looked up at her friend. "That was the one Nicholas's father supported."

"Nicholas?"

"Lord Penbrose." She smiled to herself.

"Mm-hmm," Eliza said with a smirk.

"Pardon me," a footman said from the library door, "but Lady Julia has requested all guests join her in the ballroom."

"Go ahead, Eliza," she said. "I need to re-shelve the book, and I want to retrieve *Pride and Prejudice* for a rereading. I shall run it to my room and then meet you in the ballroom."

"Are you sure? I could wait for you."

"I am sure. There is no need for both of us to be late," Sybil said with a smile.

"Very well." Eliza left the room to join the other ladies and gentlemen in the ballroom.

Sybil placed the book upon the shelf by the desk, then turned to the books on the back wall where she knew the novels to be stored. The sound of the door clicking shut startled her. Eliza had left it open.

Turning around, Mr. Tom Fairchild stood several feet away, a polite smile upon his face.

"Oh! Mr. Fairchild, you surprised me," she said, a hand over her heart.

"I hope, Miss Greenwald, it is a pleasant surprise." His tone made Sybil's senses jump to attention. Her eyes flitted to the closed door behind the gentleman, and Diana's story flew to the forefront of her thoughts.

She tried to dismiss it. After all, Mr. Fairchild had shown her no marked deference. He was probably just here to return a book he had borrowed. Looking down at his hands, she saw they were empty. She searched her mind for a polite way to answer his question.

"It is always nice to see you," she finally said. "Unfortunately, I am expected in the ballroom to help with the decorations, so I must be on my way." She walked as calmly as possible toward the door. "I hope you are able to find what you have come to the library for. Good day."

Mr. Fairchild's hand shot out and grasped her forearm before she was able to pass by him. With a pleading smile upon his face, he said, "Oh, do stay for a moment, Miss Greenwald. I had hoped to speak with you on something of great importance."

The eerie foreboding she had first sensed about him returned, and while she was sure Mr. Fairchild's smile was supposed to be charming, at the moment it looked almost predatory.

"I am sorry, Mr. Fairchild, perhaps another time. I really am needed in the ballroom."

His grip only tightened, the false civility dropping entirely from his expression. "I think not," he said coldly. The change in demeanor was so swift that Sybil would not have believed a moment before he had appeared so amiable.

Trying to gather her courage, she straightened her posture to her full height. "Unhand me, sir."

"My, but you do have pluck." He squeezed her arm. "I do like women with a bit of spirit."

She stepped back, then thinking better of it, stepped toward him. It caught him off guard and his eyes widened, but then the smile on his face grew and his grip loosened. Taking advantage of the moment, she quickly moved back again, yanking her arm from his grasp.

Mr. Fairchild was faster than her, though, taking a quick step in front of her so she could not advance any further toward the door. Pulling back out of his reach, she made a quick perusal of the room for an alternative way around him.

"Miss Greenwald," he said, slowly advancing toward her. She stepped backwards, trying to stay out of his grasp. "I would like to extend you an offer of marriage."

Sybil stopped her backward movement, startled by his words. "What?"

Mr. Fairchild took advantage of her surprise and lunged forward, grabbing hold of her wrists which she had inadvertently thrown up to ward off his attack. Sybil stumbled back with the force of the pressure he exerted, the back of her head along with her lower back connecting with the shelves behind her. Pain shot up her back and throughout her head. She took a moment to right herself.

Mr. Fairchild only pressed himself harder against her, trapping her arms and his hands between them both. Standing only a few inches taller, he peered almost directly into her face, his far stronger body stopping her forward escape.

"Stop it, Mr. Fairchild," Sybil growled. The pain no longer distracted her but fueled her anger. Blood pulsed through her veins as her muscles tensed under his grip. Every part of her filled with an intense energy. She wanted to punch him or claw his eyes out.

"Unhand me. Now!" she demanded.

"Or what?" Sheer enjoyment danced in his muddy blue eyes. Sybil struggled against him, trying in vain to free herself. She could smell onion and spirits upon his disgusting hot breath. Doing the only thing she could think of, she spat in his face.

One hand let go as he reached up to wipe the spit away. She took the opportunity to lean hard to the side, pulling her body out from under his weight. Unfortunately, he maintained enough wherewithal to keep hold of her other wrist, yanking her backward when she tried to run for the door.

Sybil stumbled, caught herself and leaned hard against his grasp. To her horror, his other hand came up to connect with the side of her face. The force of the contact caused her head to whip around, banging her cheek into the side of the nearby shelves.

Yanking her again before she caught her wits, Mr. Fairchild trapped her body between him and the wall next to the bookcase, the little corner being the only space in the room that could have possibly trapped her so completely.

Sybil's hands were wedged against his chest, his left arm wrapped about her waist. His right hand held the back of her neck painfully, hair caught between his fingers.

"Why are you doing this?" she hissed, pain radiating all over her body.

"Is it not obvious, Miss Greenwald? I have asked you to marry me, and you are resisting."

Sybil did not know why, but she let out a bark of sardonic laughter. "And this is how you hope to convince me?"

"You will agree to marry me, Sybil."

"You do not have permission to use my Christian name, sir."

"I shall use far more than that, Miss Sybil Greenwald." He pressed his body even harder upon hers. She struggled against the pressure, feeling panic rise up her chest and into her throat.

"Why me?" she said through clenched teeth. "Why not a London lady? One with title and money. I am sure you could ruin one of them into marrying you."

"Because none of them will get me both a fortune and revenge," he said, an edge of steel to his voice.

Sybil tried to process his words. How had he learned of her fortune? Then her mind raced forward through the rest of his statement.

"Revenge?" she squeaked out. Her thoughts rushed to Nicholas.

"Yes. My cousin stole everything that was important to me when he claimed the earldom, and now I shall return the favor."

"My father will never let you marry me."

"He will have to when I am done with you, for no one else will want you."

"No." Sybil's voice shook on the whispered word. Tears pricked the back of her eyes as his meaning sunk in.

"Yes. I cannot wait to see the devastation on Nicholas's face when he realizes the woman he loves belongs to me. It will be agony. A lifetime of agony to repay him for the pain he has caused me."

A scream gathered in her throat and burst forth before she even realized what she was doing.

Mr. Fairchild's hand clapped over her mouth, covering her nose in the process. Sybil tried to take a breath, but to no avail. Shifting her body as much as possible, she tried to kick at him, but she was trapped.

Sparks of light dotted the edge of her vision. A prayer screamed up from the depths of her heart to the heavens before blackness engulfed her.

*Dear God, save me!*

Nicholas entered the library, Lord Ansley at his side. His uncle and Mr. Williams followed close behind with Mr. Martin bringing up the rear. With Bradley and Anthony's absence, they had needed more men, and, thankfully, Ansley and Martin had been more than willing to help capture his uncle and cousin in their deceit.

In a stroke of luck, Tom had made it easy on them, excusing himself to the library not fifteen minutes ago.

Caraway had given the signal before leaving to attend to 'personal matters.' If all went well, it would be a quiet arrest, and none of the guests would be aware of the upheaval in the house.

"What the devil!" Ansley exclaimed from beside him. Nicholas, who had been subtly trying to reassure himself that his uncle still followed behind, swung his gaze around. To his horror, Tom stood near the back of the library, his arms wrapped around a woman in an amorous embrace.

Tom pulled his mouth away from the woman's and she sagged against him, probably in embarrassment at being caught.

"What is all this about, Tom?" his uncle exclaimed from behind him, but the words sounded odd. Nicholas had the strange impression of an actor on a stage, as if the words were rehearsed.

"It looks as if we have been found out, my love," Tom said, glancing at the gathering of gentleman.

The woman in his arms did not move. *Strange.*

Her face was turned away from him, but something about her was familiar. Tom had not necessarily shown a deference to any young lady that he knew of, even though several had definitely shown interest in him. Nicholas's eyes widened. He knew that cream-colored gown, jade comb, and especially those dark tresses.

"I sure hope you plan on marrying the poor girl after such a display," Uncle Fairchild said loudly, "for she is fairly ruined for anyone else."

Nicholas's heart leapt into his throat, a loud rushing sound filling his ears. His feet froze to the floor. Something was wrong. Sybil would never submit to such treatment, not from Tom. She would fight, and fight hard. Why was she being so submissive?

"Let her go, Tom," Nicholas said, a quiet threat in his voice.

"I think not. Miss Greenwald is perfectly comfortable where she is. Besides, your presence is upsetting her. I think it best you leave so we can continue our conversation about our future in private." Turning to his father, he said, "I fully intend on making Miss Greenwald my wife, Father. I have already asked her."

"You will do no such thing!" Nicholas shouted. "Unhand her!"

Sybil didn't even stir an inch. Something was definitely wrong. If she truly desired to marry Tom, she would say so herself, not lie mutely against his chest.

"I think not," Tom said, a sneer upon his lips. "We're perfectly situated as we are."

Nicholas's control snapped, and he rushed forward attempting to reach for Sybil, but his cousin spun her away from his grasp. The momentum of the action caused her head to loll back before falling again on Tom's chest.

The blood Nicholas saw upon her lips infuriated him. "What have you done to her?" He roared, lunging for Sybil at the same moment Mr. Martin and Ansley flanked Tom upon either side, latching onto his arms.

The struggle was over quickly as the other two gentleman pulled Tom's arms from around Sybil. Nicholas held her firmly as her unconscious body fell against him.

Gently, he laid her upon the floor, inspecting her face as he cradled her head in his arms. A bruise was forming on her left cheek, and blood lined her lips.

Sound from the door alerted him to the presence of other guests. So much for gathering everyone in the ballroom.

Mr. Greenwald pushed through the crowd and rushed to where Nicholas knelt on the floor with Sybil. His hand came up to rest on her forehead and then her cheek. Sybil's breath came out relaxed and even.

"I believe she has only swooned," Nicholas said to him in hushed tones. Mr. Greenwald nodded his agreement, then turned to the room at large.

"Who the devil has done this to my daughter?" he growled.

"I am sure it was only an accident," Uncle Fairchild said placatingly. "The boy has every intention of marrying her, so you need not worry about her reputation."

"The devil he will!" Mr. Greenwald roared. He glared at Tom who was still being restrained. "I will meet you with pistols at dawn before I ever let a scoundrel such as yourself marry my only child."

"Dueling is illegal, Mr. Greenwald," Uncle Fairchild said in a condescending tone. Oh, the irony of that statement. So was embezzlement, blackmail, and extortion, but that had not stopped him from doing all of them over the last decade.

"I am sure we can come to some sort of agreement, sir," he continued placidly.

Mr. Greenwald stalked over to the man, fists clenched. "There is no agreement that could ever be reached that would cause me to agree to my daughter marrying a veritable brute."

"But Mr. Greenwald," Mr. Williams said, "we saw her locked in an amorous embrace with Mr. Tom Fairchild. Her reputation is fairly in tatters."

"Not of her own free will, as you most obviously can see." Mr. Greenwald stepped menacingly toward the smaller gentleman. Mr. Williams took his cue, clamped his mouth shut, and stepped back, not willing to receive a fist from the furious father.

"But who would want her now?" Uncle Fairchild asked, as if Sybil had suddenly become tainted goods, not worthy of any other man's attentions. "She must marry my son for her own good."

Mr. Greenwald raised his arms as if he was ready to pummel the man for his impertinent suggestion. Nicholas knew he had to do something to stop this madness.

"Tom cannot marry Miss Greenwald," he said loudly, drawing the attention of the room.

"Why not?" Tom spat out, still firmly in Ainsley and Martin's grasp.

The room went silent with Nicholas's next words.

"Because I have already offered for her."

# Chapter Thirty-Six

Sybil tried to reach through the blackness to the voices arguing all around her. Somehow, she knew she was the subject, but try as she might, she could not open her eyes. Her father's angry voice registered in her mind. *Papa!* She tried to call out to him, hoping he would save her. Why did she need to be saved? She couldn't remember, but the sense of urgency was screaming from deep inside her soul.

Someone declared her ruined and insisted she marry his son. No! Her mind protested, giving her strength to fight through the oppressive darkness.

Eyes flying wide open, her gaze landed on Nicholas's face.

"Tom cannot marry Miss Greenwald," his calm voice declared.

"Why not?" an angry voice said from somewhere across the room.

"Because I have already offered for her."

Murmurs of confusion filled the room, but in the chaos, Nicholas's eyes found hers. They momentarily widened in surprise, then softened. Those earth-toned eyes continued to stare directly into hers, lighting a blaze in her heart that she knew would never extinguish. The look, the moment, was almost perfect—until her memories assailed her.

Had she been compromised? What had happened after the blackness enfolded her? Had Mr. Fairchild...? Sybil could not finish the thought. She took stock of her faculties. Other than the pain in her lower back, face, and head, nothing else felt different.

"How do you feel?" Nicholas asked quietly.

Before she could respond, however, her father whirled around and rushed to her side.

"You are awake, my dear. Are you well?"

Mr. Tom Fairchild's petulant voice rose above the questions. "You are lying. I do not believe you have offered for her at all, Nicholas."

Sybil could see her father shoot a glare at the younger man. "Yes, he has." Then locking gazes with Nicholas, he nodded.

What was going on? In her memory, Nicholas had made no such offer. Unless...

A disturbance at the door drew both men's attention. She turned her aching head ever so slightly to see Lord Caraway and Mr. John Fairchild push their way through the throng.

Looking back at her father, wrinkles formed on his brow as he observed the gathered throng.

"We need to get her out of here, Penbrose. Her reputation has suffered enough," he insisted.

Nicholas nodded in agreement, then examined the newcomers. "John. I believe my mother wished to show our guests her progress in the ballroom. Would you be so kind as to show them the way?"

The slender blond-haired man nodded and turned to the group at large. "I am sure Lady Julia is quite distressed at our tardiness. Shall we join the others?"

A few grumbles met his words, but the crowd began to depart, except for the three men at the back.

"What is going on here?" The elder Mr. Fairchild demanded from a few paces away. "Why is Mr. Morris here, and who are these other two fellows? I thought we were here to discuss business, not entertain the rabble."

The castigating expression the older man directed toward Nicholas was openly accusatory. Mr. Fairchild appeared confident, but the nervous way he spun the ring upon his right-hand finger suggested otherwise.

Unease pervaded in the room. Something was off about this situation, but Sybil could not quite place it.

The three men stepped in, and the last man shut the door. Two of the men were not dressed as the rest of the party but appeared to be common laborers. The third man looked the part of a gentleman, if a little less finely attired.

"Can you sit up?" Nicholas asked, tension evident in the way his eyes pinched at the corners.

"I believe so." She pulled her body up at the same time he supported her upper back. "In fact, if you will help me, I believe I can stand."

Tucking her legs to the side and arranging her skirt so she would not get tangled, Sybil was about to rise when another commotion broke out.

Mr. Tom Fairchild struggled fiercely against the two men holding him and Mr. Fairchild backed up until he almost touched the bookshelves.

"What is going on?" she heard her father ask Nicholas.

Nicholas let go of her and rose to his feet. "Protect your daughter, Mr. Greenwald," he said ominously before stepping past them both.

"It has been brought to my attention, Mr. Fairchild," one of the men near the door said after Mr. Tom Fairchild had been subdued, "that you have been stealing money from your father's estate for nigh unto a decade."

"That is a weighty accusation, Mr. Morris," Mr. Fairchild responded. His hands shook slightly as he continued to spin the gold ring upon his finger. "I do not believe there is any proof of such ridiculous rumors, and I am sorry my nephew would denigrate himself to make such a claim. You see, he is still upset that I questioned his legitimacy to the earldom, but any man would under such circumstances, wouldn't you agree?"

Sybil stared wide-eyed at him. Mr. Fairchild had been the one to steal from Nicholas? She could hardly believe it. Why would a man of wealth and consequence need to turn to thievery?

The smile of camaraderie Mr. Fairchild directed toward Mr. Morris seemed forced, but Mr. Morris relaxed his stance slightly. Sybil remembered Nicholas saying his uncle could be polite and charming when he chose to be, and with money and good looks, he had won his way into some of the best of Society. His silky words, however, reminded her of a snake as it slithered its way through the grass, hoping no one would notice its actual target.

"Aye," Mr. Morris said, "I think any man would question, but that is neither here nor there, for it is not Lord Penbrose's word on which I am relying."

"And what, pray tell, could anyone have against me?"

"The ledgers of Penbrose House. The words of a blackmailed, threatened, and abused steward, as well of those of your own son."

Mr. Fairchild's fierce gaze shot to Mr. Tom Fairchild, who only stared back at him in surprise. He gave his father an almost imperceptible shake of his head, then smoothed his facial expression into bored unconcern.

"Not that retch of a man." Mr. Morris indicated Sybil's attacker with a sweep of his hand. "The other one. The one who seems to have a modicum of morals and a decent backbone, no thanks to you or your father."

Mr. Fairchild's eyes narrowed into slits as he dropped his hands to his sides, clenching and unclenching the fingers that held his gold ring. "Ledgers can be falsified, servants are liars, and John is nothing but a sniveling drunk who has a penchant for the gaming tables."

"Yes," Mr. Morris said, "but the secondary bank account opened under Penbrose estates, which was used to receive regular deposits from the original account and kept completely secret from everyone but you, Mr. Gates, and your father's solicitor, or rather his apprentice, was not fabricated and does not lie. The ledgers do, however, back up the findings in the secondary account."

Mr. Tom Fairchild took that moment to leap toward the door, but he did not make it more than two steps before Lord Caraway and Mr. Martin subdued him again.

Mr. Fairchild glared at his oldest son. It would seem the younger man was not as good at remaining calm under pressure as his sire.

Things were coming together in Sybil's mind. Mr. Morris must be the squire, or perhaps a magistrate.

Mr. Morris eyed Tom a moment with unconcealed loathing. "Is there something you wish to say, young man? Your position is even more dire than your father's. You realize that forcing yourself upon a woman is punishable by death under the law."

Mr. Tom Fairchild's eyes widened, and he stammered. "She was..." A glare from the magistrate stopped his sentence. "That is," he tried again, "I did not..." He swallowed hard before continuing. "The lady's virtue is still intact."

"That does not change your past, and I have it on good authority that you have forced yourself on women before. So would you like to enlighten us any further on you and your father's dealings?"

Tom's mouth became a veritable floodgate. "He has been using the servants for years to line his pockets with Penbrose House coffers. A cook, an undergardener, the steward, anyone he could pay off or blackmail—"

Uncle Fairchild stepped forward, cutting off anything more Tom might say. "This is preposterous. Why would I steal from my own estate? I was to inherit, if you recall. Mr. Gates is the actual thief, and he has already been charged. He is at this very moment in Newgate prison waiting for transport."

Nicholas spoke up from several steps away. "Actually, it is thanks to Mr. Gates that we have any and all of these records. He was nothing if not thorough in keeping good accounts."

Mr. Fairchild cast him a look so filled with ire, Sybil shivered at the sight.

"As a further legal education, which your family seems to be in sore need of," Mr. Morris said dryly, "it is also illegal to threaten a man's life and livelihood for your own personal gain, *Mr. Fairchild.*"

Noise of a scuffle near the door pulled the attention off Nicholas's uncle. Apparently, while everyone's attention had been focused on Mr. Fairchild, Mr. Williams had slowly made his way toward the door of the library. The only other person not caught unaware was the constable near the exit. His quiet escape now blocked by the burly man, Mr. Williams turned back to the room at large.

"Mr. Williams, come join us," Mr. Morris said in a congenial voice that would not fool anyone. *Where did Mr. Williams fit in all of this?*

The tense man took several steps toward the magistrate but stopped short, resting his hand upon the back of one of the wingback chairs. There was a slight tremble in the man's hand.

"I think, Lord Penbrose," Mr. Morris turned to Nicholas, "we have sufficient evidence to arrest Mr. Fairchild and Mr. Tom Fairchild. Mr. Williams should also be detained for questioning." The magistrate's words rung with finality. Something seemed to snap within the room.

Tom began kicking at the legs of the two men who held him, Mr. Williams grabbed the vase on the table next to him and lobbed it at the constable near the door, who in turn pulled out his club as his companion rushed Mr. Williams from behind.

While the other two men fought wildly with the men near them, Mr. Fairchild, hemmed in by Mr. Morris, Lord Caraway, and Nicholas, stood calmly with his hands in the pockets of his dinner jacket, a look of challenge in his eyes.

"All right, Mr. Fairchild," Mr. Morris said with authority, "how about we do this like gentleman, shall we? If you come peacefully, we can leave without causing a scene."

"And that is supposed to comfort me? With or without a scene, it will still cause a scandal, you realize." This last statement was directed at Nicholas. "It will follow you around Penbrose, perhaps for all your years. What then? Do you really want your sisters to be tainted by your actions?"

It was true, Sybil realized. They all would be implicated in this, but the alternative was far worse.

Nicholas took a step toward his uncle, but Mr. Fairchild reached inside his dinner jacket and retrieved not one but two pistols. The sound of the weapons cocking stopped the progress of all three men around him.

Fear licked at Sybil's heart before the hot anger sank in, and she scrabbled to her feet. She had not suffered through these last few years and gotten this close to happiness only to have it snatched away.

A hand grasped her upper arm, and she looked to the right to see her father shake his head imperceptibility. She glared at him, but knew he was right. What could she do against two pistols?

She could only see Nicholas's profile, the muscle in his jaw bulging as he clenched and unclenched it. One of the weapons was pointed directly at him.

"Now," Mr. Fairchild said, "Shall we do this as gentlemen? You will all kindly step aside and I shall leave you to your discussion. I, however, am quite through with the subject and no longer feel my presence is appreciated at this house party. So, if you will excuse me." He motioned for everyone to move with the guns.

Nicholas slowly backed away. Lord Caraway did the same. Mr. Morris was the only man who stood his ground, not in the least surprised by the turn of events.

"Step away from the door," Mr. Fairchild called to the constables who held Mr. Williams not five paces from the closed library door.

They started to shuffle to the side, but Mr. Fairchild shook his head. "No, come this way." Motioning with the pistol in his right hand, he pointed to a place several paces to the left of Nicholas.

As they were moving into position, Mr. Fairchild took several steps toward the door. Pivoting around, he kept his pistols trained on the group, alternating his target between each one of them as he backed toward the exit.

"What about me?" Mr. Tom Fairchild sniveled, his arms pinned to his back by Mr. Martin and Lord Ansley.

"You are no longer my problem, boy. You got yourself into this mess, get yourself out of it."

*This could not be happening*, Sybil's mind screamed as she took a step forward. Her father's grip tightened almost painfully on her arm.

Mr. Fairchild could not just calmly walk out of Penbrose House. If he left today, they would probably never find him.

"You will never convince the courts or the Prince Regent that you are the true heir if you flee the country," Nicholas said, taking a step toward his uncle's position.

A mirthless chuckle escaped Mr. Fairchild's lips. "That is because I never was. Why else would I need the money?"

"You knew?" Nicholas sputtered.

"Of course I knew," The older man sneered. "*Dear* Miss Grant, my mother's lady's maid, called me to her deathbed to share the terrible truth," sarcasm lacing his cold voice. "She always did have a soft spot for me. It seems she did not want her *poor boy* to be caught unawares."

"Then why challenge the will?"

"Because it would have appeared strange if I had not." His condescending smile sent a shiver up Sybil's spine.

Mr. Fairchild was within reach of the door. Sybil sucked in her breath when he leveled a pistol in Nicholas's direction and pulled the trigger. Nicholas dove at the same moment the pistol's blast sounded in the room.

His body jerked mid-jump and a scream ripped from her throat as her heart crashed into her ribs.

Nicholas landed with a thud on the rug beside the wingback chairs, his still form causing Sybil's eyes to fill with tears. Ice filled her limbs and she felt frozen in her place. This could not be happening. Not now. Not when they were so close. Her legs suddenly refused to hold her up and she fell to her knees. Sobs racked her body and she buried her face in her hands.

# Chapter Thirty-Seven

Searing pain shot through Nicholas's arm just before he landed on the decorative rug. Never before had he been so grateful for this rug. The small amount of cushion it provided made it easier not to flinch with his fall.

Holding completely still so as to appear dead, he hoped his uncle's need for vengeance would be relieved and he would leave the rest of the room's occupants alone. Sybil's scream and subsequent tears tore at his heart, but he needed his uncle to believe he had won.

A clang reverberated through the room. From between the legs of the chair, he saw the pistol skitter across the floor, freeing up his uncle's hand to open the door.

"I will take my leave now. Do enjoy the rest of your day," Nicholas heard him say dryly before the door swung open and his uncle's polished Hessian boots slowly backed through the opening.

In a flash, something shot out from the bottom of the door frame, and suddenly his uncle's boots were struggling for purchase. Slipping on the polished wood floors, he landed with a thud upon his back. The report of the pistol sounded at nearly the same instant Uncle Fairchild's back hit the floor.

A shower of dirt and debris fell down a moment later. Men came running from several directions in the house. Nicholas saw his bailiff fall on his uncle, shackles already in hand, clamping one around each of the stunned man's wrists before he could even gather the wherewithal to fight.

Nicholas struggled to his feet, the stinging intensifying in his right arm when he tried to place weight upon it. Finally he gained a standing position and placed a hand over his upper arm where blood soaked through his sleeve.

Movement and the glimpse of a blue dress caught his attention. Miss Bawden bent over a subdued Mr. Fairchild, her hand upon her chest.

"Oh, dear me," she said in a loud apologetic voice, "Do excuse me, Mr. Fairchild, my foot seems to have a mind of its own and often lands where it ought not." The grin upon the woman's face as she straightened, however, conveyed she was anything but apologetic.

Nicholas returned her grin. It would seem Miss Bawden's pluck had no end, for the woman simply nodded toward him and sauntered off as if she were on an evening stroll.

Something slammed into him, and arms wrapped around his middle, causing him to grimace in pain. A dark head was buried in his chest. Sybil! Nicholas had never seen a more beautiful sight.

Slowly, he wrapped his good arm about her shaking shoulders as her sobs filled the room.

"I thought you were dead," she wept into his chest.

"As you can see... or perhaps feel," he said impishly as he gave her a gentle squeeze, "I am very much alive."

A soggy chuckle shook her shoulders. Pulling back to look at her face, his heart pinched anew at the bruise upon her cheek and the blood he saw on her face. It was more than before. Had she been hurt again?

"Nicholas." she said, stepping out of his embrace as her fingers came tenderly up to touch his arm. "There is blood everywhere."

Sybil's fingers grasped his jacket sleeve and a loud ripping sound filled the room.

"Sybil!" Mr. Greenwald cautioned from across the room.

"He is hurt, Papa. Surely the rules of propriety can wait."

A second rip sounded as she pulled open his shirt sleeve. Tender fingers touched the hot skin surrounding his wound, and magically, the sting did not seem quite so terrible.

Caraway extended his handkerchief out to Sybil, and she dabbed at the wound, clearing the blood away. Nicholas could not help the smile that spread across his face. Most ladies of his acquaintance would be disgusted or perhaps even swoon at the sight of so much blood, but not Sybil. She was all business and no nonsense in this moment.

"He's lucky. It looks like it just grazed him," Caraway said, inspecting the wound with Sybil.

Sybil merely nodded, then pressed the handkerchief firmly against the open wound. The pressure caused the wound to sting anew.

Hissing through his teeth, he said, "I liked the gentle touch better."

Caraway chuckled and shook his head, a knowing grin covering his face.

Sybil narrowed her eyes at him, but the slight smile that pulled at the corner of her lips let him know she really didn't mind his teasing.

"We need to stop the bleeding," she said, pressing just a little harder.

Wilson rushed into the room at that moment, a harried-looking Mrs. Phillips close on his heels.

"Oh, dear!" The housekeeper exclaimed. "I shall have someone run for the surgeon right away."

Nicholas nodded. "Could you also assure my mother that I am well, Mrs. Phillips? I am sure she heard the gunfire and is beyond worried."

"Yes, my lord." She spun on her heels and left the bustling room.

"Wilson. Please send for my solicitor. We have business that cannot wait."

"Yes, my lord," he said with a bow and turned toward the door.

"Oh, and Wilson," Nicholas said, causing the burly man to stop and turn back. "Please send word to the kitchen that I am in need of some willow bark tea."

"Of course, my lord."

After Wilson left, Nicholas turned his attention back to Sybil, only to have it called away by Mr. Morris.

"Might I have a word with you, Lord Penbrose?" the magistrate inquired. "Privately."

Sybil glared at the man, fire in her green eyes. "Perhaps, Mr. Morris, you may not have noticed," she said through her teeth, "but Lord Penbrose has been *shot*."

Nicholas would have laughed if he had not been so enthralled with the woman in front of him. It was incredible being on the receiving end of Sybil's care and concern. The flash and fire that lit her from within was ready to go to battle on his behalf, and he loved her for it.

Placing a gentle hand over hers, he said softly, "I'll be all right, Sybil."

Her blazing eyes shot to his, and he was sure she would fight him, but some of her bravado faded the second their eyes locked. Something passed between them, a sort of unspoken agreement. She nodded, and he took up the job of applying pressure to his arm.

"You should probably have Porter see to your lip."

Sybil's fingers came up and gently probed the split. "I believe you are correct. I probably look a sight."

The magistrate paced several steps away, impatient to get on with their business. Nicholas wanted to reassure her. Wanted to tell her she was always beautiful. Wanted to hold her and soothe away her pain, but he knew the constraints they were under. Things needed to be seen to right away.

"Ride with me?" he asked quietly.

Sybil searched his eyes, and he hoped she saw what she was looking for.

"When?"

"Thursday at eight. I have things that I need to see to tonight and tomorrow, but I should be home late tomorrow evening."

She nodded slowly. "Thursday."

Then without another word, she walked to where her father hovered. Taking his proffered arm, she left without a backwards glance.

Porter dabbed lightly at the cut upon Sybil's upper lip. Her father sat upon the window seat, a look of concern upon his face.

"And that is the last thing you remember?" he asked.

"Yes," she said quietly.

"Well, my dear, it seems God heard your prayer."

"Yes, I am indeed fortunate he was listening," she said solemnly. Porter moved to remove the pins from her hair. With each tress that fell, the ache in her head lessened. "But I am not sure why. It is not as though I deserve it."

"Why do you say that?" Her father rose from his perch to stand by the dressing table.

"Because I am indeed selfish," she whispered. "Selfish and filled with bitterness. I have been angry toward God, toward you, toward everyone since Mama died."

"I am sorry, Sybil. I should never have said that to you. It was unkind of me, and, if truth be told, completely selfish on my part."

Sybil turned upon the bench to look at her father. "But it's true, Papa. I only thought of myself and how this house party would affect me. Your words helped me see that. I was so unused to hearing the word no from your lips that it fairly shook me to not get my way. It was pretentious of me to think I could simply demand we leave and you would comply."

Gently, he picked up her hand and cradled it in his own. "We are quite the pair, poppet. I was so selfish in my wants that I convinced myself this party would be good for you. I have all but ignored your comings and goings these past weeks, too caught up in my own pleasant pursuits to even recognize the danger you were in. So, if you were a bit selfish, the only person I have to blame is myself."

"I do not blame you, Papa. You have as much a right to enjoyment in life as I, and it was good for me to remember that." Sybil cupped her other hand around her father's larger one. "You were right, you know. I did need this time to resolve my past."

"And have you?" A teasing grin lit his face.

"Perhaps?" Her smile faded.

"Perhaps? I would think there is no *perhaps* about it. It seemed quite settled downstairs in the library."

"But Papa," she dropped his hands and facing forward on the bench, "I think Lord Penbrose was only acting the gentleman. I would not want to force the man into an arrangement he did not truly desire."

"If that man does not desire you, I have become both deaf and blind. His love was so clearly evident in both word and deed that no one could have been left in doubt of his affection for you."

"You believe he loves me?" Hope filled her chest.

"Without a shadow of a doubt." He laid a hand upon her shoulder.

Sybil placed her own hand upon her father's once more.

Gazing down at her hand on his, her father said, "As for God. It is my own belief that if he is our Heavenly Father, that he loves you as much as your earthly father, most likely more. And I would have come to your rescue whether you were angry with me or not. My love for you is not contingent upon yours for me, Sybil. Even if we had not spoken for years, if you called out to me for help, I would come running. If I would come to your rescue with how imperfect I am, would not a perfect Father do the same and much more?"

Her papa's words brought a sudden epiphany. All this time, she had thought she had been angry at God, but the root was far deeper. She had worried God had forgotten her. Thought he had not heard her plea to save her mother. While she still could not completely understand why Mama had to die so young, she knew that God had reached out to her today. She had not been forgotten.

A warmth spread through her heart granting her peace, a type of peace she had not felt since before her mother fell ill. It was not as if the pain of losing Mama had suddenly evaporated. But somehow, an unseen hand had reached into her heart and helped hold up the weight so she might feel a moment's relief from grief's ever-present pressure.

A small knock brought both Sybil and Mr. Greenwald's attention to the door. Porter rushed to open it, cracking the door to inquire of the person's business on the other side. Sybil was surprised to hear Lady Julia's voice.

"I will leave you to your company, my dear," her father said before bidding the other lady good day and exiting the room.

Lady Julia stepped in, motherly concern on her face. "Miss Greenwald. I hope you will forgive me. My son has just informed me of your dreadful experience, and I am come to inquire after your wellbeing, but I can see for myself you have been badly abused."

Tears pricked the corners of Sybil's eyes. It had indeed been dreadful. Terrifying, in fact, and while she had tried to keep up a mask of strength in front of her papa, she could feel it slipping with Lady Julia's concern.

When the first tear splashed onto her cheeks, Lady Julia's feet came unglued from the floor and she rushed to Sybil, wrapping the girl in her arms and guiding her to the edge of the bed. Sybil wept on Lady Julia's shoulder, for how long, she did not know.

"I am terribly sorry, Lady Julia. I have quite ruined the sleeve of your evening gown," Sybil eyed the dark wet patch she had left on Lady Julia's beautiful burgundy gown.

"Do not trouble yourself, Miss Greenwald," Lady Julia said, taking Sybil's hands in her own. "Might I call you Sybil, at least for this moment while we are alone?"

"I would like that very much."

"And you may call me Julia."

"Oh, I could not. It would feel almost disrespectful."

Lady Julia nodded her head, accepting Sybil's explanation. "One gown, Sybil, is the same as the next. It is made of lifeless materials that have no real impact upon you or me. But a person... a person is made of a mind, a heart, and a soul. And those three things are far more precious than anything I might put upon my person. I promised you I would be here so you might not be alone, and here I am."

Just when Sybil thought she had no more tears to cry, another slipped down her cheek, but this time it was one borne of appreciation. She managed a wobbly smile through her tears. "Thank you, Lady Julia."

"You are very welcome, my dear," she said, tenderly placing one hand on the side of Sybil's uninjured cheek.

"Now," she said, dropping her hand, "do you wish to join us for dinner, or would you rather a tray be sent up?"

"I do not think I am quite presentable for company, and I do not wish to cause a stir."

"I see. I will have Aba send up one of her ointments for that lip. It will aid in the healing process and make it not so painful."

"Thank you, again."

"You are most welcome," Lady Julia said with a soft smile, as she rose from the bed. "I will have a tray sent up. I hope you are able to get some much-needed rest."

# Chapter Thirty-Eight

T he trial the next morning, like that of the steward, was swift. Nicholas was grateful Mr. Morris was an honorable man. Many of England's magistrates were no better than common crooks. But Mr. Morris looked at all the evidence in front of him, acknowledged the testimonies of John and the steward, as well as those of Lords Caraway and Ansley. In the end, it was left up to Nicholas to decide the punishment he would pursue in the Assize courts at the Old Bailey in London.

His uncle and cousin could be hanged. It was rare for people of such high standing, but Uncle Fairchild's crime was so egregious that Nicholas doubted anyone would defend him.

In the end, Nicholas chose to have them transported, just as he had with the steward. The magistrate agreed to release Mr. Gates into Nicholas's custody and have Mr. Fairchild and Tom take the steward's place on the transport to Newgate prison. It could be months before their case could be heard, but they would find no leniency.

"As for repayment," the magistrate said, "Mr. Fairchild's estate shall return to the Penbrose earldom from which they were originally derived, providing restitution for the thirty thousand pounds stolen by Mr. Fairchild."

"That is preposterous!" Mr. Fairchild shouted from his seat. "Downing Way is worth far more than thirty thousand pounds."

"Yes, but we must think of interest, Mr. Fairchild," Mr. Morris said, a smug expression upon his face. "Besides, you should be grateful to be walking away with your life. Your nephew does not have to be so kind."

The reminder of a death sentence silenced Mr. Fairchild. While Nicholas was interested in regaining some of the lost assets from Penbrose House, another idea had taken hold of his mind.

"Your Honor, might I ask that only the money be extracted from my uncle's estate?" he said.

A self-satisfied smirk crossed his uncle's arrogant face.

Tom, who stood beside his father, looked intrigued. Nicholas's cousin had not said more than ten words in his own defense, taking his sentencing with much more grace and honor than his own father had.

"It is your estate," Mr. Morris said. "You may do with it as you wish."

"Then I would like the remainder of the estate to be given to Mr. John Fairchild," Nicholas said. Mr. Morris nodded in consent.

John's eyes shot to him, a question in their depths. Nicholas nodded, acknowledging that he was completely serious.

Uncle Fairchild started cursing.

"Silence!" Mr. Morris barked. Uncle Fairchild clamped his mouth shut.

"If there is nothing else," the magistrate said, "I believe we can adjourn."

Uncle Fairchild glared mutinously at Mr. Morris but said nothing. Mr. Gates, on the other hand, who had been brought from the gaol for the trial, looked like he might burst into tears.

The man was much thinner than when he'd first entered. Nicholas could even see how gaunt his cheeks had become since the last time he had visited. A bath and several good meals would be needed before the old steward recovered from his time behind bars.

Nicholas was unsure what he would do with Mr. Gates. He no longer needed a steward, having already hired a very competent man to run Penbrose House. But he could return the man's previous funds, money that had been seized when he'd been accused of theft. It was enough that the older gentleman could probably retire comfortably with his wife, if he was prudent.

John made his way to Nicholas through the few people gathered about the room. Taking Nicholas's hand firmly in his, he shook it. Nicholas flinched, realizing he'd offered the hand connected to his injured arm.

"Sorry," John said. "But you have left me speechless. Do you truly wish for me to have Downing Way?"

"I would not have said it, John, if I had not meant it. I believe you will do well with the property. It and the people there will flourish under your care."

"I feel like I am getting a second chance to make something of myself." He dropped Nicholas's hand and stepped back. Rubbing the back of his neck. "I am not sure I deserve it."

"Perhaps not, which is why you must measure up to the living. Show me over this next year that you can care for the estate as it ought to be, and I will give you one of Mirage's colts to add to your stables."

John's eyes lit up with excitement. "I see you are not averse to stooping to bribery," he said with mock seriousness.

"Is it working?"

"Most definitely." John smiled.

Both their gazes were drawn to the back of the room as the doors were thrown open to escort Mr. Fairchild and Tom out. Nicholas wished things had turned out differently between them, but he could see no other way to have peace for them all.

"Nicholas," John said, "may I at least give them some funds from the estate to help them begin anew in the penal colonies?"

In that moment, Nicholas's heart broke for John. No matter how much he had been manipulated and controlled by his father, no matter how much his brother had cost him in reputation, they were still John's family. It would be hard for him to see them shipped off, quite possibly never to be heard of again.

"It is up to you, John. I will not stand in your way."

"Thank you," he said quietly, still staring after the retreating forms of his brother and father.

Nicholas arrived home much sooner than he had expected. If he hurried, he would still have plenty of time to dress for dinner.

Cresting the top of the stairs, he turned toward his own rooms only to find Sybil sitting on the window seat of one of the alcoves that overlooked the gardens. She stood when he approached, looking him over from head to toe. Nicholas was not used to such open regard. It made him a bit self-conscious. Her eyes landed upon his wounded arm, and she stepped forward, hand outstretched, as if to touch the bandaged limb hidden under his coat.

"How are you feeling?"

"Sore and a bit hungry, but otherwise well."

In truth, the bullet had laid open three or four inches of skin and muscle a half-inch deep. He was exceedingly lucky he had anticipated his uncle's ire, or he would not be standing here now.

Sybil's hand remained outstretched, uncertainty in her eyes. Nicholas stepped forward, allowing her hand to rest upon his elbow just below the injury. She stared at her own hand resting upon his arm before she looked up into his eyes.

"Thank you," she said in a small voice. "I had not thought... that is, I did not think..." Her red-rimmed eyes shimmered with unshed tears. "I did not think defending my honor would lead to this."

Nicholas raised his uninjured arm and rested his hand upon her cheek. She leaned into his touch, apology written across her face.

"Sybil," he said, "this wound had nothing to do with protecting you, but if it had, I would have done so most willingly. This and much more." A tear slipped down her pale cheek and ran in a direct course to where Nicholas's thumb lay.

Gently, he wiped it away. "Truthfully, my uncle has probably been aching to rid himself of me for the last three years, at least."

She shuddered under his touch, whether from pleasure or the thought of what might have happened, he could not tell. He took a step closer to her, and her eyes lifted from his arm to his face.

"About what you said, in the library," she began, then stopped.

"What I said in the library?" he encouraged.

"Never mind." Color touched her cheeks. "It is almost time for dinner, and you still need to dress."

Nicholas took in the peach dress she wore, the gauzy layers seeming to float about her. Her dark hair was piled on top of her head like a crown of curls. She started to take a step back from him, and without thought, he reached out with his good hand and caught her about the waist.

She inhaled at his touch but did not look away.

"Sybil, I—" What? What could he say? He could not declare himself here. Not yet, anyway.

His eyes darted to her lips, focusing on the little crack at the corner. He desperately wanted to kiss her, but he did not want to hurt her either. However, Sybil was assessing his lips as well.

Pulling her just the slightest bit closer, he stared down into her emerald eyes, losing himself in their depths.

"Just kiss her, already," Miss Bawden's voice said from down the hall. "I am trying to get to the drawing room, and I cannot proceed until you two clear the hallway."

Nicholas and Sybil laughed, the moment completely broken. Gently, he kissed her forehead, then peered back at Miss Bawden.

"Well, that was a flat disappointment," she said with an expression that clearly said he had done it wrong.

Sybil giggled. Nicholas loved the sound of it.

"I am sorry to have ruined your entertainment, Miss Bawden." His apology was met with a snort and a smirk from the young lady.

"Yes, well. Just make sure it does not happen again." She brushed past him, grabbed Sybil's arm, and led the furiously blushing woman away.

# Chapter Thirty-Nine

Sybil made her way to the breakfast parlor the next morning, her mind consumed with thoughts of the night before. After the evening's entertainments, she had been on her way to bed with Eliza at her side, when she had spied her father in a small parlor locked in an intimate embrace with Lady Evelyn.

When her father saw her standing in the hall, he asked for congratulations as Lady Evelyn had just accepted his proposal.

Thinking back now, Sybil realized she could have responded with more tact, but she had just stared at them. Finally, she had given a short, rather lifeless felicitation, then carried on to her room.

Eliza had inquired whether she might like to talk a while, but Sybil had refused, insisting she would be fine, and she just needed some rest.

Now, however, she was not sure if that had actually helped. She was happy for her father, she truly was, but the thought of living with the happy couple made her heart ache. It would be hard seeing Lady Evelyn step into her mother's place, and she would not even have Porter—Maria—there to comfort her. Her dear maid would be off living her happily-ever-after with Mr. Brown.

"Sybil," a voice said from behind her. Turning around, she saw her father hurrying toward her. "Can we speak a moment?"

"I suppose," she said, not knowing if she was ready for this conversation.

Gesturing toward the door closest them, Sybil was surprised to see it was the music room. She entered the room, but instead of sitting, she stood near the door.

"I was a little disappointed in you last evening, Sybil. You cannot have been completely unaware of my affection for Lyn."

"Yes, but two and a half weeks, Papa. You proposed marriage after only two and a half weeks!"

"Life is short, Sybil. Your mother's death was a hard reminder of that. I have loved Lyn my entire life, and now fate has brought her back to me."

"Your entire life?" she said, still trying to grasp the situation. She had thought she was prepared; she had been reminding herself daily that this was coming, but somehow it still brought pain. "What about Mama?"

"I loved your mama, but she is gone now."

"But how can you say you have loved Lady Evelyn your entire life, and yet claim to have loved Mama as well?"

"Do you remember the story I told you in the carriage on the day we arrived at this house party?"

"I believe so."

"Do you remember that Lady Evelyn was forced to marry Lord Caraway at the end of her first season? That there was a young man she was forbidden to marry?"

"That was you?" Sybil hissed.

He nodded. "I lost her to her father's greed. Honestly, I did not think I would ever be able to recover, but your mother came along, and she pieced my heart back together again. I loved her for it. It was not the same love as I felt for Lyn, but a more mature, self-sacrificing love. Your mother was always one who believed fate was God's way of making things right in the end, and truly, I thought meeting her *was* God's way of making things well again."

"But now?"

"Now God has turned fate again and given me back the heart that was once mine."

Sybil's legs trembled beneath her. While she could not wrap her mind about what her father was saying, she could not fault him. Taking several steps into the room, she slumped onto a chair, the train of her riding habit bunching uncomfortably underneath her as she relieved her legs so she might focus on the tumult of her mind.

"I know it is hard to understand, but I need to live again, and so do you. It is what your mother would have wanted for us both."

The all-too-familiar sensation of tears stung her eyes, but she refused to let them fall. Mama had obviously not wanted her happiness, or she would have encouraged her to marry Nicholas years ago.

Looking up, she saw compassion in her father's eyes, and the first tear fell.

"Why did she insist I marry a lord, then? You are a good man, and you have no title. Why?" she growled, her heart aching.

"While your mother was a good woman, she was not perfect. She regretted it, you know."

"Regretted what?" Sybil said through angry tears.

"Regretted that you threw away happiness only to please her."

"I threw it away?" she said in disbelief.

"Sybil, you have always had a mind of your own. If you had truly wanted Lord Penbrose back then, you would have taken his offer."

She let his words sink in. Was it true?

"When I said I thought you were still too young for a season, I was only looking out for you. I did not want you to get hurt, Poppet. I knew you did not know your own mind yet, and I worried for you."

The tears came hard. She *had* been the one to throw it away. Mama would not have disowned her or looked down upon her for her choice. She had just been too scared of disappointing the woman she'd admired most of all in the world.

Papa's arms encircled her and she hugged him back. "I'm sorry," she sobbed into his coat. "I have been so bitter and angry. I want you to be happy."

"I will be." He pulled back and handed her a linen. "And so shall you. We'll make this work, Sybil. It will be strange at first, but I believe you and Lady Evelyn will get on well."

She nodded, dabbing at her tears.

"Now, I believe there is a young lord who is waiting to take you out riding," he said with a twinkle in his eye.

Sybil was surprised that he knew. She had not told him, and she didn't think he had overheard them in the library. He was right, however—Nicholas was waiting, and she needed to dry her eyes before seeing him.

She was late. Checking briefly in the breakfast room to make sure Nicholas was not waiting there for her, she rushed on out to the stables.

Tempest pranced about her lead as Cormac led her from the stables, saddled and ready to ride. Nicholas stood not far off, gently rubbing Rogue's sleek black neck.

"I do apologize," Sybil said when she came within hearing, stopping several yards away to let down her habit.

Nicholas raised his gaze from the horse and handed the reins to a groom. As he strode toward her, Sybil was mesmerized by his tall, athletic build. He reached her at the very same moment Cormac brought Tempest to her side, and in one swift movement, he grasped her waist and lifted her to sit upon the mare's back.

The surprise of the action and the intimacy of such a gesture nearly stole her breath away.

"Good morning," he finally said, smiling up at her. She wanted to respond, but Tempest chose that moment to skitter to the side, and Sybil had to put her focus into settling her mount. She would have rather spent time settling into Nicholas's hazel-eyed gaze, but Tempest was still Tempest.

Then she remembered his arm. "You should not have done that. You could injure yourself further or break your stitches."

"Holding you was well worth the risk," he said, then turned on his heels and strode back to his horse.

Once Nicholas was mounted, they made their way to the west pasture to burn off some of Tempest's energy, racing to and from the field's treelined edge. Rogue made the run twice, but it took Tempest four times before she settled.

Nicholas was oddly quiet during this exercise. No banter or jests emerged, just soft compliments on her riding skill. It was odd, really, to see him so subdued. Was he in pain?

With Tempest now manageable, they made their way toward the old stone church. Nicholas's silence was beginning to wear on Sybil. She did not mind a comfortable quiet ride, but this hush was fraught with tension. Should she suggest they turn back? It was the logical thing to do, but she could not bring herself to do it.

"I believe it is your turn to ask the next question," she finally offered, hoping to pull Nicholas from his reverie.

"Yes. It is," he agreed, but said no more.

"It will not work," she said with a smile. "I will not ask another question just to break your silence."

He chuckled and his shoulders seemed to relax. "I was merely forming the next question in my mind. Nothing more."

"Says the man who wiled out multiple questions in just such a manner."

He grinned. "Very well. What is your favorite color?"

Sybil was surprised at the innocuous question. After his last direct line of approach, she had been bracing herself. Glancing down at her red riding habit, her lips tugged into a smile.

"I like red. Though, perhaps, not this bright," she indicated her habit, "but a darker, more subdued color."

"Like that of a deep red rose, perhaps?"

"Indeed. Like the ones flanking the fountain in the Penbrose garden."

Nicholas smiled. "I have been partial to those myself. I always know when I am nearing the fountain and they are in bloom; they give off the most wonderful scent. A mixture of sweet and spice."

"Yes, they are heavenly," she agreed, but she could think of nothing more to say. Several more minutes passed by as she waited for his next question, the grey structure of the old church coming more into focus the farther they rode.

"You have six more questions." She hoped he would take his cue.

"Six?"

"Do not tell me you lost count?" Truthfully, she was not actually sure if she had remembered correctly either. "If I had known, I would have been relieved from answering any more questions at all."

"Is that what you want?" he asked, his face a little too serious for her liking.

"No, but I do like to win. And that most definitely would be a win over the wily Lord Penbrose."

A smile returned to his face. "Well, then I'd best make good use of my six remaining questions."

They had reached the church, and in an unspoken understanding, they stopped their mounts to look at it. Nicholas suddenly dismounted, surprising Sybil when he came to the side of her horse and reached up.

"Care to walk for a bit?"

She nodded, noting that for once, Tempest stood completely still, her eyes half-lidded in rest. Placing the reins on her mare's neck, Sybil reached down and steadied herself on Nicholas's shoulders, trying to place as much weight on her hands as possible so he could help her dismount with less pressure on his arm. With his hands about her waist, she slipped from the saddle and settled on the ground before him.

Their gazes locked for the briefest moment before Nicholas stepped back, robbing her of his warmth.

Cormac approached, and she handed him Tempest's reins. Gathering her habit, she pinned it up so they could stroll about the grounds. The grass was unkempt and the bushes overgrown, but the flowers bursting through the patches of green were lovely.

"I am sorry about your uncle," she finally ventured, wondering if yesterday's proceedings had truly taxed him so much.

He nodded, reaching down and plucking a wildflower from the tall grass. Spinning the stem of the little purple blossom, he said, "I have never been close to the man. His lifestyle and morals have never been in keeping with my own. It was hard, however, to see Tom carted away. I cannot help but think of how we use to play together as young boys before we all went off to school."

Sybil stared at Nicholas as he examined the flower. He was so good. He had not complained about the scandal this situation would bring upon himself and his sisters, nor had he sought for the maximum punishment for his wayward uncle and cousin.

"Perhaps your cousin will learn something from this situation. Is it possible he could make something of himself in the penal colonies?"

"I hope so," he said slowly, "but let us not spend any more of our time discussing my family. I would like to put it behind me. Do you know the name of this flower?"

She stepped closer. "It looks like a cornflower."

Nicholas pulled his eyes away from the flower and met her gaze. Lifting his hand, he tucked the purple bloom behind her ear. The warmth of his fingers trailed past her ear and brushed her neck before he pulled his hand away.

"Thank you," she said softly.

Nodding his head, he offered her his arm. She took it as they began strolling about the church. Sunlight peeked through the clouds and illuminated the one stain glass window that remained of the old grey building. Green moss clung to the stones that had started to blacken with age. It was oddly enchanting.

"I believe I have nine more questions?'

"Nine?" Sybil laughed. "Are you hoping I have lost count?"

"No. Only trying to get more questions for myself."

Oh, he *was* wily. "I refuse to fall for any more of your tricks, your lordship."

"Are we back to 'lording' me again?"

"If it can get me another question."

He laughed. "Very well, here is your next question. Will you open my mother's ball with me?"

Sybil stopped, pulling him to a halt with her. "Me?"

"You are the woman I asked."

"I understand that. It is only the question caught me off guard. I thought you would have asked one of the other young ladies by now."

"No, I find I only ask one lady questions at this house party."

His smirk really was irresistible. "I see, well she had best accept, or you will be left in want of a partner."

"Will she also dance the supper set with me?"

"I suppose, if only to keep you from dining alone."

"And will she answer every question I ask her for the rest of our lives?"

Her breath caught in her throat. She was not sure exactly what he was getting at, but hope welled up within her like a fountain that could not be restrained.

Taking both her hands in his, he stepped closer, bringing their joined hands up to rest upon his chest. Sybil could feel the steady beat of his heart under her fingers. She looked up into his eyes as they searched her face. They flitted from her forehead to her chin and then back to her eyes. He gazed at her for one long moment and her heart picked up speed at the intensity she saw there.

"I would like to continue this game, of a question for a question, from this day forward, and for the rest of our lives. I want to exchange questions with you every day, so we may come to know each other's deepest hopes and dreams. But that is not all I want. I want to share chocolate and coffee with you over breakfast. I want to ride races with you. I want to read books, discuss politics, and quite literally change the world with you."

Sybil ducked her head, feeling a tear trickle down her cheek. She had cried more today than she had in the last month. A warm gloved finger tucked under her chin and slowly lifted her face to his eye level.

"I was not bluffing, Sybil, when I told my uncle and the room at large that I had offered for you. It may have been two years ago, but the offer still stands. I want you for my wife."

Sybil pulled one hand from his to catch the sob that broke her throat. Holding one hand over her mouth, she nodded mutely.

"Is that a yes?" he asked, a smile beginning to spread across his face.

Pulling her hand away from her mouth, she swallowed. "Yes, Nicholas. That is a yes."

"Finally," he shouted, and pulled her into a firm embrace.

Sybil laughed through her tears. She could not agree more.

Nicholas stepped back, his hands coming up to cup her tear-streaked face. Tipping his head slightly, he captured her lips in a fervent kiss. Sybil sucked in her breath at the intensity and returned his kiss with relish. Stepping forward into his touch, she wrapped her arms about his waist, and the world melted away.

It was just the two of them, their lips sealing their love and their hearts beating in time as their souls reached out and claimed each other for the rest of forever.

<h1 style="text-align:center">Epilogue</h1>

"Thank you, Wilson," Nicholas said to his butler, having just come in from the early September day. His hunt with John had been successful. There would be roast pheasant tonight for dinner.

"The post came while you were away, my lord," Wilson said, holding out a silver tray.

"Ah, good. By chance, do you know where Lady Penbrose might be?" He smiled to himself. He still loved the sound of that name upon his lips.

"In the library, I presume. It *is* the afternoon."

"Very good," he said with a grin.

Entering the library, he could not see a single person present, but he knew better. Walking to the second chair by the fire, he bent down and peeked his head around. Tucked back as far as she could sit was Sybil, her head leaning against the side of the wingback chair, a book propped in her hands.

She looked so pretty and peaceful there, but poor Aida would be distraught to see the beautiful hair style she had created crushed against another chair back. It was probably the girl's biggest trial as Sybil's lady's maid.

"Hello, my love," he said quietly, enjoying the surprise on her face.

She glanced up at him with a big smile. "You are home!" Setting the book in her lap, she leaned forward. He rewarded her with a brief peck on the lips before standing straight and making his way to the other chair.

"What are we reading today?"

"A book called *Mansfield Park*. Eliza suggested it in her last letter. I have read a few from this author before, so I am sure it will be good. I see you have the post."

Nicholas had almost forgotten he held the letters in his hand. Flipping through the envelopes, he saw one from Bradley. Setting the others on the table between them, he said, "This one is from Tuck."

"Ah, how is Bradley?" she asked, compassion filling her voice. Things had been difficult for their friend since his brother's passing, but hopefully, he would see improvements soon.

"I guess we should open it and find out." He broke the seal and began perusing the letter. "He says he is well."

He read through the first page in silence. "It looks as if he is needing some help."

"With what?"

"He is asking for information on running an estate. It seems his brother left the place in some financial difficulty." It was no secret Bradley was still struggling with his brother's death, mostly with the chaos the man had left not only financially, but emotionally.

"From what you have said of his older brother, it does not surprise me."

"Nor I," he said, distracted. What would happen to the elder Mr. Lenning's wife and young daughters? The estate was also still trying to support Bradley's mother and his two younger sisters. It was not as if Bradley would cast them out, but how would he start a family of his own?

"This is interesting," he said, reading the next section of the letter.

"What?" Sybil rose from her chair to stand next to him and read over his shoulder. Nicholas took advantage of the situation and snaked his arm out around her waist, toppling her onto his lap. She squealed and giggled as he righted her in his arms.

"He says you need to spend much more time in your husband's arms."

"He does not, Nicholas." She playfully pushed against his chest.

"No, but he should have." He chuckled. Then snuggling her close, he brushed his lips across hers. She leaned into his kiss, and he completely forget the letter he still held as he crushed it against her back to pull her closer.

She pulled back laughing. "I shall never know what the letter says if you abuse it so."

"It says he saw Miss Diana in Venworth," he said as he trailed kisses along her cheek.

"He did?" Sybil pulled back to look directly at him.

"See for yourself." He handed her the letter.

Sybil sat up on his lap to read through the missive herself. Apparently, Lord Brock had sent Diana to visit her mother's cousin. Good. His friend's last letter had been one of distress, requiring Nicholas to impart some much needed information for leverage with Lord Brock. Why, however, the man did not just send Diana back to her mother was beyond him. There was no need for Lord Brock to keep such a tight hold on the girl, especially when she had a loving mother to care for her.

"He says here that the Williamses were in town around the time he removed himself to Fallow Hall. What did you find out about Mr. Williams?" she asked.

"Oh, he had nothing do with my uncle Fairchild's scheme, he just happens to be a bit of a coward." He smiled. "Apparently, the man really did not like confrontation and the tense situation in the library got to his nerves."

"What will you do about Bradley's request?" She stood and straightened her skirts. Nicholas felt the loss almost immediately, but he promised himself he would not be petulant and beg her to return to her previous perch.

"Lady Hamdon's brother, Lord Gladsby, lives not far from Venworth and is very adept at bringing estates back to full production. They are acquainted. I will write Gladsby. Maybe he can take Bradley under his wing, as Mr. Martin did for me when I first inherited Fairfield Manor. It will take some time, but I think eventually Gladsby could help him right things. Plus, he has much more time on his hands," Nicholas said, standing.

She turned to face him. "Oh, he does?"

"Well, yes. He is a baron of small estate, and I have several I must manage, plus the man does not have a wife to keep him busy." He slowly inched toward Sybil.

"I suppose you are *so* very busy with all those estates." The corner of her mouth lifted into a smirk. "You have far too much to do. I should just leave you to your work."

She stepped back and tried to sneak around the chairs.

"Oh, no you don't, you little minx," he said, snatching her about the waist as she began scurrying from the room. Her laughter filled the air as he pulled her into his arms. The sound of it filled his heart with joy. She was here, in his home, as his wife. A dream he'd thought would never come true.

"I will never be too busy for you, Lady Penbrose." He brushed a stray lock of hair behind her ear and gazed into her laughing green eyes.

"I am glad to hear it," she said, suddenly serious. "I love you, Nicholas."

"And I you," Nicholas said against her lips before kissing her completely senseless.

# Author's Notes

This book has been years in the making. It started twenty years ago when my husband decided to abandon his pre-med major and instead pursue a degree in history. I was relieved and distressed all at once. But because I am a supportive spouse, I agreed to take a vow of poverty and follow him as he pursued his multiple degrees in the humanities field. Do you know what I learned along the way? I actually like history.

Truthfully, I already knew I did, but over the years I have learned how much. His job as a professor has introduced me to parts of history that I never would have pursued on my own. The most prominent is Black history.

In 2010 my husband published his dissertation on indentured servitude of Black people in the Illinois Country. That paper took a village to write. Between my husband, aiding professors, records curators, and yours truly, (sorry I was a terrible beta reader, honey) it finally saw the light of day. The biggest piece of information I took from that paper was that indentured servitude was really just a fancy, somewhat-legal way of keeping people in slavery.

That paper lit a spark in me. Over time, I branched out my study to include England and its part in the Transatlantic trade. From there I studied topics like sugar plantations, the harvesting of cacao beans, the Haitian revolt, and how piracy helped many Black people achieve freedom.

The initial idea for this book came from the story Nicholas tells of his father in the Caribbean. It is based off the above-mentioned research topics. Originally, I included the detailed story from my mind. Then I realized it was more Jonas's story than Nicholas's and it was trimmed down to its current size. But the story is important because it's the place where Nicholas is most impacted and begins his fight for good. From there, my story built and grew. The real secret to Nicholas's heart was Sybil's willingness to fight alongside him. Her innate fire and passion made her the perfect partner.

While Sybil and Nicholas are fictitious characters, several of the people in this book are not.

*-Mrs. Davinier*, the woman Jonas Fairchild meets, is the married name of Dito Elizabeth Belle, great niece to the 1st Earl of Mansfield. Born the illegitimate daughter of an enslaved black woman and an English soldier, she spent her early life in the Caribbean and eventually was moved to England to live with her great uncle. The Earl of Mansfield is one of several aristocrats who called for a change in England's laws concerning the slave trade. While Dito was not treated exactly the same as family, she was given far more consideration than most black relatives. Upon the earl's death she was given a yearly annuity of 100 pounds and a lump sum of 500 pounds.

*-William Wilberforce*, the man Jonas Fairchild supports, was the most prominent force in passing the Slave Trade Act of 1807 which stopped England's participation in the transport of enslaved people across the Atlantic. A politician and philanthropist, he fought his entire life for the moral treatment of the suppressed. He died in 1833, three days after hearing the news that England had completely abolished slavery.

*-Ignatius Sancho* was one of the first Black men to hold a vote in England. He lived from 1729-1780 and was supported in Society by the 2nd Duke of Montagu. His letters were gathered and published postmortem in 1782.

*-Francis Williams*, a scholar and poet, was also supported in Society by the 2nd Duke of Montagu. However, in time Francis returned to Jamaica, his birthplace, to set up a school for free Blacks. His work in education was

groundbreaking as there were no schools for Black people in Jamaica prior to his arrival.

-*Toussaint Louverture* was a general and politician who played a prominent role in the Haitian Revolution. Born into slavery in 1743, he was freed sometime between 1772-1776. He fought for Haiti's freedom from 1793 until his death in 1803, just nine months before the Revolution succeeded.

-*Olaudah Equiano's* (Gustavus Vassa) memoirs of his time in slavery were quite possibly the biggest catalyst in the abolishment of the transatlantic slave trade. Stolen from his family at 11 and sold into slavery, he was eventually able to buy his freedom. As a member of the abolitionist group, Sons of Africa, he campaigned for freedom until his death in 1797.

While Jane Austen is not mentioned in this book, it is important to note that several of her works are. I did not add her name because she first published her books under the pen name *A Lady*. Therefore, during this time period readers did not know who to give credit for these wonderful stories.

Other historical facts in this book include the information on Napoleon's Seventh Coalition or the Hundred Days. This was Napoleon's last march which ended at Waterloo. The information was included in my story to add context so the reader can understand where it sits in history. The secondary reason for adding this information was to give a little background to where Fredrick, the last of the Merry Men of Eton, is at this point in time. While he plays a very small role in the first two books, he is not absent. Never you fear readers, he will make his grand entrance in book three.

The towns of Kettering, Whitney, Oxford, and London are real. Kettering at this time specialized in shoes and so it had an ample number of cobblers. It exists in Northamptonshire, a real county, known for its abundance of beautiful churches.

Penbrose House and many of the other places in this book are fictitious, but I did base this house heavily off Castle Ashby House and Kirby Hall. Both are real country homes in Northamptonshire. One day I hope to visit them in person.

I did a lot of research on the laws of inheritance, as well as the punishment for stealing from a peer. While the initial theft may not have gotten Mr. Thomas Fairchild hanged— due to his relation to an earl as well as the money he could have bargained with— his attempt to kill Nicholas would not have been looked on lightly and would have sent him to the noose if Nicholas did not interfere. Crimes at this time and their punishment were mostly handled by the victim. Such a direct assault on a peer, though, would have angered the whole aristocracy.

Most everything else in this book were products of my imagination. My story is set within the strictures of 19th century English Society. Any misrepresentation was not intentional. It was my hope to portray all characters in the most historically accurate way. All descriptions were researched and written with the best of intentions. If there is anything in my work that seems like a slight to any person, place, or thing, I truly apologize. It was not my intent.

Thank you, dear reader, for choosing my book. I truly appreciate it. For additional information about my research please contact me at teahthewriter@gmail.com.

*No cats were hurt in the making of this book.*

# Acknowledgements

Many helped with the process of writing and editing this book. I would like to recognize a few key people.

To my mother-in-law Saundra, thanks for being so excited to share my work with friends. I'm pretty sure half of my sales on my last book were somehow connected with you singing my praises. Your love and support means so much to me as I chase this crazy dream.

My neighbor and friend Lisa, you have been one of my biggest fans from day one. You believe in me even when I don't. Thanks girl! I love you.

To Author Sally Britton, thank you for always answering my questions no matter how ridiculous or how late. It's so nice to know there is someone who has my back when the negative voices of the world are beating me down.

I had several great beta readers, but a huge thanks goes to Author Brooke Losee. You were one of my biggest supporters. Your helpful hints and funny comments kept me going when I just wanted to trash the whole story.

Author Katie Stone you listened when this story broke me, then reminded me that I am good enough. Thank you so much for always knowing how to help me feel better.

To my Alpha Reader Johanna Brown. I still can't believe you plowed through this book when it was such a mess. Then, because you are amazing, you plowed through the rewritten copy. Lots has changed since you last read it, so if you're ever bored you might want to pick it up a third time...or not. I love you girl. Thanks for always being there for me.

I cannot forget my amazing Critique Partner Molly Stratford. When things were getting down to the wire you stepped in and pulled over time, not only as a beta but also as a therapist and friend. I can't tell you how much that meant to me.

Lastly to my husband, Donovan. Thanks for knowing when to hold me and when to push me into action. If it were not for your support, I would not be able to achieve even a tenth of what I have this last year. You are incredible in every single way.

# About Author

## Teah Kemp Weight

Greetings reader! I am so honored that you took time to read my book. It has been a true labor of love. There will be many other books to come. I would love to share them with you! Please sign up for my newsletterwhere you will find sales, giveaways, and special offers— like my upcoming free Novella.

A little about me, I grew up on a ranch in eastern Utah changing sprinkler lines, herding cattle, training horses and bailing hay. In high school I participated in choir, drama and dance. It was during this time I won my first award for writing.

I had planned on pursuing a career in English literature, but life threw me a curve ball and I found myself raising a large family as I followed the love of my life through several states as he pursued a doctorate in history and began teaching.

Twenty years, four states, seven children, and multiple universities later, I have put pen to paper—actually fingers to keys—and started writing again.

I am an avid reader of historical romance, but I also enjoy a good romantic comedy. I hope to create many more stories set in various time periods of history. Currently, most of my stories are set in the Regency period of the Georgian era.

I currently live in South Texas with my Prince Charming. We have seven children and far too many pets. When not writing, you can generally find me being a mother. Such is life with so many children, but I also enjoy horses, mountains, fall foliage and chocolate.

# Also By

<br>

<u>Merry Men of Eton</u>

Secrets of a Baron's Daughter

<u>Coming Soon</u>
**Secrets of Fallow Hall**

Mr. Bradley Lenning's brother left him an estate, a family, and world of hurt when he suddenly died. Caught between duty and desire he's forced to chose between the obligations he already has and helping the woman he's rapidly falling for.

Diana Cattering has known more pain in her twenty years then anyone aught. Trapped with an abusive cousin and a conniving uncle she's unexpectedly granted a short chance at freedom. There is one stipulation. She must never speak to the man her heart is growing to love.

Take a chance on this forbidden love.

www.ingramcontent.com/pod-product-compliance
Lightning Source LLC
Chambersburg PA
CBHW072044190726
48294CB00005B/1397